The Dead Sagas

Volume II

A Ritual of Flesh

Lee C Conley

Books by Lee C Conley
from
Wolves of Valour Publications

The Dead Sagas
A Ritual of Bone
A Ritual of Flesh

A Ritual of Flesh
from
Wolves of Valour Publications

Written by Lee C Conley
First Edition 2020

ISBN:
978-1-9993750-6-5

Cover art by Andrey Vasilchenko
and
Cover layout and cartography by Lee C Conley

www.leeconleyauthor.com

ACKNOWLEDGMENTS

Thank you to my family for the support, my incredible wife Laura for putting up with the whole process and to my little girls, Luna and Anya, for making me smile in those moments of doubt. Thanks also to Mum and Dad, and to Nan, for all the support.

Thank you to my amazing editor Alicia Wanstall-Burke for all her hard work, her critical eye helped turn this rambling yarn into something polished I am proud of. Thanks to my cover artist Andrey Vasilchenko for the awesome artwork. Thank you to R.J. Bayley for his amazing audiobook narration. A huge thank you to my beta team and proofing squad: Lisa Maughan, Steve D. Howarth, Damien Larkin, Jo Rachel Rainbow-Henson, Michael Baker, Nigel Potts, Nancy Foster and Peter Mitchell. A big thank you to Michael Evan for all the publicity work and managing to get me featured on all those podcasts and interviews.

Thank you to all the members of The British and Irish Writing Community, in particular my fellow team members who run both the community and our Bard of the Isles Magazine. That's you, Damo (again), Phil Parker, and Jenny Hannaford-Jennings, but also to all my other friends in the group for all the support and encouragement.

Thanks to all the great writers who I am proud to call a friend and have given me their thoughts on A Ritual of Bone and their continued support while writing A Ritual of Flesh: In particular, Michael Baker, Jacob Sannox, C.F. Welburn, J.P. Ashman, D.M. Murray, Jordan Loyal Short, Phil Williams, Jamie Edmundson, Daniel Kelly and Dyrk Ashton to name just a few. You guys are all awesome.

Thanks to Rob J. Hayes for his help and promos. Thanks to everyone who may or may not be part of a certain non-existent cabal and to Tom Smith, whom this book is also secretly dedicated to. Thanks to Kareem Mahfouz and everyone in his Fantasy Writers Bar group.

To all the great bloggers, podcast hosts and reviewers — without you all us indie authors are nothing. There are too many to list you all but thank you to: Timy at RockstarLit Book Asylum and Justine Bergman from Whispers and Wonder for hosting my cover reveal and their constant support, Nils Shukla, Laura Hughes, and all the Fantasy Hive guys, G.R. Matthews, Julia Kitvaria Sarene, and Richard Marpole from Fantasy Faction. Alex Khlopenko and Julie Rea from Three Crows Magazine. Thank you to Jamie Davis, Ryan Kirk and E.G. Stone for having me on your podcasts. Thanks to Phil Exon at the Super Relaxed Fantasy club, David Walters at FanFiAddict, the guys at Fantasy Book Review, the staff at BristolCon for letting me and Damo do our workshop, Fantasy/Sci-fi Focus for hosting the video Q&As and readings, the organisers at QuaranCon for putting me on that amazing panel, Paul at Bookends & Bagends, Alex at Spells and Spaceships, Angel Haze at Indie Fantasy Addicts, Matt at DarksideReads, Edward Gwynne for the sword chats, and also Mark Coulter, Paul Torr, Steve Caldwell and Alan Behan for posting about and recommending my book—yeah I saw, thanks guys. There are so many people who have supported my work these past years, and if I have missed anyone I am sorry but I truly do appreciate it so thank you—none of it would be possible without you.

Thank you all and I hope you enjoy this book.

For my girls.
Laura, Luna and Anya.

And of course,
a cat named
Macumba

The Dead Sagas

The Story So Far...

A Ritual of Bone

Amongst the ancient crumbling ruins of the High Passes a young apprentice of the College ventures out into the night to study the moon. He feels something out there with him, and overcome by an unsettling sense of watching eyes, he runs from the unseen menace, tripping and snapping his ankle in the darkness.

The apprentice is found by his masters and taken back to their camp. His master, Eldrick, and Master Logan are encamped in the remote location to, amongst other things, conduct a macabre study of anatomy. With his leg in ruins he is unable to perform his duties and the following morning Eldrick informs him he no longer has need of him at the camp. He will have to return south to the College. The apprentice spends the morning brooding over this news and busies himself in his work until Truda, a fellow apprentice, returns from an expedition across the border to war-torn Cydor. She returns with a cart full of corpses for Eldrick to continue his grisly studies and speaks of the worsening war over the border. The apprentice begins to notice his feelings for her when he becomes jealous over her attentions to one of her sell-sword escorts. He then finds himself alone for the rest of the day as he awaits his final night in the camp.

Part of the College study in the ruins was an ancient ritual known as the Bone Ritual, a ritual that allegedly allows communion with the ancestors. The apprentice witnessed the ritual first hand and saw Master Eldrick summon a soul back to its bones, and then later that night watches another attempt, this one raising a corpse which tries to attack him. But something else was disturbed, they have accidentally awakened an ancient darkness which seems to have slowly warped his master's mind. The wounded apprentice is shaken by the experience and leaves for the College the following morning with their findings.

Far to the west, a hunter named Bjorn is sent to look into a series of disappearances and rumour of a beast. He finds an abandoned village and strange tracks, which he follows into an ambush and is captured. He awakens to find himself bound beside a strange Wildman and the dead villagers he was trying to find. Bjorn escapes, releasing the Wildman also, and discovers that his attackers are stone-age cannibals, known in the ancient Sagas as the Stonemen.

These Stonemen were driven away hundreds of years ago but appear to have returned and are now attacking the northern border of Arnar, hunting its people and eating them. He must make it back to Oldstones to report the terrible news to High Lord Archeon. The Wildman who Bjorn freed from captivity is following him, haunting his every step, and pursues Bjorn as they both evade the cannibals and escape to the safety of Arnar.

Aboard the trade ship *Glyassin,* a sickness is killing the crew. The ship sails home from the arid shores of distant Myhar and brings its deadly cargo back to the port town of Anchorage in southern Arnar.

Nym and her brother Finn live in poverty on the streets of Anchorage and are forced to accept the charity of a one armed tavern keeper named Jor, an old friend of their parents. Nym must sell herself for silver just to buy food to survive and the experience haunts her. She notices a strange witch-seer watching her in the street and hurries away to find her brother. After the town-guard stop a fight between Cydorian sailors, Jor and an old friend, a warrior of the town guard named Wilhelm, witness the sickness for themselves as a man dies bleeding in the street before them.

Back in the north, after the apprentice departs, and unbeknownst to him, Eldrick plans another ritual attempt. As the College scholars raise the dead in the High Passes, local warriors on guard nearby, under the command of Lord Arnulf, hear a warning bell ringing out from the High Passes and begin to investigate.

They are attacked by the walking dead and the scouting party is killed. Arnulf, with his best warrior, Hafgan, beside him, finds one his men from the scouting party dead, and after encountering some of the dead himself, retreats to await reinforcements from his friend Lord Fergus. Help arrives as they wait in the lowlands at the Waystone, Fergus comes with his shield-maiden warriors led by Astrid, the Death Nymph, and together they all intend to go back to find answers. A nearby farmstead known as Hern's Farm is found deserted; the folk there have been massacred. They discover a lone survivor, a young wounded girl, who in turn bites one of Fergus's men, Olad, as she struggles to escape him.

As they make camp to prepare to return to the mountains, Hafgan and the young warrior Erran discuss the history of Lord Fergus's chief warrior, the deadly shield-maiden Astrid, known also as the Death Nymph. Despite Hafgan's warnings Erran tries his luck and approaches the warrior woman to ask her to spar with him, and even manages to survive the encounter with his manhood intact, although her warriors are not best pleased.

During the darkness of night, the wounded girl's cursed brother attacks, and is slain. The girl turns savage also and attacks, but is killed by Erran. To the horror of all present, both corpses then rise again and attack the bewildered warriors. It is soon realised that those killed by the dead return from the grave themselves, but those only wounded become 'Cursed Ones', terrible bestial savages that in turn return from the dead upon their demise. When the dawn comes the wounded warrior Olad has disappeared. The warriors of Arnar are unsettled but venture up into the passes to find answers and destroy any remaining dead.

Arnulf and Fergus discover the college camp, and there find the great hound which once belonged to Master Logan. The creature seems to be the camps lone survivor and is named Fear by Arnulf. At the hidden campsite Arnulf and Fergus discover the bell which had rung out and caused Arnulf to send men to investigate, they are also attacked by Olad, now a Cursed One, but he is slain by Hafgan.

The final College ritual appears to have been the cause of the evil Arnulf encountered in those fell passes, and must have somehow raised the dead, but the restless dead seem to have attacked the scholars also, killing everyone at the camp. While investigating the camp's surroundings, Arnulf and Fergus discover evidence of the rituals, and appalled, return home with evidence of the College's involvement.

Bjorn finally corners the Wildman and warns him to stop following him. The Wildman cannot speak his language and persists regardless. After several encounters they eventually form an uneasy friendship. Bjorn accompanied by his strange new ally hurries back to his employer to warn him of the cannibal's attacks.

Back in Arn, the sickness spreads through the port of Anchorage and ravages the heartland of the realm. In an attempt to stem the tide the local folk attempt a ritual, a plea to the gods, beseeching the gods to save them from the terrible plague. At the ritual Nym sees the king's daughter for the first time, but she is also in turn being watched again by the strange witch-seer that she has caught staring at her over the past few days. Sick folk from the town interrupt the ritual and many of the townsfolk flee, Nym, Finn, and Jor amongst them. As they make their way home, a guard in service to Anchorage's lord, the huscarl Lord Warrick, warns his old friend Jor that the plague is spreading and tells them to seek refuge in the nearby capital, the city of Arn, and so they flee Anchorage.

Arnulf returns to his town, Ravenshold, and his hall, named the Motte, to discover the dead and Cursed Ones have spread and attacked, destroying his home, killing many of his folk including his family, who burned alive in his hall. Grief stricken, Arnulf gathers their ashes and takes their remains to his family crypts accompanied by Ewolf, his son and only surviving family. Hafgan learns that Ewolf has been bitten and follows his lord to keep watch over him. Hafgan sees Ewolf attempt to kill his father but is stopped by the surprise horns of an approaching host of warriors.

High Lord Angus, Fergus's father, has marched his men to aid the folk of Ravenshold. With him comes Calimir, his advisor and a man of the College. Arnulf and the other warriors from the passes confront Calimir and accuse all members of the College with the crimes of sorcery and raising the dead, blaming them for the loss of his family and the destruction of his town. In the night the townsfolk of Ravenshold attack Calimir as he sleeps and slit his throat.

Arnulf gets permission from Angus to venture south to the capital to inform the king of the College's terrible studies and reveal what they have done. Arnulf's only surviving family member is his son, Ewolf, who after being bitten has begun to succumb to the curse and has become a Cursed One. Arnulf seeks vengeance but must do what he can to save his son.

As A Ritual of Bone ends we find Bjorn is heading to his employer High Lord Archeon at Oldstones to warn of the cannibals. Nym, Finn and Jor follow Wilhelm's advice and flee Anchorage for the assumed safety of the capital, Arn. The Apprentice is being haunted by the dark flickering shadows and the apparition of a dark hooded figure that stalks, not only his dreams, but his waking life also, as he journeys south for the capital of Arn and the College. The book ends with Arnulf, Fergus and their warriors heading south to the plague ravaged capital of Arn as the evil of the risen dead spreads. As they depart Ravenshold, they see the body of Calimir hung from a tree, a sign that the people of the north share Arnulf's blame of the College. Arnulf hears news from a passing patrol that the dead have been sighted nearby, and Hafgan declares, "It's spreading... Gods save us."

11

DRAMATIS PERSONAE

The College

College folk of The High Passes
The apprentice – apprentice of Master Eldrick.
Master Eldrick – master of the College, scholar of healing lore.
Master Logan – a master of the College.
Apprentice Truda – apprentice to Master Logan.

Folk at the College in Arn
Master Luthor – scholar of The First Sons, scholar of the scriptorium and master of languages.
Scholar Gideon – scholar of languages.
Jhas p'her – known as Jasper, the dark man of Myhar, once an oar slave.
Apprentice Duncan – an apprentice of the College, previous apprentice of Eldrick and apprentice to Luthor.
Apprentice Elgar – apprentice of Master Luthor.
Wes – acolyte of the College.
Eoin – acolyte of the College.
Master Hobar – a master physician.
Apprentice Enid – apprentice of Master Hobar.
Vinaeus of Telis – visiting scholar from Telis.
Master Edwith – a scholar of matters concerning the gods and religious rites.
Master Ardben – a master of the College.
Master Hoartwyn - a master of the College.

The Council
Councillor Merwyl – College elder, elected speaker.
Councillor Uriah – College elder.
Councillor Rodrik – College elder, and the College representative in Rhagnal's court.
Councillor Caleb – College elder.
Councillor Sareb – College elder.
Councillor Sareya – College elder, keeper of the archives.
Councillor Asha – College elder, scholar of mystic studies.
Councillor Harek – College elder.
Councillor Symon – College elder.

Warriors of the North

Arnulf's warriors
Arnulf – Lord Ravenhold and the Motte.
Hafgan – Arnulf's chief sworn warrior.
Arnulf's warriors lost in the passes – *Hagen, Darek, Branik.*
Erran - Arnulf's sworn warrior.
Fear – Arnulf's hound.

Fergus's warriors
Fergus – Lord of Weirdell.
Astrid – The Death Nymph & Fergus's sworn warrior.
Hild – one of Astrid's shieldmaidens, sworn to Lord Fergus.
Olad - Fergus's sworn warrior, became a Cursed One and slain in the
    Passes.
The shield-maidens of the Death Nymph – formidable warriors led by Astrid
the Death Nymph, sworn to Fergus.

Folk of Eymsford
Angus – High Lord of The Borders & the Old Lands, and Fergus's father.
Calimir – man of the College and advisor to Angus, murdered in the
    North.

Folk of Ravenshold
Aeslin – Arnulf's wife.
Idony – Arnulf's daughter.
Ewolf – Arnulf's son and warrior of the Motte.
Engle – Castellan of the Motte.

Folk of Arn & The Bane River Delta

Folk of Anchorage
Nym – street urchin of Anchorage.
Finn – street urchin of Anchorage.
Jor – tavern keeper in Anchorage.
Wilhelm - sworn warrior of Lord Warrick.
Ox – sworn warrior of Lord Warrick.
Lord Warrick – Lord of Anchorage and huscarl to the king.
The Witch-seer – a mystic of Anchorage.

Folk of Arn

Seth – musician and son of Jor.
King Rhagnal – King of Arnar.
Chancellor Alfric – Chancellor of Arnar, advisor to King Rhagnal.
Prince Harald – son of King Rhagnal.
Alethea – daughter of King Rhagnal.
Olga – Alethea's maid.
Frana – wife of King Rhagnal.
Roark – a street ganger.
Skag – a drunk of Arn.
Whistler – a bargeman.
Wolter & Mirim – old couple of Arn.
Edith & Elsie – mother and daughter in Arn.
Barden – driver of a dead cart.
The king's huscarls: *Jarvi, Aellar, Offa* – sworn warriors of the king.
Ramona – a mystic in Arn.
Edgar – young warrior, sworn warrior of Lord Warrick.

Folk of Stoneshore

Galen – man of Stoneshore, fisherman and grave digger.
Mal - man of Stoneshore, fisherman and grave digger.
Roloff – tavern keeper in Stoneshore.
Touthless Maud – drunk of Stoneshore.
Marik – drunk of Stoneshore.
Old Char – drunk of Stoneshore.
Lord Aefric – Lord of Stoneshore.

Folk of Western Arnar

Folk of the Wilds

Bjorn the hunter – famed master hunter and tracker.
Tung the Wildman – a wildman from the Barrens.
Khyra – a woods witch.

Warriors of the West

Lord Kervan – Lord of Pinedelve.
High Lord Archeon – Lord of Oldstones, High Lord of the Western Mark
and the Frontier.
Daeluf – Captain of Oldstones, sworn to High Lord Archeon.
Hrothgar – Lord of High Stones Hall.

Raiders and Rebels in the West
Niall
Seb
Hale
Pike

Folk of Cydor

King Leofric – King of Cydor.
Lord Jarlson – Rebel leader and pretender to Cydor's crown.

The Gods of Arnar

Old Night – God of Death.
Varg – God of war and hunting.
Hjort – The Hart of Horns, God of the hunted and luck.
Bheur – Goddess of winter and snow.
The Maiden – One of The Three, Goddess of beauty and youth.
The Mother - One of The Three, Goddess of childbirth and love.
The Crone - One of The Three, Goddess of age and wisdom.

The Dead Sagas

VOLUME II

A RITUAL OF FLESH

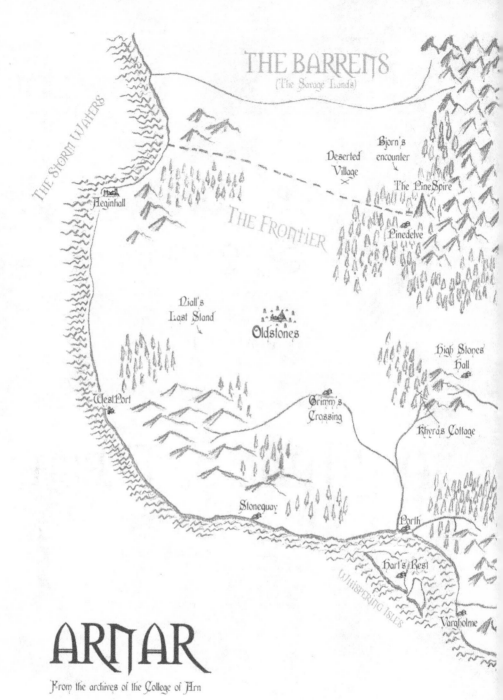

THE BARRENS
(The Savage Lands)

THE STORM WATERS

Bjorn's
encounter

Deserted
Village ✕

Heginhall

The PineSpire

THE FRONTIER

Pinedelve

Niall's
Last Stand

Oldstones

High Stones
Hall

WestPort

Grimm's
Crossing

Rhyra's Cottage

Stonequay

Porth

WHISPERING ISLES

Harl's Rest

Varaholme

ARNAR

From the archives of the College of Arn

By Master Areion
Master Cartographer and Scholar of Charts

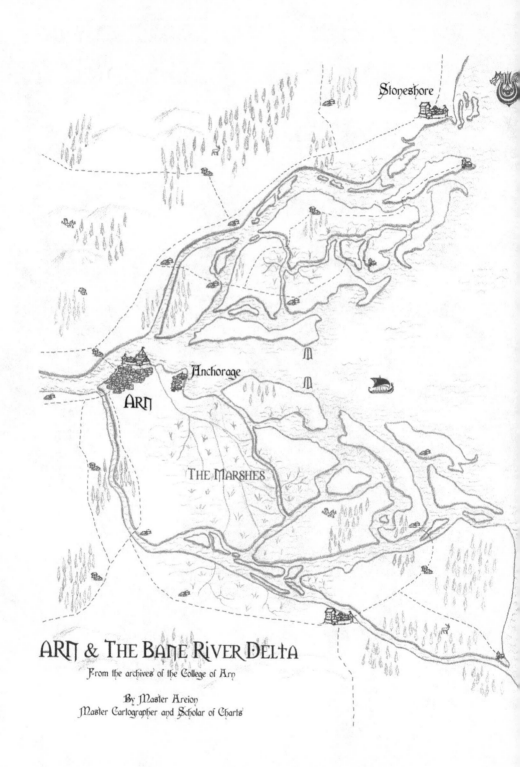

Stoneshore

Anchorage

ARN

THE MARSHES

ARN & THE BANE RIVER DELTA

From the archives of the College of Arn

By Master Areion
Master Cartographer and Scholar of Charts

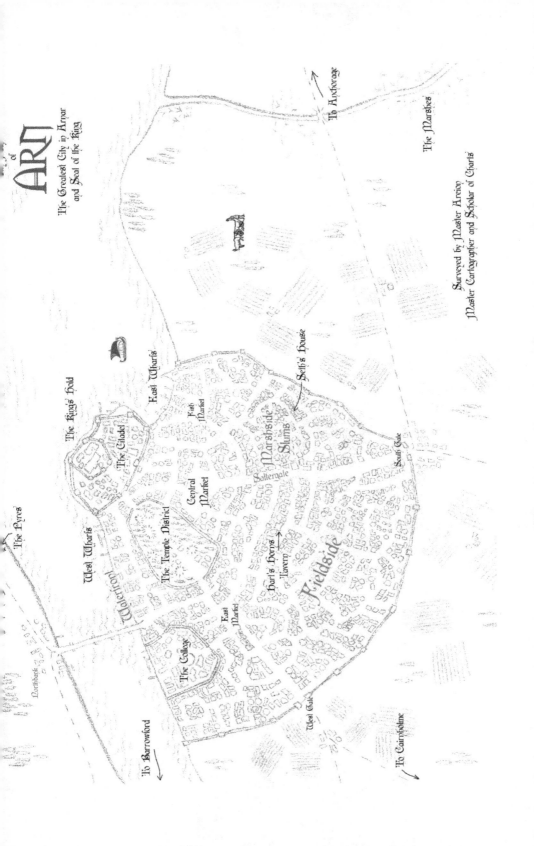

ARD
of

The Greatest City in Arnor
and Seal of the King

Surveyed by Master Arvioy
Master Cartographer and Scholar of Charts

The Pyres

Northbank

To Barrowford

The King's Hold

The Citadel

East Wharfs

West Wharfs

Waterfront

The Temple District

The College

Central Market

Fish Market

East Market

Marshside Slums

Sellergate

Seth's House

Dari's Bone's
Tavern

Fieldside

West Gate

South Gate

To Cairnholme

The Marshes

To Anchorage

Part One

Dark Tidings

CHAPTER ONE

The Grave Pits

Rain lashed down and dripped from the wooden eaves of the nearby buildings. Galen drove the shovel into the earth with his boot. The wet ground gave easily. He heaved another shovel full of soil onto the pile, the small mound beside him growing larger as he slowly dug the pit deeper.

Thunder rolled overhead and the rain seemed to grow heavier, as if the gods themselves were trying to spite him. He was drenched and his boots covered in mud, water pooling at his feet as he stood at the bottom of the pit. He heaved another shovel full of sodden dirt onto the pile.

The clouds hung thick and heavy above him, and though dusk was just settling in, the hour seemed much later. Galen had been told to get the pits dug before nightfall, and had laboured away a long day in the mud. The storm came in after midday, rolling in from the sea to darken the sky and to pour down torrents of rain upon him as he toiled.

His feet sank deeper as he shifted his weight and water rose slowly towards his ankles. He would not finish this last one today, not in this terrible rain. Giving up, he clambered out of the hole and planted his shovel in the heap of earth beside him. The rain dripping from the end of his nose and from his hair, his clothes heavy with thick mud, he hurried over to the shelter of an old outbuilding standing in the yard.

The weary timber awning had open sides, but the roof was turfed over a lattice of woven branches. It huddled against the back of a long, low thatched building that faced the street beyond. Although quite open to the elements, the little lean-to seemed to hold off the worst of the rain.

Galen pulled on his cloak and looked out into the downpour. Puddles had formed across the yard and at the bottoms of the pits he had laboured all day to dig. The street adjoining appeared empty, the glow of hearth fires visible through the shutters and doorways of the thatched houses, great pools of water forming in the churned up road.

A wain rolled into view, pulled along the muddy street by an old horse. He watched it turn into the yard and come to a stop.

'Another three here, Gale,' called the driver. 'Two from the row on the dale road and another of Enid's boys, poor thing. They say she's sick now too.'

'Dark times, Mal. That's over two dozen this week,' he replied.

Mal climbed down from the cart and hurried under the shelter. 'They say it's got worse at Anchorage, and it's the same in the villages as it is here.'

'Any word on when we will be back to sea?'

'It's not looking good, Gale. Old Stefar's sick now. Without a boat master, and half the crew down with it... Well, if they end up like these poor souls,' Mal motioned towards the grim cargo in the back of his cart, 'we won't be back at sea for days, perhaps even weeks.'

Galen sighed at the thought. They had already been stuck in Stoneshore for two weeks, with no sign yet of when they might be heading out again.

The pair stood in silence watching the rain drip from the roof. The thought of burying more folk he had known his entire life made his heart heavy. He looked around at the pits. *This was no place to bury the dead.* The first victims had been interred the traditional way, beneath cairns and mounds, some were burnt on pyres as was their family's wishes, but now there was just too many. Now folk shared a mass burial, in pits dug in a spare lot at the edge of town. It seemed wrong to him. It was no way to honour the dead. The downpour dampened his spirits further. He was eager to get this grim task done for the day. Galen cleared his throat. 'Come on then. Let's finish this quick and get warm.'

They moved to the back of the cart. There lay the afternoon's dead—three victims of the blood sickness that had descended on the town. The bodies were bound in old linens, dark blood soaking through where their faces should be. A Buckner man was unbound. Galen knew that family, everyone did. The corpse's face indeed seemed familiar, but with the bloody staring eyes and a gaping, gore choked mouth, which one he was Galen couldn't tell.

The rain continued to hammer down as they placed the bodies into one of the burial pits. Galen began to cover them with earth, his shovel biting into the sloppy mud and dumping it with a splatter. Mal pitched in, and they covered the corpses but had not even half covered them before they made a hasty retreat back to the shelter. Galen grimaced as he surveyed their work. He knew tomorrow would bring yet more dead. They would be laid on top of those he had just covered until the pit was filled. Then he would begin digging and filling all over again, more pits for the dead.

'I'll finish the rest tomorrow. I've had my fill of mud for to-day,' called Galen.

Mal nodded. 'Aye, let's get out of this rain.'

They unhitched the old horse from the blood-stained wain and led it back to the lord's stable.

There was a still quiet over the town of Stoneshore, a sense of dread hanging heavy in the hearts of the people living here, drawn down by the strange and terrible sickness that had swept into town without mercy. The first sick had appeared nearly a moon past, more were falling to it as each day passed. Galen and Mal walked the silent streets with their hoods raised and their cloaks drawn close about them, passing the doors of darkened houses which had been marked with warnings of death.

Galen had never known a sickness like this, and he had lived in the small fishing town since he was a boy. Folk had thought it was a flux at first, until the first of them had died screaming, their eyes bleeding, vomiting blood until they collapsed, still and silent. He was a fisherman by trade, but with the sickness taking its toll, most of the boats had been unable to put to sea. Just like the rest of the able-bodied crews, he had been forced to find other work until this all blew over, and there seemed no shortage of grave pits that needed digging.

He peered out from under his hood and looked down the nar-row twisting street. Somewhere down there, it intersected with the main sea road that led to the great town of Arn. He knew the old sea road ran south along the coast to Arn. He had never ven-tured far down that road, and had rarely been to Arn at all, but their fishing boat had visited its nearby port many times; a place known as Anchorage.

Stoneshore's round, low walled buildings glistened in the faint light of a few hissing torches, some more intricate than others, constructed from two or more round buildings, sometimes overlapping and connected with low walls of mud. The larger houses along the street had wooden doorways carved with elaborate patterns and images, and were sometimes built from stone. Galen looked uneasily at the crude skulls daubed on many of the doorways in red paint, markings of the sickness. He hurried onward, eager to distance himself from the ominous devices.

They reached the crossroads at the town's centre. Along the west road and lining the central market square were several long rectangular buildings, some with two storeys, all built with thick wooden frames and walls of mud, clay and dung that had set hard and solid over a wicker weave. One such structure was a tavern on the market square, and they hastily made their way inside and out of the rain.

'Galen? Mal? Look at you both!' a loud voice exclaimed. 'Come in quick, get out of that rain. You look half drowned.'

Roloff, the tavern keeper, waddled over with a strained smile on his fat round face, and beckoned them to a table near the hearth. The fire gave off a thin smoke that collected amongst the rafters and drifted out through the door and shuttered windows. There were tables and stools set about the place, although many were empty. Those brave souls who dared congregate in the tavern sat apart, their conversation no more than a murmur. All seemed fearful of getting too close to one another.

The tavern had noticeably quietened as they had entered and people eyed them fearfully. They knew those who had been collecting and handling the dead. Galen and his old shipmate were covered in mud and soaked through, and there was no other reason for folk to be about in this weather. Roloff served them ales and food as they warmed themselves, but Galen noticed even he kept his distance, quickly dumping the plates and tankards and then sharply stepping back. Galen and Mal had frequented this place for years, he thought Roloff a friend, but in his fear he was no different from the others. They ate quietly as they dried off and before long the quiet talk resumed.

'Heard you lads took Enid's other boy today.' The voice of an old woman reached them from across the room. 'That's sad. And her old man Jak last week.' It was Toothless Maud who spoke from her usual corner, though no one ever dared call her that within earshot. Galen noticed long ago she seemed to always be found that corner, day or night.

'Aye.' Mal nodded, keeping his eyes on the contents of his mug. 'We buried him with the others, and I hear she's sick now too.'

'The gods are cruel at times, replied the old crone. Her voice was sibilant, most of her teeth gone exept one prominent front tooth. 'Old Night has no pity,' she added before taking a sup from her tankard.

'Aye, I saw the marks on her door, but she's still there,' said another man from a nearby table. 'Heard a man earlier too,' he continued, 'said he heard word, it came off a ship at Anchorage. Said they found 'em all dead in the taverns by the docks. Said that's where it started, I hear.'

The folk of the tavern looked at each other nervously, the general murmur of conversation dying.

'Shut your mouth, Marik!' snarled Roloff in a sour tone. 'You trying to drive off all my business? Does anyone in here look sick?' He turned to the grave diggers. 'You lads sick? No? See, no one here is sick, not even them! So shut your mouth and stop trying to scare folks.'

Marik gaped at the unexpected outburst. 'I didn't mean nothing, just saying what I heard,'

The tavern keeper glared at him before storming away into a back room.

'I didn't mean nothing by it,' Marik muttered again.

Galen took a bite from the heel of bread he had been served, and frowned down at his bowl. The bread was stale and the stew, although hot, was watery and scant on anything other than root vegetables.

'See, I heard some news...' said an old man with a long grey beard who sat by himself. Galen knew him as Old Char. The old man waited until he had their attention and then went on. 'I've heard that to the north, in the Old Lands, there's rumour of dead men. Dead men walking, and a curse upon the land.'

Mal caught Galen's eye and raised an eyebrow as he listened.

'That's absurd, old man,' blurted Marik. 'Dead men walking? Ha! Mayhap the sickness has spread to the north too? That would be grim tidings if this curse blights the whole realm.'

'I'm not sure, lad, but it does sound that way. Dark are the rumours and I heard another thing too, 'bout the war away to the north in Cydor. Heard Lord Jarlson marched on Three Bridges and holds the town south of the river, but their king has sent a force to meet him. Could be there will be a great battle in Cydor.'

'I heard the same,' chimed Toothless Maud. 'And I heard Jarlson brought a host of mercenaries along with his own men. They say he pushed the king's forces back to the bridges.'

'Course it could have already happened, the talk is a week old at least.' The old man shrugged and scratched at his wiry beard. 'We'll hear soon enough, if any more ships dare come here.'

Galen nursed his tankard, only vaguely listening to the tavern's talk. He had little cares for what was happening north of the borders in Cydor, or the dealings of mercenaries from the east. As far as he was concerned Arnar's old enemy could tear itself to pieces. It was the terrible things happening here in Stoneshore that tugged at his thoughts as he sat smeared in drying grave dirt. He let them talk and offered no comment, if that talk gave some small distraction, it was welcome.

'Well the Cydors have never had any love for us, let them slaughter each other,' said Roloff, waddling back into the taproom.

'Aye, and that Jarlson's certainly no friend of Arnar,' rumbled Old Char. 'I heard a few of our raids hit his lands this year and last. Some clever buggers realised the south lands of Cydor are in rebellion and so are fair game. I heard of a few lords raiding there, but the king's trying to put a stop to it. Don't want it to look like Arnar's taking a side in it.'

'Best to stay out of it, aye,' agreed the fat tavern keeper.

'Great changes are afoot in Cydor, perhaps a new king?' said Marik. 'If Jarlson takes the throne, could mean a war for us too.'

'Aye, tis dark times,' said Roloff. The storm outside announced its presence with a loud rumble of thunder. 'But whatever Cydor's fate,' continued the tavern keeper with a glance at the roof, 'it'll mean less trade and more trouble for a long time yet, and that ain't good for us.'

People grumbled their various agreements.

'There are already fewer folks travelling the roads with this sickness about,' continued Roloff, 'and they're avoiding the towns. The merchants will be hit even harder. The lads in the fields have seen folks passing through the countryside and joining the road again away from the town.'

'They fear the sickness, and wouldn't you, lad?' asked Toothless Maud before returning her gaze to her tankard.

The folk of the tavern had almost forgotten their plight as talk had turned their minds to other things, to the troubles and gossip of other distant lands. But at the mention of the illness, the atmosphere turned icy, heavy foreboding settling in the room.

A piercing scream of despair ripped through the air outside, echoing down the street from somewhere nearby. The mournful wails of a woman silenced the tavern, and cold, creeping fear again stole amongst them.

'Another one taken to Old Night, may the gods have mercy,' muttered Maud.

'I heard Old Shef has taken ill too. Sounds like you boys will be digging graves for some time yet.' A man nearby waved his tankard unsteadily towards the pair seated near the fire.

Mal nodded sadly. 'Aye, he's in the hands of the gods now. A grim hope though. They have been cruel of late. Old Night seems to ever prevail. His dark halls must be getting full.' He paused and sighed. 'I fear the boats will have too few men in the coming months. Many are without crew and sit silent at the dock, and with the nets empty, food will be scarce.'

Marik nodded. 'It's the same with the landsmen, many are —'

A large man ducked through the low tavern door and the room fell silent again. He wore a long grey cloak that dripped from the rain, worn over the livery of the town guard and a harness of mail. He removed a dripping peaked helmet and set it on a table.

'Attention!' His commanding voice echoed off the hard walls. 'The high lords of Arn have commanded the roads to be closed, and the gates of all towns around Arn to be sealed. Travel between the towns and villages is now forbidden, except by leave of each town lord. All ports are closed; no ships will sail or make berth here without leave of our Lord Aefric or a special writ. Folk are not to wander the streets without purpose and are commanded to bring out their dead.'

The big guard's eyes drifted across the faces of the tavern patrons and came to rest on Galen and Mal, seated by the fire. Galen recognised him as one of the guards who kept an eye on the work crews. 'Thus commands Aefric, Lord of Stoneshore.' The guard's shoulders dropped as he let out a sigh. 'May the gods have mercy on us.'

The fat tavern keeper hurried towards him. 'They can't shut us in like rats. This will ruin us!' he exclaimed in a shrill voice.

'Be calm, man.' The guard dismissed Roloff's worry with a gruff grunt. 'This terrible sickness will pass. It must. The folk of Arnar will endure. The ports and roads will soon be open, but the high lords cannot risk Arn, or the realm. This red horror has spread quickly, and we must do what we can to stop it. We must endure and look to the gods. Be glad the taverns are still open at all.'

The tavern keeper shrank back and slumped down on a chair as the guard turned his gaze back to the muddy pair by the fire. 'You lads, you're from the work crews?'

Mal nodded. Galen watched the guard approach, but he didn't get too close. Galen ached all over from his day of grim labour, even lifting his head to the man seemed an effort.

'Did you return your tools?' asked the guard. 'We were told they were to be returned to the quartermasters you borrowed them from.'

Galen leaned back in his chair and threw a weary look at Mal, who shrugged. With a glance back at the guard, Galen mirrored his mate's gesture. He felt bone tired and filthy beyond measure. With all this going on, why were they worried about a few shovels? 'The horse we took back, but the shovels are still at the yard. With the rain, I totally forgot.'

'Make sure you go get them before you return home or they will make you pay for them, I'm sure,' advised the guard, offering them a sympathetic smile.

The guard turned and left, followed by several others, probably keen to return to whatever family they had left, or perhaps just eager to get away from the lingering threat of the sickness. In the stillness left behind, Galen heard the voices of the guards as they moved along the street beyond, calling out the decree of their lord for the townsfolk to hear.

Galen drained his tankard and after bidding his companion farewell, rose and made his way out into the storm. The lightning had eased a little, but rain still washed across the town, coming down in sheets. The evening sky was made even darker by the clouds, hanging in dark curtains before the stars, the only light flickering from the torches of the guards as they hurried along the muddy streets.

With a groan, he remembered the shovels, and instead of turning for home, he plucked a torch from its sconce outside the tavern and made his way back to the yard and to the pits he had laboured in all day. Soaked through once more, he entered the yard and noticed another cart standing abandoned beside the other. The shrouded, blood stained bodies lay stacked in the back of the wagon, ready to be buried in the morning.

How did a fisherman end up here with such a macabre duty? he thought.

His torch hissed as the rain lashed down. Searching the yard for the shovels, his gaze eventually fell upon the ground beside the cart. Galen frowned. One of the linen shrouds had come away and lay soiled and damp in a muddy puddle. He glanced quickly at the bodies again. He may not be used to seeing the dead, even after his recent days of grim labour, but he knew how they were *supposed* to look. A body lay sprawled on top of the others strangely, its shrouds disturbed.

Looters?

He took a careful step closer. There were strange wounds in the exposed skin. Small chunks had been torn from the cold flesh, as if some animal had got at it while it lay unattended. *Dogs perhaps?*

It was then he heard scratching in the gloomy yard behind him. He turned slowly, catching sight of movement. There was something in one of the pits.

Quiet, tentative steps brought him closer, until he saw someone stooped at the bottom of the pit. The thin figure had long blond hair; or was it grey? It was hard to say. Galen lowered the head of the torch toward the figure in the pit, illuminating the interloper. Its lank hair was pale, almost white, but the torch gave it a flickering ruddy hue. It hung down in the mud as the figure crouched low, trailing around in the filth beside something at the figure's feet.

It was a body; one of the victims of the foul sickness. Galen saw it was one of the bodies he and Mal had buried only a few hours before, a body that had been likely living that morning, still fresh from its death bed.

Galen recoiled. *What are they doing?*

Whoever it was, they didn't notice as he slowly approached, the figure totally engrossed in the remains of the poor soul in the pit.

'You there!' called Galen, his voice shaking. 'What are you doing? I'll call for the guard.'

The figure froze, then slowly turned its head.

Galen took a step back in horror.

Blood smeared the man's face. It covered his hands and was splattered through his long, pale hair, almost indistinguishable from the mud caking the lank ends. Was it one of the dying?

'Are you sick? Stay back!' he warned, lowering the flaming head toward the figure.

The figure's eyes were dark and malevolent. It stared back but said nothing, looking more like a nightmare creature than a man. And he was chewing something. A dark trickle of blood ran down his chin.

Galen's eyes widened as he realised the man was no looter. The body at his feet lay torn open, its innards spilled into the mud. The man kept chewing.

He is eating the dead.

The thin, blood-smeared figure suddenly hissed at Galen like a feral cat and shrank back on all fours like some kind of animal. One of its legs looked deformed, it skewed awkwardly in its grotesque ruin. Its top lip curled and it snarled. Perhaps it said a word, he couldn't tell, then it leapt from the pit and raced off into the shadows between the buildings with a hunched loping gait.

Galen stood over the pit, heart pounding, his eyes locked on the shadows where the creature had vanished. His gaze slowly returned to the pit and fixed on the grisly remains. *That thing was eating them, it was eating the dead!* Water dribbled down his face unnoticed. Galen thought about what the old man had told them. *What if the talk in the tavern was true? Of dead men walking, and a curse upon the land. But that thing didn't look dead, that was some kind of ghoulish creature.* He stood frozen in terror. *What if it comes back?* Without a second thought, he spun on his heel and fled.

Thrust into a mound of disturbed earth, the shovels stood forgotten, and Galen sprinted through the mud and rain towards the flickers of torchlight moving down the street.

CHAPTER TWO

Oldstones

The crisp blue sky had been cloudless all day. The low sun shone brightly but did nothing to lift the bite of the cold air. The winter snows could not be far away.

A huge weather front had begun to roll in from the west as the day drew on, cleaving the sky in two for as far as the eye could see. The ominous cloud bank rose up what seemed like leagues into the sky, like a dark roiling cliff-face stretching into the heavens. It brought with it the final rains of autumn which would no doubt turn to hail and then snow in the coming weeks. Behind him to the east, the sky over the rolling hills and forest remained clear and blue.

Bjorn rode his horse to the brow of the rocky hill. The Wildman waited there for him, perched on a rock beside the track, crouched into a squat. The Wildman answered to Tung, although there were still only a few shared words and gestures of understanding between the two of them. He was a curious creature, wearing an assortment of pelts and skins, his hair a riotous tangle of knots that seemed to blend into his beard. Tung used ash to daub his skin with strange symbols. Bjorn had first thought him a savage; a primitive.

The hunter regarded his companion a moment. *But was he really so primitive?* Bjorn had never seen anyone with such skill in bushcraft. He had watched him hunt, seen him fashion beautiful and deadly weapons from nothing but stones and sticks. The hunter suddenly realised his opinion of Tung had certainly begun to change. Although strange to his eyes, perhaps Tung was no savage, perhaps he was just different, a man on a wilder path to even himself.

The Wildman liked to range ahead as he desired, and Bjorn often found him waiting beside the road for him to catch up. Tung's sheer stamina had left the hunter in awe this past week. He was indeed indomitable, never seeming to tire, his steady padding jog easily keeping pace with Bjorn's horse day upon day, yet still he could break into a quick run at any time and disappear into the wilderness ahead. The hunter had never known fortitude like it.

Tung sat watching the encroaching darkness creeping across the panoramic sky-scape, then threw a glance at Bjorn as the hunter reined in beside him to survey the land.

'It's Oldstones, friend,' said Bjorn, pointing.

The Wildman regarded him blankly for a moment before following the hunter's gesture down into the wide valley spread out before them. Tung made a low hooting sound.

There was a town below, spread around the base of a craggy hilltop rising from the valley floor. Even from this distance the hunter could see the shallow gorge which clove through the town and forked around the foot of the hill. It tapered off into narrow ravines which appeared to run between the buildings, as if some mighty force had thrust the bare rock of the hill up through the town and split the ground asunder around it.

This was Oldstones.

The town drew its name from the hundreds of megalithic standing stones scattered across the valley around the craggy spire. Some were lone menhirs while others were set in rows, grids and circles. There were several old longbarrows littering the valley too, and folk had found ancient cairns and dolmens, all interspersed by hundreds upon hundreds of the strange standing stones. They had been there long before the folk of Arnar had settled these lands, relics of an older time, their purpose known only to the gods.

'Come, friend. Civilization awaits us,' said Bjorn with a grimace. The hunter nudged his horse forward and rode onward. Tung sprung down from his vantage point and once again resumed his measured jogging beside Bjorn's horse. Approaching from the east, Bjorn could make out the wooden walls and palisades ringing the town, parts intersected by the natural defences of the grey stone cliff-faces, their tops fashioned into ramparts.

Timber watchtowers loomed into the sky, huge banners floating in the breeze, guards no doubt maintaining a vigil, watching over the approaches to the gates and the stony sentinels surrounding the walls.

The sight of those palisades was a relief. It had been months since he had rode out in search of a mysterious beast and the truth behind the disappearences along the border. What he found instead was a nightmare. The nagging fear still gnawed at him, a fear of cannibal Stonemen appearing from the trees behind him in pursuit. His recent nights had been haunted by memories of that charred, half-eaten arm, of hearing those braying hunting horns. It gave him chills to remember it. Those palisades offered safety, and the end to his task.

The track took them close to the first of the menhirs. Three stood in crooked order by the roadside, different sizes and shapes, yet they were of the same dark grey stone, and Bjorn stared at them as he passed. They were overgrown; patches of brambles and tall grass choking the ground around them. The smooth dark rock seemed contoured with dozens of irregular flat sides, and the stones appeared to lean and twist, like drunks in a tavern.

There were other stones further beyond them, some adorning the rises of the low slopes leading towards Oldstones' east gate. A herd of goats grazed on a hillside nearby, the goatherd resting lazily against a fallen menhir as his flock roamed amongst the weather worn stones. There were other animals at pasture around the stone strewn valley; flocks of sheep in the distance and tan coloured cattle inside the wattle fence of a farmstead nestled alongside the east road.

As the pair drew nearer to the town's walls, Bjorn made out the shapes of guards upon their high ramparts. The east gate slowly swung open. A horn blew behind the palisades and Bjorn reined in, uncertain. Tung slowed to a stop and looked around in wonder.

A column of riders emerged, banners of many colours in their midst. The glint of steel reflected the light of the late autumn sun, not yet obscured by the blanket of heavy cloud. Warriors in their hundreds marched in the rider's wake — a small army.

Bjorn watched on, apprehension turning to curiosity as the host filed out from the gate and swung onto the south road, but Tung seemed agitated, grunting and sniffing at the air as if trying to sense the intent of the soldiers.

'They're not coming our way, friend,' said Bjorn to his companion. 'But I do wonder... They can only be going south or west by that road.'

He expected no answer from Tung. He never did. Bjorn had no doubt the Wildman understood some of his words, but his strange follower rarely tried to speak. Tung seemed quick to pick up a little of Bjorn's language, a few basic names for things but nothing more. Bjorn had in turn begun to recognise the strange sounds Tung had been repeating, though he had yet to assign any meaning to them. Both of them wore only dense, blank looks in their eyes whenever they tried to speak with each other, each attempt usually ending in frustration.

Nudging his horse once more towards the fork where the east and south roads met just outside the east gates, Bjorn and his companion reached the intersection in the road as the tail end of the host marched away. The hooves of the horses and the step of hundreds of footfalls had left the south road a mess of churned mud. The large wooden gates of Oldstones remained open and townsfolk spilled out to watch the host disappear into the distance. Some likely had loved ones amongst them, others just watched out of curiosity.

Guards stood about the open gate, banners of yellow and black hanging from the palisade to either side. Most of the guards wore a tabard of the same colours over a motley assortment of armour. *The best warriors must have marched out*, noted the hunter as he surveyed the men at the gate.

Withered corpses hung chained from nearby menhirs, all in easy view of the east gate. Half a dozen recently demised men hung limp from a gallows which stood outside the city gates, and beside them, an empty gibbet hung creaking on its chain in the breeze. Criminals, most like, their fate displayed for all to see. A grisly reminder of the law in these lands.

Tung stared up at the dead men fearfully, then moved around to Bjorn's other side as they passed, placing the hunter between himself and the hanging dead. A trader's cart, which had been patiently waiting beside the road as the host passed, now rolled up to the gates. The driver sat laughing with one of the guards as Bjorn reined in behind it, drawing the attention of another guard who threw a wary glance at Tung.

Tung was bewildered, wandering over to the palisade to lay his hands on the wooden logs, gazing up at the ramparts above. He hooted and bobbed his head.

So it seems the Wildman truly has never seen palisades or been close to a town such as this? Bjorn wondered, *Is he truly one of the Stonemen from the legends?* The question had often haunted his thoughts these past weeks.

'Get away from there!' barked another guard, suddenly noticing the strange Wildman for himself. Tung shrank back and sank onto all fours as the guard approached.

'I'm sorry, friend. He is with me. Don't worry, he is harmless,' said Bjorn in apology. 'Though, he's likely mad.' *Why say that?* Bjorn pondered his choice of words. Were they to mask Tung's suspected origins? He strangely felt the need to protect the Wildman from the prejudices of his own harsh world.

The guard eyed Tung for a long moment, then turned his attention to Bjorn. 'And you are?'

'I am Bjorn the hunter. I'm returning to Lord Archeon and have urgent news for him. He's expecting me.'

The guard looked him over, as if trying to decide whether or not to believe him. 'Best get on then, but keep an eye on him.' The guard nodded sharply at Tung and waved them through.

Bjorn whistled and beckoned, and Tung approached apprehensively. It was hard to tell how the Wildman would react to being inside the town. Was it a good idea to bring him in at all? Bjorn reckoned he had little choice — he'd been unable to stop the Wildman following him so far. What could he do now, short of having him restrained and locked up somewhere? That also might not end well. He simply had to do his best to keep Tung out of trouble.

He sighed.

'Follow,' Bjorn commanded sternly, before clicking his tongue and urging his horse onward through the gate. Tung seemed to catch his meaning and followed quietly, nervously eyeing the steel weapons of the gate guards as he passed beneath the gateway.

On first glance Oldstones looked very much the same as any other Arnar settlement. The outskirts were a sprawl of old wooden round houses and mixed with the more modern wooden buildings which had sprung up as Oldstones had swollen to its current size. Taverns, merchants and smiths lined the main street, plying their trade, and a herd of cattle was being driven into a large shed built up against the inside of the palisade.

It seemed as if quite a crowd had gathered to watch the warriors march out, one that was now dispersing as folk went back to their business. Bjorn picked his way through the milling townsfolk, most wise enough to stand aside and allow his horse through. The Wildman drew many curious looks as he padded along beside the hunter's horse, his head swinging about, eyes taking in the sights of a town for what had to be the first time. More than once something caught Tung's attention, and Bjorn had to call him back as he tried to wander off.

Yet while the outskirts of Oldstones seemed no more unusual than a dozen other towns he had visited, Bjorn remembered Oldstones to be a strange place, and not just because of the ancient stones strewn through the valley. The older central districts were like nowhere else he had ever been.

He led the awe-struck Wildman over a sturdy bridge spanning one of the wide ravines. Below, within the gorges, folk had built homes against the sheer stone walls. The deep winding ravines became thin, winding streets. Sprawling buildings climbed several levels, and some buildings reached up the walls to the full height of the ravine, joining houses on ground with the level above. Overhead in the narrower sections of ravine, bridges spanned the gaps between rooftops and gangways ran between the taverns and merchant shops in a maze of walkways. This was the district known as the Crags.

They passed through another gated palisade, built in a gap between rocky bluffs, and made their way up towards the high crags at the town's summit. The rocky streets were riddled with caves and gullies, buildings hewn long ago from the solid rock itself and built upon further in recent times. Natural cave mouths had been built over, revealing only the front walls of the buildings concealed within, many reaching deep into the hillside. Of all the roads, the winding boulevard of old stone-pile buildings leading to the summit was known to be oldest, and the lord's hall was to be found at its centre.

Oldstones seemed to be a place long lived in, occupied well before the warriors of Arnar had driven people like Tung away and claimed it for themselves, the ancient stone first cut by a people now long passed from memory. It was one of the largest towns on the northern frontier and had become the centre of government in the west, the seat of the High Lord Archeon. Bjorn was eager to report back to the high lord and put this business behind him.

***

The chamberlain led Bjorn and Tung through dark corridors that led deep beneath the hillside, stopping before a large carved door with iron edging.

'The lord is likely busy, hunter, but I will inform him you are here.' The chamberlain gestured at the doors as a guard swung it open. 'Please follow me.'

The guards eyed Tung suspiciously and followed the pair inside, taking up watchful positions beside the door.

The wide hall was stone walled, with torches ensconced along its length. Black and yellow banners bearing the high lord's colours adorned the patterned beams overhead, but other than that, the room's decoration was tastefully modest. A few folk occupied the hall, and eyes turned curiously towards them.

The Wildman scuttled between the tables behind Bjorn, peering about and inspecting everyday items that must have been brand new to him. The tables, the doors, buildings of wood and stone, paperweights, bowls and utensils of metal rather than stone—such basic trivial things to Bjorn, but likely a mystery to this poor soul. Tung stared at the strange and wonderful surroundings in a curious awe.

The bustling chamberlain led them along the length of the hall towards a raised dais occupied by the lord's empty chair, then beyond that and through a curtained partition. A small hearth crackled beside a large desk where High Lord Archeon stood frowning down at a collection of open ledgers. A pair of men stood beside him—chamberlains by the look—no, perhaps clerks, thought Bjorn.

Archeon had a lean, serious face and looked well into his fiftieth year, despite his hair retaining its dark colour, save for a shock of grey here and there. He wore it cut short and his face was clean shaven. The hunter motioned for Tung to halt and the Wildman sank into a crouch. The high lord gave them barely more than a casual glance before looking back down at the ledgers. He

39

frowned and placed a finger on the pages before him.

'Does this seem a little low to you?' murmured Archeon.

'Similar to previous weeks, lord,' replied one of the clerks.

'Aye,' said Archeon, looking up at the man. 'But, we've just had seven of my banner men march out, who knows how many hundreds of warriors, all here most of the week. Every other ledger shows a much larger increase this week, except this one.' Archeon stabbed his finger angrily at the page.

'Yes, lord,' agreed the clerk hastily.

'Who tallied this?' muttered the high lord as he ran his finger along the page. 'Broka! Go and get this Broka from the low market to come and see me.' The clerk immediately rose and made to leave the chamber. 'He is either incompetent or a thief. This just won't do,' rumbled Archeon.

'Of course, lord. I will see to it.' The clerk bowed and rushed from the room as the chamberlain scurried to Archeon's shoulder and whispered in his ear.

'Yes, I saw,' Archeon replied dryly, glancing again at Bjorn. 'A moment, Bjorn.' The chamberlain scuttled away to wait quietly to one side while Lord Archeon took another long look over the ledger before him. 'Yes, these seem mostly in order. I will finish with them later.'

The clerk beside him nodded and gathered up several papers and books, then disappeared into a corridor.

'So, Bjorn,' said Archeon. 'The hunter has returned. Did you bring me my beast?'

'No, m'lord.' Bjorn attempted to swallow away his words of failure but found his mouth suddenly dry. 'There was no beast.'

'No beast? Shame,' said Archeon as he poured himself a wine. 'Would you like some, or we have ale if you prefer?'

'A wine,' he replied gratefully. 'I rarely drink good wine these days.'

Archeon nodded to someone unnoticed in the shadows. A servant hurried forward and filled Bjorn a long tin cup full of pale wine.

'It's good,' declared Archeon. Then his eyes narrowed. 'But, I sent you to find a beast, hunter, to find out the truth of these disappearences on my border, and you're telling me there is no beast?' He frowned. 'So, what *did* you find?'

'I do think I found the truth of the matter,' replied Bjorn. The

Wildman chose that moment to make a low cooing sound and Archeon's attention fixed on Bjorn's strange companion. The hunter cringed at Tung's interruption. *Don't bring attention to yourself, friend. Not here, not now.*

'And who is this?' enquired Archeon, the corner of his mouth twitching with a smirk.

'A Wildman, lord. A primitive from the Barrens beyond the border.'

'Is he sane?' asked Archeon, watching Tung with one brow raised as he sniffed a nearby curtain.

'For the most part,' replied the hunter stifling a smile.

'Has he something to do with all this...' Archeon whisked his hand in the air, searching for the words. 'The disappearances?'

'It's a long story.'

'Well, I'll hear it,' said Archeon as he made himself comfortable in the large chair behind his desk.

'As I said, m'lord, I found no sign of any beast, and no one who could claim to have seen it. Just rumours. No tracks, or signs, or anything. I do not believe there is a beast–that much was purely talk.'

Archeon frowned. 'There have been many reports coming in with the merchants about this beast, a lot of talk of the folk it's taken. Are you saying it is all rumour?'

'Alas m'lord, I found no trace of a beast.' Bjorn shook his head, glancing quickly at Tung, who was attempting to lick an unlit tallow candle. 'But I did confirm the disappearances. There were many I spoke to who knew others who had vanished, all of them out near the borders, and beyond them also. I found empty farmsteads and hamlets, but yes, only talk and rumour of a beast.'

Archeon nodded seriously. 'Did you discover what happened to them? The folk who lived there?'

'I think so,' said Bjorn. This should have been a triumphant moment, but instead it was sucked dry and empty by the thought of what he had seen.

Archeon sat forward in interest and Bjorn began carefully. 'I found one such deserted hamlet, well over the border. It was abandoned. There were no bodies, no livestock either, but tools and items strewn all over the ground as if dropped in a hurry.'

'Probably brigands,' commented a voice.

Bjorn jolted with surprise as he realised a finely mailed man had been sat across the room, silent and unnoticed in the shadows.

'Daeluf, the captain of my guard.' Archeon introduced the warrior with a gesture. He sat on a bench almost hidden from view, listening in. He wore a fine mail coat, his helmet upon the table beside him.

Bjorn nodded at the man. 'We met briefly on my last visit, lord.' He had seen his face before. He remembered the silver scar that snaked down one cheek. Daeluf had a serious face, much like his lord, and wore his dark hair cropped short.

'Aye, my reports tell us they are mostly brigands living out there,' said Daeluf. 'I would not be surprised if it was one of their camps you discovered, hunter.'

'Perhaps, friend,' Bjorn nodded again thoughtfully. 'But there are also many folk who have settled the land out there—frontiersmen and the like. It seemed like a small village, not a brigand's camp.'

Daeluf grunted.

Bjorn ignored his derision and turned back to address the high lord. 'I picked up a strange trail leading off into the wilds, though. It led east towards the foothills of the Spine.'

'You ventured that far east?' The lord seemed a little sceptical at that.

'It led to...' He trailed off, uncertain. *They will think me a madman.* After a moment of thought he took a breath. 'There were savages out there. Stonemen, like in the old stories.'

'Stonemen?' echoed Archeon and raised his eyebrows at the chamberlain who stepped forward with a glint of interest in his eyes.

'Aye, lord. I was attacked. There are tribes of them out there.'

The high lord looked sceptically at Bjorn but did not speak. *He doesn't believe me.*

'Lord, you paid me for my skills in the wild, but still, they ambushed *me*, took me completely by surprise in the wilderness. They appeared like ghosts. I have hunted those parts before and never have I seen or heard of such a people out there, ever!'

'Did you find our missing folk?' asked Archeon seriously.

'I found some, lord. All dead. They had hunted them down.'

'That is ghastly,' exclaimed the chamberlain. 'Poor devils, killed for sport.'

'No, you misunderstand me. There is more to it. It wasn't for sport. They were eating them, eating *people!*' said Bjorn. 'Hunting our folk like game.'

The chamberlain gasped and looked repulsed.

'By the gods,' murmured Archeon, his expression darkening.

'It was a hunting party that took me. They had me trussed up like a deer on a hunt. There were others, Arnar folk.'

'Were they definitely *our* people?'

Born noted the doubtful look in Archeon's eyes had gone, replaced by a grave seriousness. *I have his attention now.*

'They were our folk, dressed in our clothes—Arnar blood in their veins, no doubt.' Bjorn was emphatic about this. This he knew to be true. 'Despite which side of the border they were from, they were our folk, Arnar's kinsmen. They were all dead. These Stonemen... They are eating people.'

'Could there be any truth to this?' asked Archeon, addressing the chamberlain beside him.

'It is written in the Great Histories,' said the chamberlain, 'that the Stonemen were pushed back and fled far to the north, away from the steel and armour of Arn and his warriors. They were said to have gone across the Barrens, to perish in the wastes. It is possible some did not...perish.' The man seemed nervous. Bjorn spied the feather brooch the chamberlain wore on his robes. *A man of the College.* Sight of that familiar symbol plucked at an old pain within the hunter.

'Do your records speak of these Stonemen devouring folk?' Archeon pressed.

The chamberlain shook his head. 'They do not. It is written in the Great Histories that the last of the Stonemen fled north many centuries ago.' He paused thoughtfully. 'Perhaps they are out there still, a people forced to survive any way possible, even if it means eating their own kind to endure.'

'Is he one of them, a man-eater?' Daeluf demanded, bristling and eyeing Tung darkly as the Wildman prodded at a wolf-skin rug.

'I am not sure,' admitted Bjorn. 'He was their prisoner and I freed him when I escaped. He fled from them also, so I doubt he lived among them. They wore skulls, he does not. Yet, he shares their look and uses the same weapons of stone. I think he may be a Stoneman, but I cannot say for sure.'

'Perhaps a different tribe,' ventured the chamberlain. 'There could be many of them, each with different ways. Who knows? There are stories of warring tribes far to the north still using stone weapons and wearing skins, thought to be the remnants of the untouched savages of old. But there is nothing in the College records that I have seen to prove it.'

Bjorn listened intently, wishing in some way he'd known this before he had ventured north. Even Tung drifted closer, captivated by the chamberlain's words, though he could not have understood them.

The chamberlain paused to shrug. 'I dismissed it. There are colleagues of mine who believe the Stonemen of the Sagas could have been what was left of the peoples untouched by the First Sons. Others think they could perhaps be descendents of the First Sons themselves, but unlike our ancestors, were a people who fell back into feral tribes after their fall. There are many theories back at the College, but little proof.'

Bjorn recognised the name. He had always thought the First Sons were just a myth. He had heard it said they were the same ancient folk who raised the strange stones littering the hilltops and wild places across all the realms of men.

'Do you think these brutes who are preying on our folk could be one of these lost tribes?' asked Archeon.

'The Sagas tell us the old tribes would fight amongst themselves and raid each other's villages, but since Arn's time they have never dared to return south and raid Arnar. They fear our steel.'

Archeon nodded seriously once more.

'So not just brigands wandering around out there,' mused Daeluf.

'I can find the records if you desire to read what we have on them, m'lord?' offered the chamberlain.

'Maybe I will,' replied Daeluf sourly. Bjorn seriously doubted the man spent his leisure time anywhere but a tavern. He certainly didn't look the type to frequent an archive.

The chamberlain walked around the desk to take a better look at the Wildman. 'You say these feral Stonemen could be his kin?' he asked Bjorn, nodding at Tung.

Bjorn regarded his companion. The Wildman was staring up into the eaves of Archeon's hall where the high lord's black and yellow banners hung limp in the still air. Tung seemed so out of place here in these halls, lessened somewhat by the grandure around him and no longer the indomitable pursuer Bjorn had admired in the wilds. He belonged to a folk left behind by the world, considered savage as beasts, and something inside the hunter found that sad. From what he had seen of Tung, the Wildman was more than that. Bjorn himself felt most at ease while in the wilds. He had a strange empathy with a people remaining wild and free.

'He is like them,' Bjorn replied thoughtfully. 'These Stonemen are not like us, their faces, their eyes — they are different. Tung does share their look, aye, and I am certain he is not of our blood. Yet, he does not act like the ones who captured me. The others I saw were more beast than man. They were cannibals, truly a savage people. He is intelligent, and has proven himself kind, and loyal.' Bjorn felt a pang of guilt at his first reaction to the Wildman, seeing now his judgement had been borne of ignorance. His hand drifted to the stone knife he wore at his belt, a fine gift, made with great skill and given in kindness.

'Very curious indeed, but Stonemen? Could they still roam beyond the borders?' The chamberlain moved towards Tung, examining him.

Bjorn stayed him with a warding hand. 'I would not get too close. He can be unpredictable. It would probably be best to treat him as you would an animal. He can be easily spooked and does not understand our ways, but as I say, he is still cunning and intelligent.'

'Is that so,' murmured the chamberlain, cautiously keeping his distance and slowly circling.

'Yes, he seems quite skilled in bush-craft. He managed to track me many leagues as no other man could. I was mounted and he on foot, yet he kept pace and sought me out. We have formed a bond this past week, a trust.'

'Impressive,' said Archeon, eyeing the Wildman as he grew still and watched them nervously, evidently aware they were talking about him. 'He has a name?'

'He answers to Tung,' replied the hunter. 'He just appeared in my camp one night and tried to talk with me. It was a strange experience. I still can't understand him, but for a few gestures and words.'

'Is it possible?' muttered the chamberlain. 'They have been gone for hundreds of years. Our ancestors purged them from these lands. How could they have survived out there?'

'Only the gods know,' said Bjorn, 'but they are returning south.'

'So, you are telling me Stonemen from the old Sagas have returned to raid my lands, and are eating my folk?' Archeon demanded.

Bjorn nodded, glancing at Tung as the Wildman flinched at the high lord's tone.

'This is grim timing, lord,' said Daeluf.

'Aye,' agreed Archeon frowning.

'There would be little help we could send to the villages until the banners return,' Daeluf continued.

'The banners are marching west, you likely saw them,' said Archeon, addressing Bjorn. 'There are few we could send to help our people in the north until they get back. Raiders on the west coast have been proving... troublesome.'

Arnar was at the far western edge of the known world, a frontier realm, and there was nothing but strange, uncharted seas to the south and west. No people other than the folk of the Barrens and the folk of Arnar toiled on the seas closer to the coast, and Bjorn was curious to know who would dare land a warband on the west coast.

Before he could ask, Archeon fixed his gaze upon him. 'Who else knows of these Stonemen?'

'I met with Lord Kervan at Pinedelve,' Bjorn told him. 'I warned him before riding here, lord. He said he would spread the word. I'm sure he will do something—send out scouts, and get his people safe.'

'That is good.' Archeon nodded, almost speaking to himself, before looking at his guard captain. 'Could Kervan not deal with this tribe? He must have a few dozen good men at least.'

Daeluf nodded in agreement.

'There were many of these cannibals, m'lord,' interrupted Bjorn. 'Not just one hunting party. Who knows how many more are heading south?'

Archeon considered the hunter's warning a moment and frowned. 'I will send word out and warn my people along the borders. I will make it known that Arnar's warriors will sweep these savages from our borders. The border lords will have to muster their own warriors and send for help from their neighbours. But I will send those who can to help hunt these man-eaters. I'm sure there are many young lads hungry for some glory. Let them hunt these beasts.'

'Aye, lord,' agreed Daeluf.

'Until we know more that is most wise, lord,' said the chamberlain.

Archeon sank back in his chair and rubbed his face. 'Sea raiders in the west, Stonemen of legend *eating* my people in the north east. Talk of plague in the capital. Cydor ripping itself apart over the Spine. These are dire times,' said Archeon shaking his head and letting go a sigh.

Plague? Had Bjorn heard that right?

'Well thank you, Bjorn. You are always welcome here. You have done me a great service, and the king also. I will see you are well rewarded, as I promised.' Archeon said formally.

Bjorn sensed it might be his time to leave the high lord to his thoughts and collect his silver. It seemed much had happened in the time he had been travelling in the wilderness. He bowed. 'A pleasure, Lord Archeon. You know how to find me if you require my services again.'

The high lord nodded and the mailed captain rose, crossing to the desk to speak briefly in Archeon's ear. The high lord flicked a glance at Bjorn and nodded to what he heard. Curious about the whispered conversation, but not willing to offend the lord and end up hanging in the gibbet before the gates for his trouble, Bjorn motioned for Tung to follow and turned back to the hall. The chamberlain moved to show them out.

'I have another job for you hunter, if you want it,' called Archeon. 'I will pay well.'

Bjorn wanted nothing more than a warm bath and a tankard of ale, keen to put all this behind him, but it was not wise to refuse such a man of power.

'Of course, Lord Archeon. I am at your service,' said the hunter turning back to the desk, forcing himself to smile. 'What would you have me do?'

Archeon smiled grimly. 'Another hunt. Not a beast this time, but a man.'

CHAPTER THREE

The Daughter of a King

The mud squelched beneath his boots. It had rained again. Ahead, a woman wailed in grief as her companions tore her away from her husband's corpse. She knelt and clutched at him, not wanting to relinquish his cold embrace, desperate for a few final moments in the arms of her love; yet another citizen fallen to the sickness.

Wilhelm pulled his scarf tighter over his face. The usual stench of the city streets had been pervaded by the underlying scent of death. It was not uncommon to see blood churned into the mud, the victims of the sickness laid out beside doorways awaiting the wagons. Some, having staggered their final steps, lay where they fell in the alleys and side streets.

He pitied the woman. Her plight had become an all too familiar sight in the capital these days. However, he found himself no longer as moved as he once had been, back before all this began. It felt wrong. He mused morbidly on his morality — he'd become dulled to the mounting sight of death around him, like a knife used too often without care or reprieve.

Two men heaved the body onto the back of a wagon then gave a shout to the driver, who flicked the reins and urged the horse on. The wagon rolled away, its wheels carving deep furrows through the wet mud and the grieving woman gave chase, sliding and stumbling, before sinking to her knees in the narrow street. Her companions surrounded her, offering consoling words of comfort but they did nothing to lessen her sobbing.

'Poor girl,' said Alethea. 'Come Olga. We should go to her.'

Olga, the princess's young handmaiden, looked around at the houses uncertainly and caught Wilhelm's eye before reluctantly following Alethea.

'Is that wise, m'lady?' Wilhelm asked. 'I have orders to keep you from harm.'

'Don't fret Wilhelm,' replied Alethea, cutting him off. She set her jaw and her eyes flashed with defiance. 'I will go where I please. Neither your Lord Warrick, nor my father can stop the gods from striking me down if they so wish. Only love and kindness will stay their hands. We will go to her.'

'Of course, m'lady, I just don't think it is wise to get too close,' pressed Wilhelm, adjusting his face scarf.

Alethea rolled her eyes and strode off towards the crying woman, lifting the hem of her dress out of the churned mud. It was a valiant attempt to prevent the ruining of the garment, but it failed. The handmaiden, Olga, followed dutifully.

Wilhelm sighed and looked back to the horses. His friend Ox held the reins of their waiting mounts, and the man shrugged before stifling a wet, chesty cough. The king's daughter had expressed her earnest desire to go down and see the state of the city of Arn for herself, to show the people that they had not been forsaken by their sovereigns. Thus, Wilhelm and his companion were bound to trudging through the mud all morning in her wake. Folk had come out to stare, ashen faces peering from their doorways as Alethea moved amongst the residents, talking to them in turn. Watching as Alethea embraced the poor woman, Wilhelm shook his head.

This is not wise.

Their route had taken them into the maze of narrow lanes and streets between the south gate and the markets. Houses were poorly maintained here, barely more than a slum, mostly thin wooden framed dwellings with a second storey jutting out to overhang the street. They had been badly walled with mud and clay, and Wilhelm saw many with dilapidated roofs and evident patches of improvised repairs.

Ox brought the horses up. 'Not the best part of town,' he said looking around the nearby houses then covering another cough.

'Aye,' replied Wilhelm after a moment. As far as he was concerned, the sprawl of the city allowed too many folk in one place. Unable to grow their own, folk in the city relied on merchants to bring their food in from the waterways, but food wasn't free. And in a place like this, there were often too many folk and not enough coin to be made. Poverty was common.

Ox hacked out another cough and spat into the mud.

Wilhelm could not help noticing that Ox had the very same spluttering cough he had heard amongst the folk he passed. He hoped it was just a cough brought on by the winter creeping in, hoped it was nothing more sinister than the seasons changing, but he felt a growing fear it was the same cough he'd heard in Anchorage, tearing at the lungs of the dying.

Folk were saying this was how it started—a cough, then the bleeding. Death comes quickly after. He had seen it in Anchorage, and now here. Wilhelm fidgeted with his face cloth, pulling it up below his eyes.

***

'They're coming, Nym!' exclaimed Finn as he burst through the door.

'Who?' she replied as she absently rolled the remaining piece of hack silver between her fingers. She had used her brother's knife to slice off sliver after sliver, until now only a fragment remained. Even though the silver had diminished with time, the memory of what she'd had to do to get it had not. Thankfully, the stink of the drunkard had eventually washed off.

'Soldiers! Out there on the street,' said her brother in a panic, closing the door behind him. 'They never come down here. Are they after me?'

Nym looked up and scowled at her brother. His face was filthy. His clothes ripped to rags. There was mud matted in his hair. Her little baby brother had become a street urchin. She rose and joined him in peering out through a crack in door.

'Look,' he said. 'There.'

'I see them. Why would they be after you? What have you stolen now, Finn?' She slapped him across the back of his head. 'I warned you to stay out of trouble. Why are you so stupid?'

He recoiled and spread his hands. 'Nothing anyone saw,' he replied, the corner of his mouth lifting in a smirk. She scowled at him and peered again through the crack.

'Oh look, here comes the old bastard too,' said Finn, glancing back at the soldiers. 'Wait, shit, they've stopped him.'

The guards were armed and wore armour beneath their cloaks, and one of the warriors had hailed Jor, stopping him as he scurried back along the street. She narrowed her eyes and watched them talk a moment.

'What's he doing?' Finn squealed in alarm as Jor pointed their way. Her brother darted over to his meagre possessions and began franticly hiding things.

Nym ignored him, studying Jor and the warrior as they continued to talk.

'I think it's the warrior from back in Anchorage, the one who warned us. The old man's friend,' Nym said, not taking her eyes from the scene through the crack. Jor smiled as he spoke, though the smile quickly faded to a grave expression.

Her brother still wasn't taking any chances. He continued to scrabble about in a corner.

'It's her,' gasped Nym, turning to gape at her brother. Finn stopped scrabbling and looked at her blankly. 'It's the princess!'

It was her for certain; Nym recognised her face from the sacrifice ritual in Anchorage. It had failed, the gods refused to listen to their pleas, and she, Jor and Finn had all fled to the city, but she remembered the princess, remembered how she had walked among the common folk and offered comfort to the sick. The soldiers were her escort. She had her hair braided again, but it was different—intricate and beautiful. Her long green dress had been stitched with pretty patterns, and she'd hitched it up out of the way as she walked through the mud, her fur shawl draped over her shoulders. She carried herself with such confidence, holding her head high, her eyes daring the men folk to defy her will, but yet so gentle and caring as she spoke to the folk in the street, taking their hands and offering kind words. She looked so pretty and strong. Nym stared, wishing she could be like that.

She watched Jor bid the warrior farewell and hurry back towards the door, moving aside as he entered.

'Who are those guards looking for?' Finn demanded of Jor before the man had time to greet them.

'No one, lad,' replied Jor, frowning suspiciously. He turned to Nym. 'You feeling better now, lass?'

'Yes, much better. I really am fine. I promise. Probably just some bad food.' He might be a bit gruff, rough around the edges, and sometimes difficult to please, but old Jor was a good sort. After their parents had died, he'd been there for her and Finn, giving them shelter and work in his tavern. He even cared enough to clip Finn around the ears for thieving. When the sickness hit Anchorage, he'd brought them with him to Arn, seeking shelter at the advice of the guard he'd been speaking to outside.

Jor frowned as he looked over her face. 'I brought you this,' he said, handing her a small bundle of cloth. Nym unwrapped it to reveal some twisted brown roots. 'Sevren-root... for your stomach.'

She smiled. 'Thank you, Jor. That is kind.'

'No worries, lass, it's easy to come by,' replied the old man.

'Is that really the princess out there?' asked Nym, peering back out the door.

'Have you been out?' demanded Jor angrily. 'I told you to stay inside.'

She had done as he asked, although Finn had snuck out briefly.

'No!' she insisted. 'I've been watching from the door.' It was something Jor had taken to doing himself recently, nervously peering out into the street at every scream or sound of a commotion.

He nodded sternly, seeming to accept her explanation. *I have seen sixteen winters and yet he still sometimes treats me as a child.*

'Who were you talking to?' asked Finn. 'We saw you talking to the guards.'

'An old friend from Anchorage, but I don't see how it's any of your business.'

Nym ignored her brother's enquiries. 'So is that *really* the princess?' asked Nym eagerly. 'It looks like her.'

Jor fixed the young lad with one last frown, then rubbed his brow with weary exasperation. 'Aye, lass, it's the king's daughter. Now, can I get through and get these soggy boots off?' He pushed past Nym, took down his heavy hood and undid his cloak. The biting cold had left his balding and wrinkled head a bright red, despite the thick cloak's hood. He scratched his head with the stump of his amputated forearm and looked around the room. The house was a hovel, two simple rooms of low crumbling mud-packed walls and a low beamed roof. The main room, in which they stood, was barely furnished, just an old table and a few chairs around a dirty hearth. This was where they had been sleeping too, their bedrolls spread out on the ground along the walls. The house's owner seemed to live a frugal life, he had few domestic possessions, and had been kind enough to let them share the meagre space. 'Isn't he back yet?' asked Jor.

'No,' said Nym, turning back to peer out through the door.

'Who was your friend, the guard?' asked Finn. He was as tenacious as he was annoying. Why was he so interested in the guard? Didn't he realise there was *royalty* in the street? 'Is he the man from back home?'

'Aye, it was Wilhelm,' replied Jor. 'He's out guarding the king's daughter. And no, he ain't out looking for your thieving arse, so just calm down. It was good to see a friendly face, though. Folk 'round here ain't the same. They don't trust us. We're outsiders to them.'

Nym glanced back over her shoulder at that and noticed the old man looking at her, a solemn frustration in his eyes. She knew what he was thinking with that look. Folk had been avoiding them since they'd arrived in Arn, or avoiding her anyway. She had been quite sick several times of late. Even Jor had been keeping his distance. Perhaps he feared she'd caught the sickness? He wasn't alone in his fear either. A veil of dread seemed to hang over the entire city, and she was terrified she was sick just like the others. Nym tried not to think about it and looked at the unwrapped bundle of roots in her hands.

Jor sighed and stooped over to peer through the door. 'Where is he?' the old man grumbled impatiently.

Nym was barely listening. She had turned back to the door, watching in fascination as the princess and her servant spoke with a filthy looking group of children.

'Can I go and speak with her too?' asked Nym hopefully. She desperately needed a distraction. This tiny house had become so claustrophobic she felt like she was choking, and she needed something to take her mind off her recent ill health.

'Certainly not!' snapped Jor. 'What would *you* say to the king's daughter?'

Nym slumped and sighed. She thought she might tell her she had a pretty dress or tell her how awed she had been to see her in Anchorage, but she didn't offer the old man a reply.

'Ah, I see him. Thank the gods,' said Jor, oblivious to her hurt frown. 'Mind out the way, lass.' Jor ushered her out of the way and stepped back as the door opened.

A tall man in his late twenties entered, his black hair worn down to his shoulders. He placed an instrument case down beside a chair before turning to look at them.

'Well, did you see him?' Jor demanded, barely giving the man time to orientate himself in the room.

'Oh, what a greeting. Not, "Hello, son. Are you well?" Just straight to business,' the man said sarcastically as he removed his cloak. He flashed a grin at Nym and her brother and sat himself down on a chair. He kicked off his boots and warmed his feet by the hearth. He made no effort to tidy his discarded boots away. Seth never seemed to make any effort to keep the room tidy – dirty plates left piled, possessions were just kicked aside until needed. He didn't seem to see the need for such trivialities such as housework, although Nym did what she could to lessen the squalor and make herself useful.

Jor's stern expression twitched into a tiny smile. 'Sorry, I'm just eager for some word. Been grim tidings of late.'

'Aye, it has,' replied Seth. 'All the more reason for a little light-hearted humour.'

Nym liked Seth; he made her laugh. He seemed kind and friendly, and had not hesitated to offer them a place to stay in his small backstreet home. Finn seemed to like him too. In fact, young Finn worshipped the very footsteps Seth left in the dirt. He followed him around like a shadow, hanging off his every word, and Seth certainly had a cheeky, slightly villainous charm her brother seemed to admire. It was not hard to imagine him at work, charming the tavern with his lute and quick wit.

Seth sank into his chair and dragged his lute case closer. Nym moved to kneel beside the hearth, stoking the embers with a stick. She watched as her young brother absently drifted towards Seth to sit down on the dusty floor beside his chair. Finn was watching Seth and the lute case expectantly.

'So, what did your man say?' his father pressed, undeterred by his son's levity.

'There might be a way if you're willing to pay.'

'As long as we can get out, I'll pay,' Jor assured him. 'Old Night's dancing all over the city. It's worse here now than when we left Anchorage.'

'And it doesn't look like it's going to get any better, either.'

Seth glanced up from his lute case. 'Did you see the wagons? There's bodies everywhere. The gates are still sealed, and they ain't opening them any time soon. They're not letting folk in or out without a lord's writ. Word is, it's spread up the coast too. Gates are sealed at every town all across the waterways. King's orders. It's really not good. Have you ever seen anything like this before?'

Jor shook his head but didn't reply, letting silence fill the room.

'I think... I think I may come with you,' said Seth with a frown. Jor had been at him for days, but Seth had seemed reluctant when Nym had heard them speak of it before. Jor clasped his son's shoulder with his remaining hand and gave him a relieved smile.

'That's good, son,' grinned Jor. 'Glad you see it now. We should all get out.'

'Where will we go?' asked Nym.

'I was thinking perhaps we should head out west past Barrowford, into the wilds. Wait 'til this blows over,' said Jor.

Seth nodded slowly. Nym had no idea where Barrowford was, but she wasn't sure she liked the sound of the wilds.

'What's out there?' protested Finn.

'Less people and less sickness,' replied Jor gravely, taking a seat across from his son by the fire. Finn sighed loudly. 'I don't wanna go. Can't we just stay?' Her brother was ever the street runner, ever since they were small. Had he ever spent any time outside the high walls and winding streets of a town or city? Had he seen farms and fields and forests? They had both spent their whole lives in Anchorage. What would he do out in the wilds where he had no people to rob. *Would probably do him some good*, she mused. The idea of wild woods and hills had always intrigued her, she had always loved trees, but the reality of actually living out there filled her with trepidation.

'No, we're gettin' out. Death comes too easy here now. You haven't seen them out there.' Jor waved a hand toward the door and the damp, fearful city beyond. 'Folk are dying — bodies piled up all over the place. I reckon this is plague.'

Seth nodded solemnly in agreement. 'I've heard a few rumours; folk are calling it blood plague, and the city healers are saying they haven't seen anything like this before.'

'If there's a chance to get out, we should do it while we can.' Jor looked at Finn, a grim set to his lips as if he understood the boy's desire to stay put, then shifted his gaze to her, lingering for a moment, as if unsure.

'He might be right, lad. Might be best to get out 'til this all blows over.' Seth scruffed Finn's hair but Finn didn't look convinced. 'Be some good opportunities when we get back too, plenty of good stuff that will need finding... claiming maybe, if you catch my meaning.' His face broke into a sly grin and he winked.

'Seth!' snapped Jor, his bald head flaming up to angry red. 'He don't need no encouragement!'

Seth grinned at Finn. 'Besides, out in the wilds I can teach you to fire a bow.'

'Who's gonna teach you?' laughed Jor.

Seth ignored the comment and gave Finn a wink as he leaned over to unclip his case.

'How soon can he get us out?' asked Jor scratching his stump of an arm.

'I'll find out more when I see him later,' said Seth, picking up his lute. 'I'm playing tonight.'

'You're going back to play? With all this going on?'

'Aye, father. Harold the Bold, who usually plays at the Hart's Horns? Well, he's taken sick. Not looking good for him by all accounts,' Seth said with a shake of his head. 'Anyways, the tavern keeper is offering double for a good player. How could I refuse?'

'Seth, come on, lad. We spoke about this. I don't want you ending up sick too. It's a bad idea.' Nym could see the anguish in Jor's face, the genuine worry etched in his creased brow and the way he rubbed at his stump with his remaining hand. She didn't blame him. She didn't fancy the idea of mingling in a close room full of folk who might be sick, but they had to eat, and work was hard to come by.

'It'll be fine, Da, really. Hart's Horns is the best tavern in Fieldside. There's a stage, plenty of room between me and the folk. It's just one night and it's good coin. If I impress him, I could get in there regular when we get back too. Would do me some good to have a steady booking.'

'It's just not safe,' warned Jor. 'I don't want any of us out there. Folk are sick everywhere now.' As if to emphasise his point, a chilling shriek echoed from somewhere nearby.

'If Old Night wants me, nothin's gonna stay his hand. Might as well get on with life in the meantime.' Seth strummed a few exploratory chords on his lute and adjusted a tuning peg, as his father stood up and paced around the room with a face like thunder. That may well be true, thought Nym, glancing at her brother, but what if Seth brought the sickness home? 'Besides,' continued Seth, 'I'll see our man there too. He reckons he can get us out for the right price. He knows people, but we're going to need the extra coin I make. I very much doubt smuggling us out is gonna come cheap.'

Seth began playing quietly, the fingers of one hand picking away while the other danced in intricate shapes along the neck of the instrument. His lute had two necks; one rising above his head, the other shorter and wider, with of the most strings. He had said what kind it was, but Nym had forgotten. The body was a highly polished black wood that faded to pale white in places. A delicate inlaid marble pattern ran across the shiny surface and the ghostly white fingerboards were inlayed with sets of black or white symbols. It was a breathtakingly beautiful thing, made all the more so as Seth made it sing, its voice low and haunting with mournful cadences and beautiful intertwining melodies.

Nym was awed by the young man's playing. He liked to boast he was the best in the city — whether that was true she could not say — but when she had heard him play on occasions such as this, she certainly believed it possible. She remembered seeing a lutist play at Jor's tavern in Anchorage, but that man had been nothing in comparison to Seth. She had begun to believe Seth had been favoured by the gods with his talent. The others sat listening quietly, the seriousness of the preceding conversation fading.

'There's another thing,' said Seth, not looking up from his lute or pausing as he played. 'I doubt you'll like it... We probably had best all go.'

'Go where?' asked Jor.

'My man, he'll need to see us all. To know what he's dealing with.'

'No! Me and you —'

'He'll only send for them later so he can see them for himself,' Seth cut his father off with a gesture at Nym and her brother. Finn sat up excitedly. 'Best get it over with.'

'No, absolutely not,' snapped Jor.

'He'll need to know we can be trusted. Dangerous work, defying the king.'

'I would come to see you play,' added Nym hopefully, deepening Jor's frown.

Seth gave her a smile. 'See, let them come, old man. You'll need to come anyway, why not us all. It could speed things along.'

Jor looked at Nym and she knew almost instantly what he was thinking. What if she was sick again? 'I don't like this.'

'You don't like anything anymore,' chided Nym lightly. She met Jor's gaze. 'Please? We've been shut in here for days.'

'I promise I will not cause any trouble,' added Finn, puffing his chest out and straightening his back in promise of being on his best behaviour.

The old tavern keeper heaved a sigh. 'Fine. I'm not your master. Do as you will, but you keep your eye on your brother. We don't need to add to our woes.'

Finn's face lit up with excitement and Seth grinned. He settled back in his chair and began another tune, his fingers dancing across his lute as he played a merry jig.

***

Wilhelm watched old Jor scurry away and enter the battered doorway of a nearby hovel. He was glad the old man had made it out of Anchorage. Still, he wasn't much better off here.

Another cart rolled past bearing the grim cargo of two twisted and blood-soaked bodies, and Wilhelm backed away. Ox coughed again as they stood aside to let it pass.

A frail looking elderly woman cried out and without further warning, collapsed against the wall of a nearby house. She hacked a terrible cough and started heaving up blood into the mud. Folk gasped and gave her a wide berth. Some stood watching her morbidly, others fled away, afraid. No one knelt to help her, except Alethea, who hurried over before Wilhelm could stop her.

'Do something!' she exclaimed, wild, pleading panic in her eyes. 'Help her!'

'No, m'lady—stay away!' called Wilhelm, knowing his plea was in vain.

She ignored him and rolled the woman onto her back. A gurgling cough sent a spray of blood onto Alethea's face, and the handmaiden found herself splashed with crimson. Olga smeared the blood across herself in a revolted attempt to clear away the gore, but Alethea seemed ignorant of the blood, weeping as she held the dying crone. Wilhelm did not want to get too close, but duty wrestled with fear. He knew he needed to get Alethea out of here.

The crowd stood in silence as the woman struggled to breathe, an eerie melody of someone playing a lute floating over the ghastly quiet, giving the scene a sense of the surreal. *Where was that music coming from?* thought Wilhelm. Wilhelm fiddled with his face scarf and watched, aghast as the old woman weakly pleaded for help, a trickle of blood now running from her eyes.

Wilhelm stared in horror at the crimson splatter on the princess's face, blood mingling with the tears streaming across her cheeks. His stomach lurched in shock. *I have to get her out of here. Now!* Ignoring protocol he grasped the princess by the wrist and hauled her away from the stricken woman. Alethea seemed dazed, making no protest as she allowed him to drag her away. She barely noticed him laying a hand on her. He had orders to follow, his lord, Warrick, and the king, would both have his balls if let any harm come to her. He should never have let her come here. *The damn lass just wouldn't listen.*

Ox coughed beside his horse. A small crowd watched them go. Wilhelm saw other folk coughing, pale drawn faces mingled amongst them. The sickness was all around him, the creeping dread of death stalking the streets.

CHAPTER FOUR

The Apprentice

L eaves still fell from the nearly bare branches, floating down
to the water. A few lingered, clinging to the branches as the
final remnants of autumn. The cold breath of the wind, the
misty mornings, and now awakening to the occasional touch of
frost, all heralded that winter was certainly upon them.

The dark waters whirled and eddied in the wake of the river
barge, and the apprentice leaned heavily on the stern rail, staring
down into the murk. The rains that always preceded the chill bite
of winter had swollen the waterway with sediment, washing it
from the surrounding farmlands upstream and leaving the water
a sluggish murky brown.

His hair hung lank and pale. It had lost all colour now, faded
from its, once rich brown to a grey white. The sights and stress of
the rituals Master Eldrick had performed back in that bleak mountain pass had taken a greater toll than he thought possible. His
sleep had become haunted of late, stalked by terrible dreams and
terrors; another ill side-effect of his recent studies. He now looked
old beyond his years, much older than a young man in his twenties, drawn and gaunt, his youthful exterior worn down with the
weight of vicissitude.

The journey south from the High Passes of the Old Lands had
been tough and uncomfortable. It had been over a moon since he
left the camp in the High Passes; ten cold nights in a painful jolting cart before boarding a cramped coastal ship, on which he was
buffeted by sharp winds and salty spray. Travelling by ship had
been unplanned but necessary. With his ankle broken, he was

bound to a cart, and he deemed it unwise to attempt a crossing of the Spine of the World. Arn's Pass was an arduous route at this time of year, and especially so for a man as injured as he was.

The trek had also been a damp one. He'd spent much of his time getting drenched alongside his taciturn companion or huddled amongst the cargo amid the lashing autumn rains. He had gladly dismissed the hired-sword once they reached the coast, keen to rid himself of the intimidating presence at his side. And with a College seal and promissory letters of payment from his master, the apprentice was confident he could manage without his guardian's services once he found a trade vessel with a captain heading south. The College was well known for paying its debts, so passage was not difficult to arrange. And so, once his cargo of reports and finds had been loaded aboard, the apprentice and the hired-sword parted ways. The man would presumably return to his comrades back at the camp, but the apprentice didn't much care — he was just glad he was gone.

For what he hoped would be the last leg of his journey, he'd found himself aboard another vessel, this one a river barge, slowly creeping through the silt laden river delta to the northeast of Arn, hoping to make berth at the College by the end of the day.

His leg throbbed painfully, and he shifted his weight in a vain attempt to ease the ache. It had not set properly, and he feared he may never walk quite as well as he had before. He hadn't been unable to stay off it during the long journey either, and weeks sat huddled and cramped in the cart, his splint broken while he'd been violently thrashing in the uneasy sleep of a fever dream, had allowed the cold to seep into the very core of his bones. He suspected the bones had fused poorly, and as a result, his ankle and lower leg now skewed off to the side at a slight angle. The whole ordeal had not been good for his healing, and the apprentice longed for the warmth of a fire and dry clothes. Whatever had possessed Master Eldrick to send him off with such an injury? He should have stayed at the camp and rested under the healing expertise of his masters.

Walking put a terrible pressure on his mangled ankle, resulting in horrendous pains shooting up his leg whenever he put any weight on it. He had developed a very noticeable limp and had begun to walk hunched over, leaning heavily on Master Logan's staff. Barely able to walk unaided, he managed only a step or two before the agony forced him to stop.

A shadow of dread flickered across his senses, a darkness that danced in his peripherals, and he glanced at the riverbank, scanning the trees. That now familiar presence was again watching him, the intense malice of unseen eyes haunting him wherever he went.

Turning, he surveyed the barge behind him, but nothing seemed out of place. He shuddered and leaned back on the stern rail. He knew he would not see anything, but he could not help sweeping his eyes over the water, carefully studying the banks on either side.

Nothing.

No lurking eyes watching from beneath the surface or from the reeds. No movement in the trees save for the chill winter breeze. Closing his eyes, he hoped to shut out the shadow still dancing at the edge of his vision. It was no use, even with his eyes clenched shut he could still feel the darkness boring into his soul. He was assailed by memories of the passes and dead faces. His head began to spin, the chilling sensation of that menacing presence became overpowering.

'You alright there, friend?'

The voice startled him out of his reverie. He opened his eyes and felt disoriented, his head spinning, his eyes adjusting to the light. His stomach knotted in shock. *How did I get here?* He seemed to have wandered along the barge and now found himself midships stood amongst barrels and sacks of what was likely grain.

He turned to the speaker and saw the bargeman eyeing him suspiciously. 'You alright? You're not sick are you?'

'No, no,' replied the apprentice, shaking his head. He rubbed his eyes as his vision cleared. 'Like I told you, I've come from The Borders up north. There's been no sickness up there.' He took a step and staggered, his hand reaching to cling to the railing as his leg buckled beneath him. *Where is my staff?* Glancing around in panic, he found his staff laying on the deck not far from where he had been standing at the stern. In his momentary lapse of memory it seems he must have found his way to the midships without it.

How was this possible?

The apprentice was left bewildered and in agony as he staggered to the rail to support himself. Logan's staff had become his crutch, his only means of walking for himself, be it painfully and slowly. He clung to rail and breathed heavily as the pain in his leg pulsated.

'Well you don't look well, lad.' The bargeman didn't look convinced.

'Please, don't worry. Really, I'm not sick. The leg is agony but I'm not sick. The first I saw of it was back at Stoneshore, but not up close, I swear. As I told you I was only in town a night and left this morning with you good folk.'

'Aye, was handy you had that College writ, with the town getting sealed up last night we would have been stuck there without it, and these supplies need getting to Arn,' he said with a gesture at the barge's other cargo. 'The crew are grateful they can get back to their families in the city too, so you have our thanks, scholar.' The bargeman offered him a weak smile, the suspicion not leaving his eyes. 'You kept clear of the sickness in Stoneshore though?'

'I kept to myself, but I saw the bodies, the carts. I stayed well away. A terrible thing... Awful.' The apprentice paused and stared over the side, wrestling with the memory of the bodies piled into wagons, the blood—victims of the sickness ravaging the town. He'd heard rumours of the sickness when he'd boarded the ship in the north, but they hadn't done the reality justice. His fingers absently wrapped around the wooden charm hung at his neck, tracing the carved swirling design of one of the old gods for air and wisdom. His father had always worn one similar, for luck and protection, and so he did also, mostly out of habit, but he often thought an old god of wisdom was quite an apt trinket for a scholar to wear. Now though, it was protection he sought from its touch. 'But I assure you I'm quite well,' he said after a pause. 'A long, wet journey has worn me down, that's all, and my leg is worse with the cold.'

The bargeman looked him up and down warily and nodded before hurrying off to speak with his fellow crewmen. The others glanced the apprentice's way as they spoke, their attempts at furtive looks speaking clearly of their suspicion and worry. They were watching for the cough, or worse a trickle of blood from their passenger's face, fearing his presence doomed them also.

The apprentice turned away from the anxious looks and glanced down, pulling his cloak tighter over his blood-stained shirt. If the crew noticed, they would surely throw him overboard or do something equally rash. To them he would be just another victim of the sickness, a stranger expected to be found laid dead in the back of a cart within the day. Not that they needed to worry. He had suffered several bad nosebleeds in his sleep on the journey south, the worst was last night, awakening from a horrific nightmare to find his hands and face covered in blood.

Last night had been so bad it had filled his mouth and he'd woken choking with blood over his clothes. The night-terror had led him to claw his face as he slept, leaving welts and scabs on his cheeks and neck and covering his hands in sticky blood. He was sure the bleeds were caused by his nightmares, they had started before he had even seen the sickness, but these folk wouldn't know that, best to keep it hidden.

With his back to the crew, he painfully clawed his way back to the stern rail, and holding it for support, he clumsily bent down on one leg and retrieved the staff. He pulled himself back up with a grunt and rested his weight on the walking staff to resume his vigil over the slowly swirling murk of the barge's wake.

This waterway led to Arn, one of many channels that flowed out from the great Bane River before it emptied into the sea as a fractured web. The city of Arn sat upon the point where the river splintered into many winding channels, and several smaller outlying towns and farmsteads occupied the large swathes of land scattered throughout the wide delta.

The barge worked its way upstream, creeping past small fishing villages and more farmsteads. The land here was fertile, crops grown on a much larger scale than in the north. Whole fields had been tilled, rather than the smaller allotments of the north, and extensive herds of livestock could be seen from the river, roaming the land where no crops grew. He remembered the land around Arn as rich with trade and produce and thus one of the most populated regions in the realm, but something seemed different.

Goods usually flowed in and out of the main port of Anchorage, just outside Arn, and he'd expected his ship would berth there, but its captain had dared not dock at the port. He'd told the apprentice that the sickness had brought a blighted change to the place, no one with their wits intact would go near it. The waterways seemed quiet, the villages near deserted. A sinister menace had descended upon his homeland. The sickness had dug its claws in deep.

An eerie wailing reached the apprentice's ears. He turned,

searching upriver for the source of the strange sound. Emerging from behind the trees that lined the bank, a small farmstead appeared, and the wailing grew louder as the barge drew level.

Amongst the squat wooden houses a woman knelt. The apprentice's heart sank into his stomach as he beheld the woman's anguish, her face distorted and twisted in grief, rocking back and forth as she cradled the limp small form of a child in her arms. Beside the houses were several freshly dug graves, and except for the grief-stricken woman, no one else stirred in the farmstead. He knew in his heart she was now alone there, with only the roaming goats and fowl as companions, and he doubted those creatures understood her terrible loss or her overwhelming isolation.

The barge passed by, the crew looking on in silence until the mournful wailing faded behind them. A heavy weight of grief settled on the apprentice, pressing in on his chest until even drawing breath hurt. The scene brought a painful memory. He remembered his own mother cradling a baby in her arms, her keening wail, a baby sister lost so young. It was so long ago but a pain that had never left him. His mother had not been left so terribly alone as this poor woman was. He turned away, cuffing tears from his eyes, and limped over to the cargo in his charge. Lowering himself down amongst the chests of artefacts and reports he had carried with him for weeks, he sat in contemplative silence. This strange sickness was unlike anything he had ever heard of. Merciless and cruel, from what he had seen in his brief time back in these lands, it appeared to be ravaging the local populous on an unthinkable scale, tearing apart families and households, remorseless and indiscriminate. Old Night's reap had been plentiful in these parts, the god of death's halls must be getting crowded of late.

A chorus of shouts went up from the bargemen working to the fore, and the apprentice saw one of them pointing into the water ahead. As another joined him, a grim curiosity outweighed the discomfort of standing, and the apprentice heaved himself to his feet with the aid of the staff and with an increasing sense of dread, went to look.

Over the rail, he caught sight of a body floating face down in the river, and his gorge threatened to rise. He could not tell if it was a man or woman, its long, lank hair drifting across the surface like the grasping tentacles of some sea creature. As the body drew closer, a wave of panic crashed over the barge workers.

'No! Don't touch it,' called a bargeman as one of his fellows moved to push it away with a landing pole. The man froze and retracted the pole, the rest of the crew standing in motionless silence as the barge slipped by and the body bumped loudly against the hull. Somehow the crew feared that it even touching the boat was a curse or fell portent.

But the sight of the floating corpse struck a different fear in the apprentice, a grim recollection of his studies in the mountains. He had hoped not to encounter such a sight again, but alas, what had begun with rumour had ended with the gruesome dead piled into the back of carts at Stoneshore. He seemed cursed to look upon the dead as often as the living.

'Look another!' exclaimed one of the crew.

This one had been caught in the protruding roots of a tree growing on the bank, its branches hanging low and limp over the water. A dead face stared up at them with empty, bloodied eye sockets, its flesh turgid and pallid, beginning to distend and bloat from the nebulous waters. One arm stretched out as if reaching toward the folk aboard the barge, while the dead man's mouth hung open at water level. Ripples from the barge's wake struck, jerking the body up and down as if it were struggling against being restrained, its gaping mouth shouting in silent protest as they slipped past.

The barge sailed on, the coastal breeze filling the wide sail and pushing the vessel slowly upstream. The riverbanks rose up around them, becoming high, steep embankments, and as the apprentice looked up, a great shadow fell over him. A wooden structure appeared overhead, a bridge built from thick beams spanning the waterway. Several such bridges spanned the rivers of the delta, serving the road network in addition to the many ferry crossings frequenting the river banks, consisting of small boats or the larger flat rafts capable of taking a cart. He held his breath as the barge passed under, the mast barely an arm's length from colliding with the supporting trusses. The presence of the large imposing bridge indicated the barge was drawing close to the city. It would not be much longer.

The river took a wide bend immediately after the bridge, and as the barge slowly traversed the corner, the source of the floating dead came into view.

Upturned, its wheels sticking out from the water, a cart had plunged down the steep banks and come to rest in the lapping shallows. It had presumably been travelling the dirt track that ran along the bank towards the bridge but had not made it.

Whether the driver had simply lost control or had themselves succumbed to the sickness it was hard to tell, but the cart had dragged the unlucky horse harnessed to it into the river as well. Deep gouges through the earth marked the descent of the cart and the struggling horse, which could be seen just beneath the surface of the water, held there by its tack.

It appeared to be one of the dead carts. Bodies had tumbled from the back of the cart and sprawled down the bank in a bloody ruin. A lone crow sat perched on one of the wheels and cawed angrily at the approaching barge, whilst another pecked purposefully down at one of the corpses on the bank.

The presence of the floating corpses in the river had now lost its macabre mystery, but the apprentice watched on, troubled. What struck him as most unusual about the whole scene was that none of the locals had arrived to attend the wreck. The bodies were being slowly claimed by the river and the crows, and at this rate, would likely never be recovered. It seemed that what would have once been a tragic calamity for a local community now went unnoticed, just another event lost and forgotten in the unfolding nightmare visited upon these lands.

The apprentice felt certain now he had not escaped the torment of his experience in the mountains. The subjects of Master Eldrick's studies haunting his every step, a parade of dead faces following wherever he went. Even here, on the doorstep of Arnar's capital, death stalked him.

The apprentice sank back down amongst his possessions and looked up into the grey clouded winter sky. Small flocks of black carrion birds wheeled through the sky overhead, mostly crows, but also, with some surprise, the apprentice noted a pair of rhaan accompanying their smaller cousins. They were normally fairly rare in these southern lands, though it was said that rhaan are the lieutenants of Old Night himself, never far from slaughter and misery, their presence ever a grim portent.

He stared down at his ruined leg, a vain attempt to put the horrors around him to the back of his mind, his thoughts turning to Truda, his friend and colleague, a fellow apprentice, she had remained in the north with Master Eldrick and Master Logan. He was struck by the image of Truda sat upon her cart back at the campsite. The comparison between that memory and the up-turned cart in the river made him shudder. He longed to see her again, to hear her wry teasing wit, and he wondered how far behind him she and the two masters were. They should have struck camp by now and be on their return journey. Master Eldrick had said he had only a few days of work left at the ruin — a week at most.

Glancing around at the crates and chests full of finds, artefacts and reports that he had protected as best he could for weeks, the apprentice hoped his master would be satisfied with his efforts. He was unlikely to be impressed with the maimed condition of his apprentice's ankle, however. The apprentice sighed and shifted the weight of his leg to a more comfortable position and sat back, watching the rhaan wheeling high overhead.

The afternoon wore on and the sun began to set, bathing the sky in its fiery hues and shifting the clouds to a foreboding shade of dusky magenta. The sail bellied and flapped as the wind picked up and the barge moved out of the protected waterway into a much wider part of the river. The water, licked by the wind, be-came choppy, forming low cresting swells which broke against the barge's hull. Four of the crew put out oars, two each side and their superior manned the tiller, calling out a rhythmic rowing chant. The apprentice made his way to the prow as the river wid-ened, eager to see his destination.

The mouth of the great river yawned in front of him as the barge crossed from the smaller waterway and began to move up into the main artery of the river. Behind him, to the east, was the sea, and the port fires of Anchorage. The harbour's two huge sen-tinel stones were tiny in the distance, set atop huge stone mega-liths thrust from the waves, marking an ancient harbour of a peo-ple long forgotten.

His gaze swung westward to the city of Arn. Nestled high on a rocky outcrop, sat the hold of the king; imposing over the land-scape, the mighty Citadel crowned skyline. It was as if not even the river could defy the authority of the formidable hold — the riv-er coursing around the base of the outcrop and splintering into the many waterways and wetlands of the estuary. Palisades ringed the hilltop in several layers enclosing a great long house with tim-ber towers spaced at intervals along the walls, banners and pennons fluttering in the breeze.

Below the daunting hilltop fort, sprawled the city of Arn. Several bridges stretched across the surrounding waterways, feeding the city as it spread along the southern banks of the river. Ships and barges crowded the jetties jutting from the banks and the smoke from countless hearth fires threaded up from low squat buildings to form a dirty haze hanging over the city.

The apprentice never ceased to be struck with a sense of awe when he beheld the sprawl of Arn from afar; the seat of power in Arnar, and his home. He had rarely seen it from this vantage point, the low winter sun a bright blazing disc through the clouds as it sank behind the fortified outcrop.

Thick plumes of smoke caught his eye, billowing from what looked like bonfires on the far northern banks. He had never seen such in all his years in Arn and he strained his eyes to make out more detail. The bonfires — no, pyres — burned fiercely, the smoke staining the sky and the setting sun a murky orange.

Has the toll of sickness been so great?

As he watched, a few carts arrived, bodies tossed into the flames without ceremony like the battlefield dead. It did not seem right.

The apprentice turned away from the northern bank and surveyed the timber battlements of the Citadel as the barge drew parallel with it. Soldiers patrolled the walkways along the palisades, the glint of steel reflecting the setting sun. The king's hold itself was said to have been built on the ruins of an ancient hill fort. The apprentice recalled hearing tales of the fortress, stories of kings and heroes long dead.

The streets and wharfs seemed strangely quiet, absent of the usual hustle and bustle as the barge approached. Few folk walked the streets and those he could see scurried like frightened animals, hurrying to the safety of a bolt hole. He saw more than one cart trundling along the abandoned streets, presumably carrying the dead. This was not the town he had left.

The College district was situated in the north-west of the city, and had its own wharfs feeding a series of compounds enclosing the College buildings.

The shadow flickered across his vision once again.

A cold shudder ran down his spine. Never far away, the malign presence weighed heavy on his shoulders, riding his soul into a town of the damned.

The College wharfs drew slowly into view and the apprentice's spirits leapt. The shadow dissipated and scattered, driven away by the elation of seeing his destination. He was so close now. The warmth of a fire, a good meal and a bath, clean clothes and a healer to tend his ankle—all within reach. No more rain or wind, no more frigid cold, no more jolting cart tracks. Despite the rigours of the journey, the aches in his limbs, despite the worry that gnawed for all the people he knew here in the College and in the city, he allowed himself a weary smile.

The wharf workers called out to the bargemen, asking first to their health and then of the cargo. All of this was exchanged over the water before the mooring lines were hurled ashore. The barge's hull bumped against the wharf and rocked slowly to a settled stop. The apprentice made his way to the boarding plank as the crew prepared to unload.

A dock worker stood aghast as his eyes fell upon the apprentice hobbling towards him. He gaped at the apprentice's twisted leg, the terrible gait it gave him, his lank hair hanging white; a nightmare figure, shambling towards him. The worker looked for a moment as though he might stop the apprentice from passing, but instead he just stood aside. After all, the apprentice wore the College symbol, and there was little the man could do.

The apprentice limped to the wharf's overseer and produced his folded paperwork, delivering instructions for the unloading of his cargo. The overseer eyed him warily, perhaps even fearfully, but after an awkward moment he nodded and waved him on. Nodding his thanks, the apprentice stood a moment, leaning on his staff, and surveyed the courtyard ahead.

He was home.

CHAPTER FIVE

Voyage into Darkness

The clash and ring of steel rang out over the windswept sea, and the prow of the fat bellied merchant ship pushed through the low swell, clawing its way through the dark waters. A crowd of people stood about on deck, watching keenly, keeping to the sides, enclosing the central deck to watch what was now becoming a morning ritual.

Arnulf leant against the railing, his greying brown hair whipping across his face in the sea wind. Hafgan stood beside him, and they watched as Erran once again fought the Death Nymph.

'He's getting better,' commented Arnulf.

Hafgan grunted and scratched his shaved head. 'Aye.' He was a big man and wore a swirling design inked over the old scar on his cheek, his arms thick with arm rings. 'Still needs to stop worrying about hitting her though. Every time he hesitates, she slips in.'

Arnulf nodded. He wasn't much of a swordsman himself, fighting with his axe when he ever had need to. Hafgan was far more skilled, and Arnulf knew few more formidable warriors with a sword. It was one of the reasons Hafgan stood where he was now at his lord's side.

Erran threw out a flurry of cuts, each neatly parried by Astrid as she slowly and calmly gave ground to his onslaught. The shield-maiden was a sight to behold. Clad in leathers, her dark brown hair was braided tightly against her head. Her eyes smouldered, framed by the dark kohl she wore on her lids and lashes, baiting Erran.

Arnulf had seen her do this a dozen times in recent days. Once again, choosing her moment wisely, she ducked around Erran and struck him hard in the ribs. He cried out in pain and frustration, clutching at his side.

Hafgan chuckled grimly. 'He doesn't learn. Every time...'

'You should show him,' Arnulf suggested.

'He hasn't been interested,' Hafgan grumbled. 'Hasn't trained with me in weeks. Let him learn the hard way, off her, until he sees sense and comes back to learn, instead of getting his arse kicked.'

Arnulf smirked at him. Since Erran had first taken up a sword, Hafgan had been training him. The boy's father was a horse merchant—a wealthy man—who had given it as a gift when Erran had first sworn to Arnulf. He still remembered Erran's face; so proud, so full of confidence. It was far too fine a blade for a warrior still so young and inexperienced. Arnulf knew the big warrior resented these fights. Perhaps he did not feel the boy ready, though Arnulf suspected he feared the young lad's poor performance. It was well known that Hafgan had been training him, and the boy's skill had some reflection on his own. And it was not reflecting well.

'Still don't rate her then,' smirked Arnulf.

Hafgan shrugged. 'I've seen better. If he only listened to me.'

Erran cried out again and Arnulf looked over to see the lad clutching his arm as the Death Nymph circled him.

The swords were blunted; Fergus, Lord of Weirdell and Arnulf's lifelong friend, had procured them from his father's master-at-arms back in Eymsford before they set sail. They left no serious wounds, just a nasty bruise—nothing worse than some broken fingers, usually. Arnulf remembered using similar swords as a lad. He had never been very good though. To him his sword was a status symbol, a badge of office, not a weapon of war.

Fergus had grinned like a mad man as he'd handed Astrid the practice swords. He was keen to see his warrior honour her word, more for the alleviation of his own boredom than anything else. There was little to do as the slow ship lumbered along the coast, and Astrid could find no excuse to put Erran off any longer. Fergus, of course, had eagerly goaded her into it.

The first morning, she'd waited for Erran and tossed the sword at his feet, then proceeded to flatten the poor lad. His first lesson — keep your sword to hand, for she could strike anytime. Fergus took great pleasure in telling the tale to any who would listen. She ambushed him the next day too, but Erran was ready this time. She still flattened him and Fergus had laughed as he, Arnulf, and the others watched with amusement.

She'd waited for Erran at dawn every morning since, on the deck of the ship, to give him a good kicking. The crew had started calling it "the dawn ritual" and gathered eagerly to watch the fight ensue.

Two of Astrid's shield-maidens watched on with faces of thunder. They seemed the only other's amongst the crowd, besides Hafgan, who watched disapprovingly. A rumour persisted of these two and their disdain for men, of their intimacy behind closed doors, and Arnulf suspected the rumours were indeed true. It was obvious to him they viewed their leader's attention of the young lad with a bitter resentment, was it because he was a man, or perhaps because they thought a warrior of her renown was lowering herself to even spar with the young warrior? He could not say but their loathing was writ plain on their faces.

Fergus however took great interest in the fights, encouraging them to continue and cheering. He placed bets and bragged of his warrior-maiden's prowess. Arnulf was welcome of the distraction too. He had wallowed in dark moods of late. The grim events in the passes had all taken a terrible toll on his mind, the impossible sight of dead men walking, those accursed remnants of some College sanctioned experiment, then to find his home razed to embers, but worst of all, the tragic loss of his wife and daughter to the flames. A hatred seethed inside him. *The College will pay, I will have my vengeance.* He suspected he was a much different man these days — brooding and sombre where he had once been quick to smile and laugh. It was good to have his old friend with him. Fergus always managed to turn everything into a spectacle with a cheery laugh. Hafgan had also been steady company, more than proving his place at Arnulf's side these last weeks. He was nothing but a steadfast and stalwart companion, a good man to the core.

'She's quick, I'll give her that.' Hafgan folded his arms over his chest, his eyes carefully following the fight as the ship rocked gently in the swell.

'Could you take her?' asked Arnulf.

73

Hafgan threw him a dark look. 'Never doubt it.'

Arnulf did not. Hafgan was his best warrior by far, indeed nothing but formidable. He had been stoic as a rock when they fought the dead, while other men quailed in fear.

A sea bird flew into the sail, its panicked cries drawing the attention of the spectators upward for a moment.

'That is a bad omen,' muttered Hafgan as the bird freed itself and winged off over the surf.

Arnulf shook his head. He'd never put much stock in omens, at least, not until he and his soldiers had encountered the impossible in the high mountain passes near his home. A cheer from one of the onlookers drew his attention back to the fight. Erran had landed a blow and sent Astrid staggering back, and he quickly followed up with a flurry of strikes. He kept her off balance as she struggled to parry, compensating as she did for the roll of the ship. The spectators began cheering encouragement.

A terrible shriek split the air and the ringing swords fell silent.

'I told you, a bad omen,' said Hafgan.

A bellow and a roar echoed up the deck, followed by a yelp from the great grey hound Arnulf had named Fear. He'd found the dog in the mountains too, alive amongst the walking dead, terrified and wary. But they had formed a bond, and the hound had accompanied him ever since. The shaggy grey-haired hound had been watching the waves crashing against the prow but the poor beast bolted at the sound, shaking with terror and cowering low against the deck amongst some coiled rope beside Arnulf.

The sound of chains clanking hard against metal bars rose from beneath the deck at their feet, something thrashing wildly inside a cage. Astrid and Erran stood with their swords lowered at their sides, looking nervously along with everyone else at the hatch to the lower deck. Arnulf could not help but notice the quick glances towards him, looks of pity that quickly flicked away as he met their eyes. The insane screaming killed the jovial atmosphere dead, the morning ritual brought to an abrupt end.

He did this sometimes. Perhaps the commotion had disturbed him. He would suddenly scream like a wild beast in the dead of night, then throw himself against the cage bars. Few slept well and none aboard could escape the sound of him thrashing at his chains in the hold, consumed with fits of bestial rage.

Arnulf turned to the rolling waters of the sea, trying in vain to ignore the sounds coming from below. He sighed and hung his head despairingly. Fear's wet nose appeared and nuzzled his hand, seeking for comfort, and Arnulf looked down into the shaggy beast's scared yellow eyes.

'It's alright, boy,' murmured Arnulf.

Is it though?

The hound seemed terrified by the inescapable screeching and primal roars wracking the ship.

He lives up to his name... Fear. It was fear that had kept the poor beast alive.

He scruffed the hound's head affectionately and looked northward over the ship's sluggish wake to the distant mountains; the Spine of the World. He had spent his entire life in view of those snowy peaks. They could always be seen no matter where he roamed in his homelands. He could count on his hands the number of times he had been out of sight of them, and now they grew ever smaller on the horizon.

Beyond those fading peaks lay his home – The Borders, the old country, the birthplace of the realm. He held his seat there, lord of a proud people. A town full of his folk, a place which he had known all his life.

But there was no home there anymore. His hall charred to embers, the town's belly ripped asunder, so many of his people just gone. His family now ashes and bones. Gone. His wife, his little girl – all gone. Gone to the halls of Old Night with his fathers of old. There was no home there anymore, only death.

The only family he had left was the screeching creature squatting in a cage in the ship's hold. Ewolf seemed barely human, more beast than man. His terrible rages and screaming ripped the silence as some demon inside him tore his mind apart. Arnulf no longer recognised the man he knew as his son. A pitiful thing full of rage and madness, preferring to feed on the rats who strayed too close rather than the food they brought him. There was no trace of Ewolf left in that creature's cold eyes. *The College will pay.*

A now familiar wave of despair washed over him, leaving him empty inside, empty of all but one thing. Arnulf craved vengeance.

His gaze lingered on the ever more distant mountains behind them. He tried to lose himself, staring into their snow-capped heights. The mountains shrunk day by day, now fading into the cloud of the horizon so one could not be easily distinguished from the other. He sighed and counted off another finger. Five times now he had been out of sight of those familiar peaks. He wondered when he would see them again, who would come back when he returned.

He turned away from the past and looked south to the calmer seas ahead of them. Their destination drew ever closer.

Not long now, he thought.

'We have come so far,' muttered Arnulf.

'Aye,' agreed Hafgan. He didn't say anything else and a silence arose between them. It wasn't an uncomfortable silence, rather a reflective one.

Arnulf thought back over their journey, of the long road to Eymsford before setting sail. It had been tedious, the cart carrying Ewolf's cage a slow burden on their progress. Something dark and terrible had been unleashed in the High Passes of the northern mountains, and Hafgan was right; it was spreading. Rumour of the dead rising, and of a murderous madness spreading ahead of them became unsettlingly frequent as they passed through the farms and villages on the road. Arnulf feared for the lands he knew, the urgency of their journey growing heavier with each passing day.

Now aboard, the ship was painfully slow too. They had been a week at sea since departing the port at Eymsford. Fergus, being the son of the high lord, had his own ships there — good ships, fast and sleek longships of war. Arnulf had hoped to make the voyage in such a ship, but alas, they had been unable to load Ewolf's cage, and had been forced to pay the captain of a merchantman to take them, a wide bellied vessel with two masts and a myriad of sails and rigging. It was slow, but a ship capable of transporting the cage.

To their west, the last of the Spine's lofty peaks thrust out from the sea, the tips of those great mountains reaching up from the waves and towering high over the tumultuous waters which lay between them. The passage through the Sea of Spires had been slower still, as the captain steered the ship through the channels with confident caution. They would have made the journey in half the time aboard a longship.

Two longships accompanied them from the high lord's fleet, ferrying warriors in escort. Fergus flew his family's banners from them, while the merchantman flew Arnulf's, the pennons of Arnar hanging from the ship masts, fluttering in the gusting winds. He often sat watching the longships rowing, dozens of oars rhythmically dipping and rising through the surf like the legs of some giant water centipede. But now the oars were still, both ships kept to half sail and their oars shipped in these narrow channels, offering some reprieve for the warriors who usually occupied the rowing benches of their escort ships. The merchantman was so sluggish in comparison, the longships had no need for oars or even full sails to keep pace in the strong breeze.

Few folk lived on these rocky shores, with few settlements scattered across the islands, and the voyagers rarely saw any signs of life besides the millions of sea birds who ruled the cliffs. There were terrible things rumoured to lurk beneath the waves, lords of their deep dominions, but they had not yet shown themselves to Arnulf and his men. They passed the odd ship, shouting greetings across the windswept waves, and the few folk they had spoken to properly had been at Wayfell Harbour.

They had only stopped the once on their passage through the Sea of Spires, making port at the harbour town nestled in a quiet bay of one of the larger islands midway through the rocky seas. Built clinging to the rocky slopes of the sheltered bay over a deep harbour, it was a rare haven amongst the treacherous waters. A halfway house and a trading hub between the old northern borderlands of Arnar and the then newly forged south, its storm-wracked buildings hung over the harbour, looking for all the world like they might tumble into the dark foaming waters crashing against the cliffsides below. The few words they had exchanged with the folk there had been grim tidings; dark news from the south.

The ships had not lingered there. Ewolf's screams could be heard echoing off the cliffs as they sat in the harbour, and the folk who made their homes in this forlorn little place did not welcome those nightmare screams. They had not been allowed to stay long, just enough time to take on supplies before taking their fell cargo on its way.

Shouts of excitement roused Arnulf from his thoughts.

'Sails!' shouted a man from the high rigging. He pointed out off the prow. A buzz of excitement rolled through the crew as they all tried to catch sight of the ship ahead.

The full bellied red and white sail of a warship came into view. It closed quickly and passed in close to the lead ship. Words were exchanged, shouts Arnulf could hear but not understand. The warship moved off and closed on the merchantman.

It had a fierce dragon carved into its prow, and the identical shields of the warriors aboard adorned the rails, the wolf sigil of the king emblazoned upon each of them. The sailors spilled the sails and slowed the ship as it drew near.

'Hail!' called a voice across the water. 'Turn back! There is plague in the city.'

Fergus stepped forward onto the prow. 'We have urgent business with the king. We must pass.'

A mailed warrior appeared, too far away to make out any features except the shining helm on his brow.

'The king has decreed it. No ships into the capital without a royal writ,' he shouted. 'Though I see you fly lordly banners of Arnar. Who are you?'

'I am Lord Fergus of Weirdell, son of the high lord. I sail with Lord Arnulf of Ravenshold and the Motte. I speak with the authority of my father, Lord Angus, High Lord of The Borders and The Old Lands. We have urgent business with the king. We need no writ.'

There was a pause and Arnulf stiffened, waiting for what might come next.

'Who do I speak with,' Fergus shouted when no reply came.

'I am sorry my lord, I am Freathwar in service to Prince Harald. We are the king's men. We were ordered by our lord to ensure none enter these waters. Forgive me. If I cannot dissuade you, we must sail ahead to announce your coming.'

'Aye, thank you.' Fergus nodded, but Arnulf wasn't sure how much of the gesture could be seen at the rail of the warship. 'Let the king know there is urgent word from his high lord. We will arrive shortly.'

'Aye, lord, that I can do. But be warned! Approach no ship marked with black flags – there is sickness on board. Sail straight to the royal docks, do not enter the city. The plague is rife.'

Fergus glanced over his shoulder at Arnulf, his usual mischievous grin replaced by a deep, furrowed frown of concern. They had heard of this plague from the people at Wayfell Harbour, talk of ships marked with black warnings, ships of dead men where none aboard survived, plague ships, but it had seemed more rumour and tavern talk than truth.

'How bad is it, Freathwar?' Fergus called back, caution and fear at the edge of his voice.

The warrior shifted his feet, and took a moment to reply, as if the mere mention of the illness made him uncomfortable. 'It's the worst anyone's ever seen on these shores. May the god's give you luck, my lord. You will need it.'

The sleek warship unfurled its sails and moved away, easily carving the swell as it turned about. Before long it was no more than a speck on the horizon, disappearing into the distance.

Dire times...

The stormy cliffs and the folk of Wayfell Harbour lay behind them, and peaks of the Spires were falling away, the sea opening before them to the south. They may have left the nightmare of the risen dead, but they were entering instead a place of plague. So they sailed onward into the grim uncertainty of what lay ahead, to bring news of the fell happenings they just left behind. It did nothing to lift anyone's spirits.

The captain claimed it wouldn't be long before they would turn into the mouth of the great Bane River and make berth at the capital. For both the crew and Arnulf it would not be soon enough, despite what they had heard about the city. Ewolf's violent raging continued, clamouring beneath their feet throughout the morning, and Arnulf had no doubt the crew were eager to have this voyage over with and put his raving shrieks of madness behind them.

For Arnulf, he would demand his answers before the king himself. He would do everything to help his son. Someone would pay for the evil befalling his people and he would find answers for Ewolf. He dared to cling to the hope the College could reverse the evil they had unleashed.

It would be told that in the north the dead walk, and darkness stalks The Old Lands. It must be dealt with as swiftly as a hammer blow before it can take root—Arnar could not play host to such evil.

Another gut-wrenching shriek tore through the sound of waves gently lapping against the hull, the terrible noise sending the shaggy hound cowering for cover once more.

Hafgan placed a reassuring hand on his lord's shoulder, and

Arnulf started. 'It will not be long now, lord.'

Ewolf shrieked again, wildly thrashing against his chains as his father hung his head, staring into the gloomy depths below. The emptiness inside him began to fill with a dark anger as he listened to the roars of his boy.

'Not long,' he repeated. *Not long, and I will have my vengeance.*

CHAPTER SIX

The College

Sitting at an easel, a scholar meticulously embellished the stretched vellum with colour. Regarding the ornate illumination, he seemed satisfied with the swirling green and red design and placed his brush down. Picking up a flattened wooden stylus, he dipped the end in ink and began scratching at the vellum sheet. Twisting his wrist with practised ease, he produced a line of elegant calligraphic text from the illuminated initial, pausing to read through the text as he finished the first line.

'Excellent work,' said an older man standing at the scholar's shoulder. The scholar nodded, then took a deep breath before beginning a new line of script. Turning, the older man regarded the two young initiates watching the scholar work. With a tilt of his head, he indicated they were to follow, and together they moved along to the next easel. This scholar's work had intricate illustrations and knot-work running down the left and right side of the page, while the illustrations showed helmed men marching over mountains and riding ships as they crashed through the waves.

'Ah... Some of your best,' said the older man. 'Who is it for?'

The second scholar placed his brush on the easel and turned. 'A lord called Eofwin. I'm not sure where from.' He paused thoughtfully. 'I'm sure the Overseer could tell you, Master Luthor. Shall I find out?'

'There's no need, lad, but he is a lucky man, this Eofwin. Aye, he will be pleased.' Master Luthor leaned over, inspecting the designs closely.

'Thank you, master,' replied the scholar.

Luthor turned to the young initiates. 'Wess, Eoin, what do you think?'

Wess, a boy of perhaps fifteen winters, stared in wide eyed wonder. The other, a younger girl, seemed uninterested, even bored. The lad had come from one of the temples, an acolyte sent to learn his letters. Eoin was the daughter of some lord to the south, and word had it he had paid the College a handsome sum to have his daughter taught to read and write. She however, had yet to show anything but disdain for what was generally considered a great privilege.

It seemed to be a growing trend among the high and mighty to send their progeny to the College, once the domain of the learned, an order dedicated to the pursuit and recording of knowledge. Now, more and more, it had become a place where the ungrateful whelps of the wealthy came to learn the revered arts of the College, only to leave when they had what they needed, making them more useful to their elders or more valuable in marriage.

'Well?' prompted the master.

'It is beautiful,' replied Wess.

Luthor's gaze flicked to the young noblewoman but she merely shrugged in reply. The master frowned at her unworthy response.

'Will you teach us to make letters like that, Master Luthor?' asked Wess, seemingly unaware of his master's disapproval at his fellow initiate, his eyes fixed on the vellum parchment.

'Perhaps eventually,' replied Luthor.

'What does it say?' asked the initiate, his eyes tracing each line of illustration.

Luthor frowned at the boy. Surely he could tell from the images, even though he could not read the words. 'It is *The Saga of Arn*. Don't you know the tale?'

'No, master...' Wess shuffled his feet and chewed at the back of his lip. 'Well, I know Arn was a great king once.'

'He was, but before that, he was a great lord of Cydor who ruled over the lands to the north we now know as The Borders. It was a very different time, some five hundred winters past.' Master Luthor settled down on a stool, wondering how the boy had reached fifteen without hearing the tale. 'The lands south of The Spine, the lands where we now sit, were said to be infested with terrible savages known as the Stonemen. Living in caves, they were more beast than man.

'The saga tells us Cydor's king gave Arn the right not just to raid the southern lands, but to claim them and expand the borders of Cydor. So, he assembled a great fleet and sailed south from Eymsford. You see, in those days The Spine was thought to be impassable. There were no routes across their great peaks back then, and those mountains were the very borders of civilisation. The only way south was by sea.

'When Arn's warriors made landfall, they discovered ancient forts and ruins believed to be of the First Sons of legend, from which all civilised men are thought to be descended. There are such ruins scattered across the known world, but that is another tale.' Looking to each initiate in turn, Luthor was pleased to see the young lad listening intently, captivated by his new master's tale.

This one shows promise.

Despite the gaping holes in his knowledge, the boy seemed eager to learn and would perhaps make a good scholar in time. The girl however, remained uninterested. Eoin looked out the window into the courtyard beyond, and Luthor paid no heed to her blatant lack of respect.

He turned to the lad. 'The warriors of Arn quickly seized lands and easily swept the Stonemen from their path. By all accounts, they stood no chance. With only sticks and primitive stone weapons, the savages were slaughtered, their lands seized for Cydor. Arn forged new colonies and outposts along the coast and then pushed south and west, driving the Stonemen before him.

'He took this very city from them. Then a city of strange ancient stone ruins, the ruins were used as a filthy den by the savages. After Arn seized the city, he built a great fort upon the ruins of an ancient hill fort, which still stands here today.' Luthor gestured out the window. The great fort could not be seen from here, but they all knew well that it stood across the city in the direction he pointed. 'He made it his capital, and named it after himself, the great southern city of Cydor.'

'So Arnar was once part of Cydor?' asked the boy.

'Aye, lad, we are all children of Cydor in a way.'

'We aren't anymore though. What happened, master?'

'Well, the great lord Arn grew rich and powerful and ruled vast lands from The Borders all the way into the south. The king became jealous and demanded he give up the land. When Arn did not, the king sought to seize the lands for himself and divide it amongst his other lords. Lord Arn, whose power now rivalled the king's, refused and declared himself King of the South. And so, a great civil war began, perhaps the greatest ever known.'

'The Wars of Forging,' said Eoin suddenly, speaking for the first time. 'My father has had many fine storytellers and bards tell of it in his hall. We've all heard the legends, the stories of old. I was forced to listen to the great deeds of this warrior, the great victories of another — who cares? Who hasn't heard it all before?'

The lad looked at the floor, crestfallen. Luthor had to admit it was odd that these tales were new to him, and the boy seemed embarrassed of his lack of schooling, his ignorance laid bare in front of this haughty noble born girl.

'War stories bore me, with their endless names and deeds.' She rolled her eyes and folded her arms. 'I liked the stories of the gods who came amongst men and caused mischief, the ones with fantastic creatures. They are much more interesting.'

'All myths as far as we know, lass,' said Luthor, seeing a chance to pique and encourage her interest at last. 'We have people here at the College who study those tales. Many have attempted to prove their truths.'

He smiled, but she shrugged and returned her gaze to the courtyard outside. Luthor sighed and looked back at the boy who had been so keen to listen.

'In any case, there was a great war, Arn prevailed and our kingdom was born. I have of course skimmed many of the details, but that is *The Saga of Arn* in short. The wars raged for generations as Cydor tried to reclaim their lost lands. Some argue the Wars of Forging are part of the Saga also, but it is truly another saga in itself. Another long chapter in the Great Histories we are compiling here at the College.

'Anyway, my young initiates, that is enough of that for now. You will study the stories in much more detail and of course learn all about the Great Histories in your time here, and perhaps even add to them. We must move on from the scriptorium and leave these good men to continue their work in peace.'

Master Luthor ushered them through a doorway and into the hallway beyond, leading them past several doors to similar rooms, all filled with scholars working at easels, the walls crammed with shelves stacked with scrolls and books.

After travelling through a complex of passageways, they arrived at another room occupied by a man at a desk studying a large book closely. Light shone through rows of high windows and onto the cob bricks that made the lower walls. The upper wall was made of wooden planks, all supported by a sturdy timber frame. Those high windows that were not shuttered spilt beams of light through the dusty air. Disturbed motes of dust were illuminated and swirled about through the light before disappearing into shadow.

He looked up as Luthor entered, acknowledging him with a nod. 'Master.'

He had a young face for a man of middle years, his age only betrayed by the receding line of his ever thinning hair. The scholar rubbed his eyes and focused on the initiates.

Luthor turned to his two young charges. 'Wess, Eoin, this is my apprentice, Elgar. He will take you through some letters.'

The scholar nodded in greeting. 'Good to meet you both. What do you want me to show them, master?'

'Get them on the clay tabs, and try them with some basic words. See how they do.'

The scholar hesitated then replied, 'Yes, master. I will do as you ask.'

'Thank you, Elgar. I have something I need to attend to.'

'Ah yes,' Elgar said suddenly, 'before I forget. Gideon came looking for you. He said to send for you as soon as possible.'

'Yes, thank you. He found me earlier. I'll leave these two in your hands. I should not be long.' Luthor rifled through several scrolls of a shelf, collected the one he sought and hurried back into the passageway. He had not gone a dozen feet when he recognised a familiar bulk lurking by a side passage. The man threw him an urgent glance and hurried over.

'Gideon, I'm coming now,' Luthor grumbled impatiently as he approached.

'Luthor, I've made some progress!' The short, bulging man whispered as he waddled to Luthor's side.

'Good,' replied Luthor. 'How is our guest?'

'He is less wary now we have found the dialect, most certainly.'

'It is a strange tongue,' said Luthor. He waved the scroll in his hand. 'I brought what there is on it, scant little though I'm afraid.'

'May I?' asked Gideon with a gesture to the scroll. 'It seems the Myhar he is using is not his native tongue, hence his peculiar dialect.' Gideon unravelled the scroll and paused to study it intensely. 'Yes, this will be helpful,' said the large man as he rolled the parchment up. 'Best studied while sitting down though.'

They continued onward and emerged into a courtyard that intersected several of the cob and timber buildings. Luthor always felt there was a neatness about the College, a sense of order and propriety that made him feel at ease. The pair made their way into another building through an entrance guarded by two of the College's hired-swords and followed a corridor to its end, where another pair of bored looking, heavy-set men stood guard at a barred door.

Gideon halted Luthor with a touch to his arm and leaned in close. 'You know, the council will be expecting our report tomorrow, and word is they are under pressure from the Crown to provide answers. Especially with all *this* going on.' He waved his hand, gesturing to the surroundings but to nothing in particular.

Luthor nodded grimly. 'Well, we will see if we can get more sense from him this time.'

The pair continued to the end of the hall and the guarded door where their guest was being held — the current subject of their study.

The guards unbarred the door and Luthor entered first. His eyes flicked around the room quickly, searching for the occupant. Luthor was always nervous when he visited; worried the foreigner might be lurking beside the door again, ready to strike and make another escape attempt.

His eyes settled on the man, and found him sitting calmly on a bed of furs and blankets in the corner.

His skin was a dark, almost onyx in colour, and his piercing eyes stared at the pair as they entered uncertainly. He had been given clothes of the local style, wearing breeches and a College tunic that hung open at the front, revealing a dark muscled chest marbled with white scars.

A tray of half eaten food lay on a side table, the remains of a heel of bread and some cheese. Apple cores littered the tray beside a small earthen flask of wine and a horn mug. Luthor noted that he had been well kept, as ordered.

The man had initially been kept in a gaol, speaking a strange tongue no one had ever heard, and there was no one about who could speak with him. Luthor had heard he was due to be sold back to a slaver until the sickness and its origins drew the attention of the city's lords. The powers that be had ordered the man be handed over to the College in the hope of some kind of interrogation, and perhaps an explanation of what this sickness was, if not a way to halt it. The council had guarded him closely, though he was technically no prisoner. The man had done nothing wrong, after all, except to come off that cursed ship at Anchorage — the only one to survive.

The black man sat absently rubbing the welts of fresh scarring around his wrists, the vestiges of the iron bands they had used to shackle him, and his eyes followed Luthor and Gideon as they moved into the room.

The council had appointed Master Luthor the task of communicating with the foreigner, as he was one of the few at the College who had travelled the lands of Myhar. Gideon had been enlisted to aid Luthor soon after, as his studies were in the languages of the world's known peoples. The pair had laboured, without much success, since their guest had been brought from the gaols, and those first few days had been frustrating. The man did little but stare at their attempts to speak with him, then caused great difficulty when first released from his restraints. Understandably, still thinking himself a prisoner in a strange land, he had seized the opportunity and tried several escape attempts.

The foreigner now seemed to have resigned himself to a more comfortable confinement, not forced to work or to row, nor kept behind bars in squalor. He had settled some, but remained wary of the College men and their attentions.

Gideon and Luthor had begun to make headway on some shared simple words, mostly with gestures, and discerned a few basic words the man understood, trying to communicate that he was no longer a slave but a guest of the College, guarded for his own safety, but the man had not shown any understanding. Luthor had deduced that the man was speaking a dialect from Myhar, but had gotten nowhere with the dialects he knew. Gideon's revelation now explained why they had been so unsuccessful.

Gideon unfurled the scroll and sat at a table, poring over the manuscript. He began muttering as he read, trying the strange vowels and words of a Myhar tongue.

Luthor stood at the large man's shoulder, one eye on the man on the bed. 'So, Gideon; you said there had been progress?'

'Ah yes. Observe,' said Gideon, placing down the unfurled scroll. He rose from his stool and moved towards the bed. '*Marakya deilem. Arak selema.*' Gideon bowed to their guest.

'*Jhas p'her deilem,*' the dark man replied, his face contorting as he struggled with Gideon's accent.

'*Gideon deilem,*' replied Gideon. With a clap of his hands he turned to his colleague, his face alight with excitement.

Luthor stepped forward and leaned over the parchment. Gideon placed his finger on a scrawled passage of text. After a momentary read, Luthor also repeated the phrase.

'*Mar-ak-ya... dei-lem.*' His pronunciation, not as proficient as Gideon's, his speech broken. '*Arak selema.*' His eyes flicked to the dark man after he spoke the last words. He waited.

The dark man nodded. '*Jhas p'her deilem.*'

'*Luthor deilem,*' responded Luthor with a smile.

'Astounding,' muttered Gideon.

Luthor stepped closer to their guest. 'Luthor,' he said placing his hands on his chest.

'*Jhas p'her,*' said the dark man, indicating towards himself with a mimicking gesture.

'Finally, we have something!' Luthor beamed at his colleague.

A wide smile cracked Gideon's face, he clapped his hands together unable to contain his excitement. Luthor retreated to the table to read the parchment again.

'What is it?' asked Luthor.

'From the *Akhaiha*, a formal greeting — religious — but mentioned several times in the texts we have. From what it states here, the work of a Master Henrich, it seems to go beyond worship, into the entire structure of their customs as a formal greeting and as a dedication to their deities. A common gesture throughout the northern regions, and possibly much of Myhar.'

'I have read of the *Akhaiha*, but it is not something I have studied in depth,' admitted Luthor.

'He seemed to react to certain words earlier, basic names of objects from my studies in the Myhar tongue. But I do not think he understood them. But still, the reaction to this dialect got me thinking. I needed this to make it work,' said Gideon, indicating the parchment. 'This is why I have been sending for you all day.'

'Is there more we can try?'

'I am not sure.' Gideon shrugged. 'I don't think it is his native tongue but perhaps there is something else. I cannot say without further study and experimentation.'

'But still, this is excellent. We have much to do,' said Luthor. 'The council will hear of our progress first thing in the morning.'

'Aye, at least now we have his name,' exclaimed Gideon excitedly. He clasped his hands together and bowed once more to the dark man, still sat quietly on the bed. '*Jhas p'her.*'

The candles nestled in the hollows lining the wall had burnt low by the time Luthor emerged from the chamber, leaving Gideon to continue their work. The bored guard forced a grimaced smile in farewell but did not speak, and Luthor hurried away down the darkened corridors back to his own chambers.

Since discovering his name, their guest had become more responsive. They had managed to coax several other exchanges, which Gideon had written down and was likely currently scouring through manuscripts to find translations. There was unfortunately scarce knowledge here in the College from those distant shores, but the challenge did not seem to deter the man.

Luthor scurried back across the courtyard and his thoughts turned to his initiates. It had grown late, and he wondered how they had done with their letters. Would his apprentice still be awaiting in the study? He doubted it at this hour.

Luthor continued quickly through the dark corridors of the College, the only light, a glimmer of moonlight from the high windows. Rounding a corner, he collided with a dark form which he sent sprawling into the adjacent wall. The shadowed figure seemed to hop on one leg, and a wooden staff skittered across the floor as the flailing figure fought for balance.

Luthor scrambled to a halt, immediately concerned he had knocked down one of the aged College men. He prayed it was not one of the council elders. His eyes focused in the gloom as the old man regained his composure, his greyed lank hair and age crippled leg becoming clear. Luthor did not recognise him.

'I am sorry, friend!' exclaimed Luthor.

'Master Luthor?' asked a familiar voice.

Luthor stared into the man's shadowed face as his eyes adjusted in the scant light. It was not as aged as he first presumed, but a face he knew yet could not place.

'By the gods,' muttered Luthor as realisation dawned. 'It's you, lad.'

Luthor stared, taken aback. Of course he knew this face, but it was not the young features of the man he remembered. It had not been that long since he had last seen him, several moons at most, just before Master Eldrick and Logan had left for their research expedition in the north. The face he saw before him was gaunt and drawn, aged beyond his years. Something haunted his eyes, hiding behind exhaustion and pain.

Luthor looked down at the apprentice's leg then hurried to collect the walking stick that had fallen from the younger man's hand. 'Dear boy... your leg. What in the god's names has happened to you? Your hair!'

'I know, master. It was a bad break.' He touched his hair, then leaned back against the wall. 'It just hasn't healed... It was a long, wet road with little rest or a proper healer. My body feels drained.'

'Aye,' frowned Luthor, passing him the staff and stepping back. 'That leg looks bad. We should get you to the healers straight away. We have some of the best within the College here. If it can be set straight, they will be the ones to do it. Has *anyone* looked at it?'

The lad shook his head. 'Not since Master Eldrick set it, and that was weeks ago. I have just returned from up north, and I have not long docked. I will get it looked at but not at this hour. It can wait till the morning.'

'Make sure you do, lad,' said Luthor. He eyed the crippled leg. It was twisted and crooked, and he could not imagine the pain of resting any weight upon it. He shuddered. 'I must ask; is the sickness bad in the north?'

'I saw it first after we rounded the Sea of Spires, heading for Stoneshore. There was no sickness in the north when I set sail, but it is terrible out in the waterways coming here. I saw horrible things... Has it hit the city? I saw pyres on the river bank?'

'Probably worse, lad,' said Luthor before he paused, his thoughts drifting to images of dead faces he had seen in the city's gutters.

'Does anyone know what it is?' enquired the apprentice. He looked weary, dark circles under his eyes.

'I wish we did. I fear a plague has descended upon us. Half the College is scratching for a way to stem the tide. Still, that is dire news. Gods protect us.' Luthor sighed. 'Anyway, it is good to see you, lad. Please give my regards to Master Eldrick. I look forward to seeing him.'

'Ah,' replied the apprentice. 'My master is likely still on the road behind me. He should be on his way back with Master Logan and the others by now. They were returning by road, but couldn't be much more than a week or so away. I cannot be sure, though. I did not make good time.'

'Oh well, lad. Welcome home, in any case. I only wish the city wasn't as troubled for your return.'

'Thank you, Master Luthor. Forgive me, but I am in sore need of my bed. A real bed.'

'Aye, I won't keep you. It is late, get some rest.' Luthor watched the young apprentice limp painfully away into the gloom. He had known the lad from his earliest years in the College, he had once been his own apprentice before he had moved to study under Eldrick—a bright lad, promising. Now he was a cripple. The young man relied on his staff heavily; it skidded and made clicking sounds on the smooth stone floor as he limped away. His gait was truly ghastly to behold, and despite his hopeful reassurances, Luthor feared he would never walk right again. He stood a moment, watching in morbid fascination, before resuming his hurried walk back through the dark corridors to his chambers.

CHAPTER SEVEN

Silver for Blood

They stumbled along the gully, tripping and sliding on wet stone, four men desperately clawing their way up on to the ridge ahead. A roiling canopy of dark cloud shifted above them. The rains had come, and the deluge hadn't eased all day.

'Fucking rain,' Niall grumbled at Hale. 'Could you not have come sooner? We could have missed all *this*.' He made an incensed gesture at the sky.

'Took time,' said Hale, wiping his dripping hair out of his eyes. 'We had to get our gear out, stash the supplies. You're lucky we got you out at all, mate. Took the best chance we could.'

'We just bled for you!' barked Seb, turning on Niall and blocking his ascent with the width of his shoulders. The others jolted to a stop behind him in the stony gully. 'Three good lads, we left back there. I saw Pegg fall. The others? Fuck knows — either dead or being strung up. You're damn lucky you're not with 'em. I certainly don't wanna be dying for ya, so get your ass moving.' Seb turned and heft himself higher into the gully.

Niall scowled. He was the earl's man. These land-folk should know their place but he stayed his tongue. Seb was right — he would likely be dead and rotting in that gibbet beside the gates if not for the bravery of these men.

He turned and threw a furtive glance over his shoulder, searching the trees behind him, then hurried on, pulling himself along with the larger boulders. The wet stone had scraped his hands bloody, his legs were tired, his boots caked in mud and his clothes were soaked and heavy. Despite all this, he urged his aching legs forward and continued his scrabbling ascent up the dripping gully.

He caught a flash of movement away to his left. A quick glimpse of a shape, a man in the trees, then it was gone. He snapped his head around.

Nothing.

'Did you see something?' asked Pike from behind him.

Niall peered off into the trees. 'I thought there was something there, just for a second.'

'It's fucking following us,' muttered Pike.

'There ain't no fucking ghost,' snarled Seb from higher up.

'It *was* a fucking ghost,' Pike insisted in an irritated voice. 'I saw it. It was just stood there looking at me, and then it vanished.'

'You didn't see anything, fool! You're just scared of the woods,' snapped Seb.

'I saw something, I swear.' Pike clutched at Niall's jacket as he clambered up beside him, 'Sounds funny, but did it look like the trees?'

Niall shook his head and pulled a look both amused and full of derision before continuing on. If he stopped for more than a few moments, he worried he may not be able to start again.

'It looked like the trees,' continued Pike, falling behind again and seemingly unbothered if anyone was listening or if any of them believed him. 'Then it was gone,' he said with a flick of his hands.

'I don't know what it was,' Niall replied, after catching his breath. 'I thought it was someone running, but there is nothing.' He stopped and searched the trees again.

'There's something out there, I'm tellin' ya. I reckon it's after us,' whispered Pike.

'There's no fucking *ghost*,' growled Seb, obviously still in earshot.

Niall raised his hand to silence them. 'What is that?'

The low call of a horn echoed through the valley, accompanied by the faint sound of barking dogs.

'Shit!' Seb spun around. 'They might have our scent.'

As one the men began franticly scrambling up the rocky gully.

'How did they catch us so fast?' Pike huffed in disbelief.

'They ain't caught us yet, lad. Might not have our scent proper yet. Go, move!' barked Seb.

'What if they do?' asked Pike in a grim tone.

'The boat isn't far, come on,' urged Seb. 'Hounds can't track us on the water.'

Niall hoped this boat they'd arranged wasn't far. He longed to get back on the water and away, not just to escape but to be back on deck. He'd spent his whole life at sea; boats were home to him and he wasn't sure he liked these old lands.

Ahead, Seb pulled himself over the last ledge and up onto the ridge. Niall would be glad to leave this cursed gully behind. It had been steep and treacherous but had taken them up through the last rocky cliffs of the high valley side, each step bringing him closer to freedom.

Finally he too climbed over the ledge and turned to look back the way they had come, the winding valley stretching out behind him. He searched the trees below for any sign of pursuit, but there were none. The faint barking of hounds rolling across the hillsides, but that was all. They would have some tough ground to cover to catch them, if they were indeed after him and his companions, and not some hunting party out after game. A network of dense and tangled valleys lay between them.

'What the fuck is *that*?' exclaimed Hale. Niall looked up and gasped.

Amongst the trees of the ridge, on the rocks ahead of them, sat a figure.

'That's him!' hissed Pike. 'The fucking ghost.'

Seb snapped out his axe from his belt, his eyes fixed on the stranger. The half-naked man sat calmly staring back.

His beard covered the lower half of his face, while his long hair hung in a tangled mess of leaves and twigs. He seemed to be wearing a loin cloth — no, pelts — and clutched a crude spear as he eyed them silently.

'Move away, friend. Let us pass.' Seb rumbled, with no hint of friendliness, stalking menacingly towards the man, his axe held low at his side. He motioned to the others and Hale moved up to join him.

'He looks like the woods,' muttered Pike as he clambered up next to Niall and unsheathed his knife. Niall could see it now. The strange man seemed to be smeared in mud and leaves and did indeed look like the woods behind him, blending perfectly with the surroundings.

Niall unhooked his own weapon from the loop on his belt and glanced down at it. The axe was not his; it had been among the weapons hidden in the stash before his escape, sequestered in the hills outside the town's walls before Seb's crew had got him out. Niall was glad of the foresight of his rescuers. Some of these men were his people, sent to live amongst the land-folk many years ago, while others were men of Arnar waiting for a chance to help their banished kin. All had been anticipating the time when the earl finally called them to arms.

The Wildman sat motionless, watching Seb and Hale creep closer. He had an eye on all of them.

There was a wet thud beside Niall.

'Ugh,' cried Pike, and the feathers of an arrow suddenly appeared from his chest. He dropped his knife and tumbled to the ground groaning.

Niall spun, scanning the trees along the ridge. *They're all around us!*

Another arrow thrummed out from the shadows and thudded into Hale's throat. His head snapped back with the impact and he collapsed into the mud, clutching his neck as blood pumped out between his fingers.

Were they waiting for us? Niall sank low behind a large rock. 'Shit,' he muttered.

He flicked a quick look at the Wildman. He was gone. No sign of him anywhere. *Like a ghost.* Niall searched for the source of the arrows and found it—a cloaked figure with a bow.

Seb had seen the bowman too, and was already creeping forward, stooping low behind the cover of the boulders littering the mouth of the gully.

An arrow clattered off the rock beside Niall and he ducked. *Shit, that was close!*

Seb suddenly charged into the trees, attempting to reach their attacker before he could loose another arrow.

From his hiding place, Niall watched as Pike pulled himself along the ground and picked up his knife, his teeth clenched in a grimace as he clutched the arrow buried in his chest. He clawed his way painfully up beside Niall to lean against the boulder, his breath shallow and gasping.

Niall popped his head up to look over the boulder, just in time to see Seb clash with the shooter, now divested of his cloak and bow, and wielding an axe in one hand and a long knife in the other. Indecision washed through Niall, and he looked frantically back at Pike then across to Hale. Pike didn't look good for much right now, so he sprang up and dashed over to Hale.

He was dead.

A knot of panic tightened in his stomach. *I don't want to die here.*

If they were to escape this Niall knew he had to help Seb, and he turned to assess their attacker.

While the strange forest man had blended with the surrounds, the bowman was a bold, dark silhouette amongst the trees. He wore the weather worn leathers and rugged clothes of a man who knew the wilds, and his dark hair hung about his shoulders, his face hard and windswept.

Niall sprung forward, axe clutched in hand, and charged to join his remaining comrade.

Seb swung his axe wide and vicious, closing in on the bowman. The attacker parried with his long knife and deftly avoided the arc of the swinging axe with a sidestep. He hacked a savage chop at Seb's chest then almost danced away as Seb stared at him dumfounded. The wound in Seb's chest bloomed red through his clothes, and before Niall could reach them, the hunter hooked Seb's knee with his axe head and yanked it up, crunching through flesh and tendons. With a cry Seb crashed to the ground, the back of his knee in ruin.

Niall skidded to a halt just out of striking distance and the attacker eyed him coldly. Niall's gaze flicked to Seb as the big man writhed on the ground, clutching his leg.

'Give yourself up, friend,' growled the huntsman. 'We have you.'

Niall gave no reply.

With a sudden feint to the right, Niall plunged left and struck at the hunter. The hunter parried the blow with his axe and came straight in with a carving chop. Niall dodged backward, only just avoiding it.

The huntsman grinned and circled him, weapons held up in guard. Niall saw no easy opening, and the hunter seemed content to let Niall make the first move.

He who strikes first often strikes last. The words of his master-at-arms echoed in his memory as he carefully decided his move, mirroring the attacker warily.

The hunter moved first. He sprang forwards and Niall swung at him as soon as he came within reach. With a smooth step around the scything axe, the hunter checked the back of Niall's arm with his long-knife and the cold steel bit his skin. The hunter's other hand brought the axe head up and thrust it into the underside of Niall's face.

His head snapped back with the impact and his vision swam with flashes of light, blurring out of focus. The axe blade raked across his face, leaving a deep gash across his cheek. He staggered backwards dazed, the blood dripping down his chin.

He's so fast, thought Niall, his head spinning as the world tilted sideways.

Seb appeared beside him, somehow back on his feet, and with a roar he returned to the fray. Despite his wounds he threw himself at the hunter, swinging another mighty blow with his axe. The bowman stepped back and frantically parried with knife and axe as Seb rained down a series of savage blows, one after another in blind fury. Seb seemed to have him on the back foot.

Suddenly a wet crunch echoed against the trees.

'Ugh,' grunted Seb, staggering towards Niall. He gawped down at the sharpened spear point protruding from his chest with widening eyes.

Niall blinked hard as the Wildman appeared from behind his comrade and tugged his spear free before swinging it around to strike the side of Seb's head with the blunt end. A blow that should have sent any man down failed to level Seb, and somehow he remained standing. Rounding dizzily on his new attacker, he swung wildly, missing his mark and staggering.

The hunter and his comrade circled him at a distance until the Wildman jabbed his spear towards him. Seb coughed a gout of blood, and despite his best efforts, his attacks lost their power and frequency as his strength waned. He was losing blood fast.

He's done for, they all are.

Niall turned and fled, leaving his wounded comrades to their fate. He plunged into the trees and ran for his life, expecting a blow from behind at any second. A quick axe in the back as he ran would at least be a more merciful death than what awaited him. He would not return to that cage to die slowly, rotting beside his comrades. If it must be death at the hands of these land-folk he would chose his fate. He would take his chances in the wilds alone—the gods had often smiled on him, why not now?

He tore through the trees as fast as his legs would carry him, blood pouring from the wound in his face. He managed to smear it into his eyes as he wiped his face with his sleeve, stumbling over roots and uneven ground, slipping on moss choked stones, but he kept his footing and urged himself onward.

He dared not look back. He heard Seb bellowing his final defiance. He would go down fighting, that one.

Niall risked a quick glance behind him as he ran.

His heart froze.

Running low to the ground, closing on him with every step, came the Wildman. A pang of panic struck him. He sprinted as hard as his legs could be forced to run.

There was a strange whirring sound. Something struck his legs, fouling his steps. There was a sharp stinging pain and he crashed into the undergrowth. His legs bound by something, Niall reached down to find a crude bola.

The Wildman loomed above him menacingly, a spear levelled at his face.

No, no...

With a quick whirl of his spear—no more than a sharp, fire hardened stick—the Wildman reversed the weapon and brought it down hard into his face. He fell into darkness.

*****

The sound came first, the clip-clop of horse's hooves on stone, accompanied by the baying and barking of hunting hounds, then the horsemen emerged from the undergrowth and picked their way through the stunted trees and shrubs onto the ridgeline. From the presence of hunting dogs, one could be fooled into expecting a hunting party, but no. Instead, these were men in an assortment of chainmail and boiled leather, the common theme among them, the black and yellow raiment of the Guard of Oldstones.

It was raining again. His hair stuck wet against his face, and he wore his fair share of mud too.

Bjorn still held his horn in his hands, tapping it gently with his dripping thumb. The horn, pale ivory shot through with blooms of a deep reddish-brown, was capped at one end with a mouth-piece wrought in silver. He placed it back on his belt now the horsemen and hounds had caught up with him.

The armoured troop trotted towards where the hunter stood, their hooves splashing through the muddy puddles, their captain at the fore in a splendid polished helm and fine armour. Daeluf drew his horse to a halt in front of Bjorn as the hunting dogs milled around barking at their quarry, laid still on the floor.

'Job done, m'lord,' said Bjorn.

Daeluf looked over the four muddy bodies laid on the ground before his horse. 'Aye, so I see. You engaged them alone?'

Bjorn gave a grim nod. 'Aye,' said the hunter as if it were but a small trivial thing. 'Just me and Tung here.'

The Wildman had been a devil in the woods. He had scouted far ahead, coming and going as they tracked the outlaws through the valleys. When he came upon them, he had shown the hunter, and when the time came, they seemed to act as one, without the need to understand each other's words. Tung revealed his obvious cunning, and though they still communicated with gestures alone, he was becoming less the savage in Bjorn's eyes as each day passed.

Bjorn looked at his companion, crouched nearby leaning on his crude fire-hardened spear. He was watching the horsemen and gave a long, low hoot.

'Took your time though, m'lord,' said Bjorn, turning back to the captain and flashing a grin. 'I thought we'd take them while we had a good chance. We had them good here—didn't have time to wait for you to catch up.'

'It was tough country.' Daeluf gestured back the way they had come. 'And in this,' he said looking up, 'the hounds were near useless.'

'Of course, m'lord,' said Bjorn with a shallow bow.

'And I've told you not to call me that, hunter. I'm no lord,' snapped Daeluf.

'Yes, m'lord,' replied Bjorn with a smirk.

Daeluf scowled at him and nodded at the four men laid face up in the mud. 'Is that all of them?'

Bjorn nodded slowly. 'None got away.'

'They are all dead?' asked the captain.

'One will live, the others maybe not.' Bjorn was certain one of them had already perished.

Daeluf dismounted and looked the four of them over. Two were bound, and one had an arrow in his chest. His breathing was shallow and wet, and Bjorn reckoned he was unlikely to survive. The other two were limp and still; one with an arrow through his throat while the big man lay covered in blood and wounds.

Daeluf gave each a kick as he walked along, and one of the bound men groaned and opened his eyes as Daeluf shoved him with an iron shod boot. The man's hair was sticky with blood, but he was still quite conscious and he glared up at them.

'Which is your man?' asked Bjorn.

'This one.' Daeluf kicked the conscious man again. 'You're in luck, hunter. You will be paid well for this one, I'm sure.'

Bjorn gave a satisfied nod. 'Dead or alive, I'll take silver for all four.'

'Aye, that you will,' replied Daeluf.

'Is that Seb?' shouted one of the mounted guardsmen.

'That it is,' Daeluf called back to the guard. He glanced at Bjorn then nodded down at the men on the ground. 'These two were in the guard. The big one called himself Seb, but gods only know if that was his real name.' He landed another swift kick to the survivor's gut, sneering down at him. 'You'll pay for this, you fucker. I'll see you back in a cage for good. You can rot there this time.'

Bjorn grimaced at thought of the gibbet he had seen by the gates of Oldstones. He hadn't cared enough to ask when given the job of hunting the men, but on seeing Daeluf's fury, his curiosity piqued. 'What did they do?'

'Spies and saboteurs; they played us false, these bastards,' snarled Daeluf without looking away from the prisoner. 'How long have you been amongst us, you honourless dog?'

The man glared up at them and bared his bloody teeth.

'Our armies will crush you, fool,' he shouted, with all his remaining strength. His accent was strange, not one Bjorn had heard. 'We will sweep you aside like a hammer from the sea. Our folk are already everywhere, already amongst you, waiting to cut your throats. The people will rise up against you. They will rise with us as we free them!'

The man's words and fervour shocked Bjorn, but not as much as his message. Did he speak true? Was there some threat lurking amongst the people of Arnar?

'You lie!' snapped Daeluf.

The prisoner said nothing more but glowered up at them, grinning like a blood-spattered maniac. Daeluf landed another savage kick for good measure, doubling the man over.

'Bind these two on a mount,' snapped the captain to the waiting horsemen. 'Bring the heads of the others. We ride for Oldstones.'

Bjorn watched as the surviving men were draped over a horse side by side and securely bound in place like a pair of deer caught on a hunt. One struggled, the other merely grunted as they heaved him over the horse's back. Bjorn turned away as a guardsman began hacking the heads off the other two — that was grim work he'd rather not watch.

The hunter looked out into the valley below. His hair dripped in the rain and the faint smell of decomposing wood and damp permeated the air. He imagined, now the rains had come, the winding valleys, gullies and gulches would quickly become a tangle of stinking mire and choking branches.

There was a series of hacking wet thuds behind him and he winced — another head for the high lord. Bjorn was growing sick of death. How many men had he sent to the noose or the chopping block for some crime or another? How many had he sent to the dirt by his own hand? Two today, likely three by morning — more dead for Old Night's hall. The prisoner would probably die a slow, grim death too, especially if the gibbet hanging at the east gate waited for the poor fool.

The man's talk of armies and rebellion echoed through his thoughts. All was not as it seemed in this. He looked over at Daeluf and saw the captain had mounted his horse beside the dismembered head of a bloody corpse. A guardsman picked it up by the hair and dumped into a sack.

Bjorn turned back to the valley and chewed the inside of his lip. Perhaps he should take his silver and go south or east for a time, live a quiet life somewhere in the woods, away from the death of guilty men. He had seen gruesome things of late. Images flicked through his mind — men feasting on the flesh of others, the faces of those he had just put to the dirt, the face of the head in that bag. There were others, men he had brought to meet the justice of lords, men who were now just as dead as these fools.

He was tired, and the thing that had once been a quiet whisper had begun to call ever louder. Perhaps it was time to seek the thing he found himself wanting more and more. Could he go back to her? Or had it been too long? He'd sent her no word, despite always meaning to, but with each day that passed it seemed more pointless.

He was certain by now she would have found another. He had wronged her after all, and left her for far too long. Why would she wait? The answer was one he had ever feared finding, but that had not stopped him thinking how he might go about it. He'd watch her for a time, just to see if she was happy. What harm would it do? She needn't see him or know he was in town, especially if it risked causing her more pain. But each time he'd thought to do it, he'd put it off, leaving years to pass between them. But perhaps it was time?

'Are you coming, hunter, or are you going to stay here in the rain? We ride direct to Oldstones,' called Daeluf. With a gesture from the captain, one of the horsemen led Bjorn's horse to him and he took the reins, greeting it with a rub on the nose. He set his foot in his stirrup and heaved himself up.

A short sharp whistle brought Bjorn the Wildman's attention and Bjorn jerked his head towards the trees. 'Are you ready for a run, my friend? Let's move.'

While fairly certain the Wildman understood nothing he said, Tung certainly recognised the jerk of the head as a signal to move out.

'To Oldstones,' said Bjorn as he nudged his horse forward, and Tung followed.

CHAPTER EIGHT

An Eye for an Eye

Nym clutched the bag of provisions closely to her chest and kept moving. It was her turn to venture out to get some food but all she'd managed to get were oats and a few root vegetables — potatoes, carrots, a turnip — nothing exciting. The street was not as crowded as she had expected but it still heaved with more people than she would have liked. The market was much the same as the main street; busy, but full of folk who were visibly cautious, nervous eyes watching those around them for any sign of the illness. The sense of dread hanging over the town was palpable, reminding her of Anchorage.

The city was supposed to be an escape from all this.

She tightened the scarf over her mouth and nose and kept her distance from the milling crowds, taking every precaution she could to protect her from the sickness. It seemed like contact with the sick transmitted the illness, burning its way through families, workmates and groups of friends, but no one knew how. Was it touch? Or did one simply have to breathe on someone else to give it to them? No one even knew if you could be sick without appearing so, carrying death with you like an invisible cloak.

She whispered her plea to the gods as she walked. 'Please don't be sick, please don't be sick.'

Her resolve battled with her roiling stomach as she walked. She prayed it was just some bad food, or perhaps the foul smells of the city, the piss and shit churned into the muddy streets, that was making her sick. Sometimes it was quite overpowering. Or was it the lingering smell of Old Night's work, the twisted bodies rotting in the autumn sun on every street corner?

The crowd parted for a rumbling cart. The grotesque lifeless husks of what were once Arn's townsfolk—neighbours, friends, men, women, children—all sprawled in the back of the cart. The sickness had no pity. It cared not who it struck down into Old Night's grasp. Despite her scarf, the smell that hit her as the cart passed was awful. Her stomach turned.

There was no holding it.

She turned and vomited onto the street, heaving up her breakfast. She continued to retch even when there was nothing left to bring up. She tried her best to avoid her clothes but still splattered her boots. Finally, the urge abated and she spat the taste of bile from her mouth and pulled her hair from her face. To her horror, the surrounding folk had stopped and stood staring at her in terror.

'I'm not sick,' she said to the nearest man. He recoiled and pushed his way through the bystanders to get away from her. 'I'm not sick...' Tears welled in her eyes. *Please gods, don't let me be sick.*

She didn't want to end up like those twisted corpses, stacked in the back of a cart. Fighting back the tears, Nym hugged her bag tighter and ran.

When she slowed, she was far from anyone who had seen her throw up in the gutter, and safe enough by her reckoning that she wouldn't be suspected of the illness. She wiped the tears from her face with the back of her sleeve and trudged onward. The dull ache of sickness in the pit of her stomach remained, but at least she didn't feel like she would vomit again for a little while.

She turned onto one of the city's main thoroughfares, the wide street known as Saltergate, which led to the wharfs. The Citadel rose above the squat buildings lining the street ahead, dominating the skyline by the river, and a patrol of guardsmen passed her by, grim-faced warriors in assorted armour carrying spears. They cast suspicious eyes over everyone, and folk kept their distance, the uniforms and the wolf head shields they each carried marking them as the king's warriors.

Nym gave the soldiers a wide berth, catching snatches of conversation as she continued on. Folk seemed agitated about something, something other than the sickness.

'How are we supposed to trade with the gates sealed?' a man growled to a woman standing to one side of the road, raising his arms in exasperation as she passed.

Nym frowned. *The gates are sealed?*

'Trapped like rats!' replied the elderly woman in a crackling voice.

Nym focused her attention on the half-heard conversations and found a common thread. Folk everywhere were all talking about the same thing — the decree from the ruling lords and perhaps some thought, from the king himself. Ahead, folk crowded around a man at an intersection in the wide street.

'Due to the sickness,' he called loudly, 'the city gates have been sealed. No person or group of persons are permitted to travel without a writ. Nym slowed at the back of the crowd, watching the man as he rolled up his scroll and moved along to shout his message at another junction.

So Seth was right, thought Nym. There had been rumours swirling for days now, recounted by Seth, but this was the first time she had heard it with her own ears. *We truly are trapped in the city.*

Hopefully Seth's plan to get them out would work, otherwise they'd be stuck here like everyone else.

Another pile of twisted bloodied corpses, a man and woman, had been dumped in the street to await a cart, discarded like scraps on a midden.

She shook her head and held her breath. *Whatever happened to honouring the dead?*

The door of the house behind the corpses had been daubed in red paint. It was a warning that screamed "beware — sickness within".

She averted her eyes, her stomach already twitching at the gruesome sight. *Not again, not here. We can't stay in the city. I don't want to end up like them.*

She felt the hairs on the back of her neck prickle, standing on end as the creeping sensation of being watched came over her. Nym spun and searched the street. Had someone reported her to the grim-faced patrol as being one of the sick? She scanned the townsfolk as they went about their business on the busy thoroughfare, then locked her gaze with a pair of eyes framed by thick kohl paint; eyes that watched her intently.

It's her. She's here. The witch-seer. Nym was sure it was the same woman. She remembered the eyes clearly. She must have made it out of Anchorage too.

The seer's hair was adorned in the same jingling trinkets, her eyelids painted with the same dusky colour, making her eyes bright and intense as she stared at Nym. She wore a black dress and her skin was darker than that usually seen in Arnar, leaving Nym to wonder if she hailed from across the sea. She wore more trinkets over her clothes, like the ones in her hair, and Nym easily imagined her reading the cards and telling fortunes in a smoky room hung with charms. Witch-seers were a secretive people— mystics, healers, witches—who folk said the gods spoke directly to. The strange woman's attention made Nym uneasy, and she shifted her feet.

Why is she watching me?

Nym's scarf slipped down and revealed her face. She smiled nervously at the woman, then pulled the cloth back into place and hurried away. She didn't dare look back to see if the woman's gaze followed her. She was eager to get back; she wanted to get ready. At least tonight she would have some distraction from the constant dread, from the sickness, and from the horrible death that had descended on the city. Seth was taking them to the tavern to meet his man. A tingle of excitement rushed through her at the thought of it. She'd never been to a real city tavern, and she looked forward to watching Seth play.

***

A man with a lean face with long stubble over his chin pulled up a chair at the table, his dark hair greased with some sort of oil. Nym could smell him from where she sat; stale sweat and only the gods knew what else. Was this really Seth's man?

Their table occupied one of the tavern's wood panelled booths, tucked into a shadowed corner on the far side of the tap room. A single candle burned in a dented lantern at the centre of the table, its ruddy light barely illuminating their faces from the gloom.

'Is this them?' the man asked, nodding at Nym, Jor and Finn.

'Aye,' replied Seth, before turning to the group. 'This is Roark.'

Roark looked each of them over, his gaze lingering on Nym for long enough to make her uncomfortable. He leered at her, show- ing several missing teeth. She managed an awkward smile then quickly looked away.

'Can you do it?' asked Jor.

'Ah, straight to business. No time for pleasantries?'

'We're eager to get going,' replied Jor. 'So, can you do it?'

'Aye, I can.' Roark leaned forward across the table. 'Have you got coin though? Two silver marks each — one for me and one for the man who'll be takin' you.'

Jor threw a shocked look at his son but Seth nodded. 'Aye, we've got the coin,' Seth assured him.

That seemed like a lot to Nym. She'd never even seen eight marks in her life.

'Let's see it then.' Roark's brows rose in surprise.

Seth flashed one of his disarming grins. 'Like we agreed; half now, for you and your man to make arrangements, and half when we're on our way.'

'Don't you trust me?' said the man with a smirk.

Seth laughed. 'I don't trust no one. But I trust you enough you'll keep your word to get paid the second half when the job's done. That's what we agreed.'

'Aye, that we did,' he replied reluctantly. 'Let's see it then.'

Glancing around to check if anyone was watching, Jor fumbled inside his clothes and nervously drew out a purse, shielding it with the stump of his arm. Nym couldn't help notice that her brother's eyes lit up as the purse came into view, and the man sitting opposite eyed it greedily. It worried her that their expressions were identical, and she nudged her brother, levelling a scowl at him. One look at the dirty, shifty looking man opposite told her she did not want Finn to end up like him, just another gutter-rat in a street gang.

Jor counted out two big silver coins, followed by two sizable chunks of hack silver. 'These'll serve?'

Roark picked up one of the lumps and turned it between his fingers, inspecting it carefully. With one of the big coins in one hand and held the hack silver in the other, he hefted them, comparing the weight. There was a long, pregnant silence and he put the metal back on the table, rubbing the long stubble on his unkempt chin.

'Reckon they will,' he said finally, an easy smile stretching across his lip.

'How long before we can leave?' asked Jor.

'Few days hopefully.'

'Not sooner?'

Roark shook his head and scraped up the silver from the table. 'It'll be by river.' He leaned in close and lowered his voice. 'My man works a barge. He has a writ, can get things in and out. He'll smuggle you out, but he ain't back in yet. Still out on the waterways. I'll make arrangements as soon as he's back in dock, then I'll send for you. Make sure you're ready.'

Jor sat back hard in his chair, the sour twist to his lips betraying his displeasure at the delay. Painting on a smile to ease the tension, Seth nodded at Roark. 'We will. You have my thanks.'

Roark looked them all over once more, then rose and walked off, slinking out quietly through a side door. Jor watched him go with a scowl on his face.

'Eight marks,' grumbled Jor as he tucked the purse back inside his shirt.

'Aye, pricey but there's a lot of risk.' Seth scratched his finger along a rough line on the table. 'Trying to get out is breaking the crown law. I heard they filled a man full of arrows as he tried to climb the walls just two days ago.'

Finn's eyes grew wide with worry. 'What if they catch us?'

The peril of the plan suddenly struck her. *If they catch us they could kill us.* The worrying thought squirmed and grew in the pit of her stomach as she chewed at her fingernails.

'They won't, lad.' Seth assured the boy with a shake of his head. He turned to his father and leaned forward. As one, the others mirrored him, huddling together over the table. 'We do have the coin, don't we? I've got my share.'

Jor offered him a weak smile. 'Aye, I got the rest. But can we trust him?'

'Probably not, but we have a deal. He'll stick to his word to get the rest of the silver, if only so folk don't hear that he ripped us off. It'd be bad for business.'

Jor grunted. 'Eight marks...'

Seth placed a hand on his father's shoulder, 'Be worth it if we don't catch the sickness.'

Jor nodded gravely.

A niggling worry grew in Nym. The old man was paying a lot on behalf of her and Finn. It was kind of him, but would Jor expect them to pay it back? How long would it take her to work off two marks? Had she just become indebted to the former tavernkeep without realising it?

She took a deep drink of her ale. It was bitter and watery but a heady sensation crept over her all the same. Nearby a man laughed loudly and she glanced over to see him sway about drunkenly on his stool, talking at the top of his voice with folk at the next table. It was a welcome sound, despite the volume. She had heard little laughter of late.

'Look how he's pouring that ale,' remarked Jor. 'I do better and only have one hand.'

Before Roark's arrival, the old man had been quietly faulting the tavern at any opportunity, comparing his own small but apparently, perfectly run little ale house with the big city pub.

'Uh huh,' agreed Nym vaguely as she looked about.

It was indeed a much larger place than she was used to, with a wide tap room, interspersed with timber columns supporting chunky beamed rafters overhead. There were rows of tables and dozens of stools and chairs which Jor's place lacked, and a large hearth burning away in the centre of it all. Dark iron braziers stood about, filled with gently smoking embers, and instead of dirty straw strewn over the floor, there were well levelled timber planks and a scattering of fresh straw by the doors. There were even decorations and furs hung on the walls between shuttered windows. It was well kept as far as Nym could see, and she wondered if the old man was merely jealous and seeking fault.

'If I had this kind of custom and space, I'd be making a killing,' continued Jor. He scowled into his mug and smacked his lips. 'This tastes like shit too.'

'They seem to have a lot of drink in,' Nym observed, referring to the wide array available for purchase behind the bar. She watched her brother carefully, while Finn watched the purses of some gamblers at a nearby table.

'A small ransom's worth, but likely fake. Nowhere has stock like that, do they, lad?' Jor grumbled at his son, but Seth did not appear to be listening. He sat on the edge of the booth seat and looked out into the bar, surveying the crowd.

Occasionally his gaze trailed shamelessly after a passing barmaid as she wove between the tables, and it seemed like they all knew him, rewarding his attention by flashing a smile in his direction. Nym watched them too. They seemed so confident as they exchanged laughs with various patrons.

'Quiet in here tonight,' said Seth. He looked at his father and grinned. 'Usually twice this in on a reaping night. Think of what you'd make if you had a place like this.' Jor scowled at the suggestion but Seth dismissed his father's lack of humour with a wave. 'I'm just hoping I get my full silver. The manager is known to be a tight arse.'

Nym ran her eyes over the crowd. If this was quiet, then it must get properly rammed in here on a good night. Everyone seemed jovial enough, a hum of conversation accented by a single louder voice. Some folk sat ominously alone, peering blankly into their drinks, drowning their sorrow, she did not doubt, and two old women huddled off to one side, gossiping over a bottle of dark liquor and pouring drams into little glasses before knocking them back.

The loud man laughed again, catching Nym's attention for the second time. He had an ugly, ropey scar down his face that carved through one of his eyes. An eye patch concealed the worst of it. The ale was settling in, her head swimming slightly as a warm sensation lapped at her awareness.

'Need something a bit stronger than this,' said Seth, pushing his ale across the table. He dug out a handful of small of coppery coins from his jacket and turned a smile on a passing serving maid, spinning one of the coins on the table. 'We'd like a bottle, please? I'll sing a song for you if you bring it over.'

The maid pretended to think about it with a mock frown before she grinned. 'Course, dear.'

She hurried away, then returned with a bottle of a dark liquid—some kind of Telik rum—and four earthenware tumblers. The maid took payment as Seth scooped up the bottle and pulled the cork free with a low pop. He gave it a sniff and wrinkled his nose.

'Boss says you can start when you're ready. And don't forget—sing me a song. I'll be listening.' The barmaid gave Seth a coy smile and then wove away between the tables.

Seth set out the tumblers and began pouring drams of the dark liquor. Jor waved his hand over Finn's to object, but Seth playfully slapped his father's hand away. 'Won't hurt him. Let them have a proper drink.'

Finn's eyes lit up as he lifted the tumbler and examined the liquid inside, imitating Seth and giving it a sniff. Nym smiled and shook her head. Jor was less amused.

'To old gods and good folk,' said Seth, raising his glass. He knocked the rum back in one and the others followed suit. It smelt foul and tasted worse, burning Nym's throat and making her belly warm. The fiery liquid made her gasp, but at least she didn't splutter like Finn, not expecting it to be so harsh. He laughed as he wiped his mouth and nose, and even Jor twitched a smile. Seth poured out another round and immediately knocked his back.

'Should you be drinking like that if you're playing, lad?' Jor frowned at his son.

Seth laughed. 'I always drink and play. Keeps me interesting.'

He poured out a third for himself, threw it down his neck and grimaced at the taste, then he grabbed the handle of his lute case and sauntered over to the stage.

It was a small stage, nothing more than a small raised platform jutting out from the wall opposite the bar, but it was a stage nonetheless. Seth settled on a lone stool, placed his long case on the floor and undid the clasps. As he lifted his lute to his knee, some of the patrons began to take notice.

Nym was ever fascinated by the strange, slender instrument, staring at it as Seth played an exploratory chord and adjusted a few of his tuning pegs. He strummed a few more times and began playing strings together, working through the long neck and checking them against the chords and notes he played on the shorter, wider neck until he seemed satisfied.

Without a word he began the opening melodies of an old and well-known song; *Eye of the Mountain Cold*. The taproom grew still as all eyes were drawn to Seth and his beautiful double-necked lute. It didn't seem that remarkable at first, Nym had heard the song a dozen times before, but as he slowly wound down on the familiar refrain, he launched into what must have been his own arrangement of the piece. With a cheeky, knowing grin, Seth played on, his hands dancing over the fretboard, adding layers of complex melodies to the well-known song. Nym watched on, stunned. It was beautiful. She'd never heard playing like it.

When Seth finally began to sing, the crowd were captivated. His voice was light, yet deep and rich, and he seemed lost as he stared into nothing while he sang.

Folk started clapping along with the beat of his song, a rowdy few singing along on the refrains, eliciting a smirk from the singer. Others started dancing.

A man whirled around drunkenly with a tankard in his hand, spilling ale on the floor as he twisted and kicked, but he was smiling. Nym and Finn began to clap and cheer. The harsh tasting rum had her vision swimming, her head felt light. She turned to Jor as she clapped and laughed with her brother. The old man wore a look of immense pride as he watched his son sing and her heart warmed to see it.

For a fleeting moment the folk in the tavern seemed to forget the plague, the suffering, the stalking death outside the door — it seemed a distant thing as Seth sang and played, carrying them away to a happier place.

Finn shuffled out of the booth and Nym darted to her feet, grabbing his arm.

'Where are you going?' asked Nym with an arched eyebrow.

'Just off for a piss,' replied Finn. His words were slurred more than she would have liked.

Jor fixed him a scowl. 'Come straight back and stay out of mischief, lad.'

'Aye, I will.' Finn feigned indignance, then grinned and pulled his arm free of his sister's grasp. She watched him disappear into the crowd, weaving through the drunken revelry. Jor's eyes followed him too, and Nym caught the look of doubt on the old man's face. Would he ever stop suspecting her brother of nefarious intent?

Seth played bawdy shanties and jigs, laughed and joked with folk as they shouted and heckled in appreciation. He played a slow ballad for the bar girl who stood watching with an empty tray clutched against her chest, dreamy eyed and a smile on her lips. A pang of vague jealously cut through Nym, though it might have been the heady liquor warping her emotions. Her gaze lingered on Seth more than usual, noting how his mop of black hair hung across his handsome features as he sang. He was good looking, no doubt, but his soft eyes, quick smile and witty words stirred something in her that she could not name.

'You know, lass,' said Jor. 'Long time ago, me and your father... Well, we were tight, me and your pa? Fought in the war. I knew your ma, too. Good people. I was sad as hell to hear about them passing, not right, too soon.' The old tavern keeper rarely talked of those times, and Nym wondered if his pride in his son had combined with the rum to turn his thoughts to family, loosening his tongue as he watched his son play.

'My pa went to war?' said Nym, eager to tease more from the old man.

'Aye, lass. We were at Aeginhall. That's where I lost this,' he said, brandishing his stump of an arm. 'That was a hard fight. If it weren't for your pa, I doubt I'd have marched back from that cursed place.'

'He saved you?'

'Pulled me from the shield wall before I went down. I owe your pa my life. It's why I'll always keep an eye out for you. You're nearly family as far as I see it. There'll always be a place under my roof for the both of you? Even your little shit of a brother.'

Nym nodded, her cheeks flushing at Jor's sudden display of affection. 'I don't know what we would've done without you. Finn is grateful too, even if he don't—.'

A sudden roar cut across their conversation and silenced the crowded taproom. Patrons whirled around to investigate the noise, and Seth's music petered out.

'What the *fuck* are you doing, boy?' bellowed a man.

Nym found the source and her heart began to pound. The one-eyed drunkard with the loud voice stood over her brother, pinning him to the bar by his throat.

It was her worst nightmare made real. *No, no, no…*

'I'll have your fingers, you little cunt,' he roared, brandishing a knife.

'No!' Nym screamed, flinging herself out of the booth but staggering to a halt as the man turned a drunken scowl on her.

Finn squealed and squirmed. 'I didn't do—' The drunkard punched Finn into silence whilst still holding the knife.

Seth's voice sliced through the silence from behind Nym. 'Easy there, big man. He's just a boy. We don't want bloodshed tonight.'

'He's a fucking *thief*!' The drunkard's face flushed red with rage, his chest heaving and his teeth bared. Nym heard Seth put his lute down and step from the stage, moving through the crowd and into her line of sight.

'I know this boy. He's not a bad lad.' Seth held out his hands like one might to a frightened horse. 'Finn, what did you take?'

'I didn't take nothing… please,' squeaked Finn.

'You little liar. I caught your hand in my pocket!' The drunk punched him again. 'Think you can pick me clean when I'm drunk, boy? Not a fucking chance. Don't you know who I *am*?'

The man staggered slightly and watched Seth approach from the corner of his eye, blinking through the haze of a heavy night of ale.

'Come now. Friend. He's with me. Let me buy you a drink and we can forget about this.' No more than a few paces from the man, Seth stopped and deployed one of those disarming smiles.

The drunk suddenly punched Finn in the belly and tossed him across a table like a ragdoll. A wordless cry escaped Nym as her brother crashed into a stool, splintering it to pieces. She took two steps, intending to help Finn, but the boy was up and out the door before she got close enough to touch him.

The stumbling drunk ignored Finn and seized Seth by his collar.

'With you, is he? What is this? Working together, trying to pull a number on us, you fucker?' snarled the man. He shoved Seth up against one of the support pillars and laid his knife at the singer's throat.

'No—' Seth managed, struggling to breathe.

The drunk slammed his forehead into Seth's face.

'No, Seth!' Nym screamed again as Jor sprang to his feet. Seth's teeth were bright red, and blood streamed from his nose. The drunk leered at Nym with a vicious grin.

'She yours, is she?' he smirked at Seth, his words slurring. He leaned in close to Seth's face. 'A pretty one. I bet she rides well, eh?'

'Don't you fucking *dare*,' Seth ground out, hands curling into fists as Nym watched. With one hand, she felt around on the table at her back, gripping a tankard as tight as she could. She wished for a knife, but the mug would do.

'I'll make sure you never lay eyes on anything so pretty again,' the drunk snarled, drawing his knife across Seth's face with a grimace of drunken spite.

Seth roared as the blade carved from one side of his face to the other, slicing across his eyes with merciless precision. He reeled away screaming, but Nym couldn't hear it. Time slowed as he spun toward her, hands clutching at his ruined face as the drunk man laughed. Bloody black pulp oozed from between his fingers.

Nym dropped the tankard and shrieked in horror.

CHAPTER NINE

The Council

The silent occupants of the room waited patiently, watching as the last and most elderly councillor shuffled to his chair. Finally, they all sat down.

'I, Councillor Merwyl, elected speaker of this council, hereby bring this session to order.' Merwyl stood at the centre of the crescent council table in robes of fine grey cloth, decorated with a pattern of woven silver. Certainly one of the College's elders, he still maintained a quick mind, his sharp blue eyes surveying the room from under bushy eyebrows.

There was a murmur of procedural agreement from the others, and the quill of the scribe began scratching on parchment as he recorded the meeting's minutes.

The council convened in a large upper chamber of the sprawling buildings that formed the main College compound. It was a wide room, lit on all sides by rows of small windows. Twelve chairs stood at the large crescent table, but today only nine elder councillors sat around it, the other chairs remaining vacant. This was the assembly who decided all important matters, and many trivial, which the College engaged itself with.

'Please note the date. 'Tis the morning of the fifth day, of the eleventh month, of this four hundred and eighty seventh year of Arnar,' droned the councillor as he took his seat. The scribe scratched away, recording his words.

Merwyl, a famed orator, had held the position of elected speaker for some years now, and while he was by no means in charge, it was his role to guide the agenda and maintain learned order in debate.

A gallery of chairs occupied the edges of the council chambers, and it was not uncommon for members of the College to attend an open session. Today, the apprentice occupied one such wooden chair. He had only been to a council meeting a handful of times, but simply being in the room recalled memories of standing between the pincers of the crescent table, awaiting acceptance to study under one of the masters. The scrutiny of those imposing scholars, bearing down upon him, was a hard thing to forget.

He absently fidgeted with his hands and looked around. There were several other members of the College sitting quietly in the gallery, listening to the opening proceedings, and he caught sight of what appeared to be a delegation of men among them. They wore strange, long, wrapped robes, and their skin was a darker bronze. He knew them to be Teliks, and assumed them to be fellow scholars—there were often Teliks in the College—come to study and to exchange knowledge.

There were other young scholars in attendance, also listening attentively. Some faces he recognised but none paid him any heed. He noted Master Luthor sat with them, nodding and smiling when the apprentice met his gaze.

Before he could nod back at the master, a dreadful darkness flickered at the edge of his vision. The apprentice turned slowly to look and flinched as his gaze fell upon a dark robed figure sitting nearby, staring straight at him.

It's here!

He jerked to his feet in alarm and shooting pain lanced up his leg as he forgot himself in his panic. Lurching backward in an awkward stumble, he cried out, drawing the attention of the council chamber suddenly to him.

'Silence in the gallery,' said Speaker Merwyl, frowning at him.

His leg continued to throb as he returned to his seat, self-consciously shrinking down, embarrassed at his sudden outburst. Blessedly, the attention on him waned as the observers lost interest and focused back on the council meeting. The apprentice threw a sheepish glance at Master Luthor, who now watched him curiously with a slight expression of concern.

The apprentice forced himself to look back to where the black robed figure had been, the same dark spectre that had been haunting his thoughts for weeks.

It was nowhere to be seen.

Instead a young scholar sat in the seat, staring at him uncertainly, no doubt wondering what she had done to startle the crippled apprentice.

He was still exhausted from the journey, that's all. It was nothing but fatigue. The apprentice scowled at his foolishness and concentrated on the council proceedings.

'Where were we?' Merwyl glanced down at the roll of parchment in front of him. 'First item is today's developments concerning the sickness, what news?'

'We have lost two more of our number this morning, despite our best precautions. Members of our College are still succumbing to this *sickness*,' said Councillor Harek.

Merwyl nodded seriously. 'Have their bodies been removed from the compound?'

'They were moved to one of our buildings outside the walls before they passed,' she replied. 'Any who are sick are moved at the first sign of symptoms.'

'Yet, the number slowly grows. We must do all we can to keep it out of the College, to keep us all safe,' chimed in Councillor Asha.

'Indeed, these are dire events, happening within our very walls.' Merwyl laid his hands on the table and sighed. 'By all accounts, it is getting worse, friends. We will no doubt hear more this very day.'

'It's spread seems uncontrollable. The local folk are dying in droves,' Councillor Caleb said from the far end of the table, his words greeted with several concerned nods. The apprentice frowned at the man, studying the odd mask he wore. It was shaped very much like a bird's beak, and his voice was slightly muffled from beneath.

'We have had word,' announced Councillor Rodrik, holding up a piece of parchment. 'The king is again demanding answers. My position at court is becoming... strained. And I fear we still have little to give him.'

'Surely we have something for him,' muttered Merwyl as he scanned the parchments before him. The king had tasked the College with not only discovering the source and cause of the sickness, but also uncovering an effective treatment, and he loathed to let another day pass with little to nothing to report. The speaker placed a pair of wire framed spectacles on his nose and peered along the lists. 'First related matter here is…. disposal of the dead. Councillor Uriah?'

One of the councillors stood. Younger than many of the elders upon the council, Councillor Uriah was perhaps only in his thirtieth or fortieth year. His hair still full, his face not lined with age, he wore a cap of deep red and plain robes of undyed mottled grey cloth trimmed with the same red fabric as his cap. It was attire designed for an intentionally humble look, without appearing shabby.

'Thank you, Speaker Merwyl. My learned friends,' Councillor Uriah said, casting his eyes across the council. 'Unfortunately, the practice we suggested does not appear to have had an effect. However, I still believe, and I am sure we can all agree, that it is best if folk continue removing the dead as soon as possible. There is still a chance it is stemming the spread of this sickness.'

'Yet we have no proof and still it spreads,' cut in Rodrik.

Uriah frowned at the interruption. 'Proof or not, the council voted. Removing the dead is the best course of action, but it is causing its own problems. There aren't enough carts, the pits are filling faster than they can be dug, and wood for the pyres is proving costly. We are just not disposing of enough. Folk have taken to dumping bodies in the waterways, which could well be fouling our drinking supply and aiding the spread.'

'Surely the water would cleanse the dead and wash them out to sea?' mused Councillor Sareb. The plump councillor spoke with a thin reedy voice. He wore a black robe trimmed in red, and his hair hung long either side of his bald, sweaty dome.

'Perhaps, but I took a boat to investigate and many lay rotting there. As the common folk say, "You do not shit where you eat," or in this case, dump the diseased dead where we drink. I suggest we recommend the dead are deposited downstream of the city.' Councillor Uriah produced a parchment from a leather envelope on the table. 'I have prepared a list of concerns regarding the matter, including your observations and suggestions. You will each have a copy for your consideration.'

A scholar came forward and passed a copy of the document to each of the councillors and was a moment of silence as they each read the list.

'This is an outrage!' exclaimed Caleb. 'Why are my findings

listed so low on the list? It is clear to me, without doubt, this spreads through the fouled smoke. The pyres are burning day and night, and a pall hangs thick over city. The smoke of the burning dead has befouled the air — it is the smoke spreading this, not the water.'

'I disagree,' said Councillor Uriah. 'This seems to have started, and spread, from Anchorage. There were no pyres there yet it ran rampant through the port then came here, smoke or no smoke. I find your most wise observations intriguing, councillor, but I do not agree with them wholly.'

Councillor Caleb snorted with derision through his beaked mask.

Uriah opened his hands to offer some consolation. 'That is not to say it isn't possible that the smoke could have some effect, but I do not believe it solely responsible.'

'Rubbish, my people have been wearing the masks and *none* have fallen sick. Not one,' declared Caleb. 'My suggestion is that these masks be worn by all here at the College, and by as many of the townsfolk who can prepare them. A mask covering both nose and mouth, stuffed with a mixture of sweet-smelling herbs and other plants with known healing properties would —'

'Is that what those ridiculous beaks are that you have your scholars wearing?' mocked Uriah.

'You dare to mock me, young man? I have sat on this council since you were a mere acolyte!'

Councillor Sareya stood up, an elderly woman with wild frizzy grey hair. 'This is proven! How dare you —'

Other councillors leapt to their feet, some shouting down their colleagues, others offering support. Someone else began loudly shouting about the gods.

The apprentice sank down in his chair, suddenly embarrassed that the Telik delegation were here to witness some of the brightest minds in the College, and indeed the realm, descend into petty bickering. All except the most elderly councillor now stood shouting over one another. Councillor Symon instead remained seated, looking around in utter confusion with a slight expression of fear. The apprentice wondered if he even knew where he was.

The apprentice glanced over to the scribe, his quill scratching furiously and his face panicked as he struggled to keep up with the furious barking of the councillors. After a good minute of effort, he gave up and looked helplessly at Speaker Merwyl.

The elected speaker stood from his chair and began knocking loudly on the polished table with a heavy gavel. 'Councillors, please!'

The clamour slowly subsided into rancorous stares of thinly veiled contempt.

'Let us act with at least *some* propriety,' said Merwyl with a touch of rebuke. 'All of you have made excellent points, and each will be considered. We will vote your suggestions and advise the king accordingly.' He looked around the table and sighed. 'The truth is we just don't know, my friends. If we bury them, might we poison the soil, as Councillor Harek suggests? If we burn them, the fumes foul our air. Or is it in the water? Is this simply the work of the gods? We are no closer to an answer than when this all began, and as Councillor Rodrik reminds us, the king looks to us for answers. Is there anything to be found in the archives about this sickness?'

'Nothing, Councillor Merwyl,' replied the wizened Sareya beside him. 'Our learned Telik colleagues from across the sea have no knowledge of it either.'

One of the Telik scholars rose from his chair in the gallery, a balding man with short hair around the side of his head. His long white robes draped across him in an intricate wrap.

'The visiting scholar, Vinaeus of Telis, addresses the council,' declared Speaker Merwyl with a bow.

'As you know,' Vinaeus began in a thick accent, 'we have sent word to the Great Library in Telis. There is possibly some record on this, perhaps our physicians have some help for the people of Arnar. But the ships take some weeks to make the crossing and return. If there is knowledge of this in our libraries, we will bring you what we have, and do what we can to facilitate some kind of agreement between our peoples.'

'Nothing is free in Telis,' muttered Sareb.

If the Telik scholar heard him, he ignored the sour councillor, gave a slow bow and returned to his seat.

'The folk are calling it a blood plague,' ventured Uriah.

'The king has been reluctant to use *that* particular word,' cautioned Councillor Rodrik. 'But it does indeed appear that we are afflicted by plague.'

'Let us take a quick vote now,' Merwyl suggested, perhaps before anyone could dispute Rodrik's claim. The apprentice shifted in his seat, his muscles aching and his back a twisted mess of knots. 'All in favour of advising the king this is indeed some kind of plague?'

Six hands rose above the councillor's heads and the scribe made a record.

'This malady will be recorded as "plague" in the records of the Great Histories. The king will be advised of our findings.' Merwyl squinted through his spectacles at the parchment before him. 'Ah, Master Luthor has an update on the survivor.'

'The man from the so called "cursed ship"?' enquired Councillor Asha curiously.

'The very same,' replied Merwyl.' Please come forward, Master.'

Luthor rose from his seat, and moved between the chairs to take the floor near the crescent shaped table.

'My learned friends and honoured councillors, thank you for the summons. It is always an honour to address the council,' Luthor said with a bow. 'We have made much progress recently, however I think it best you see for yourselves. Scholar Gideon awaits with our guest...'

'He's here?' exclaimed Councillor Caleb.

'Ah, excellent,' Councillor Uriah said, rubbing his hands together. 'I have been most curious about our guest. Send him in.'

Luthor nodded to a young acolyte near the door, who promptly hurried out and returned with a fat little man who the apprentice assumed to be Gideon. The man waddled nervously into the chamber and looked around as all the eyes in the room turned to watch him. A murmur of excitement rippled through the observers as a much taller man entered in Gideon's wake.

The apprentice had never seen such a man. His skin was as dark as ebony, the whites of his eyes stark in contrast to his face. His muscular physique was apparent, even from beneath his clothes, and the apprentice thought he looked rather peculiar dressed in Arnar style. The man was flanked by two cautious guards—a wise precaution perhaps, but the man did not seem aggressive. In fact, he was unbound and glanced around calmly.

'May I present my colleague, Scholar Gideon,' Luthor introduced the fat man, who nodded to the councillor's table.

Merwyl cleared his throat and glared at the scribe. 'Please note

Scholar Gideon will be addressing the council with Master Luthor.' The scribe tore his gaze from their newest guest and
scratched frantically at the paper.

'Is he safe?' Caleb asked, fearfully eyeing the big dark man.

'Oh, yes,' replied Luthor. 'He's quite friendly.'

'*Friendly?*' Caleb repeated, turning a dubious look on the councillor beside him.

Ignoring Caleb, Luthor turned to the others. 'Gideon and I
have made a major breakthrough in speaking with him.'

'Fascinating,' whispered Uriah, examining their guest closely.

'Indeed, councillor. We have discovered a common dialect,
and have pulled everything on it we could from the archives.
What we had was scant to be honest, but it was enough to converse on a basic level. Observe.'

Luthor approached the man and spoke in a strange tongue.

'*Mar-akya deilem,*' He gave a slight bow. '*Arak selema.*'

'*Jhas p'her deilem,*' replied the foreigner.

'*Luthor Deilem,*' finished Luthor, then turned to face the council
with a smile.

'What does it mean,' asked Merwyl.

'It means his name is Jhas p'her.'.

'We have begun calling him Jasper,' said Gideon, speaking for
the first time. 'He seems quite happy for us to do so.'

'I see,' replied Merwyl. He adjusted the spectacles perched on
his nose to peer closer at Jasper. 'I must say I have never met a
man from Myhar. Hello there, Jasper,' said the elected speaker
with an awkward wave. 'It is a pleasure to meet you.'

Jasper gave Merwyl a long look, neither warm nor cold, and
the apprentice wondered what he must think of them all.

'He can't understand you, you old fool,' sneered Caleb. 'Can
he?'

'No, councillor, I don't think so. We have only just begun to
understand more about him, but in a short time he has picked up
a surprising amount of our language.'

'Some of *our* language, you say?' Uriah asked with obvious interest.

'Councillor, if I may,' interrupted Gideon. 'Jasper here has
been on-board an Arnar merchant vessel for perhaps several
weeks. He has been with us here for several more. I think he has
picked up a lot more than he initially let on. He seems very quick

to be honest. I think he understands more than we know.'

'Impressive,' commented Uriah.

'Does he have any knowledge of this sickness?' Rodrik cut across the curiosity of the others, bringing the council back to the matter at hand.

'We have not quite got that far, but we will do our best to find out,' replied Luthor.

'Do what you can, Luthor. If he knows anything it is paramount we know too.'

'On hearing the dire reports of this council, I certainly agree,' replied Luthor, 'We will do our —'

Jasper suddenly took a few steps towards the council table and the guards bristled. Jasper stopped at that and bowed low before the councillors with his hands clasped together.

'Old ones... Hello... I... *Jhas p'her*,' he said with a single thump to his chest and there was a gasp as he spoke. '*Jhas p'her deilem.*'

His voice was deep and rich in the stunned silence of the council chamber, only the frantic scratching of the scribe's quill echoing against the walls. Jasper bowed again and turned to follow Gideon, as the little scholar glancing in surprise at Luthor as he shepherded Jasper from the room.

'Fascinating indeed,' murmured Councillor Sareya.

Try as he might, Master Luthor was unable to conceal a grin at his guest's unexpected words as he watched them leave.

'Er, ah... well,' Speaker Merwyl stuttered. 'Excellent. As I was saying, Master Luthor; please continue your work. He is a fascinating fellow — quite impressive.'

'Thank you, councillor.' Luthor gave a small bow. 'At the rate we have progressed, I am confident we will have more soon. If it pleases this council, I will remain to observe the remainder of the session.'

'Of course, Master Luthor. Be seated,' replied Merwyl with a gesture to the gallery.

***

The apprentice yawned. He had forgotten how tedious council meetings could be, old men and women who loved the sound of their own voices, droning on and on, the quill of the council scribe endlessly scratching away.

With the matter of the plague seemingly dealt with for the day, the meeting turned to more mundane topics. Councillor Rodrik demanded an immediate closed council session as soon as they were adjourned, apparently he had received a concerning dispatch from Eymsford. The apprentice was curious about what it could possibly be, he had just travelled from the north and all had seemed well in those lands, but Rodrik would not speak of it in public, it was obviously only for the Council's ears.

Several other speakers came and went, giving reports, petitioning for funds. There was even a disciplinary action, and the apprentice sat up for that one. He watched as the accused stood wringing his hands while the council weighed his case — a matter of using College coin to buy a few months of expensive wine. It dragged on, not nearly as interesting as it first appeared.

Another flicker of darkness pervaded the edge of his vision and an oppressive gloom settled over his thoughts. He felt his stomach slowly tighten as the feeling of being watched crept over him once more. He looked around, searching the other chairs in the gallery, half expecting to see the hooded figure which haunted his imagination.

It is just my imagination. By the gods I need sleep. He suspected he could easily sleep out the week, and then perhaps his mind would return to some kind of normality. He slumped back in his chair as his weary mind drifted off.

'Apprentice!' shouted a loud voice.

His attention snapped back into focus. The room was once again staring at him. Had he fallen asleep?

'You would do well to pay attention when called. You are Master Eldrick's apprentice?' asked Speaker Merwyl.

He was affronted with smirks of amusement and disapproving shakes of the head from the other occupants of the gallery and his stomach knotted ever tighter. His face must have been a mask of panic.

'Yes... yes, I apologise, councillor,' managed the apprentice. 'I speak for my Master Eldrick. I have —'

'Yes, yes,' dismissed Merwyl. 'Please, it is customary to take the floor before the table.' Merwyl impatiently indicated the yawning open floor at the centre of the chamber.

The apprentice swallowed a lump from his throat. His mouth suddenly drier than a dusty tomb. He fumbled his staff and it clat-

tered on the floor. Planting it securely, he heaved himself painfully upright. There was a murmur around the room as the apprentice struggled to his feet and he grimaced as each step lanced his
leg with pain. It seemed to take forever for him to hobble out onto
the chamber floor.

'Varg's balls, lad. What have you done to yourself,' asked
Councillor Uriah with a touch of concern to his stern voice.

'That's a bad break. It will need re-breaking to have a chance of
setting it right,' Sareya commented dubiously.

'Aye,' said the apprentice. 'Master Eldrick set it in a splint, but
I had another... accident.' He paused and looked about before
continuing, 'The road was not kind to it.'

'I see,' replied Sareya with a look of concern

Speaker Merwyl cleared his throat loudly. 'You have my sympathies, but to the matter at hand. You are here on behalf of Master Eldrick?'

The apprentice nodded.

'Please note Master Eldrick's apprentice...' he paused and
turned to the apprentice. 'My apologies, lad. What is your name?

'Er... Duncan, sir.'

Merwyl smiled at him awkwardly and turned back to the waiting scribe. 'Please note Apprentice Duncan, speaking on behalf of
Master Eldrick.'

The scribe's quill scratched loudly in the silent room and Merwyl motioned for him to speak. Duncan licked at dry lips, suddenly lost for words, the nine members of the council all watching
expectantly. This was the part he had been dreading.

'Our expedition was, by all accounts, a great success,' he began. 'We did extensive work.' What else could he say? *It was cold,
wet, dark, in a horrible place, where most of his master's work made his
stomach heave.* No, he could hardly say that.

'I do wonder, Apprentice, why is Eldrick not here with you,'
asked Councillor Asha.

'He had a few small matters of curiosity to settle before his return. The work is all but finished, Master Eldrick and Master Logan sent me ahead with the bulk of their findings. With my injury,
I was of little use to him.'

'I see.'

'I thought they might arrive before me, but I expect they are
only a matter of days behind me. I am to begin recording and

cataloguing our work and present you this.' Duncan held out a roll of parchment in sealed oil cloth.

'I see,' replied Merwyl. 'Let's have it.' He unwrapped the oilskin and removed its contents. He examined Eldrick's letter, peering along his nose through his spectacles. 'You have copies for the council?'

The apprentice hesitated. 'Er, no, sir.'

'Your master did not instruct you to bring copies for the council's consideration?' Merwyl frowned. 'Considering Eldrick has sat upon this council a number of times, I am surprised he did not give you proper instructions of council conduct.'

Duncan flustered for a response.

'Perhaps he expected you to already be aware of the procedure,' sneered Councillor Sareb. 'How many years have you studied under Eldrick now, boy?'

'Three years, four this winter,' replied the apprentice.

'And in that time, you have not learned proper council conduct?' he tutted.

Duncan had hoped to simply come in, speak and leave, but this meeting was turning out as bad as he had feared — nine councillors picking him apart while he stood defenceless. He had no answer.

To his relief Councillor Sareya came to his aid. 'Almost four years? I expect you will be made a full Master Scholar soon.'

'I hope so, councillor,' Duncan squeaked out, this throat tight with nerves. 'I have learned much with all my masters.' He turned to Merwyl. 'I do apologise; there will be copies for your consideration in the future.'

Merwyl grunted and passed the documents along the table. 'An interesting list indeed though.'

'Yes, Master Logan made extensive notes on the area, charts, wildlife. We undertook a study of the ruins — First Sons we believe. It was incredible... a gloomy place, though.'

'And Eldrick's business?' asked Merwyl. 'Was your Master successful in finding the specimens he required?'

'Yes, he was,' said the apprentice. The memory of those grisly dead bodies, those *specimens*, made him grimace.

'That is good, although there has been no shortage of specimens here of late, what with this plague,' rumbled Uriah.

'You were up near the Cydor border? Quite a way to go. We

hear the war is bad over there?' enquired Councillor Harek.

'I did not cross the border, but those of our team who did found many specimens for study, so we deduced the fighting had been intense. Master Eldrick's work on *The Body of Man* has been extensive, if not gruesome. His skill in medicine and healing lore is most impressive, I am honoured to study with him.'

'You should be,' said Caleb. 'Your master's skills are well known, and in these dark times he is sorely needed back here at the College where he belongs. I'm sure many of us are eager for your master's thoughts on the current sickness. You will no doubt be engaged in working on it when he returns.'

'What is this? *The Bone Ritual?*' scoffed Sareb, the parchment in his hand.

Duncan cleared his throat. He'd known this would come up, and that he would have to speak to it, but the raw memories shook his voice. 'It was incredible, really. Master Eldrick does not wish for me to divulge too much until his return. You see, it is on-going research and —'

'*The Bone Ritual* is a mummery of priests and witchdoctors, there is no truth to it,' snapped Sareb.

'Not every truth is contained in books, or of this world,' countered Councillor Asha. She wore feathers in her hair and rows of beads. Duncan thought her to be a high priestess or one of the shaman leaders. From mystics and forest witches, to great historians, physicians and scholars; the council were all learned in their fields of expertise and renowned for their wisdom. 'There is more wisdom in the gods than from your records, friend.' She turned to the apprentice with a kind smile. 'I for one will be most interested in your master's curiosities and findings.'

'As I sure many will,' said Merwyl diplomatically. 'May I remind my learned colleagues that all knowledge is respected here, especially on this council.'

Sareb scowled and grunted, and the gathered councillors descended into bickering, vying for the cleverest comment, all oblivious to the apprentice's discomfort. He stood on his good leg and leant his weight heavily on his staff, clutching it with both hands. It felt like he had been standing there for an eternity; his body tired, his hands aching, and his leg throbbing. He would have given anything to sit down, unnoticed by the staring eyes of his peers.

He kept his crippled leg lifted off the floor, dangling uselessly. It was crooked, unnaturally twisted — grotesque. He knew it, and he knew everyone watching him thought it too. The observers stared at his disfigured leg, whispering, unable to meet his eye. All the while Merwyl fought to bring the council back to order.

A councillor finally spoke above the others with a question and Duncan turned to answer. Sitting in the councillor's place was the dark robed figure.

Duncan flinched back, nearly losing his balance with the staff.

Does no one else see it?

He stared at it, completely transfixed. As usual he could not make out any features below the hood. A pool of darkness looked out at him, still and unmoving. It just stared.

'Are you listening, boy?' said Caleb scornfully. 'Speak when you're spoken to.'

He shook his head clear. A quick glance revealed the figure was gone, and in its place Councillor Harek sat staring at him.

'Ah… yes, of course,' replied the apprentice shakily.

'Are you alright, lad?' asked Merwyl. 'You look terribly pale.'

'He looks a mess,' commented Sareya.

'I… I am not myself. My leg… I am so tired from the long journey.' He paused. 'I apologise, councillors. I thought it my duty to report to the council immediately, as was my instruction.'

'Well, thank you. Your master should be proud, but your duty is now to yourself, apprentice,' Councillor Asha's voice held a note of compassion, or was it pity? 'Get yourself to a physician. Let us hope there is something that can be done…' She trailed off and managed a doubtful smile.

Definitely pity.

'It is a shame Master Eldrick is not here. He is one of our best healers,' said Uriah.

'We can continue this at another time,' said Merwyl. 'You have completed your task. I look forward to hearing more on your master's findings. You are excused for now. We can resume this when you are well.'

'And lucid,' muttered Sareb.

Relief washed through Duncan. It was nearly over. He heaved himself around and lurched towards the chamber doors, limping on his good leg, his staff clicking loudly on the stone floor. He made agonisingly slow progress, the pressure of the council's gaze heavy on his back; the entire chamber silent as they watched him hobble to the door. He caught Master Luthor's eye, watching with that same concerned look on his face.

The door swung shut slowly behind him and Duncan sighed deeply. Leaning heavily on his staff, the apprentice limped and skittered his way slowly along the corridor, eager to leave behind the scrutiny of the Council's scornful regard and the darkness that ever watched him, that hooded apparition haunting his every step.

CHAPTER TEN

The Throne Hall

It was not as cold in the Throne Hall as it had been recently. The court had become busier since the crisis began, the sickness ravaging the capital and its surrounding areas, and today the Throne Hall was packed with nervous courtiers and noblemen, all hoping for the latest word on the calamity. Despite the wide wooden arches spanning overhead, there were still too many bodies crowding the old hall, too much hot air being spouted. The Throne Hall was stifling.

Wilhelm loosened the scarf he kept over his face, his brow beading with sweat beneath his helmet. It kept sliding about if he didn't keep his head up. He didn't want to tighten the damn thing, desperate for even a little bit of air flow. His mail hung heavy, and he was certain his under-mail padding was soaked in big patches on his chest and back. It was already stained and stinking, and probably high time he got a new one.

But despite his discomfort, Wilhelm stood dutifully still. Today he accompanied his lord, Huscarl Warrick, who sat not far off at a table beside the throne. The king's chair had been moved off its dais to the head of a large table on the Throne Hall's main floor where he and his lords ate and drank. He saw Princess Alethea moving between groups of noblewomen, all dressed in their fine expensive gowns, a far cry from the rags and filth of those folk they saw in the plague-ridden streets. The princess looked ashen and tired, perhaps the stifling heat of the packed Throne Hall taking its toll.

Wilhelm's legs began to ache, but he was used to standing for long periods. It was part of the job. A patrol was always better, stretching his legs and wandering about, keeping an eye on folk, but not in these times. With this sickness about, he was much more at ease behind the palisades and ramparts of the Citadel.

He threw a glance at the man beside him. He stood leaning on his spear, looking out across the hall, the sigil of one of the king's sons, Harald, stitched to his tabard. The man caught his eye and shrugged.

The court was a bustle of concerned noblemen lately, but rather than lifting his boredom, the talk at the court was troubling. Wilhelm had begun to share the same uncertain apprehension as the worried nobles. The more he heard on this sickness, the direr it all felt. There was little known of its source, nor of how to treat it. Folk were scared and dying in droves. There was some degree of safety inside the king's hold since the common folk and any sick had been barred. Wilhelm was glad he wasn't walking the streets today.

Across the court floor, a robed councillor addressed the court and his king.

'We have urgent news, sire.' Wilhelm knew him as Councillor Rodrik of the College, a wiry little man in deep green robes. 'We received a letter by ship from Eymsford. After discussing it in closed council we decided to inform you immediately.'

The king waved him on.

'The reports from the north are dire indeed, sire. College folk have been attacked throughout the Old Lands, some murdered.'

King Rhagnal listened from his high-backed throne, dressed in a plain but finely made tunic and pair of breeches, his shoulder length brown hair was crowned with a wide circlet of ornate silver. He fiddled with a scabbarded sword on the table before him as Rodrik spoke.

Rodrik swallowed so hard Wilhelm saw the man's throat contract. He was a bundle of nerves, this one. 'There is some concern that such attacks could occur here.'

'Why would you think that?' asked the king as he pulled part of the blade free and eased it back into its scabbard.

'The College is being blamed for events transpiring north of the Spine.'

'What events? This *plague*?' The king's eyes never left Rodrik's face.

'While the events seem related, we are unsure if it is any more than coincidence.' Rodrik chewed the back of his lip and glanced around, as if someone nearby might be able to take the burden of this report from him. 'In truth we don't know, sire, the letter spoke of the attacks but gave little reason why. It could be plague in the Old Lands, but perhaps something else...'

Wilhelm watched the king's face contort with disbelief. Plague was a word none wanted to hear, but the rest of the report was preposterous.

Rodrik hurried to fill the king's stunned silence. 'I must stress that we cannot confirm any of these reports, or if the sickness has spread that far north. All we can assume is that folk are exaggerating from their fear.'

The king's brow furrowed further. 'And these attacks?'

'The attacks are an outrage, sire,' said Rodrik angrily. 'We are doing all we can to stop its spread — nearly every scholar in the College is currently dedicated to finding a solution, a cure. We are not to blame for any of this. Please, as representative of the Council, I humbly ask you to do something to protect our people.'

'What exactly do your reports say, councillor?' asked the chancellor, seated beside King Rhagnal. Chancellor Alfric was a well-built man in his fifties, he had perhaps ten years on the king, his strong face showing lines of age, but his cropped blond hair showed no sign of greying.

Rodrik shrugged. 'Not much other than mention of the attacks, and the names of prominent College members who have been victimised. Our folk up there fear for their safety, the local folk are blaming them and...'

'And?' pressed the chancellor.

'And a rather cryptic mention at the end of the dispatch. "*The dead are upon us*".'

'The dead are upon us?' repeated Alfric with an arched eyebrow.

'Indeed,' replied Councillor Rodrik. 'We assume it is mention of this plague. Death is upon them? Death spreads, perhaps? We believe it to be the first report of this terrible plague north of the Spine, but we have no other reports of the sickness elsewhere in the Old Lands.'

'If this sickness has already spread north, by the gods, it could spread across the whole realm,' gasped Huscarl Warrick.

Wilhelm watched his lord's brow furrow, a deep look of concern on his face.

King Rhagnal ignored Warrick's words. 'Are there any reports from out west, chancellor?'

'Nothing of sickness, sire.' Alfric shook his head. 'Archeon keeps up regular dispatches. He is dealing with a sizable group of brigands on the coast and has raised his banners to deal with them. It seems to be in hand. He mentioned a series of disappearances which he is investigating, some issues with piracy, a few other more mundane reports but that is all. He has also extended an offer of supplies.'

'The man has vast resources,' commented Warrick.

'I know only too well his *vast resources*,' snapped the king. 'Do you forget we fought against each other in the war of succession? The man came close to my throne. Vast resources...' the king muttered. 'We will have need of his *resources*, I have no doubt.'

The chancellor cleared his throat. 'He has shown the crown nothing but loyalty since his defeat. The lords of Arnar will always be known for their honour.'

A mumbling of agreement ran over the court.

Chancellor Alfric threw a look at Rodrik. 'There is no reason to believe for certain that the pestilence has spread west or north, until we have confirmed reports.'

The king nodded slowly.

'Is there word from High Lord Angus in the north?'

'Aye, there is word his envoys are on their way, sire,' replied Alfric. 'Harald, you had the report?'

A finely dressed young warrior stepped forward. Harald bore a striking resemblance to his father, the king. 'Aye, we intercepted High Lord Angus' envoys this morning. They are bound for the capital by sea. They will be making port soon.'

'Good, then we can have the truth of it. We cannot rely on cryptic messages from an unproven source.' Alfric fixed the councillor with another long look.

Wilhelm shifted his weight as he listened, hoping court would be called to an end soon so he can go a sit down with an ale. This College man certainly seemed rattled by these attacks. He wondered what was going on up there in the north, the last thing they needed was civil unrest amid this plague. He muttered a prayer to Hjort that this would all soon pass.

'There is some pressing news I can confirm though, sire,' said the chancellor

'Oh?' replied the king looking up from his sword.

'The rumours of the war in Cydor are true, my king. We have received word that King Leofric was defeated at Three Bridges.'

Wilhelm looked up with interest.

'The city fell and he has withdrawn the remainder of his forces to the capital. Lord Jarlson is already laying siege to what is left of the royal forces there, reports say Leofric is vastly outnumbered. The capital is expected to fall at any time—it may already have done so.'

'So, there is to be a new king in Cydor,' mused Prince Harald.

The king nodded. 'The line of the old kings will be broken. A new era for Cydor.'

'Many will not accept Jarlson as king,' added Huscarl Warrick.

'There are reports of fierce fighting,' said Alfric. 'It appears the long war is far from over.'

'When has there *not* been fierce fighting?' said Rhagnal. 'That war has raged all my life. I cannot begin to imagine peace in that place. Can you?'

The chancellor shook his head. 'I fear the Cydor we once knew will never be whole again.'

'All for the better,' muttered the king.

Wilhelm noticed Alethea drift near to her father's table. 'Surely peace is always better,' she commented as she overheard his words.

'Don't be a fool, girl,' snapped Rhagnal. 'Jarlson has long and openly spoken of the re-conquest of Cydor's territories. If Cydor somehow found peace, and Jarlson sits on the throne, open war with us will not be far behind.'

She shrugged and moved off to resume her quiet conversation with the other courtiers.

Wilhelm now longed for that tankard, something to take his mind from all this troubling talk of war and plague. It seemed there was no good news to be had anywhere in Arnar of late.

There was a pause as the king resumed tinkering with his scabbard and Councillor Rodrik shuffled his feet in the silence. 'If there is indeed plague in the north, we might be left weakened against our old enemy. Should we not—'

'We have stood apart for hundreds of years,' said Rhagnal, interrupting the councillor and dismissing his comments with a sharp gesture. 'The Borders cannot be taken. They were Arn's lands in the old times, we are his people. Jarvi?' The king looked about for one of his warriors. 'You're from the north, what say you?

The man stepped forward, one of the huscarls. 'Sire, as it was written; *These are old lands...*'

'Aye, yes,' said Rhagnal with a smirk, 'I knew you would start with that "*Lands which stood firm against the kings of Cydor, ravaged and yet held... We the proud, a people of warriors,*' recited the king. '*Ever ready to hold these lands forever more.*' Rhagnal laughed, 'I bet you border folk recite that Saga before every damn meal.'

'Don't you doubt it, sire,' grinned the Huscarl with a fist on his chest. 'I've heard of men back home even saying it before and after they fuck.' He laughed.

There was a ripple of laughter across the court.

'Don't fear, councillor,' said the king. 'Our northern border lands will always be Arnar. The folk of the Old Lands will hold the watch, plague or no plague. They will stand and if needs be, and the realm stands with them.'

Rodrik nodded bleakly, but Wilhelm saw his uncertainty in the way he wrung his hands together. 'But these inbound envoys from Eymsford, sire, and this talk of "the dead are upon us". What if we are already under attack?'

The king's eyebrows knitted, suddenly troubled.

'There is no proof!' snapped Chancellor Alfric. 'You look for trouble where there is no certainty! You speak of Cydor invading our lands, of plague in the north—where is your proof? You are a fear monger.' The chancellor levelled a finger a Rodrik. 'Keep your mouth shut until you can speak with certainty. We have enough here to trouble us without you adding to our worries.'

'All I say is that we should be prepared for either eventuality; that is all, sire,' pleaded Rodrik.

Huscarl Warrick nodded agreement. 'The chancellor is right. Until we hear otherwise, it is folly to speculate.'

There was a sudden commotion amongst the court as the great doors of the Throne Hall were suddenly swung open. Wilhelm craned his neck to catch sight of the source of the intrusion and spotted a herald hurrying to the stairs leading down from the gallery onto the court's floor.

'My king and lords of the court!' shouted the herald. 'May I present Lord Fergus of Weirdell, son of High Lord Angus. And with him, Lord Arnulf of the Motte, also of the Old Lands. They speak for High Lord Angus, Lord Protector of the Old Lands.'

***

Arnulf watched the heavy doors swing open and his stomach knotted as the herald announced their arrival. Surprise rippled through the court as everyone inside turned to him and his companions.

Beyond the heavy doors stood the king's yawning Throne Hall, as old as Arnar itself, built over the ancient stone ruins of a long-forgotten people. Stairs led down on to a crowded lower level and Arnulf's eyes were drawn to the far end of the old hall. There was an empty dais where he expected to see a regal looking figure on a large throne. Instead it stood empty.

He moved into the Throne Hall, following the directions of the herald and Lord Fergus. At the foot of the stairs there was a lowered banqueting hall, rows of tables stretched out along its length. A single, long table occupied the centre before the dais, a large central avenue remaining open before the king's table. Braziers and torches burned about the room, providing light and warmth. Not that it needed heating. The place was stifling, and a wave of heat hit Arnulf's face as he entered.

Many well-dressed folk who Arnulf took for noblemen crowded around the long-table, attended by a host of advisers and servants milling amongst them. The edges of the Hall were raised into a gallery lined with courtiers, and at the far edges of the room guards stood watch in polished armour and mail. Above his head hung hundreds of banners, a myriad of colour representing all the lords of Arnar sworn to the throne. Arnulf scanned amongst them to find his own—a black axe on red—but he could not spot it, instead turning his attention back to the Throne Hall.

The folk at the table looked grand in their fine clothes and armour. The lords of the capital wielded an impressive display of wealth, and their wealth displayed their power. There were warriors amongst them, the king's huscarls, many of them lords themselves, known to be some of the greatest fighters in Arnar. The title of huscarl, to be one of the king's own sworn guard, was an enormous honour.

Arnulf had only ever seen the Throne Hall once before, many years ago as they gathered the banners to march on Aeginhall in the west. He had never met the king, never spoken a word to him, and today he was wracked with nerves. This place had more grandeur and majesty than the high lord's hall in Eymsford. In his mail and furs, he felt like a rough stone in comparison to the polished jewels of the lords of the capital.

It was then he spotted the king, sitting upon his throne at the head of the long table. He did not look as Arnulf expected. He'd thought to find someone older, someone grander. Someone with a big beard and a full mane of hair set with a gleaming crown. He'd expected a man with lavish, expensive clothes and glinting rings on his fingers, but instead what he saw was a man like any other. The king could have been warrior-lord of Arnar, and Arnulf liked the look of him. He hoped the king was not too far removed from the folk he ruled over, a man of honour and not too haughty, though he suspected he would soon find out.

'It is an honour to receive our brothers in the north,' called King Rhagnal, rising from his throne as Arnulf descended the stairs onto the floor of the court.

Fergus led the way towards the king's table, and folk moved aside to let them approach.

'Greetings, my king,' said Fergus, bowing deeply.

'Lord Fergus, it has been some years.' Rhagnal nodded a greeting as Fergus straightened. 'I hope you and your father are well.'

'We are, sire.' Fergus gave the king a grateful smile.

'And look who else has arrived!' Rhagnal grinned, spotting Astrid among Fergus's retinue. 'Do my eyes deceive me, or has the Death Nymph returned to my hall? And still a beauty for my sore eyes.'

Arnulf glanced at Astrid, noting her stiff nod in reply to the king, and he wondered if perhaps his attempt at a compliment had fallen flat.

Rhagnal did not appear to notice or care, and turned to address the group as a whole. 'Welcome, all of you! This is my son Harald, Prince of Arnar,' said King Rhagnal, indicating a young man in fine armour. 'My lady wife, Frana, and my daughter, Alethea.' The two women offered Fergus and Arnulf courteous smiles. The younger, a rare beauty indeed, her long golden hair woven intricately, Arnulf couldn't help noticing her smile seemed more strained, her complexion a little pallid and drawn. He wondered what ailed her. 'My advisors, Lord Chancellor Alfric, Lord Huscarls, Warrick, Aellar, Offa,' continued the king indicating each nobleman sat around his table in turn. Each nodded in greeting as introduced.

'My king, this is my good friend, Lord Arnulf,' said Fergus.

Arnulf shifted on his feet and gave an awkward bow. 'My king.'

'A pleasure, Arnulf, even despite the circumstances.' King Rhagnal opened his hand towards the table. 'Please have some wine or ale.'

'Thank you, sire,' said Fergus, moving forwards as servants arrived to pour drinks and distribute them to the arrivals. Arnulf gladly accepted a tankard and a gentle murmur of conversation resumed in the hall, rippling through the gathered courtiers. 'My father sends his greetings, but we bring dark news from the north.'

'Let's hear it,' said Rhagnal, sitting back in his throne. The conversation died down then, leaving Arnulf supping loudly at his ale.

'Arnulf is a Lord of the Watch,' said Fergus motioning Arnulf to speak.

Swallowing his mouthful, Arnulf found himself the centre of attention. 'It has been my duty to command one of the watch posts on the border. The watch were attacked, sire.'

'It has begun,' called someone in alarm. 'Cydor is attacking!'

'No,' said Arnulf evenly, holding up a hand for calm. 'It was not the old enemy.'

'Then who?' asked the older man, who Rhagnal had introduced as Chancellor Alfric.

'We were attacked from within our own lands.'

A collective gasp echoed around the hall.

'Brigands!' exclaimed the huscarl named Warrick. 'How dare they be so bold. I expect you dealt with them.'

'No,' said Arnulf. There was a confused silence, slowly filling with whispers as folk muttered amongst themselves.

The king sat forward. 'A Lord of the Watch would not be here accompanied by the son of the high lord if the threat were merely brigands, Warrick. We have had nothing but vague reports and cryptic messages sent to the College. What is happening in my northlands?'

Arnulf took a steadying breath before speaking.

Here it comes. They will think us madmen.

'An evil unlike any other has been unleashed in my homeland, sire. I would not believe it if I had not seen it with my own eyes...'

Arnulf looked at his companions and steeled himself.

'We were attacked by the dead.'

CHAPTER ELEVEN

Hubris in Vengeance

Someone stifled a laugh, realising too late it was not meant as a joke.

When the king did not speak, Arnulf thought he had better fill the silence with something. 'The dead walk. They have risen from Old Night's halls, and they attacked my watch up in the mountains.'

'You mean to tell us the *dead* have risen from their graves and are walking around?' asked Huscarl Jarvi.

They think me a fool, a madman.

Arnulf nodded. 'Yes, I saw it with my own eyes. We all did.'

Jarvi snorted a laugh, then the entire hall erupted in sporadic laughter. Arnulf's cheeks flushed. He never thought to stand before the king telling such a fairy tale. The king, however, remained still and completive, studying Arnulf carefully. He raised his hand for silence. 'You are serious?'

He stood in a crowded hall, surrounded by his companions, yet under the gaze of the king and his powerful nobles, as he claimed the impossible like a raving fool, he could not feel more alone and exposed.

Arnulf nodded. 'I would not be here if I were not so.'

There was a heavy pause as the King Rhagnal regarded Arnulf, weighing his words.

'Everyone, leave us,' commanded the king in a loud voice, his eyes not leaving Arnulf. 'You stay and hear this,' he said, motioning for his advisors to remain seated. 'Councillor Rodrik you too.'

Folk murmured and whispered as the hall slowly emptied, noblemen and courtiers stared at Arnulf and his companions, some with looks of mocking amusement, no doubt expecting the king to explode in a rage for mocking his court when the doors finally closed. Others frowned, indignant at the ejection, and a few wore masks of deep concern as they filed out of the hall.

The *boom* of the heavy doors slamming shut echoed through the empty Throne Hall.

The tone of Rhagnal's voice became measured and foreboding. 'You are a Lord of The Borders. You swear this on your family's honour, on the honour of Angus, your sworn lord?'

'The dead walk, sire,' replied Arnulf, squaring his shoulders and lifting his chin, daring the remaining advisors to laugh. Many around the table did not seem convinced, murmuring whispers and snickering at his expense, but he knew what he had seen.

Arnulf's gaze fell on a robed man the king had named as Rodrik, who had now taken a seat at the table amongst the other advisors. He was wearing a quill brooch he recognised — the symbol of the College.

It was College men who had caused this. College men that had cost him his family. College men meddling in things that should have been left alone.

The laughter seemed a distant sound as his focus narrowed on the College man. He glared at the man but held his impulse to unleash his rage in front of the king.

'I saw it too, my king.' Hafgan spoke up from the gathered retinue, stepping forward for the first time, bolstering his lord over the court's derision. 'The dead walk, and they kill, then more rise to fill their ranks.'

'Silence!' commanded the king, quelling the sneers of courtiers. 'I will hear their tale.'

'Surely you don't believe this, sire' scoffed Chancellor Alfric.

Hafgan rounded on the Chancellor. 'Have you ever put an axe through someone, or taken a limb, then watched them get back up as if nothing had happened?' snarled Hafgan turning to confront the others seated at the table. 'They feel no pain, no remorse. They just kill; unrelenting, unwavering.'

'Who are you, friend?' asked the king.

'I am Hafgan, sworn to my Lord Arnulf. I saw it all and stood beside him as we fought the dead.'

'You saw this, Fergus?' asked the king incredulously.

Fergus hesitated, glancing around at the scornful, disbelieving faces, the amused looks of the famous huscarls. Did he fear to risk his honour on this insane tale?

Finally, he nodded.

'Aye, I saw it, sire.' The red-haired lord gave a weak smile to his old friend Arnulf.

All the while, Arnulf fought to control the fury rising inside him as he glowered at the man in College garb. He feared he would say something he would later regret, so he held his tongue and nodded for Hafgan to continue in his stead.

'Our town was attacked, my lord's hall burned to the ground,' seethed Hafgan, his voice strained, each word arduous, as if it pained him to admit what had happened, as if it was somehow his failing. His gaze rested on Arnulf, and was filled with regret and veiled pity. 'Lord Arnulf lost his family, and we lost many of our kin. Many became... cursed.'

'Cursed?'

'Our folk back in the north call them the Cursed Ones,' explained Fergus.

'Show him,' Arnulf growled through clenched teeth, and Hafgan signalled to Erran. The lad hurried back up the stairs and through the heavy wooden doors.

Both doors soon swung wide open. The room fell silent as a towering box shaped object was slowly carried into the hall by Arnulf's warriors. They bore it into the hushed Throne Hall, carrying it forwards with wooden poles resting on their shoulders, a tarp concealing its contents. The warriors carefully placed it on the floor then backed away, the crowd jostling quietly to get a better look.

'What is this?' asked the king, the apprehension plain in his voice.

Arnulf swallowed back a ball of grief that had formed in his throat and found his mouth dry. 'One of the cursed, sire,' rasped Arnulf, unable to bring himself to look at the covered cage.

Huscarl Warrick sharply rose from his chair, 'My king, what if it is plague? They have brought the sickness here! We cannot risk—'

A bestial roar shook the Throne Hall. Warrick sank into his chair in shock, the tarp shaking violently. The sound of chains thrashing wildly crashed and clunked as if some wild thing fought against them. Guards and noblemen alike shrank back from the tarp covered litter, and the king leapt to his feet in alarm.

Arnulf gave a nod and one of his men cautiously crept forward, snatching the tarp away and hastily retreating to a safer distance.

The iron bars of a cage were revealed, and within squatted a thin, wretched creature which, suddenly exposed, froze and glared at the staring audience. It crouched, wrapped in chains which were fastened to the cage's wooden floor and roof, and wore clothes that were torn and filthy rags, stained with its own excrement and blood. The creature glowered at its surroundings, its eyes finally meeting Arnulf's and fixing upon them.

There was a tense pause before it erupted into a screaming, violent rage, thrashing against its bonds in frustrated fury. The chains encircled the creature entirely and blood ran from beneath the manacles on its wrists and ankles as it fought to free itself.

Despite the noise, the violence and the stink, King Rhagnal stepped forwards and slowly approached the cage. 'By the gods, what is it?' he muttered.

'This, sire... is my son,' murmured Arnulf, his voice thick with emotion. 'His name is Ewolf.'

Arnulf fought a wave of despair. What had his poor boy become? Every time he laid eyes upon his son, his hope waned a little more; the hope of returning his son to the man he had once been becoming ever more remote. He was unable to prevent a tear escaping down his cheek.

The king looked at Arnulf with a profound pity. 'I am sorry Lord Arnulf, this is no fate for a man of Arnar.'

'How did this curse befall him?' asked Chancellor Alfric.

Arnulf was unable to speak, his throat tightening. He stared into the cold dead eyes of the creature, searching for any remaining trace of his son.

Hafgan spoke instead. 'The dead, sire. Folk not killed become cursed. The Cursed Ones become these raving beasts, no longer men. They rend and kill, sometimes with only their bare hands, and then feast on the flesh of the fallen.'

'By the gods,' muttered the king, his attention returning to the creature before him.

'They threw themselves at our warriors,' continued Hafgan, 'many not fearing to charge straight onto our spears. Many of our warriors died against their reckless hate, and it appears that when these Cursed Ones die, they too return and the walking dead grow in number.' He paused, sighing deeply. 'I fear this fell darkness is spreading across the Old Lands as we speak, despite our best efforts to destroy them.'

Ewolf let loose an ear-piercing shriek and the king winced. 'I have seen enough. Please take him away.'

Hafgan threw the tarp back over the cage as Ewolf fought against his bonds, and the warriors stepped forwards to bear the wretched creature from the Throne Hall, his screams echoing back to the Hall long after the heavy doors had closed behind him.

'What in Varg's name could have caused this?' exclaimed Prince Harald, still visibly shaken.

'We should summon the priests of Old Night. Perhaps there is some legend or prophesy they know of?' suggested Chancellor Alfric.

There were nods of agreement from the king's advisors, but none from those who had travelled from the north.

'We don't know what this is, but we think we know who does, sire,' Arnulf growled, pinning Councillor Rodrik with a vehement glare.

The councillor became noticeably uncomfortable under Arnulf's unwavering glare.

'The dead are upon us...' muttered the king. He turned to level a steady gaze at the councillor. 'Rodrik, it seems to me this might have something to do with the attacks you spoke of, would you not agree? If you know something... anything about what these men are claiming, you *will* tell me now.'

'I can assure you, lord, we know nothing of this.' Rodrik's eyes widened and his hands came up in a defensive, pleading gesture. 'If there was any record of such a thing in the histories, it would be widely known in the College. I have never heard —'

'Don't give me that, you little worm!' roared Arnulf, losing his temper completely and slamming his fist down loudly on the table, heedless of Rhagnal and the other onlookers. 'We know what you've been doing! Tell me what you know of your man Eldrick.'

'Eldrick?' whimpered Rodrik.

'You heard.' snarled Arnulf. He flexed his fingers, taking a menacing step towards the councillor. All his pain, all his rage, his impotence at being unable to save his son, his frustration with the denials of a man who clearly knew more than he was letting on, all boiled to the surface, and he barely held himself in check.

'Lord Arnulf!' snapped King Rhagnal. 'You forget yourself.'

Arnulf halted, embarrassment flushing his face.

'I don't know you, but I do know Rodrik. He is a member of my court and speaks for the College. I don't know how you do things in the north, but I will not have you threatening this man.'

Arnulf dropped to one knee. 'I apologise, my king. Please forgive me. My anger got the better of me.'

'You will explain yourself.' Rhagnal folded his arms. 'What have you got against this man?'

'I have nothing against him, sire, but his *College,*' sneered Arnulf, unable to keep the venom from his voice, 'are responsible for all these dark happenings. It was the actions of the College that killed my lady wife. My little girl… They did *that* to my son.' He stabbed his finger at the doors to the Hall.

'I hope you have proof to back up these accusations, Lord Arnulf,' said Chancellor Alfric.

Arnulf looked up into the face of the king, registering his anger, and beside him, the chancellor, his brow furrowed with a deep frown. Councillor Rodrik looked indignant, but it was nothing more than a vain attempt to mask his fear. Others scowled at his breach of proper conduct before the king.

This is not going well. It was time to show the king the truth.

He stood, bowing his head to the king as he did, hoping the man knew he meant no disrespect. 'Where is the book?'

Hafgan produced a huge tome and handed it to Arnulf, who hoisted it with a thud onto the table. He opened the thick cover to reveal the first page and turned it towards Rhagnal. Folk crowded in to see, peering at the open grimoire.

Arnulf pressed a finger against the bottom of the page. It clearly showed, the intricate quill emblem marked in red ink, the seal of the College, and a name—Eldrick. Rodrik took an instinctive step back.

'We found this in the High Passes, sire, near to where we were attacked by the dead. There was an encampment up there, and whoever made it left much of their work, all of it clearly marked as with these seals. There is little doubt the College had a hand in this.'

He leafed through the vellum pages to the detailed drawings

of macabre images; sketches of dissections and dismembered limbs annotated by a scrawled script. 'We also found the leavings of these cruel experiments, and something that looked to be a type of hideous ritual. There was an altar and bodies, parts of folk all laid out. It wasn't right.' He shuddered. 'It was all hidden up there in a forgotten, haunted place so no one could see it. Stone circles and old tombs — a place where the old gods still sleep. It was a terrible place to set foot, sire.'

He turned to Hafgan. 'Hand me the blade?'

The big warrior drew a dagger from his cloak. It was a twisted, evil looking thing with a black hilt, and Hafgan held it up for those nearby to examine.

'This is the very blade we found at the site of this foul ritual. The *very blade* used in these unspeakable acts.' Arnulf took the dagger from Hafgan and placed it beside the heavy tome, offering them to the king. 'We found dozens of bodies, all cut open and chopped up... There were pits for the dead... but they weren't dead. They were monsters, dead men but not. Some foul sorcery had been attempted there, like something from legend.' He shook the memories away. 'We brought these as proof of who was responsible, to make sure they answer for what they have unleashed upon us. This darkness has spilt into our lands, and it spreads further with every rotting step.'

Councillor Rodrik stood dumbfounded, his mouth opening and closing silently like a camberfish in a net as he stared down at the sickening drawings.

He can't even deny it, thought Arnulf.

'They're all dead?' Rodrik whispered, his face draining of all colour.

'There were no survivors,' Hafgan told him grimly.

'You knew these folk? demanded the king. 'And what of these rituals? Did you know of them too?'

Rodrik nodded, but stepped forwards. 'Sire, if I may...' He reached for the grimoire and began leafing through the pages, his expression shifting from shock to outright horror. 'As far as I know, Master Eldrick was conducting research for medicine, furthering the knowledge of our physicians, our surgeons. He was a famed healer himself — one of our best. Though his work may seem gruesome, I am certain it was intended for good. Certainly none of these poor souls met a dark end at his hands. They were likely already dead. None would have suffered.'

'Tell that to our kinsfolk!' snarled Hafgan.

'And this?' pressed Arnulf, gesturing to pages of strange inscriptions and symbols. The sight of the weird glyphs sent a ripple of revulsion through those looking on.

'I don't know,' admitted Rodrik, still trembling and pale. 'I must consult with my colleagues on the council immediately. We will have records of Master Eldrick's research. There will be an explanation, I am sure.'

'What?' exclaimed Arnulf with a derisive laugh. 'And give you time to go off and cover yourselves with lies? Please, sire; we found it all in the passes. The College were there. *They* did this.'

Rodrik looked up quickly and glanced between Arnulf and the king. 'Eldrick's apprentice returned and presented himself at the council just this morning. He will surely have an explanation.'

'He was there? He was in the passes?' Arnulf hardly thought it could be true. How had the lad survived?

'By all accounts, but I don't know the details. The information he presented was incomplete, but I am sure he will know something. I will find out and bring you answers.'

Arnulf's blood began to boil and he fought to stop himself from throttling the weaselly little bastard in front of him. 'If this apprentice had *anything* to do with this, I will kill the bastard myself!'

'Arnulf,' Fergus cautioned with a nervous glance at the king. He spoke before his old friend had a chance to say something he would regret. 'Sire, we beseech you; heed our words and bring this apprentice before us all for questioning.'

'I can assure you the boy will be innocent.' Rodrik nodded fervently, as if that single gesture would allay their fears. 'There will be an explanation for all this. Eldrick and his folk were likely as much a victim to this evil as your kin.'

Arnulf snapped.

'You dare talk about my family, you *bastard*!' He lunged forward to seize the councillor, but Hafgan caught him, restrained him with seemingly impossible strength.

'No lord, don't,' he whispered calmly in Arnulf's ear.

'Lord Arnulf!' bellowed King Rhagnal. 'I warned you. Guards! Seize that man. I will not have this in my hall. You dishonour yourself, Arnulf.'

Arnulf glowered at the councillor as half a dozen mailed war-riors surrounded him with their hands on the hilts of their swords. He made no move and let them take his arms without struggle, glaring at Rodrik all the while. The king might detain him, but he would be heard. 'The folk of the north know what you bastards have done. We will have our justice!'

The king dismissed him with a flick of his hand and the guards led him away.

'It will not be long before word spreads. Folk will know you for what you are!' Arnulf shouted over his shoulder. 'I will see to it the truth is known, you filthy cunt.'

'Get him out!' roared the king.

***

Fergus watched as the guards escorted Arnulf up the stairs. Arnulf did not struggle but was taken quickly away, leaving a stunned silence in his wake. Hafgan and Arnulf's other warriors looked uncomfortable, only able to watch while their lord was led away.

Fergus shared their unease. *This was not a good start.*

Councillor Rodrik remained as he was, his hands trembling, but seemed relieved that Arnulf had been led away. Slowly, the scholar sank into his chair.

King Rhagnal's eyes settled upon Fergus and he swallowed a knot of nerves.

'I am truly sorry, my king.' Fergus bowed deeply, his apology sincere. 'Arnulf is a good man, and one of my oldest friends. His entire world has been turned to ash, he has lost everything. I hope you can forgive him.'

Rhagnal frowned. He was obviously angry but still troubled at what he had just heard and seen. 'There is no excuse. He is a Lord of Arnar and in his king's court.' The king's anger softened. 'Yet what has happened is a terrible thing. He has my sympathies, but he will act with honour in my hall.'

'Indeed, my king,' agreed Fergus with a bow. 'Please though, don't let Arnulf's actions distract us from the issue at hand.' He gestured at the grimoire. 'My father sent us to tell you what we saw and this evidence is damning. He asks his king to hear us and believe us. All that you have heard is true.'

Rhagnal studied Fergus, a long look that seemed to extend into eternity, where the choices to be made rested on the edge of a blade. Which way would the king tip? Towards Fergus and Arnulf and the folk of the north, or the College?

'The dead truly walk?' asked the king, his voice low, his arms crossed before his chest.

'I saw them, sire.'

Rhagnal turned Astrid, addressing the shield-maiden directly. 'And you?'

She nodded grimly.

Fergus took his moment. If Rhagnal could be swayed to act against the College, it was now. 'If the College has indeed allowed this dabbling in these dark arts, my father, High Lord Angus, asks his king to have them brought to justice for crimes against our lands and Arnar.'

Rodrik quailed at the suggestion, but Fergus continued, 'Those responsible must be punished and those innocent amongst them must do what they can to banish this evil.'

The king frowned for a long moment, Fergus holding his breath.

'Aye, I am honour bound to hear you. And while I know you to be a man of honour, I can't quite...' He shook his head, uncertain. 'It sounds like a myth, some fireside tale, but if my one of my high lords, his son, and many more all swear it...' Rhagnal gave Fergus a firm nod. 'The College will answer for this, and we will have the truth.'

Rodrik's shoulders dropped and he seemed to shrink in his chair. 'We will my king.'

'It appears the source of the attacks against the College has been confirmed too, councillor,' said Chancellor Alfric. 'If word has spread amongst folk in the north, word will spread here too. On top of everything, we are now forced to deal with *this*?' The chancellor leaned towards Rodrik, a menacing sort of movement that caused the scholar to shrink ever further into the chair. 'Let me tell you now, Rodrik; when the low-folk hear of this, your College could be finished. I assume the majority of your folk are innocent, but if any of you are entangled in this, I counsel you to cast them out, brand them as mad renegades, and do all that you can to separate them from the College.'

Alfric turned to the king. 'And it will be necessary to distance the crown from this before it gets out of hand, sire. It will be a shame. The College have proven themselves most useful in recent years.'

The king clasped his hands behind his back and began to pace slowly, a troubled frown on his face. Fergus watched and wondered what the man must be thinking. Could Rhagnal afford to cut ties with the College? Could the College survive without the funding and publicly visible trust of the crown? More than that, how many lords and ladies of Arnar would send their children to those hallowed halls to be educated once this travesty became known?

'Sire, these accusations are an outrage!' squealed the councillor. 'Sorcery and fell arts? They cannot be? These are things of myth.'

Rhagnal paused his pacing and glared at Councillor Rodrik with a look that could have levelled a mountain. 'I hope for all our sakes that you are right, councillor.'

'I—I must speak with the council immediately. I will take the grimoire for further study, so we might discover what transpired in the north. May I take my leave, sire?'

Fergus took a quick step forward and planted his hand on the grimoire. If he let it out of his sight now, what were the chances it might never be seen again? 'Arnulf will not be happy with that, my king. He does not trust them, and frankly neither do I. What assurances have we that they will not destroy or bury the evidence?'

'Arnulf has no say here, Lord Fergus,' snapped Rhagnal. He made a sharp gesture towards Rodrik with his hand. 'Take it and go. Find the truth of this.'

Fergus scowled as the little robed man snatched up the leatherbound tome and hurried from the hall. With effort he turned back to King Rhagnal and tried his best smile, almost certain it must look like a grimace. 'Sire, is there *any* possibility that the College are hiding something? What's to stop them hiding the truth of this to save themselves?'

'I fear he may be right, my king,' admitted the chancellor. 'We should take precautions, just in case.'

The king nodded grimly, rubbing at his forehead as if he fought with a headache. 'Do what you think best.'

'Have him followed,' the chancellor instructed Huscarl Warrick. 'I want eyes in the College, and certainly on this apprentice Rodrik spoke of. If he was there, he knows something, and we need that information. It might be necessary to take matters into our own hands if the situation begins to spiral.'

'Aye,' agreed the king. He continued to pace, a frown etched deep in his brow. 'The dead are upon us,' he muttered shaking his head. 'I can hardly believe what I'm hearing.' He turned back to his lords. 'I want the truth of this, and if what these men claim is true, College or no, I'll have their heads. Find who is responsible.'

CHAPTER TWELVE

Broken Bodies & Shattered Hopes

Where am I?

He had no memory of this place, or how he got there, yet it seemed strangely familiar. He walked onwards through the darkness and swirling mist. There was something up ahead. He walked closer — a tree, its branches forked out low to the ground and twisted into gnarled hands of wood and twig. It was bare of leaves. Again, there was something about it that seemed unsettlingly familiar.

His feet were as bare as the tree's limbs, the hard earth beneath his toes, but he could not see the ground. His eyes couldn't penetrate the oppressive gloom much further than a few feet ahead, an open sea of blackness swirling with thick fog. The mist made sinister shapes for a fleeting second before shifting away, leaving him nervously wondering if there had been anything there at all.

'Duncan,' came a whisper through the mist.

'Who's there?' called the apprentice.

There was no reply.

Did I really hear that… or is my mind playing tricks on me? Doubt began to set in.

He ventured onward, a standing stone loomed out of the mist. He reached out to touch it, tracing his fingers across the menhir's intricately carved patterns and knots.

'Beautiful,' he murmured as he ran his hands over the stone. The stone was grainy and the scent of damp and moss was powerful but not unpleasant.

'Duncan,' whispered the voice.

He started and turned. It was as if someone had crept up and whispered straight into his ear. Yet there was no one to be seen, just the swirling tendrils of mist fading into the gloom. His heart pounded.

'Who's there? Show yourself!' Duncan shouted.

'As you wish,' wheezed the voice. It was barely more than a whisper but seemed to penetrate the mist from every direction.

A face emerged, a grotesque crimson mask hovering at eye level and glaring through the tumultuous fog. The apprentice recoiled with a gasp.

Its skin had been flayed away, hanging in ragged flaps at the sides, leaving the red ruin beneath exposed. Without cheeks or lips the face wore a manic skeletal grin, and without lids its eyes were flared in a permanent, intense glare. It was a terrible, grotesque visage of nightmare gore.

The apprentice froze, his pulse beating loudly in his ears. The face hung there, seemingly disembodied in the gloom, staring wordlessly at him. His feet were planted to the ground, unable to take a step back though he tried to move with all his might.

The skeletal grin broke and it slowly opened its mouth.

With an unearthly screech the face plunged towards him, hurtling forwards.

His trance broken, Duncan ran, franticly stumbling over uneven ground obscured by the cloying darkness and its ethereal mist. He ran past the shadows of more standing stones , staggering in panic as the howling shriek behind him became a malevolent cackling laugh.

The fog pulled back and the darkness receded. A red sky appeared and heaved overhead with dark purple clouds. Duncan skidded to a halt, awed by what he saw before him. A wide plain opened up around him, littered with motionless figures.

Dead bodies.

Thousands of them, stretching off into the horizon. He gaped, unable to take it in, struck dumb by the smell; a charnel house stink, the smell of rot. His stomach heaved and he gaged hard at the stench.

With tentative steps, he moved slowly amongst them, trying as best he could not to step on them. He recognised many of their faces. It seemed as though everyone he had ever known lay cold and still about his feet amongst the nameless majority. Some lay in a peaceful repose, others bore terrible wounds, limbs severed and strewn around, all of a grim reminder of his master's experiments.

Maggots writhed in open mouths and clouds of flies hung in the air. Their buzzing filled the silence with an awful resonance.

Some kind of huge monolithic structure rose in the distance, mounds and stones at its foot. Lightning flashed in the clouds above but there was no rain. He might have thought it beautiful if not for the stomach churning collection of corpses around him.

Thousands of crows circled in the roiling alien sky, the dark shapes swooping to peck at the eyes of the dead. A huge rhann flapped down and perched on a nearby corpse. The stories said it was Old Night's bird, a harbinger of death, a feared omen in Arnar. It fixed its beady eyes on him and cawed loudly as if to warn him away. It was a low throaty sound, proclaiming its conquest of the dead on which it perched. It craned its neck towards the body and began ripping at the corpse with its hooked beak. He shuddered and turned away.

To see a rhann this close was rare, but Duncan had often seen the crows at their grim work, the leavings of his master's experiments providing fresh meat for their sharp beaks. The eyes go first, and then the soft tissue around the mouth, but eventually the carrion birds would devour all this decomposing flesh, no matter how rotten it became.

All at once, the birds took flight, cawing and shrieking wildly as they ascended and the apprentice spun around.

His eyes settled on the distant monolith and its court of mounds. A darkness shimmered in air between here and there, and he could not gauge its distance. As he watched, it coalesced into a stygian ethereal form.

Was it a figure? He could not tell for sure, but it took a shape that might have been vaguely human. As it drifted closer, the shadow thickened. It was impenetrable to his eyes, like staring into an opaque obsidian abyss.

It raised what could have been arms, shrouded in wispy tendrils of darkest shadow, and the plain came to life. Where once the dead lay still and the only movement had been from the feasting of scavengers, things began to move.

What? How can that…

A bolt of shock tore through him, twisting from his gut and paralysing him. Unable to move he could only watch as the corpses rose, tottering unsteadily to their feet. Some turned and fell on the others, tearing away bloody mouthfuls of dead flesh from their companions.

One nearby had its face buried in the bowels of a carcass, horrible chewing sounds echoing through the icy air, like cattle chewing cud, as the dead thing gorged. A corpse that had once been a woman looked up at him, her chin dripping with congealed, black blood. She plunged her face back down into the gory remains of an old colleague he recognised. The dead paid him no heed and continued their charnel banquet.

The shadowy form drifted ever closer. 'Apprentice,' it said in a sibilant whisper.

Duncan froze, his eyes fixed on the approaching darkness.

'Am I dead?' whispered the apprentice. 'Is this my death?'

There was a low chuckle. 'No,' replied the figure. 'You *are* death.'

A blinding pain exploded in his leg, and Duncan cried out, jerking away. He glanced down to see a dead face staring up at him, maggots swarming over the pustule ridden face, and a gaping tear in his lower leg. The corpse looked like he had been dead a long time, his rotting flesh barely clinging to his bones. The dead man held Duncan's leg in his decaying hands, and leaned back before sinking his teeth into the apprentice's calf, tearing away another mouthful with a spray of blood. The apprentice screamed as the agony tore through his leg and the corpse pulled him down.

***

Duncan woke with a scream, his leg throbbing.

Just a dream.

He gulped air as the terrible dead face faded from his mind in the light of day, the College infirmary materialising around him.

He clutched at his leg, desperate to ease the agony. He still wore the fresh robe he had changed into before hobbling to the infirmaries. Probing fingers found thick, heavy bandages encasing his ankle, re-broken and straightened by the College physicians. A fresh set of splints had been tightly bound into the bandages, immobilising it completely, and he was under strict instruction to apply weight to the joint. His head still swam from the concoction the physicians had given to send him off to sleep, sparing him the shock and pain of the procedure. The ethelroot he had been chewing for the pain had made his tongue numb and he barely remembered them working on his leg, glad his senses had been dulled and hazy.

He sat up and eased back the cover to examine his leg. Although the pain was terrible, he was relieved to see the bandages and splints held and his leg did indeed look straight. His ankle no longer splayed at a strange angle, and for a moment he dared to hope his leg would recover. He was in safe hands at the College — there were few better places to be with his injuries.

Laying back on his cot and pulling up the covers, he glanced around the room. The other cots in the room were empty except one, occupied by a man with a bandaged face. The man sat perfectly still and looked to be asleep. Duncan didn't recall being brought in here, but his mind had been addled at the time. The room seemed clean and well kept, and he was more than happy to lay there while the disorienting effects of the medicine wore off. He made a mental note to enquire about what they had given him for his own observations. Herb lore and medicine had been a large part of his studies under Master Eldrick.

'Bad dreams, friend?'

The apprentice looked up. It appeared his companion had not been asleep after all. He had a young man's voice but it was hard to tell his age with his face hidden beneath blood-soaked bandages, his eyes covered and his black hair poking up from above the wrappings.

'Dark dreams indeed. I am glad to be awake. They say ethelroot can have that effect though. I am sorry, I thought you were asleep. I hope I didn't wake you,' Duncan apologised.

'No worries, I wasn't asleep. I heard them bring you in. What are you in here for? Can't see for myself.' He gestured to his face. 'Blinded.'

'I'm sorry to hear that,' the apprentice replied. His words seemed thick in his mouth, his numb tongue slow to respond. 'Er, my leg. They reset my broken leg.'

'A broken leg?' asked the blind man. 'Let me guess — a farm worker?'

'Why do you say that?' Duncan looked at the man, slightly bewildered.

'I know a man who broke his leg too, not two weeks back, stumbled in a furrow while walking a plough and twisted it so bad it broke.'

'That is unfortunate.' Duncan came from a farming family; he knew well enough that a farmer would struggle to feed their family with an injury like that. He still felt the mix of guilt and appreciation at the cost to his family for him, the younger brother with little inheritance, to join the College, and how hard that year must have been just so he too could have a future.

'It's all a bit unfortunate,' the man said with a derisive laugh. 'The whole fucking world is unfortunate these days.'

The apprentice nodded grimly before remembering the man couldn't see him. 'I'm with the College, actually,' he told him, answering his question.

'Oh really?' The man turned toward him with an air of surprise. 'How ever did a College man manage to break his leg? I thought it was all dusty papers and reading words in here.'

'It's a long story,' replied Duncan. 'But you're not wrong about the papers and reading.'

'Sorry, where are my manners. The name's Seth. I'd shake your hand but,' he waved at his face again, 'I can't see a thing. Physician says I've lost one eye completely.'

'I'm sorry to hear that, Seth. I'm Duncan—it's good to meet you. I'd come shake yours but can't walk over there.'

They both chuckled and Seth's face broke into a friendly smile below his stained bandages.

'You've got to laugh, haven't you?' A touch of sorrow crept into Seth's voice. 'I hope to the gods I can get some sight back in the eye I've got left. I don't want to be blind.'

The apprentice felt a deep pang of sympathy for him. He couldn't be far off his own age one way or the other, and he knew for certain he'd rather a crippled leg than blindness. He couldn't imagine that.

There seemed to be a lot of blood and puss soaking through where Seth's eyes should have been. Duncan didn't like the poor man's chances of regaining his sight at all.

'Let me guess now.' Duncan hurried to change the subject. 'You were a smith? All those white-hot sparks flying about, is that how it happened?'

Seth laughed. 'No, no. I play the lute... at least I used to. This was no accident. There was a disagreement at an alehouse and I came off worse.'

'By the gods, that's terrible!'

'I really don't know what I'll do now.' Seth gave a dejected sort of shrug. 'Folk at the taverns don't want a disfigured blind man playing for them.'

'Surely it's how you sound that counts?' Duncan offered hopefully.

'I suppose you're right,' said Seth. He didn't sound at all convinced.

'Can you still play… without needing to see, I mean?'

'Probably… at least I hope so,' said Seth. 'Do you see my case nearby? I told them to bring it. It never leaves my side.'

The apprentice glanced around the little of the floor beside the man's bed.

'Aye, it's just there, to your right.'

The blind man groped around, reaching over the side of his cot until his fingers found the polished wood of the case.

'Ah there she is,' said Seth with a warm smile. 'She's always there when I need her, and she's never let me down.' His fingers found the latches and he flipped them open with practised ease, lifting out a beautiful ebon-hued lute and carefully placed it on his lap.

'She is indeed beautiful,' Duncan said in awe.

'Not as half as she sounds,' replied Seth, cradling the instrument. He drifted a hand over the strings and strummed them. 'Let's see if I can still make her sing.' The blind man began quietly playing, and the apprentice was taken aback by the low, soul wrenching melody which began to fill the room. A little smile tugged at the corner of Seth's mouth.

'You play well, friend,' the apprentice told him.

'Aye, thank you. My heart can rest easy now she's in my hands again.'

'Do you know *Ingvar's Shields*? I always loved that one,' asked Duncan. It had been an age since he'd heard it. His father would often sing it on the long winter nights as they huddled by the hearth when he was little, he and his brother would sing the refrain filled with childhood dreams of valour and honour.

'Aye, I do.' Seth played the well-known refrain followed by a rich chord.

Duncan grinned, even though the blind man could not see it. 'That's the one.'

Seth played absently for some time as they continued to speak, both stuck in their cots in this quiet corner of the College infirmaries. Duncan told him of how he had come to be injured, but left aside the finer points about his master's experiments, and in turn he heard about Seth's bar fight. The company was welcome and lessened the sorrow of pain.

The door at the far end of the room clicked open and their conversation trailed off as a physician dressed in a robe and cowl entered.

'He's in here,' the man was saying as he opened the door.

The apprentice recognised him, but he returned no hint of recognition when he met his gaze. *Do I really look so different now?*

He quickly lost his train of thought as a girl stepped through the door. She had clear, pale skin and long blonde hair tied back in a collection of braids. She was slight, and the sharp angles of her beautiful face framed bright blue eyes. He couldn't help but stare.

Her eyes lit up as she saw Seth, and a pang of envy snapped in Duncan's chest. The musician was a lucky man to have a young lass look at him like that.

'Seth!' she exclaimed. 'Are you all right?'

'Aye, lass, better. They told me there's still a chance one eye may heal.' Seth smiled and gestured at his bandaged eyes. 'One eye is lost though.'

She gasped.

'Ah...' the physician began. 'There is a small chance, yes, but only time will tell. Pray for the favour of the gods.'

'Is there any more you can do?' asked the girl.

'We have done all we can. He needs rest, and as I said, some time.' The physician smiled weakly and Duncan thought he looked doubtful. The apprentice's heart sank for his new acquaintance. He would likely never see again, but no one had the courage to tell the poor man.

The physician looked over at the apprentice. 'Ah, Apprentice Duncan — you're awake. That's good. I hope the pain is bearable.'

'Just about,' replied the apprentice, shifting his leg from under the covers and wincing at the lance of hot pain up his shin.

'There was someone looking for you earlier. I will fetch the message shortly.'

The apprentice nodded, curious about who would be looking for him. Perhaps his master had returned? 'Thank you.'

'When can Seth leave?' asked the girl as the physician turned to leave.

'Well, we have drained his eye and dressed the wounds. It should be re-dressed now the worst of the bleeding has stopped. I will see to it, and then he may return home.' The physician smiled at the young woman and then closed the door behind him, leaving the three of them alone.

'That sounds hopeful, at least.' The girl spoke words of reassurance, but as she stepped closer to Seth's cot, one hand rose to her lips in shock. Her face could not hide her distress at the sight of the blood and gunk that had seeped through Seth's bandages. The blind man smiled at her, oblivious of her concern. 'Your father wants you back at the house as soon as you're able,' she threw a glance at the apprentice and lowered her voice. 'We could get word at any time. We have to be ready. And, he doesn't think it's safe here, with all the sick folk.'

'I don't think the sick are allowed in the College,' replied Seth. 'I heard them talking—they're being sent somewhere else. They won't risk it.'

'Aye, lass,' added the apprentice, unable to stop himself even if it meant revealing his eavesdropping. 'There's no sickness here, just broken bodies.'

The girl eyed him warily.

'Ah, Nym, meet Duncan. He's an apprentice here at the College.'

'Hello,' said Nym with a polite but cool nod.

She's stunning, thought the apprentice. He'd not encountered a girl in some time and a strange impulsive desire began to grow inside him.

Seth continued on, oblivious to Duncan's thoughts. 'He's been fine company this afternoon. Is it still daylight out there? I really have no idea.'

'It is.' Nym's eyes welled up with tears but she fought them back.

'He broke his leg while on an expedition up in the Spine, can you believe it?' continued Seth, still unaware of Nym's distress over his injuries. She glanced over at Duncan, taking in his bandaged leg then his face and hair, but quickly looked away. It was as if she hadn't truly noticed him before, but on closer inspection, was repulsed.

She's afraid of me. Am I really so grotesque to behold? He reached up and slid a lock of his hair between his fingers. It was almost completely white now, and he dreaded to think how haggard and strange he must look. The apprentice sighed. *I could never have a girl like her looking like this.*

He thought of Truda and realised he longed to see her again. What would she think of him now? As he stared at the pretty girl in front of him, the insidious feeling of desire grew stronger.

'Well I hope you recover soon,' said Nym, trying to avoid the apprentice's eyes.

'Did the old man not come with you?' asked Seth.

'No, he stayed in case we hear anything from Roark. He won't let Finn out of his sight either.' She paused to take a deep breath and perhaps to steady her voice. 'I'm so sorry, Seth. Finn never meant for this to happen. Will you ever forgive him?'

'Who, the boy? He needs a good hiding, but what's done is done. I know he never meant no harm. The gods steer us in mysterious ways. It all happens to their plan, so who do I blame? The gods? Finn? Myself for getting involved in the first place...' Seth trailed off, sinking back against his pillows, cradling his lute. 'I'm surprised he let you come alone, though. I hope you stayed away from the crowds.'

'I came along the main street, but it was near deserted. Just a few folk keeping to themselves and those horrible carts...'

'I saw the bodies and the carts on my way in,' commented the apprentice. 'Is it really that bad out there?'

'Aye, it really is,' replied Seth, his lips in a grim line.

'I hope you haven't lost anyone you know?'

Seth turned his head towards Duncan's voice. 'No family, but many folk I know have gone to Old Night. The city is being ravaged by this sickness. I hear of more and more each day, dead and gone.'

The door clicked open and the physician returned carrying fresh bandages and a bowl of steaming water. He placed the bowl on a table beside his blinded patient.

'Apprentice Duncan,' said the physician, turning towards him. 'I have been told you have been summoned before the council, and it is apparently quite urgent. You are to go immediately.'

'But I was just there this morning.' Duncan frowned. 'I hope it's news of my master, Eldrick. Perhaps he has returned.'

'Eldrick!' exclaimed the man. 'So you are *that* apprentice? I am sorry I didn't recognise you. You look... different since I last saw you.' The apprentice grunted as the physician set about attending to Seth as he spoke. 'In any case, the council await. You'll need those crutches against the wall there. Try to stay off the leg and I'll have your old staff and something for the pain brought to your quarters.'

Duncan waved his offer away. 'You have my thanks, but you won't need to. My master's rooms are well stocked with all manner of medicines. I can see to it myself. I would appreciate the staff, though.' It had become his closest companion over the last few weeks, a gift given to him from the kindness of Master Logan.

'As you wish. I hope you recover swiftly, apprentice. If you change your mind you know where to find us.'

Surprised and somewhat taken aback by his sudden discharge from the infirmary, Duncan pulled back his covers and swung his legs to the side with a wince. The inevitable lance of agony shot through his leg as the blood rushed back to his ankle. His head swam as he fought a wave of dizziness that came with the disturbance of his repose, and he grimaced, pausing until it passed. The physician turned his full attention to Seth. With a quiet warning, he began to gently unravel the bandages from his face.

The apprentice reached out, grasped the crutches and, keeping his freshly bound leg raised off the floor, slowly pulled himself up to stand on one leg. Releasing a held breath, Duncan managed to get himself upright without knocking his foot or sending another bolt of pain shooting through him.

He sighed. *Here we go again.*

He looked over to the cot where the physician had almost finished removing the bandages from Seth's face. The beginnings of a dark scab had been revealed, and the smudged stains of dried blood and fluid on his cheek bones.

'Well, Seth,' said Duncan. 'I hope the gods look down upon you and see it fair to return your sight.'

Seth smiled and turned towards his voice.

'Keep still,' muttered the physician.

'Thank you, Duncan. And I hope your leg heals straight this

A Ritual of Flesh

time. Good luck with your council.'

'May Hart's blessings be with you,' the apprentice murmured as he took his first laboured step towards the door.

'And with you,' replied his blinded companion.

At the door, Duncan heard Nym gasp and he stopped to look back. The bandage had been removed, revealing the man's face. He was more than simply blinded — he was gruesomely disfigured. A deep slash ran from temple to temple straight through his eyes, a thick ropey scar forming under the scabs and stitches. His right eye had been removed, leaving behind a gaping hole, and his left was encased in a swollen scab. Nym's hands came back to her face then, a vain attempt to stifle the trembling of her lips and the tears as the physician began dabbing a wet cloth around Seth's wounds.

May the gods be with you, friend.

He touched the old charm hung around his neck before heaving his weight onto the crutches and limping away.

CHAPTER THIRTEEN

One Last Job

The other prisoner lasted longer than Bjorn had guessed. It took two nights before he was found cold and dead when the guards checked in the morning. Then there were three heads in the sack, the body discarded beside the road.

They kept to the high ground, following the ridgelines and striking out for the nearest road that would take them back to Oldstones. Bjorn sighed with relief when they finally found a road. He was usually a man of the wilds, but the road meant they would make better time, and he was eager to collect his silver and get out of this rain.

The Wildman jogged easily beside Bjorn's horse. Tung's endurance was breath-taking. For two more nights and three days they rode, the rain pouring ceaselessly, yet Tung ran on. Soaked through to the skin, Bjorn couldn't understand how the man found the energy. The only thing keeping the hunter going was the thought of the tavern hearths in Oldstones.

Bjorn reined his horse in beside the first of the menhirs littering the plain around Oldstones. The Wildman paused, waiting for him beside the ancient stone. Daeluf and the warriors of Oldstones rode in a group not far behind him, and Bjorn turned to watch as they rode up.

'Nearly there, hunter. Archeon will be pleased,' said Daeluf from the head of the group. The last remaining prisoner, the only survivor, bobbed awkwardly, limp as a dead fish over the saddle of their spare horse.

It won't be long until he's with Old Night. He forced down a pang of guilt with a cold, grim resolve. *The life of a man, weighted with silver. So be it...*

***

'Bastards,' muttered Archeon. 'Fucking sea raiders in my guard.' He slammed his fist down on his desk. 'Sea raiders!' he bellowed.

'Forgive me lord, but who are they?' asked Bjorn.

'I'm surprised you haven't heard the rumours yet.' Daeluf gave him a look of genuine surprise.

Archeon scowled and made a dismissive gesture with his hand as if he wished to sweep the problem away. 'Raiders from the west. A horde of them have landed on the coast.'

'Aye, but what has this to do with the men I hunted? I understood that they were merely common outlaws.' Bjorn folded his arms. He didn't want to offend the lord, but he'd wondered the entire journey back if there was something else going on. 'Was I deceived?'

'You have my apologies, Bjorn,' Archeon conceded with a shake of his head. 'This was a... a sensitive matter. The existence of an enemy amongst us, and *here* of all places, is not something we wanted widely known.'

Bjorn frowned but nodded.

'You performed most satisfactorily, hunter. Your reward will be doubled for your efforts, but I must ask for your complete discretion on the matter.'

'Of course, my lord. You have my word,' said Bjorn with a slight bow. 'May I ask where these raiders have come from? There is nothing out there to the west, just cold seas. What enemy could be raiding our lands?'

Archeon and Daeluf exchanged glances. The high lord shrugged and gestured for his captain to take the question.

Daeluf cleared his throat and hesitated. 'We fear they are survivors from the old rebellion.'

'From Aeginhall?' asked Bjorn, his eyes widening.

'Aye,' Daeluf said with a nod. 'It's been nearly twenty years since Aeginhall. In truth we thought none would have survived after they fled, and we never would have thought they would dare come back.'

Bjorn nodded thoughtfully. He was young when the rebellion burned through the western lands of Arnar. He was no sworn warrior, he did not see the fighting himself, but he had heard the tales. The rebels seized every town from Stonequay to Aeginhall on the west coast and tried to forge a free state. They paid a heavy price for their hubris. The king marched west, banners from all over Arnar at his back. The final battle had been Aeginhall, the rebellion crushed when the king marched on that forlorn fortress by the sea. There was a great slaughter there, hundreds put to the sword — a dark, bloody memory for Arnar.

'The survivors and folk sympathetic to their cause escaped as the city fell, fearing the reprisal of the king's fury.' Daeluf shrugged. 'Gods, half the low folk in the region supported the separatists and many fled into the western seas. They must have scattered onto islands in the Storm Waters.'

The westerlands have not forgotten the blood spilt there, friend. Bjorn knew folk still whispered of that foolish cause on some ale soaked nights.

'And now they are back,' added Archeon, swirling his wine in his goblet. 'Their numbers are unlike anything we could have imagined. They are armed, organised, well equipped. Don't ask me how or by whom, but someone is funding them. I cannot let this happen in my lands. We have committed much of our strength to crushing them.'

'It is of great concern that they have infiltrated this far inland. They likely are well informed on our disposition,' said Daeluf.

Archeon steepled his hands thoughtfully and leaned back in his chair. 'You see now why we could not tell you everything, hunter? There is a good chance more of their spies reside within these very walls, and we must play our cards close to our chests.'

Bjorn shrugged a shoulder. He'd been used like a tool, wielded like a sword for reasons he was forbidden to understand. He wasn't sure he appreciated the sentiment, but he was hardly in a position to argue. 'I might not like being lied to, my lord, but I see your reasons. I'm sure your silver will lessen the blow.' A dark smile crept onto his lips.

'Indeed,' said Archeon, raising his eyebrows. 'There is more on offer if you remain in my service, hunter?'

'Perhaps,' said Bjorn. He picked an apple from a bowl on the desk and gave a sharp whistle. Tung looked around and Bjorn tossed the fruit to him. The Wildman bobbed his head manically. Bjorn's hand hovered over a bowl of sliced ham. The memory of a charred arm flashed in his mind, images of men feasting on the flesh of their prisoners, grease running down their pronounced jaws. His fingers recoiled. *No, not meat.*

He forced his gaze away from the bowl and back to Archeon. 'I have someone I need to see. A meeting that is long overdue. This was to be my last job before I go. It has been an honour to serve you, lord, but I can't stay.'

'I see.' Archeon stared at him over his steepled fingers, his gaze unwavering. 'I had hoped you would return to the north.'

'Why?' asked Bjorn sharply. He had no desire to return there.

Archeon's eyes flicked to Tung and back. The Wildman had settled on a fur rug and sat eating the apple, the high lord's guards watching him carefully.

'We have lost contact with several villages on the borders.'

Bjorn stared at the high lord. *That's very bad news.*

'And we received word from your friend, Lord Kervan, just after you left. He confirmed the presence of the savages. Kervan planned to move north with his men but another rider came in last night. Kervan has not been heard from.' Archeon indicated to a letter on his desk. 'It does not look good. It appears these savages are striking into Arnar. Several of my lords are reporting attacks by these… Stonemen.'

Bjorn clenched his jaw, resisting the urge to step away from the lord's desk.

'I had hoped you would go north to advise my banner-men,' continued Archeon. 'I will rally my eastern lords to strike in force and show these savages cold Arnar steel. You have experience with them, and you keep this one with you.' Archeon gestured at Tung as he sat quietly on the floor eating the apple.

'Forgive me, my lord, but I fear I would be of little use to your warriors,' Bjorn insisted with a shake of his head. Could he admit that he had no desire to ever cross paths with the cannibals in the wild lands of the border? 'I hunt, I track, but I know nothing of war and arms, of strategy,'

'That's a shame,' said Archeon calmly, but disappointment edged into his voice. He poured himself a glass of wine. 'I've got Stonemen attacking in the north, fucking sea raiders fermenting old notions of rebellion and pillaging in the west, and to top it all off, there's word of plague in the capital. The realm's going to the dogs, and it's up to scant few of us to hold it all together.' He drained his glass and sighed. 'If you will not go north, can I persuade you instead to take one final task? Nothing dangerous, I assure you.'

Bjorn chewed the back of his lip and thought for a moment. What was the harm in hearing it? As long as it took him away from the cannibals lurking in the north, he would at least hear him. 'Aye, my lord. What is it?'

'Will you go to the capital for an audience with our *king*?' He sneered the last word.

It was no secret High Lord Archeon and King Rhagnal had an uncomfortable history. The king had defeated him in the last war of succession, and while Archeon could have taken the crown for himself if the fates had decided differently, he was forced to kneel. He'd retained his position as high lord, as is customary after the succession, but there was little love between them. Any loyalty to the crown from the high lord came only from a sense of duty on Archeon's part.

'The king, lord?' asked Bjorn. Had he heard him right? There was a rumour of plague in the south?

'I need someone I trust to take word of our situation. It's getting out of hand and the king must be informed.' Archeon grimaced.

'It is no weakness, lord,' Daeluf re-assured him.

Archeon sighed and nodded reluctantly. He obviously did not want to seem weak in front of his old adversary but had little choice. 'Aye, we need men if we are to fight on two fronts. Hunter, I would ask you to go before Rhagnal and tell him what you have seen, as a witness to both these Stonemen and the cannibals you encountered. Also tell him of your part in the hunting down of the agents of these... raiders, rebels—call them what you will. The word of a man of renown such as yourself will carry more weight at court. Just tell them what is happening to the people out there. We need the banners of Arnar to march west. The king must know how dire the situation is.'

Old rivalries died hard, and Bjorn knew this would be seen as a capitulation by the high lord. The king would look like the saviour and hero, while Archeon would appear a beggar. At least by sending Bjorn, the high lord saved some face by avoiding a direct request for help. It was the only way to keep his honour intact.

Bjorn rubbed at his chin, scratching the stubble of his beard. 'I think I understand, my lord, but this *will* be dangerous, especially if the rumours of plague are to be believed.' He left the statement hanging, allowing the unspoken implication to sink in.

A smirk slowly split the high lord's stern visage. 'Of course, you'd be well compensated for the risk.'

'In advance, if that does not offend?' Bjorn pressed. 'I'll not be returning to these parts for some time.'

Archeon looked long and hard at him, understanding his meaning. 'As long as you fulfil your word, hunter, I see no harm in that. You have proven your honour to me many times now, and I know you would never wish to sully your reputation.'

'That would be *unwise*,' Daeluf put in quietly.

That's a threat. Veiled, but a threat all the same. Still, south was where he wanted to be. *She isn't far from the capital...*

The hunter made his decision. 'An audience with the king, and a good weight of silver? How could I refuse?'

Part Two

A Ritual of Flesh

CHAPTER FOURTEEN

Whispers

Click, click, click.

The crutches tapped loudly on the wooden floor as Duncan heaved himself along the silent corridor. His leg throbbed with every step, shooting pain tearing up his leg and into his guts. He felt sick, his head swimming from the strange numbing effect of the ethelroot. It was dark outside now, evening creeping in while he waited.

He had announced himself to the council clerk but had been made to wait an hour or more in an uncomfortable corner of the clerk's office while the council assembled and he was finally called to enter the chambers. At the sound of his name, Duncan had hauled himself out of the hard chair and begun a slow hobble along the corridor towards the council chamber.

Apprentice, hissed a sibilant voice.

He stopped and turned awkwardly, glancing back to the clerk's desk. The ageing scholar had his head down scribbling in a ledger. He became aware the apprentice had stopped and looked up.

'Yes?' asked the clerk with a slightly irritated tone.

'Did you say something?' Duncan's gaze darted around the room, searching the shadows.

The man's frown deepened. 'I did not. Please move along. I have work to do, and they are waiting for you.' The clerk whisked his hand at Duncan, dismissing him, and he suspected the man was not best pleased with having to attend to council duties at this time of an evening; a time of day he would not normally be required.

The apprentice turned back to the heavy doors at the end of the corridor, the passageway seeming to stretch away into the distance. Surely it hadn't always been so long? With a sigh and a grunt, he continued laboriously towards the doors. He had become quite accustomed to hobbling in recent weeks, but the pain had now returned to the same vicious intensity as when he had first broken his ankle in the north.

A bead of sweat rolled down the side of his face, but he had no free hand to wipe it away. It continued its course towards his chin and he resigned himself to the knowledge that wherever he walked in the coming days, it would seem agonisingly distant.

'Damn this agony,' he ground out.

It will pass… all things do, came the whispered voice.

He jerked to a stop and threw a look back at the clerk. The man had resumed scratching with his quill and showed no sign of hearing the voice. It was familiar, recalled from the depths of the ethelroot-induced dream, and he shivered, his stomach churning from the drugs and the fear.

The apprentice frowned. He shook his head as if to clear it. It must be his own thoughts whispering at him, he thought, some queer effect of the drugs they had given him. It was as if his dreams and thoughts had spilled into his waking mind.

Benches lined the corridor to the chamber, usually filled with scholars waiting to petition the council. They all stood empty now; this session being called much later than usual, and at odds with protocol. Duncan cursed the clerk. The man had looked down his nose and refused to tell him why he'd been summoned, leaving him to wonder what could be so important that they had gathered the College elders twice in one day.

An ominous quiet hung in the hallway, and his knock at the chamber door sounded overly loud against the cold stone walls. The door swung open slowly. Another clerk appeared and ushered him inside before stepping into the corridor and closing the doors behind him, leaving the lone apprentice to the mercy of the council.

He had never been to a closed session and the room was unsettlingly quiet and almost empty. The councillors sat in their usual places, and at the centre of the chamber, another table had been set to one side of the speaking floor, three strange looking men occupying chairs behind it. They were richly dressed and did not appear to be from the College. They looked like noblemen, serious and wealthy, each of them flanked by several burly warriors. He eyed the guards, noting the wolf's head of Varg on their livery. These were royal guards — king's men.

Why are there warriors at the Council? Why are there noblemen here? Did I knock on the wrong door? His stomach knotted and he shuffled forwards. Another bead of sweat trickled down his face. Were the terrifyingly formidable men at the table huscarls? He couldn't recall ever seeing a huscarl up close, but he knew their reputation. These were not men to be trifled with.

The apprentice glanced around and noticed the gallery was not entirely empty. A lone figure sat awaiting his arrival.

Master Luthor?

Why had Master Luthor also been summoned? The master offered him a slight nod and Duncan swallowed a ball of anxiety from his throat as Councillor Merwyl rose to his feet.

'Apprentice Duncan, thank you for joining us. Please take a seat. I understand you have come from the infirmary?' Merwyl indicated to a lone chair waiting before the council's crescent shaped table and Duncan sank gratefully into it. An attendant hurried from a corner with another chair and a cushion, helping Duncan to lift his injured leg to an elevated position before scurrying away. 'Your leg looks to be in better condition,' said Merwyl, leaning forwards to examine the apprentice's new splint and bandaged leg. 'I wish you a swift recovery.'

'Thank you, councillor,' replied the apprentice, too nervous and nauseous to utter more than a whisper.

'I, Councillor Merwyl, current elected speaker of this council, hereby convene this session. May I remind all in attendance that this is a closed session which will be recorded. The matters before this council shall not be discussed beyond this room. Do you all understand?'

There was a mumble of agreement across the room. The quill of the council's scribe scratched on parchment as he began his record.

'Apprentice Duncan, studying under Master Eldrick, has been summoned before the council and will speak,' Merwyl proclaimed for the benefit of the scribe. 'I suppose you wondering why we have summoned you?'

He nodded anxiously, his mouth too dry to form words.

'I apologise for disturbing your recovery, but we have some pressing business concerning your recent expedition.'

Duncan cleared his throat when Merwyl did not elaborate. 'How can I help the council?'

'We have reviewed the records on your master's application for funds as well as his proposed itinerary and the reports you presented this morning.' The councillor hesitated and looked to his colleagues and the observing noblemen. 'There are inconsistencies... questions that require answers.'

The apprentice frowned. He'd read some of the reports. He'd written some of them too. Eldrick had been clear about his intentions and findings, so what could it be that they found questionable?

Merwyl returned to his seat and another councillor took the floor; a little bald man in a dark red robe who Duncan recognised as Councillor Rodrik.

'We all know your master's area of expertise,' began Rodrik, 'but we require more clarity on his current studies?'

Beware, apprentice, hissed the voice in his mind. Duncan shook his head to clear it, but a sharp little claw snagged on his consciousness.

Rodrik lifted a sheet of parchment from the table. 'It states in the application records and in your own reports that the expedition took you to a place known as the High Passes, at the edges of the Spine of the World, in the northern borders of our realm. Is that so?'

'Yes,' said the apprentice, shifting in his seat.

'Why was your master in these High Passes? Why travel so far from home?' The councillor gave the apprentice a measured look down his nose.

'Master Eldrick's work is of a sensitive nature.' Duncan looked at each of the councillors in turn. No point in sugar coating it. They knew what Eldrick specialised in, but what of the huscarls? How would they react? 'It is controversial, and he needed a remote place with a supply of human bodies on which to conduct his studies.'

'The anatomy work he proposed before this council?'

'Indeed, councillor,' replied the apprentice, fighting back a ball of nerves from his throat. 'Master Eldrick felt the dissection of animals and beasts was of no further use to his study of healing. He needed human corpses, as the council was aware.'

Rodrik threw a nervous glance at the table of noble observers, but Duncan pressed on. 'Eldrick decided it was better to position himself somewhat nearer the war-torn border with Cydor, rather than in the city. While people die quite frequently here, one way or the other, it was thought folk would not take kindly to anyone meddling with their deceased loved ones.'

'Quite so,' grumbled Councillor Caleb. 'If it were discovered, folk would see evil at work, rather than the pursuit of true knowledge.'

'The folk can be foolish,' Councillor Sareya pointed out. The woman still wore her dark green robe as she had that morning. 'This council would never have risked the mob or harming both College persons and property.'

'This is why Eldrick chose the northern lands bordering Cydor.' Duncan shrugged and relaxed the muscle of his thigh, rubbing it with his hand. 'It was reasoned that war dead are rarely claimed, and never in great numbers, so Truda and Master Logan led expeditions across the border to collect bodies from the Cydorian battlefields.'

Councillor Rodrik rifled through several leaves of parchment. 'That is quite dangerous. There is no mention of this intention in the initial petition.'

The apprentice's heart rate began to climb. Eldrick had told him all their actions had been approved by the council. Had they broken some law or treaty in their gathering of subjects for his master's study? Were these warriors here to arrest him? They'd throw him in some stinking gaol to rot for his unwitting part in all this, he was certain. Fear crept from a dark place in the pit of his stomach.

'I—I never went with them, sir,' he stammered, asserting his innocence.

Rodrik seemed unmoved. 'There are many places more easily accessible than the High Passes. Why traverse the mountains?'

'Master Logan suggested it, I believe.'

'Master Logan? He is a respected man at this College. Do you know why he made this suggestion to your master?'

'Logan spoke of a rumour, an old place high in the hills beyond his family's lands. He said it was a place the local people did not go for it was said to be cursed. The rumour was, it was a for-gotten ruin and he had long been curious to go and see it for him-self. Master Logan guessed it was one, perhaps two days ride from The Borders, which turned out quite accurate.'

Rodrik nodded. 'I see. And, do you know anything of Logan's interest in the site?'

'Master Logan often spoke of his desire to chart and possibly excavate the ruins up there in order to learn more of its origins and the ancient peoples who dwelt there. He seemed quite eager to finally see it. I can only presume it had long been of curiosity to him.'

'And this work of Logan's is recorded also?'

'Of course, councillor.' Duncan nodded quickly, eager to please. Surely the council believed him? 'Master Logan conducted a survey and it's recorded in the findings I delivered.'

The councillor scratched his ear thoughtfully then scribbled a note on the parchment before him. 'Were there any other studies your expedition engaged in?'

The apprentice thought a moment. 'I worked on a theory of moon cycles, and there was a study on the local fauna by Master Logan. Apprentice Truda had her studies but she did not discuss them much...' He hesitated. 'My master also sought the truth of the Bone Ritual.'

'The Bone Ritual again?' scoffed Councillor Sareb, his jowly reddened face twisting into a sneer.

'Indeed, councillor. Eldrick has long held theories on the mat-ter, inspired by the text of the First Sons. He used Master Luthor's translations.' The apprentice nodded to Luthor, sitting in the gal-lery. 'He swore they were the most promising. One of the factors he considered before he took me on in fact, was because I had once been apprenticed to Master Luthor.'

Luthor gave the apprentice a grave smile and a nod.

Something is wrong, thought Duncan. *Has my master been arrest-ed?* What if he said something that incriminated Eldrick without realising?

'Master Luthor's name was indeed cited in the reports we read, hence why he has been summoned' said Merwyl, tilting his head towards the gallery. Master Luthor nodded in acknowledgement once more, but again said nothing. He seemed calm, unphased by the questioning or its direction, and Duncan wondered if the master knew something he did not.

'Luthor's work is most notable,' grumbled Councillor Sareb. 'There are things we agree on but I daresay the translation is flawed. Mine is much—'

'Your work is also most impressive, Councillor Sareb,' Merwyl cut in, 'but many have tried and failed to decipher those ancient texts for centuries.' He turned to the apprentice. 'What was Eldrick's interest in the ritual?'

Duncan glanced at the assembled councillors and then at the huscarls, eyeing the weapons of their guards. He was on thin ice here. How much did they already know? 'There was a text he was working on, derived from an old stone rubbing of First Son glyphs. Eldrick used Master Luthor's work to come to some interesting and intriguing findings.'

Merwyl's brows rose. 'Oh?'

'He believed the modern Bone Ritual used by the priests today could date back to an ancient practice, possibly as far back as the First Sons. He believed translation of the rubbing was the key.'

'I see,' said Merwyl with interest. 'Do go on,' he said with a gesture at the apprentice.

'There are records and accounts from long ago, but he thought the modern ritual had... how did he put it? "Lost all resemblance of what it once was". So, when we came to the passes and surveyed the ruins, both masters agreed it was likely a First Sons site. Then Master Eldrick found something, some glyphs he recognised from his work. While he was there, he thought to investigate his findings further. He greatly desired to see if he could recreate the ancient ritual, to know the truth of it.'

'There is no mention of this in the expedition proposal,' Rodrik pointed out, looking through his stack of parchments.

'Master Luthor, are you aware of these *texts* that Eldrick was using?' asked Merwyl.

'I am not,' replied Luthor with a frown. 'Master Eldrick and I have discussed my work at length in the past, but he never mentioned any new texts. Apprentice Duncan do you have a record of these texts?'

'We do, Master Luthor. It will be in my master's findings and research.'

'Well then,' continued Luthor, 'I could certainly take a look and compile a report for the council.'

'Ah... I think I would be better suited to this task,' interrupted Sareb.

Merwyl scowled at the councillor. 'You are not our only scholar on the matter of the First Sons, Sareb. The lad is right—Master Luthor is one of our leading minds on the matter, and it was his translations Eldrick worked with. It would make sense if Luthor were to lead this research.'

'If I may, councillor,' interrupted the apprentice. 'With my master's permission, I am sure I can make his work available to both of you for further study.'

'With your master's *permission*?' snapped Sareb with vehemence.

The apprentice instantly wished he had never said anything, he was merely trying to be helpful.

'Who are you to dictate such terms to us boy?' snarled the councillor. 'If this council demands to see his work, you will produce it.' He slammed his hand down on the table.

Merwyl raised his hand for silence.

'I think that would be a wise decision,' said the Speaker. Merwyl looked at the table of noblemen. The centre man nodded his agreement to Councillor Merwyl. 'Indeed apprentice, you will make the research available to both Master Luthor and Councillor Sareb for further study.'

They must not dabble with your master's work, apprentice, warned the voice in his head. *They are unworthy of its secrets.*

'I am more than willing to assist,' Duncan put in, ignoring the voice and its demands. Merwyl inclined his head at the apprentice, accepting his offer over the blustering disapproval of Sareb, who seemed to think he had been overlooked for some great and noble task.

You are a fool, apprentice. You will doom yourself, hissed the voice.

'We have diverged from our purpose!' Rodrik shouted across the gathering. 'I see no relevance in discussing this ritual.'

'I disagree,' said one of the noblemen, speaking for the first time and rising to his feet. He was an older man, and wore his blond hair short and well groomed. About his neck hung a thick necklace of gold and silver, a display of wealth the apprentice had never seen the like of in all his years.

'Chancellor Alfric addresses the council,' Merwyl announced for the scribe.

'Correct me if I am wrong, but this Bone Ritual is used by the priests of the dead to commune with the spirits of our ancestors,' the chancellor said, surveying the room carefully. 'It is an attempt to raise a soul and bind it to its former bones, essentially raising the dead?'

Councillor Uriah came to his feet. 'Indeed, lord, but there is no substance to these priests and their claims of the ritual. It is a ritual of superstition, a mummery of worship. It has never actually raised the bones to life or allowed anyone to prove a commune with the ancestors.'

'The priests claim they hear the voices of the dead, and that they alone can hear it,' said Councillor Caleb, a look of doubt on his face. For all their insistence, the priests were humoured rather than believed by most at the College. Duncan had seen vehement adherence to the teachings in rural areas though, usually among the uneducated masses.

'Convenient,' muttered Uriah in a moment of rare agreement with his colleague.

'It is a matter of *faith*,' argued Councillor Asha.

'Yes, and a matter many here do not subscribe to without any proof,' retorted Caleb.

'I would not be so quick to insult and dishonour the gods, councillors,' snapped the chancellor, glaring at the scholars. He reached for a pendant hung around his neck.

Chancellor Alfric's gaze found Duncan then, studying him for a long moment. The chancellor's scrutiny was unwavering, and the apprentice self-consciously pushed his lank hair back from his face, the locks devoid of life and colour, as dry as straw against his fingers. His skin was clammy with sweat, made all the worse by the silent regard of this powerful lord.

'You know me?' asked Alfric, addressing the apprentice.

'Y—yes, Lord Chancellor, though I have never seen you before today.'

Alfric looked down his long, straight nose, pinning Duncan with a hard stare. 'Then you know that to lie to me is to lie to the king himself? And, if you were to lie to the king, he would have your head.' A tremor shivered through Duncan and his hand tightened on the arm rest of the chair, but he nodded despite the fear. 'I have questions for you, and you will answer me truthfully.'

Beware, apprentice, hissed the voice.

Alfric took his seat again and settled into it, the assembled councillors dead silent but watching every move. 'Was your master's attempt at this *Bone Ritual* successful?'

The apprentice hesitated. A cold wave washed through him and his throat tightened, strangling his answer. It was as if he had been shoved out of his own body, no longer in control of his voice or limbs, yet words fell from his lips.

'My master believes it was, my lord. He wrote as much in the reports, but I did not ever see it.' It was his voice, but he had not chosen the lie. Twice he had seen those cold bones rise like a terrible puppet, as if drawn up by strings.

He wanted to scream, to thrash and kick until he regained control but instead his limbs refused to answer, the cold grip of another presence forcing him to watch from behind his eyes.

The chancellor frowned and he held the apprentice's eye a long moment. 'Have you ever seen the dead walk?'

The question caught the apprentice completely off guard. The memory of that final ritual had haunted him for weeks, the image of the dead man crawling and clawing through the dirt towards him. He could almost still feel its cold grasp as it seized his leg. He shuddered and pushed the thought away.

Without instruction, his face twisted into a bemused look and he shook his head. 'That is not possible, my lord. The dead do not walk.'

'Well there are men who claim they have,' replied Alfric, deadly serious. The chancellor studied the apprentice closely, staring into his eyes, searching for some falsehood. 'Warriors of Arnar have claimed they were attacked in the High Passes by dead men — the same passes where your master was conducting research. Two lords have travelled south to accuse the College of sorcery, claiming to have found *your* encampment, and they have evidence of the College's presence. Rodrik, you have the book?'

'I do, my lord. The council has examined it briefly,' Rodrik said, his voice shaking, but not as violently as Duncan's hands. What was happening? How could he be answering Alfric, his voice speaking without his control?

'Let us see it,' said the chancellor.

Rodrik produced a large leather-bound book and the apprentice's stomach knotted at the sight of it.

Eldrick's grimoire.

'Those same lords found this book, and the tales they tell of what they discovered with it are truly terrible.' The chancellor began to pace, his voice menacingly low. 'Not only do they claim to have seen the dead walk, but to have found evidence of fell happenings — foul rituals — and they talk of a terrible madness that makes beasts of men. I saw one of these beasts, one of these Cursed Ones, with my own eyes, and they tell me this evil is spreading across the north. Now, Apprentice... Duncan was it?'

The apprentice nodded, his hands cold and clammy, and his eyes bulging as he watched the chancellor pacing slowly, drawing closer and closer to where he sat, looming before the chair where his bound foot lay perched on a pillow.

'Listen closely, Apprentice Duncan. These men travelled a very long way to speak with our king and have levelled these *accusations* at the College, knowing full well what that means. There have already been attacks on College members in the north as a result of all this, and the people demand vengeance. The cursed creature brought before us is the *son* of one of these lords, and they rightfully demand anyone with any connection to this be swiftly met with the king's justice.' The chancellor stopped beside Duncan's wounded foot and he instinctively leaned away. 'And it looks like they mean *you*.'

CHAPTER FIFTEEN

An Instrument of Darkness

The apprentice had no reply, he merely opened and closed his mouth like a fish out of water.

Beware, apprentice; they seek to place blame on your head, whispered the voice. *Deny it all.*

'Now,' Alfric said, resuming his predatory pacing. The casual nonchalance in his stride belied the steely conviction in his eyes. He meant to find the truth in all this, and he'd tear apart anyone who stood in his way. 'If you want to live, you will tell me exactly what your master was doing up in the High Passes. Now, you tell me, and speak true — have you ever seen the dead walk?'

Again, Duncan spoke without meaning to, twitching slightly as he fought to close his mouth. 'I would not lie to you, my lord. I saw no such thing. But there is something I must tell you.'

Chancellor Alfric paused at that and the eyes of the gathered councillors, guards, noblemen and Master Luthor all bored into him. Bracing himself against the onslaught, he let the words out, relenting and resigning his will.

'I think my worst fears may have come to pass.' His head shook, a display of sadness he wasn't sure he felt. 'In truth, I had no stomach for my master's work. I was unable to watch his dissections. It was wrong, carving up dead men even in the pursuit of knowledge — it was against the gods. Truda took my place instead, and I had no part in it. My master was most disappointed with me; furious, in fact. But there is more. He was not himself, and I feared his mind was slipping. I saw his research and was forced to study his work. He would conduct strange experiments on the dead. He planned strange rituals and magic.' He fought to assert control over his body, over his tongue, horrified at the words coming out of his mouth. They were all lies, such terrible lies, but he was forced into the background, watching on, paralysed in his own mind.

'I argued with Eldrick and said I would have no part in his plans, that they were not just against the laws of this realm, but against the laws of the gods themselves. When I refused him, he attacked me in a blind rage. He pushed me, and that is the truth of how I broke my leg. He... he dismissed me back to the College and threatened that if I revealed his work or what he had done to me he would have me cast from the College, or worse.'

'By the gods,' exclaimed Councillor Uriah.

'Indeed,' murmured Merwyl. 'This is dark news.'

'What of the others?' demanded Rodrik. 'What was their part?'

Duncan's shoulders shrugged. 'Master Logan and Truda had no objections. They merely watched as he cast me away.' The apprentice watched the shock twist the features of the councillor's faces, several shaking their heads and glancing at each other in disbelief. The room slipped into a stunned silence.

Chancellor Alfric stared at Duncan. 'You would swear this to the gods?'

'I swear it's the truth,' he replied, returning the chancellor's glare despite screaming on the inside. This was not the truth! This was a barefaced lie, a cluster of evil untruths mixed with enough fact that even he would have trouble unravelling the fiction from the tale. He hadn't approved of his master's experiments, but he would never claim Eldrick had hurt him, or that he had cast him out.

The chancellor turned to Rodrik. 'What do you make of this?'

Rodrik considered the apprentice carefully. 'The boy seems to be telling the truth.' There were slow nods of agreement from several of the councillors.

Alfric threw another piercing look at Duncan. 'I agree,' he said after a long pause.

'I immediately move to have Master Eldrick cast from this College, his actions are unspeakable!' shouted Councillor Caleb, leaping to his feet. 'His actions are in no way sanctioned by this council.'

'I second that!' shouted Sareb. 'And Logan and his apprentice too. We cannot have such a rogues in our midst. These crimes cannot be condoned by this College.'

This was for the best, apprentice, the whisper assured him as the council erupted in heated debate. *Do you not see? There was no other way. They wanted your head; your life was forfeit. We must keep the secrets safe. Say nothing and live.*

The apprentice shook violently as the presence eased away from him and he returned to the forefront of his consciousness. Nobody noticed though, consumed as they were with damning his masters and his friend. He felt sick in the pit of his belly. What had he done?

Amongst the frenzied shouts, the chancellor spoke quietly with Councillor Rodrik, and the occasional glance was thrown in Duncan's direction. Luthor watched on from the gallery, his face still a mask of grave concern. He managed a thin smile and nodded at Duncan, a gesture meant to reassure him after what he had just done. If only Luthor knew the truth of it. He had lied to the council, to the chancellor, to the king. He was a dead man if they ever discovered the truth. Panic gripped him, squeezing the air from his chest. What would happen when his master returned? Had Eldrick already been taken to a dungeon or cell somewhere, this meeting meant to serve as his trial?

'Councillors,' Duncan said as loudly as he could. No one heard him. He shouted again and slowly the din fell away and attention returned to him once more. 'I apologise, but what is to become of Master Eldrick upon his return?'

Alfric frowned at Duncan then glanced at Rodrik. 'He doesn't know?'

Rodrik shook his head. 'I haven't told them.'

'Know what?' demanded Merwyl.

A pregnant silence hung over the council chambers.

'They found no one alive at the campsite,' Alfric told him. 'All dead.'

There were gasps from members of the council.

'All dead...' Duncan repeated as the shock of the news hit him like a landslide. His master was dead, and Logan... and Truda. All gone.

His stomach churned. He had just dishonoured their memories with his words, and all to save himself. Tears stung his eyes, blurring his vision as the councillors murmured amongst themselves.

'What will become of me?' Duncan murmured, holding back his grief.

'Will the crown be pursuing its justice on this young man, since the others cannot answer for their crimes?' asked Merwyl.

The chancellor considered the question for what felt like hours, Duncan's stomach slowly rising with every passing moment.

'It will be decided by the king,' replied Alfric finally. 'But I think the boy speaks the truth, and my word has weight with his majesty. He may be of some use in unravelling all this, and he may be our only hope of curing the curse. He must be placed under watch for his own protection, of course. I must insist that the king's own guard be assigned to him.' He turned back to the council. 'He is our *only* witness, to prove both the crimes and your professed innocence. It is in all our interests to keep him safe until the king decides otherwise.'

'As you command, lord chancellor,' Merwyl said with a bow.

'The king also commands this College to investigate the work of this rogue master. Councillor Rodrik has been appointed by the king to lead this and you will all report to him.'

'Of course, lord,' replied Rodrik, also with a bow.

'See that you send your best healers to examine this cursed man brought from the north. If the truth can be found and the man saved it will go far to proving your loyalty to the realm.' Alfric eyed each scholar at the table. 'Do you understand?'

Merwyl and Rodrik and all of those gathered nodded in unison.

'This most learned council is at your disposal, lord.' Councillor Merwyl almost grovelled, and despite his horror at his actions and his despair at the news of his masters and Truda, Duncan cringed. It pained him to see the College struck so low.

'Excellent,' said the chancellor. 'I expect your first report by the morning.'

'Of course, lord,' Rodrik agreed.

Lord Chancellor Alfric returned to his table and spoke quietly with the two other noblemen. One of them gestured to the nearby guards before rising to his feet. Two warriors approached Duncan and he shrank back, realising what they were doing, their mail and weapons rattling with every step as they descended upon him. His heart hammered as the pair flanked his seat and another three warriors moved to wait by the chamber doors.

Satisfied, the chancellor and the nobles departed the council chamber with their remaining guards, Alfric throwing another long look at the apprentice as he strode past. The doors closed heavily and plunged the council chamber in silence as all present digested what they had just heard.

'What will become of me,' asked the apprentice in a meek voice.

'Well if it were up to me, I'd cast their accomplice out!' Councillor Sareb snarled, putting voice to his disbelief of Duncan's story. 'By the gods, what were you and your colleagues playing at? You have brought the king's displeasure down on *our* heads, and now they will be poking around, investigating any scholar working on First Sons' texts, looking for renegade fools like Eldrick.'

'No one has said anything of the kind,' argued Merwyl.

Sareb slammed his hand down on the table. 'It's a damn disgrace! Putting all I have worked for in jeopardy!' He shook his head. 'This is all we need. If it were up to me –'

'Well it's not up to you, Sareb,' Merwyl snapped. Duncan was numb, only half listening as they debated his future, despite their inability to make any decisions about it. He was at the mercy of the king now.

'I don't believe a thing he says,' sneered Sareb. He levelled a finger at the apprentice. 'You claim you weren't involved, an apprentice not involved in his masters studies, rubbish. I for one think you a liar. A damn liar.'

'Easy Sareb,' cautioned Merwyl.

Councillor Sareb's face purpled. 'This crippled bastard, is a disgrace,' he bellowed. The apprentice shrunk away from his words. 'He should be cast out. He will bring ruin to this College.'

'Well the chancellor commands we keep him,' said Merwyl, rising to his feet.

'Well I'll have nothing to do with this. I've spoken my mind, you know what I think on this. Do as you will, but I don't trust him, and don't come crying to me when the people turn on us for this.' Sareb rose to his feet, 'If this is the only matter we are discussing, I will take my leave.'

'Sareb...'

The Councillor stormed off leaving an empty chair at the council table.

Merwyl stared after Sareb with a frown and a slight shake of his head.

A long and awkward silence reigned over the council chamber. Eventually it was the Elected Speaker, Merwyl, who broke the silence. He cleared his throat, drawing Duncan's eyes to his face. 'You were close to finishing your apprenticeship with Master Eldrick, if I recall our previous meeting?'

'Indeed, sir,' whispered the apprentice, shaken by Councillor Sareb's outburst. How many others in the College would share his sentiments? 'He had already presented me with my grimoire. I was hoping he would sign my apprenticeship as complete upon his return.'

Merwyl glanced at his notes. 'Who were your previous masters?'

'Master Bjarl and Master Luthor,' replied the apprentice.

'So, you were a Hart's step from being appointed as a master. Pity...' Merwyl shook his head and the apprentice blinked in confusion.

'Pity?' he asked, already fearing he knew the answer.

'This council cannot grant you the title of master without the third and final apprenticeship signed. It is a pity, as you had all but completed it. There is also the matter of Eldrick's actions to be considered. He has been cast from our halls and the apprentice of an outcast, albeit a dead one, cannot be made a master...'

'But—'

'I'm sorry, apprentice. The tenets of the College must be adhered to.'

Seething anger rose in Duncan, white hot and boiling. He clenched his teeth before he said something stupid.

They deny you the title of master, which is yours by right, hissed the voice. *They fear you, they fear your knowledge, your power. You saw the secrets with your own eyes, you will be master of them all, this I promise, apprentice.*

In the gallery, Luthor came to his feet. 'Is there nothing to be done for the lad, in light of the current situation?'

Merwyl shot him a dark look. 'I think I speak for all the gathered councillors when I say it would not be wise to appoint this young man to the place of a master amid such dire controversy.'

'He's lucky to not be in chains,' said Rodrik, and there was a murmur of agreement around the council table.

'Please,' Duncan pleaded. 'Don't make me start over.'

'I'd take him on, should the council agree?' Luthor offered, and the apprentice let a tiny flame of hope flare in his chest. 'He could study under me, and should he be acquitted by the king, I could assess his performance and sign off his apprenticeship.'

'Perhaps,' ventured Councillor Uriah. 'He could work under Master Luthor and as the chancellor suggested, he may be of assistance unravelling his previous master's work.'

'We will vote on it,' Merwyl announced. 'All in favour... and against... The motion is passed five to three. Apprentice Duncan you will continue your studies under Master Luthor and assist him in any way you can with Eldrick's work.'

The apprentice looked up at Luthor, but his expression was unreadable. It was a last ditch attempt to save him and he was grateful for it, but he wondered what Luthor really thought about once again being saddled with him, especially now he sat at the centre of such a terrible controversy.

For a long while, the only sound in the chamber was the scratching of the scribe's quill on parchment.

'There is also the matter of the creature brought to the court,' said Rodrik, breaking the silence.

A wave of fatigue crashed into Duncan and he slumped back against his chair, his hand slipping from the arm rest as he fought to sit up straight before his elders.

'Councillors,' Luthor interrupted. 'It seems my new apprentice is fading. If you have no further need of him, might I suggest he return to his chambers to continue his recovery?'

'Yes, yes,' waved Merwyl. 'We will send for you if we have need of him further.'

Luthor descended from the gallery and approached the apprentice, throwing an uncertain glance at the warriors standing by the young man's shoulders. He leaned close and spoke as he helped Duncan to stand and arrange himself on his crutches. 'You are dismissed, apprentice. Return to your quarters and get some rest. I have a few matters to discuss with the council. I will send for you in the morning.'

'Yes master,' replied the apprentice weakly. Duncan turned and hobbled towards the heavy doors of the council chamber, leaving his new master alone on the floor of the chamber. His new guards followed him, their presence immediately unsettling as they hovered just behind him and matched his pace.

The council door closed behind him. He couldn't process it all now, his mind was a mess. He concentrated instead on keeping his balance as he once again slowly limped along the long corridor stretching ahead of him.

He was so tired, and deep inside, he harboured a growing fear for his sanity. That cursed voice whispering in his thoughts could not be normal, nor could it be real. A cold shiver rushed through him and the shadows flickered at the edge of his vision.

He needed rest, that was all. He would be fine in the morning.

Despite the all-consuming numbness in his body, his leg throbbed with each laboured step. His ears were full of the thudding sound of his pulse, his skin tingling with shock from hearing of the demise of his friends and the evil they had unleashed. He felt their loss as keenly as the pain in his ankle, but for Truda most of all. Tears pooled in his eyes as he realised he would never see her again. Anger bubbled in him too, fury at seeing his apprenticeship terminated and the station of master denied him after all his hard work. He had done *nothing* wrong, and he reeled from Councillor Sareb's harsh words.

But he was right, he thought. *It was all lies.*

CHAPTER SIXTEEN

The Prisoner

Water dripped from the ceiling into little puddles on the stone floor.

It must be raining, thought Arnulf as he sat on a stool with his fur cloak pulled around him. The cell was cold and damp and smelled of wet stone and piss. He reckoned he must be some distance underground, and yet, the rainwater still found its way through the earth to drip from the roof above.

Hafgan sat dutifully opposite his cell, insisting on remaining by his side while he sat in the damp confines of the stinking cell. A guard stood nearby and kept a watchful eye on them both while leaning lazily on his spear, he had tried to refuse Hafgan at first, but the big warrior growled a threat and the guard had thought better of it and let him stay. So far, the man had ignored any attempt at conversation. Hafgan had begun whistling a tune to break the oppressive quiet, but Arnulf had silenced him with a glare.

Whether his choice of song was intentional or not, Arnulf could not bear to listen to it. It was a tune Aeslin had loved — it was her song — he was still reeling from the loss of his wife and it cut deeply to hear it without her here. His mind wandered to dark places as he sat in the dank gloom, places of mourning he had dragged himself free from and had no wish to return to. He had long since calmed down — the chill of a gaol had that effect on a man — and he sat brooding, regretting his actions in the Throne Hall. He fought a shiver and tightened his cloak about him.

'It's a good omen that the water drips, lord,' said Hafgan,

breaking the silence.

'Doesn't feel like a good omen to me,' grumbled Arnulf.

'The land above has water. This is good even if the cell weeps for you. It wants you to be free.'

Arnulf glowered at him. 'You're a superstitious bastard, you know that?' he leaned back against the wet stone of the wall and sighed. 'So, they took the book? It was our only proof and we let it go.'

'Aye, lord, and that foul dagger too.' Hafgan shrugged. 'We could hardly defy the king though.'

'They will return it to the College no doubt for *examination*,' Arnulf sneered the last word.

'We still have this.' Hafgan glanced at the guard whose attention was on something far off down the corridor, then reached inside his coat and eased the corner of a blood-stained journal into view.

Arnulf's heart lifted. 'The journal!' he exclaimed. It was the very one they had found upon the ritual altar up in the ruins.

Hafgan smiled and nodded. 'We still have some proof yet, lord.'

The whine and boom of a door opening and closing reverberated from above and the sound of approaching footsteps echoed down the narrow stone passageway leading to his cell. Both he and Hafgan straightened, craning their necks to see who it might be.

The guard snapped to attention as King Rhagnal ducked through the low entrance to the passageway, and Hafgan quickly rose to his feet and bowed his head. A fur cloak adorned Rhagnal's wide shoulders, and he seemed to fill the narrow passage.

It was dark down here, the only light coming from a crackling torch ensconced on the wall, and the king's face appeared mostly in shadow. He nodded to the guard and then to Hafgan before he turned to regard Arnulf inside the gaol cell, his features stern, almost chiselled from stone in the flickering light.

Arnulf slipped from the stool to kneel on the wet flagstones, his head bowed.

'Lord Arnulf,' said the king.

'My king,' replied Arnulf without looking up, a wave of apprehension and shame washing over him.

'I do not like having to imprison my sworn lords behind bars.

What do you have to say for yourself?'

'I am sorry, my king. You have my most sincere apologies. My behaviour was inexcusable.'

'Quite so,' Rhagnal agreed, his voice gruff against the cold stone. 'Look at me, Arnulf.'

Arnulf raised his gaze and ruefully met his king's eyes. Rhagnal studied him a moment and sighed.

'Get up and stand before me, man.'

Arnulf did as he was told, clasping his hands behind his back, standing firm and tall.

'I take no pleasure in seeing you in here,' Rhagnal insisted, casting a look around the damp cell. 'I am sorry for your family... for your son. It is a terrible thing that has befallen you, and I understand your need for vengeance. It will be dealt with. We have already sent word north to ask for more news and to extend my full support to the lords.'

'And what of the College?' Arnulf could not resist asking.

'They will be dealt with also,' the king replied, the lines of his face hardening. 'It must be said Arnulf — if you ever dare threaten anyone in my court again, I will send you down here to rot. Do you understand? You will stay away from the College. I do not want to hear that you have taken it upon yourself to exact some kind of justice on folk there without proper process.'

'I understand, my king.' Arnulf lowered his gaze again and clenched his jaw. He was not happy about leaving his retribution in another's hands.

'Your friend Fergus spoke highly of you and has begged me to hear you, so I will. You will issue apologies as and when directed.'

'Yes, sire,' agreed Arnulf.

'You have been down here long enough, I think. Though before I have you released, I want your word that there will be no repeat of this, and that you will not lay a finger on Rodrik or any other member of the College.'

Arnulf chewed at the inside of his lip. It galled him, and went against all his instincts and honour, but he would obey his king. 'I swear it.'

King Rhagnal regarded him a moment and then gestured to the guard to unlock the cell door. The king stepped back and as the guard produced a large ring of heavy keys, Rhagnal threw a glance at Hafgan. 'Is this your man?'

'He is, sire,' Arnulf nodded. Despite himself, he itched to be free of the cell and its stink. He wanted a hot meal and a bath to wash away the grime. He wanted the warmth of a fire and to be away from the drip, drip, drip of the ceiling.

Rhagnal nodded at the big warrior. 'I remember you from my hall. Remind me of your name?'

'Hafgan, my king.'

'Ah, yes. Your loyalty is an asset,' remarked the king. 'To remain by your lord's side, even in this dark place, is a thing of honour.' The cell door creaked open and the king made room for Arnulf to exit into the passageway. 'Come, Arnulf; walk with me.'

King Rhagnal led them along the dark corridor and began to ascend a set of winding stone stairs, worn in places from countless footfalls. Torches burned on the walls at regular intervals, but not so close as to properly light the narrow tunnels. They had not been lit when Arnulf had been brought down here, and he suspected they were only lit for Rhagnal's benefit and not something that was maintained.

Two of the king's bodyguards met them at the stairs, famed huscarls, who led them up the stairs and into another set of winding passages. Hafgan walked behind the huscarls, seeming to fill the passage with his large frame, stooping under the low stone ceiling in the narrower parts.

'There are many of these stone tunnels beneath my halls,' Rhagnal told them, and Arnulf wondered if he spoke simply to fill the silence, or because he actually wanted him to know the curiosity of the place. It seemed odd to converse so casually with a released prisoner, but who was he to judge. 'No one knows exactly who built them, or when, but they are surely ancient. They were here long before Arn built his great hall here. Incredible, aren't they?'

'It is,' agreed Arnulf, glancing at what little he could see in the sparse light.

'Still, it is not a kingly place. I rarely venture down here. It's like a crypt,' he said after a moment. 'Fergus tells me you are from an ancient and honourable line, Lord Arnulf. Lord of the Motte, he tells me. I have read of your Motte — the un-breachable fortress. They say it never fell during the Forging.'

'That *was* true, my king.' His voice wavered, and his heart skipped, weighed down with sorrow and shame. 'But insane monsters did breach its walls, and now my halls are burnt to the ground. I have failed my fathers.'

'No, Arnulf. Your walls held in the end. The Banners of Arnar never fell over the Motte. That is how the chroniclers will write it in the Sagas and histories.'

Arnulf smiled weakly. How many times had the truth been bent or twisted to suit those writing the histories?

'Will you return north and exact your vengeance on these dead things haunting your lands? I will ensure you have enough men.'

'No, my king, I cannot.' Arnulf shook his head. 'I will remain in the city to see out this business with the College. And I must find a way to save my son.'

'If anyone can help him it will be the College, the very people who appear to have wronged you. They alone understand what happened out there, and they are your only hope. *Our* only hope if what you say is true and these creatures stalk the north.

Arnulf scowled, forcing himself to keep walking when all he wanted to do was spin around and confront the king. The College were nothing more than self-serving elites who spent their time with their noses buried in books and meddling in things best left alone.

Rhagnal glanced at Arnulf and registered his visible displeasure. 'The College are not evil, Arnulf. This rogue and his fellow renegade scholars — their kind are reviled by the College. The council will not allow this kind of work to continue. I will see to it that any involved are punished and cast out, you have my word.'

'But, sire —'

'No, Arnulf,' Rhagnal made a sharp gesture with his hand and cut Arnulf off before he could build a head of steam. 'I understand your hate, but the College is *needed*. I cannot have trouble here, not now. They are also *my* only hope for answers to this terrible plague.' He scoffed. 'Plague, they are calling it. Have you seen it out there? It's beyond grim, and I need the College on my side to fight this horror. I cannot have my one of my lords threatening them or spilling blood within their walls in the name of vengeance. I need them.'

Arnulf frowned, his jaw tightening, but he nodded, resigning to his king's wishes. A sense defeat clawed his heart.

'I will make sure everything that can be done to help your lad is done,' the king assured him, as if that might repair the damage done.

The ancient stone passageway ended with a wooden door and one of the huscarls moved ahead to open it for the king. Light spilled into the passage as the door creaked open and they emerged into a richly furnished hallway somewhere within King Rhagnal's hall.

'You are welcome here,' said the king, turning to him as a huscarl closed the door. 'As long as you are tempered and act with honour, you may stay as my guest. But you will stay away from the College. I forbid you to set foot there, do you understand?'

Arnulf grimaced. 'Yes, my king.'

'Now, I have much to attend to but I will no doubt see you again very soon. Go and get some rest. I will have word brought to you if we discover anything further.'

The king turned and left, walking away along the hallway, trailed by his huscarls.

Arnulf watched him go, frustration welling in his chest. He would not disobey his king's command, but he would seek his vengeance. This he swore.

CHAPTER SEVENTEEN

The Sleepwalker

'Where in Varg's fucking name is he?' Wilhelm muttered, staring up the corridor. It was dark, and he had no idea what the hour was, but he was pretty sure he should have been relieved by now. He yawned. 'If that bastard's still asleep, I'll have his balls nailed to a tree.'

He stood guard outside the chamber of the College apprentice who had been up in the passes, participating in some sort of fell magic. But as the dark hours of the night passed him by, he grew weary, standing in the hallway half awake, half in a snoozing reverie.

Wilhelm missed his old friend Ox. The little man was sick with the plague and lay dying in a cot. Last Wilhelm heard he was still alive, but he feared his old friend would not last much longer. Wrapped up in blankets was no way for a warrior to die. Wilhelm was greatly saddened to think of what was to come.

In Ox's place, Lord Warrick had sent some young idiot to stand guard with him. The lad was called Edgar, and so far he'd proven himself totally incompetent, which was to be expected from the son of a soft, rich bastard. The boy wouldn't stand a chance if he found himself in a scrap, and if Wilhelm had a say in it, he'd be nowhere near the fool if it ever came to that. It was Edgar he waited on now, and the little shit had left him standing in the dark far longer than he should have.

A loud thump broke through his thoughts. He blinked the drowsiness from his eyes and threw look along the corridor. It was quiet, empty. Furniture crashed behind him and he spun around to look at the door. The sound had come from within the apprentice's chambers.

'Shit,' he hissed as a panic flashed through him, his hands tightening around his spear. Had some intruder snuck inside? Had someone gotten past him unnoticed?

He grabbed at the door handle without knocking and pushed. It opened, revealing a dark room, lit only by faint moonlight from an uncovered window.

Wilhelm sighed with relief. There was no intruder – it was only the College lad stumbling around in the dark.

'You alright in there, boy?' Wilhelm whispered from the doorway. The apprentice stopped and turned a shadowed face towards him. His posture seemed strange, all hunched over with his head tilted to one side. 'Everything alright, lad?'

The apprentice did not reply. He just stood there, still as stone, as if frozen in place.

Wilhelm leaned back a little, frowning at the boy's face. His features were hidden in deep shadow, distorted by the weak light from the hallway. Wilhelm plucked a torch from a sconce beside the door and lifted it to spill ruddy light into the chamber, illuminating the apprentice's face.

His eyes were barely more than slits, his jaw slack and his mouth hanging open.

Wilhelm waved a hand in front of the boy's face. 'Dammit,' he muttered under his breath. 'The fool's asleep.'

It was said to be unwise to wake a sleepwalker, but he had to do something to stop the boy crashing around his room.

He raised his voice slightly but not so loud as to wake him. 'Go back to bed, lad... Go on, off to bed with you.'

The apprentice did not move, and stared back with half closed eyes. The tiny sliver that Wilhelm could see was white, as if his eyes had rolled back in his head. Wilhelm shivered and stood for a long moment in the doorway, wondering what to do next.

The apprentice lurched forwards and began to stagger unsteadily towards his bed, his head hung low. Wilhelm narrowed his eyes against the gloom and noticed the boy seemed to be walking unaided.

That's gonna hurt when the poor bugger wakes up, he thought with a grimace.

Satisfied there was no danger to the lad, he slowly pulled the door closed and stood for a moment, listening. The still quiet of night had returned to the corridor; only the guttering torch could be heard. The guardsman shivered again, unsettled at the oppressive silence and his peculiar encounter with his sleeping charge. He glanced down the passageway, suddenly very keen to be away from this dark hallway.

It was not long before a flicker of light illuminated the far end of the corridor and the sound of footsteps echoed against the walls.

'About bloody time,' he snapped as Edgar appeared.

'Why, am I late?' replied the young guardsman in an innocent voice.

'You know damn well you are,' snarled Wilhelm. 'If it happens again you'll be sorry, you mark my words.'

'Easy there,' said Edgar, raising his hands. 'Don't be like that. It can't be much past midnight, surely. Must just be the hours stretching long and slow. I swear it.'

He would have liked to punch his smirking face into a bloody pulp right there, but he knew this wet piece of shit wasn't worth it. Instead, he scowled and held his tongue.

Wilhelm jerked his thumb at the door. 'I just caught him walking about, asleep on his feet. Keep your ear out for him in case he does it again.'

'Sure will,' replied Edgar, yawning as he sat on a stool by the door.

'Don't you be falling asleep on guard, lad,' Wilhelm warned. 'It's a dozen lashes if you're caught. Not nice, I promise you.'

Edgar scoffed at him and leaned back against the wall. 'You get on your way. I've got this.'

Wilhelm cast a sour glance at the young guardsman. He had his doubts, but to hell with it. It wasn't his problem. He just wanted something to eat and some sleep. 'Midnight, my arse,' he muttered as he stalked off along the dark corridor. Weary, footsore and heavy eyed, he was just glad to be done for the night.

***

Beams of sunlight streamed into his chambers, the bright light finally dragging Duncan free of sleep. It had been another restless night cursed with more terrible dreams.

He vividly recalled the nightmares, filled with the shambling dead and plains littered with endless bodies, strange skies overhead and sinister monoliths in the distance. He had dreamt of the council too, and their leering, disgusted faces — Councillor Sareb bellowing another savage rebuke at him, denying him, mocking him. The memory of the council was a fresh wound, and anger bubbled within him, threatening to boil over whenever he thought of Councillor Sareb's spiteful glare and the silent judgement of the others.

In another nightmare, he sat at a macabre feast, eating unspeakable things, but it too began to fade into obscurity. The last thing he remembered was Truda, her face dissolving before his eyes as the morning sunlight shone through his window.

The apprentice looked around his chambers. It had quickly become a cluttered mess since his return. It was cold and his breath misted slightly. He pulled the blanket over his head to shield his bleary eyes from the brightness, and sighed.

Would he really never see Truda, or indeed any of them, again? He'd thought her pretty, though other young men at the College did not seem to regard her as a great beauty, and he would miss her face, her wry smile as she teased him. He'd never told Truda of his feelings for her, never entirely certain he had any until recently, but he suspected she had her suspicions — the way she used to toy with him, it was almost like she knew before he did. There would never be a chance to tell her now. She was dead, and he was full of hopeless regret.

He winced as he tried to move his leg. A vicious pain assaulted him and his ankle throbbed. He bent forward to examine it, but was dismayed to find the bound splints looked disturbed and the bandages were somehow dirty. The ever-present pain had intensified this morning, only then remembering it had just been rebroken the previous day. Duncan groaned, waiting for the throbbing to ease. He was however glad to finally be back in his own bed, for whatever small comfort it gave him.

Duncan licked his lips and tasted the strange, bitter tang of iron. He cursed and sat up. 'Not again!' he groaned.

He touched his nose and examined his fingers, gasping at the sticky film of blood on his skin. Not just a little — he was practically painted with it. This was no small nosebleed.

He threw back the covers. There was blood everywhere; his

hands, down the front of his shirt, all over the blankets.

A cold panic clutched his heart.

Was he sick?

It had been impossible to look away from the corpses he had seen on his journey to the city, hard not to notice the ghastly, fatal effects of the plague. The blood loss was incredible, the terrifying crimson flood that signalled the death throes staining the faces and bodies of the folk unfortunate enough to catch it.

The realisation slowly dawned on him — he wasn't dead. From what he had learnt, the blood came in the final stages, and he had been suffering these nosebleeds for days, if not weeks. If he truly had the blood plague, he would already be a corpse. He didn't even feel sick — quite the opposite in fact. Other than his dark mood from the events of the previous day and the pain and intermittent nausea from his throbbing leg, he felt much better this morning.

It was just another nosebleed, albeit worse than usual. He peeled off his shirt and tossed the bloody ruin on the floor. How had this much blood come flooding out while he slept? Gripping his crutches, he pulled himself up from the bed and tottered over to a side board, filling a basin with fresh water from a jug. Balancing on his good leg and precariously touching the big toe of his injured foot to the floor, he began to wash the blood away, the water turned crimson almost instantly.

A ghastly mask stared back at him from the surface of a dirty mirror on the wall. Most of the sticky, half dried blood clung to the skin around his mouth, and a fair amount had stained his teeth. It was caked in the strands of his pale thin hair, and he had little choice but to lean over the basin and plunge his face into the water, scrubbing hard with a cloth to dislodge the gore.

He would have to dispose of the soiled shirt and bed covers without anyone seeing them. Folk would all too readily assume he was sick if they saw the blood. It would do him no good for rumours to spread, especially given his current situation with the council.

A knock at the door made him look up with a start.

'One moment! I'm coming,' he called, frantically hobbling back across the room to stuff bloodied clothes and blankets into a bag. He tossed a clean cloth over the basin — he would have to empty that later — then limped on his crutches towards the door.

***

Master Luthor strode along the corridor towards the apprentice's chambers, catching sight of the guard outside the door. The man sat slumped on the stool and looked to be dozing.

Luthor gave the leg of the guard's stool a light kick and the guard shook himself awake. 'Wil—,' the guard muttered, sitting up and rubbing his eyes. He cast around, then looked up at Luthor. 'Oh, hello.'

'Are you supposed to be asleep on duty?' Luthor asked with a frown.

'Wasn't asleep,' replied the guard.

Luthor raised a dubious brow at the guard, a young lad barely old enough to grow a beard, then turned to knock loudly on the apprentice's door. A muffled call came from within.

Good. The lad's awake.

As he waited for his new apprentice to answer, he noticed a dark smear on the door, but before he could examine it further, the door opened.

'Apprentice Duncan, good morning,' said Luthor with a smile.

'Master,' nodded the apprentice. Duncan stood leaning on his crutches, sweating from exertion and bare-chested, his face still wet from his morning wash. Luthor blinked rapidly, shocked by the gaunt and bony young man he saw before him.

'I trust you slept well,' he asked, looking past the lad into his chambers.

'Much better, master,' replied Duncan. He smiled weakly. 'It's good to be back in my own bed — good to be back at the College, to be honest. I've had quite enough of bumping around in carts and sea-boats to last a lifetime.'

Luthor laughed. 'I can imagine. You look better than you did yesterday, but you're still a little pale. Are you sure you're alright?' Luthor leaned forward, his attention drawn to a dark mark on the young man's neck. 'Wait, is that blood?'

'I had a nosebleed,' he said, wiping his neck and glancing away, avoiding Luthor's gaze. 'Nothing to worry about. It happens quite a bit. I don't really want folk knowing though; there's a lot of fear in the air. Anything to do with blood will send folk running.'

Luthor wrestled away the prickle of apprehension that slivered over his skin at the thought of sickness, his scholarly judgement eventually overruling impulsive alarm. The lad was right; if the blood was due to sickness he would be dead already. *Just a nose-bleed then.* 'Aye, probably for the best,' he replied. 'Are you well enough to get started? We've got some work to do.'

'Yes master. I think work will do me good.' Duncan nodded, offering another weak smile.

'Good, get dressed then. The dawn is growing old and the council will soon be asking for a report.'

'Yes master, I will just be a moment.' The apprentice moved away, letting the door swing closed as he limped back into his chambers. As the door shut Luthor realised the smear on the timber was likely blood.

He turned to the guard. 'Did the lad leave his room in the night?'

'No,' the young guard replied, hastily shaking his head. 'I took over at midnight and didn't hear a peep from him all night.'

Luthor regarded him doubtfully but nodded. The fool had likely been asleep. The door opened again and the apprentice hopped out into the corridor, aided by his crutches, now dressed in a plain robe.

'My apologies, master. I am not as fast as I was, with this leg as it is.' Duncan did his best to keep up, and Luthor shortened his stride, keeping their pace leisurely as they made their way along the corridor. The guard trailed along behind at a slight distance.

'How is the leg feeling today, Duncan?' He glanced at him, watching him wince with each jolting step.

'Painful is one word for it,' Duncan ground out between clenched teeth. 'I have some hope now, though. It may yet heal. I was worried—it set awfully crooked while on the road. Thought I might be doomed to be a cripple. But still, with the god's luck...'

'Aye.' Luthor nodded.

His study chambers weren't far, located across a courtyard from the dormitory wing. There seemed less of the usual bustle around the College these days. The sickness in the city had changed the atmosphere—where groups of scholars had once stood conversing, now the corridors and open spaces seemed hauntingly empty. Folk scurried about nervously, keeping to themselves. Luthor led the apprentice past several scholars wearing strange hooked beak-like masks. He guessed they were students of Councillor Caleb, or at least subscribers of his fouled air theories.

The masks enclosed most of the face, the nose piece elongated and designed to be stuffed with sweet smelling medicinal herbs, tapered off into something resembling the beak of some grotesque carrion bird. Councillor Caleb espoused the notion that the herbs masked the foul air and kept the blood plague at bay. Folk were eager to take any precaution and the unsettling looking fashion had been taken up by many at the College.

Luthor pressed his lips into a line and shook his head. He had no idea if the masks helped, but they seemed an extreme measure based on little evidence. They emerged into the empty courtyard and he led the apprentice towards his door.

'It's been a while,' said Luthor over his shoulder.

'You're still working from the same rooms?' Duncan asked, pausing as his new master fiddled with the lock.

'Aye, lad.' Luthor shoved the door, cursing the stiff hinges under his breath. 'Not much changes around here.'

'Feels like coming home, master,' the apprentice said with a pained smile, hobbling inside. The guard followed them into a short hallway but remained by the entry, eyeing the apprentice as Luthor shut the door.

The porters had already been in, leaving several crates, sealed bags and sacks on the floor of his study.

'I hope it's all here, lad,' Luthor murmured, following Duncan up the hall and into the room. He perched his hands on his hips and surveyed the clutter. He'd requested the findings of Eldrick's expedition but was surprised at the sheer amount they had brought.

He turned to the apprentice and with a raised eyebrow. 'This may take some time.'

The apprentice limped between the crates, checking the contents of each, lifting a lid and peering inside. The crate was packed with wrapped items, specimens and relics no doubt. Duncan seemed to mutter as he made his way through the crates, as if shifting through his thoughts aloud, untangling memories to make sure everything was there. Luthor frowned and lowered himself into the high-backed chair behind his desk. He had known many men with that strange habit, but Duncan had not been one of them. The lad was not the same boy he had once known.

The apprentice leaned down to run a hand over the artefacts and ledgers, appearing to draw some comfort from the safe delivery of the familiar items, which he had no doubt kept safe for weeks during his journey south.

Duncan finally turned to Luthor. 'Hopefully it won't take too long, master. It all appears to be here, at least. Master Eldrick instructed me to check and catalogue every item we loaded... It was the last task he ever gave me.' The apprentice stood staring at the crates, a heavy silence stretching out between them. The apprentice looked lost and forlorn, Luthor felt for his new apprentice. He had never seen the lad so out of sorts. The recent news of his old master, and the fate of his colleagues, weighed heavy on him.

'I'm sorry about Eldrick... and the others,' ventured Luthor. 'Eldrick was a good man before...'

'You have nothing to be sorry for, master.' Duncan shook his head vigorously, as if shaking some dark memory clear of his eyes. 'I on the other hand could have done something... Something more to stop him, to reason...' He trailed off into silence.

'I doubt there was much you could have done, lad,' offered Luthor. 'It was fate. The gods spared *you*, sent *you* back. Maybe they have a design for you, lad. Maybe, Duncan, they let you return to help bring an end to the darkness Eldrick unleashed in the world.'

'Perhaps,' replied the apprentice distantly.

There was another pause. It seemed he would say nothing more.

'Well, I'm glad to have you back in my service. You were always a most apt pupil.'

'Thank you, master,' he replied, managing a smile.

Luthor regarded the stacked crates and bags of research, leaning an elbow on the arm of his chair and resting his chin on his palm. 'I don't know where to begin with all this.'

'Anywhere you like, master. I know where it's all packed.'

Luthor stroked his short-kept beard thoughtfully. Might as well dive straight in with both hands. No point nibbling at the edges. They simply didn't have the time. 'Well, let's get to the heart of it. Start with this work using my translation, this Bone Ritual...'

CHAPTER EIGHTEEN

Plague's Toll

Wilhelm approached and stood to attention before his lord's desk while Lord Warrick sat in a high back chair, quill in hand, writing in a heavy bound ledger. Warrick cast a quick glance up from his work.

'Ah, Wilhelm,' he said, acknowledging the guardsman before returning his attention to the open ledger. Lord Warrick was younger than Wilhelm and kept his lean face clean shaven and his hair short, his leather tunic trimmed with fine knotwork stamped across the surface. Despite his relative youth, Lord Warrick carried an air of authority, every bit a lord and a man of renowned reputation as a warrior and as a leader of men.

As Warrick finished scribbling, Wilhelm glanced around the room. His lord's office was plain, though he kept many books and scrolls on shelves along the walls, as was expected of a man of learning, he supposed. Other than a silver wine goblet and a bear skin rug, the only decorations were the sigils on the wall. The royal sigil of Varg's wolf head, the same image emblazoned on his own shield, hung behind Warrick's desk along with his own personal crest of a coiled eel. The two sigils were made of carved and lacquered wood and hung on polished oak mounts.

'Sorry to disturb you, lord. My report would have been earlier but I... overslept.'

'Not like you, Wilhelm,' Warrick said without looking up.

'It was a late night, lord,' replied Wilhlem with a scowl. 'That damn fool Edgar took his time relieving me. I got little rest.'

Warrick set down his quill and offered his sworn man a thin

smile. 'And, how is the young lad getting on? Does he attend his duties well?'

'Barely, lord.' Wilhelm wondered how best to convey Edgar's performance to Lord Warrick. Pampered little shit might cover it, but spoiled brat fit the bill as well. 'He's a wet piece of shit, if I may beg your pardon.'

Warrick chuckled and shook his head. 'I don't doubt it. I put him with you for good reason. If any of my men can make a warrior of the pup, it's you.'

Wilhelm managed a smile in return. It was a compliment, but it still left him saddled with an idiot. 'I will endure, lord.'

'Good man. I'll leave him in your capable hands. How are things at the College? They are making us welcome, I hope?'

'Yes, lord. A bunch of gutless pen-pushers though—I doubt they could lift a sword between them. They quiver to even look at us. But they have been amiable.'

'And the boy?' Warrick's brow rose slowly and Wilhelm wondered what the lord truly thought of the lad who had returned from the north. Did he believe all that Lords Arnulf and Fergus had said in the Throne Hall? It was difficult to reconcile, yet they had evidence, and the lord's son… He had become a beast. That was impossible to ignore, and Wilhelm did not imagine his lord or king would do so.

'He's been quiet, under guard night and day. He's just some cripple, lord. He doesn't get up to much.'

'Ensure it stays that way,' said Warrick seriously. He picked up his quill and scratched at the ledger again.

'Aye, lord, it will be done.'

Warrick nodded. 'Any word on their progress, with the Cursed One, or the plague?'

'I'm not sure, lord, I'll keep an ear out.'

'I want to know as soon as something changes. That Councillor Rodrik reports to us directly, but I'd like my own set of eyes and ears about the place.' He kept his eyes on his work but shook his head. 'A warrior has honour, *that* I can trust. A scholar out to cover his own backside? Gods forgive me if I'm not overwhelmed with confidence. Just keep an eye on them down there.'

'Yes, lord.' Wilhelm shuffled his feet, his throat tightening a little. Did he dare ask after his sick comrade? 'I'll be glad when Ox is back to duty, lord. Have you heard how he fares?'

Warrick held his gaze for a good while, carefully laying the quill down. Eventually he sighed and looked away at the bookshelves. Wilhelm's stomach knotted.

'I am sorry, Wilhelm. I had word earlier this morning. Ox succumbed to the sickness in the night. He is with the gods.'

It was the news he had been dreading and it struck his heart like a hammer blow. He maintained his composure, gnawing at the back of his lip, and Lord Warrick's gaze became sympathetic. He knew his men. He knew the bond they shared.

'He was a good man, one of my best. I am sorry, Wilhelm; I know you were close.'

Wilhelm stood wordlessly, processing the news of his friend's fate.

'I shall send another man to command those stationed at the College,' Warrick offered, reaching for a leaf of parchment to write a message. 'Give you a few hours to yourself?'

Wilhelm steeled himself before answering. 'Thank you, lord, but that won't be necessary. He'd accuse me of skiving off if he were here. In any case, he's with Old Night and I have duties to attend to.'

Lord Warrick nodded. 'As you wish. Your fortitude serves you honourably in these dark days. We will raise a cup in his name in the hall tonight.'

Wilhelm nodded gratefully but found his tongue had become too thick in his mouth to form words.

'I've lost three men this week,' said Warrick, draining his goblet, then turning it absently on the desk. 'Many more are sick. Alethea is abed as we speak.'

'The princess?' That rocked Wilhelm from his grief. He stared at the lord, sure he had not heard right. Had she fallen ill while she walked the city streets, guarded by him and his men? Was it his fault? Should he have done more to keep her far from the hands of the infected? What-if's and should-have-done's tumbled through his head.

'Aye, the poor lass. She is a dear friend to me. The king is beside himself, of course. I fear the worst,' Warrick said gravely. 'I fear the palisades of the Citadel are no longer enough to keep this plague at bay. Unless the gods intervene, those "gutless pen-pushers" as you so eloquently described them could well be our only hope for a cure.'

Wilhelm had no reply, still reeling at the loss of his friend.

'And they must find it quickly,' continued Warrick. 'I fear the Lady Alethea does not have long if she has indeed fallen victim to this *plague*.' He almost spat the last word. 'You must keep the peace at the College until a cure is found. We can ill afford any more trouble.'

'Trouble, lord?' asked Wilhelm, slightly puzzled.

Warrick glanced at him with a frown 'I'm surprised you haven't heard. News reached us of a death at the College last night. I hoped you could look into it upon your return. Crowds are stirring up trouble outside the College too—word has spread that they had a hand in what is happening in the north and rightly or wrongly, folk are connecting that to the plague. We've sent the city guard to disperse them.'

'I go to sleep for a few hours and all this happens,' said Wilhelm. There had been nothing to report from his small corner of the College, other than the apprentice sleepwalking around his room. Yet apparently death stalked its halls. It must have happened on Edgar's watch, and there was no doubt the fool had slept through it. 'Is there anything you want me to do? Me and the lads could—'

'No, Wilhelm, your task remains; guard that apprentice and report back any news as I have asked.'

'It will be done, m'lord. I will ensure the boy is kept safe. Is that all, lord?'

Lord Warrick pondered a moment. 'Yes, you'd best be on your way. Keep the lads in check.'

'I will, m'lord.' Wilhelm gave a small bow with a fist to his chest in salute, then turned for the door. What would he find when he returned to the College? People were on edge across the city, and the news of the events in the north could well be the spark that lit the tinderbox.

It wasn't far from the Citadel's lower gates to the jetties. Wilhelm and the other guardsmen had been using a launch from one of the small piers to reach the College, a seemingly safer route than risking the plague-ridden streets. He pulled his hood up, hoping for some small protection from the plague, and left the supposed safety of the Citadel, passing through the lower gate and into the street beyond. His boots squelched into the churned mud of the well-trodden thoroughfare.

His breath misted. The cold had crept in, the mornings now sparkling with a veneer of frost, some still glistening in patches of shadow even as the morning grew, the frigid cold clinging to the air. While the heat of summer would have been a living hell, the chill did little to freshen the odours of the city.

The usual stench of Arn's streets, the piss and shit of beast and man alike, the lingering scent of fish mongers and butchers, bakeries and flower stalls, a few spice hawkers and in the distance, tanneries, now mingled with a much more ominous odour. Either the collections had reduced or the bodies had become so numerous that folk simply dumped the dead unceremoniously in the gutters. Outside the squat, rundown houses the twisted, mud smeared dead lay waiting for a passing cart that had not yet arrived.

Folk gave the piles a wide berth. Wilhelm tried to avert his eyes but despite his best efforts, he found himself staring at their faces. Lifeless gazes and features frozen into twisted expressions of horror stared back, blood crusted around eyes, mouths and noses, clothing stained black with gore and the muck of the street. Hideously distorted limbs, stiffened in death into grotesque poses — it should have terrified him, but he had become numb to the death around him.

Wilhelm imagined his old friend Ox laid in such a pose. Choking on blood in a rickety cot was no way for a warrior to pass. Would his old comrade be dumped in the filth of a gutter to await the rumbling wheels of a cart, or would the garrison at least have the decency to carry him to a pyre? He feared that was unlikely. There was too much to do, too many others to worry after to waste time on one dead man.

The look on his face must have been dark, for folk made way and let him pass like a ship's prow moves through waves. Any that strayed too close received a harsh bark to stand aside. With his shield strapped to his back and brandishing a spear in hand, none were fool enough to ignore his warnings.

The river lapped against its banks as Wilhelm stepped onto the wooden planks of the pier and jerked a nod at the boatman. He handed him a coin.

'College again?' asked the man in a thick inland accent. He sounded like he could have been from Barrowford, upriver, but Wilhelm had never been there himself.

'Aye,' replied Wilhelm as he stepped into the little boat. 'Shall I take an oar again?'

'Be my guest, friend, if it gets you there faster.' The boatman shrugged. 'Coin's the same either way.'

Wilhelm sat at the bench and heaved one of the oars onto his knees. The boatman pushed off into the river and sat down beside him. They pulled in unison and surged forwards, leaving the little jetty behind. The buildings alongside the river slid past with each pull of the oars, the sky overhead thick with grey cloud. It would not be long before the snows came.

There was a sudden thump against the hull of the launch.

'Shit,' exclaimed the boatman, leaning over one side and recoiling, his face screwed up in disgust. 'Don't touch it with the oars.'

Wilhelm peered over to see a body bobbing in the water. The current carried the launch onward and Wilhelm stared as the body turned and rolled from the impact with the hull.

He blinked and thought for a moment the floating corpse had Ox's face. Was this where his old friend had been dumped? He shook his head clear and looked again. The face was that of an old man. He sighed, part in relief, part in sorrow.

Ox had fallen sick some days back, not long after their foray into the city with the princess. Wilhelm had thought it a foolish thing to do at the time, and he was certain that day in the filthy slums was where Ox had been marked by the plague's deathly touch. Now the princess had fallen ill he was certain of it—the stupid girl. She was a kind soul, but she paid no heed to any warnings, and now Ox was dead because she'd dragged them out into the heart of the sickness.

Ox was not the first among the guard to fall sick, and had been taken to a guardhouse outside of the Citadel. It was not thought wise to allow any sick inside the Citadel's palisades. It was the last time Wilhelm had seen him.

Ox had been a good friend, a companion of many long years. He had stood shoulder to shoulder with him, shield to shield and axe in hand in many a fight – at Aeginhall, in the succession, through two wars he had been by his side. He had sailed with him in Warrick's raids. Ox had his back more times than he cared to remember. They had both served the king and their Lord Huscarl for many winters and now he was gone. Wilhelm kept pulling on the oar, his mind distant on old memories.

The boat bumped against the College jetty and the boatman threw a rope over a protruding bollard. He hauled the launch against the pier and Wilhelm stepped off onto the dock. The College docks were enclosed within the compound walls, a private access for the delivery of supplies and travel up and down river for the scholars. He gave his thanks to the boatman and strode towards the buildings. He needed to find his fellow guardsmen, and more importantly his charge, the apprentice.

Not far from the living quarters where he'd left Edgar on guard, shouts echoed from the walls and he stopped, spinning towards the sound and hurrying to investigate. Edgar could damn well wait.

The commotion seemed to be coming from one of the main gates, and as he approached, Wilhelm caught sight of the sell-swords the College employed, standing on the platform over the gate. He climbed the stairs of the wooden gantry to look down into the streets beyond.

A large crowd had gathered, jostling and facing off with the city guard deployed between them and gate. They were attempting to quell the crowd, but the townsfolk shouted curses and threw the occasional object at the struggling guards.

'What in the gods name is going on out there?' Wilhelm demanded.

One of the College sell-swords looked him over. 'Fuck knows,' he replied, returning his attention to the milling crowd below.

A dark object sailed up towards them and clattered against the compound's walls, falling just short of Wilhelm's position on the gantry. Most of the men on the gantry flinched away, but Wilhelm held his ground, glaring at the mob.

'I've seen you lads coming and going these last few days,' sneered the sell-sword, stepping forward again as if he hadn't just shrunk back from a piece of thrown rubbish. 'What are the king's men doing poking around here? This is *our* turf.'

'King's business. Nothing you boys need to worry about,' replied Wilhelm casually.

'Has it got anything to do with that kid who just came back from up north?' the man pressed, nodding towards the College buildings. 'Folk are saying the College did fell things up there. Offended the gods, and all. Brought the plague down on us.'

'Folk have got the wrong idea,' Wilhelm said slowly, recalling his lord's warnings. The College may have been up to no good in the mountains, but he had a job to do. 'Folk shouldn't listen to rumour,' he added.

The sell-sword grunted as he swung his gaze back to the mob below.

Seeing a chance to weed out information, Wilhelm ventured a question, 'I hear there was a death last night?'

'Aye,' replied the sell-sword, eyes narrowed at the crowd, scanning their faces with derision. 'Word is one of the councillors is dead. Could be from the sickness or one of this lot got in and killed the bastard. No one's said for sure.'

'Really?' said Wilhelm in surprise. He wasn't sure what he'd expected, but this wasn't it. A councillor? They were the elderly folk he'd seen at the meeting the day before, all gathered in the chamber to question the apprentice.

'I heard he was messed up pretty bad when they found him too,' another sell-sword put in from further down the gantry. 'Like he'd been attacked by a hound or something. They're all keeping it pretty quiet though.'

'Probably wise...' Wilhelm muttered, glancing down at the mob again.

Someone below shouted something incoherent and launched another missile up towards them. One of the city guards jabbed the offender in the face with butt of his spear and a violent scuffle broke out. Shouts rose up as the city guard viciously beat down the unrest, their commander shouting for the crowd to disperse immediately and threatening bloodshed.

'Getting messy down there. You lads stay safe,' Wilhelm said dismissively to the sell-swords as he turned to descend the wooden stairs. He wasn't going to stick around to watch.

'Oh, don't you worry 'bout us, king's man,' one of them called after him, and he left them to supervise the violence erupting outside the gates.

News of a councillor's death was deeply troubling, especially if one of the angry townsfolk was responsible and not the sickness. It was not impossible someone could have snuck in, scaled the walls in the dead of night and murdered him in his sleep, but the question remained why? Did they blame that councillor directly for the events outside these walls? Or had they had the simple misfortune of being in the wrong place and the wrong time? Lord

Warrick was right — they had to remain vigilant.

He frowned and hurried off to find Edgar and his charge. With a mob at the gates, his job had just become all the more complicated.

CHAPTER NINETEEN

There's Always Hope

He stared into the crackling flames of the hearth and hummed the song that had haunted him for weeks. *Her song.*

Arnulf raised the horn tankard to his lips and paused. The dark crimson liquid was fragrant but edged with a bitter tang. Telik wine — he had rarely drunk anything this luxurious, his head hazy, his cheeks slightly numbed. *Perhaps I have had my fill.* Sadly the wine did little to numb the ragged, raw hole left behind by the loss of his family.

Fear let out a whining yawn and Arnulf scratched the hound behind the ears. When satisfied, the hound yawned again and lowered himself in front of Arnulf's deerskin chair, curling up before the heat of the fire.

There was a *crack* and a *pop* as a log shifted in the hearth, fingers of flame and the orange glow of coals slowly devouring the firewood. Arnulf's eyes never left those flames. *They were consumed by the fire.*

A tear rolled down his cheek. *Aeslin...* He could not force the image of her face from his mind. Her smile, her beautiful hair; all consumed by the raging inferno, like the log in the hearth, reduced to ashes. *Ashes and dust.*

There was another face in the flames. *Idony...*

Cherished memories played before his eyes.

A laugh as joyous as spring leaves catching the first light of the summer sun. His ears filled with that laugh, and he thought of the forest nymphs frolicking over a babbling brook. His daughter

214

had laughed with an almost manic glee as he chased her through the woods, her eyes alight with mischief as she hid behind a tree. Ducking one way and peering around, then darting the other way as he drew near. All the while giggling as she made her escape. *Idony... My little princess.*

She had a smile that could warm winter itself, eyes the colour of a bright summer sky, and an inexhaustible selfless love for all things.

Why, gods? Why did you take them from me?

He watched the memory of Idony catch on the tip of a flame, looked on as it contorted and writhed in the heat, just as she would have done, disappearing into the blackened ruin of the hall. *Ashes and dust...*

He choked on a sob and drained his tankard. No amount of wine or ale could dull his pain, or extinguish the flames.

There was a knock at the door.

'My lord?' It was Hafgan's muffled voice.

Arnulf didn't reply, his eyes never leaving the flickering fire. He wiped away the tears with the back of his sleeve, then heard the door open and close. He didn't look up as a hand clasped his shoulder.

'Why, Haf?' Arnulf asked, not expecting an answer. 'Why were they taken from me?'

There was no reply, just the companionable silence of the big warrior. Hafgan squeezed his shoulder in a gesture of silent consolation.

Eventually Hafgan spoke, 'I'm sorry, lord. I wish I had answers to comfort you. The gods can be cruel.'

'What did I ever do to them? I have *always* honoured them, yet they saw fit to take everything.'

'It is little comfort, but Aeslin and Idony are in the halls of our ancestors. You'll see them again one day... There's still Ewolf.'

Arnulf tightened his grip on the tankard, his knuckles paling.

'Please, lord. The lad will be well again... you must believe it.'

Arnulf snarled and hurled the tankard into the flames. Fear jumped up in alarm as the vessel clattered against the hot stone, cinders and embers bursting from the hearth.

'What do you suggest?' Arnulf slammed his fist onto the arm of his chair. 'We let those bastards *experiment* on my son like one of those corpses we found in the passes? What could they possibly do? What if they make things worse?' His throat tightened and the final words came out strangled, worn thin by grief.

'There is a hope, lord,' Hafgan insisted. 'There are good folk at the College, I am sure; folk who will want to see Ewolf returned to health.'

'Is there?' He turned to Hafgan, his vision blurred by tears. Arnulf saw a sad look of pity in the big warrior's eyes. 'Is there?'

'There is always hope, lord.'

'I want to see him,' Arnulf demanded, suddenly desperate to lay eyes on his boy. Hafgan nodded.

It had become a morbid ritual in the days since Arnulf had been released by the king, he and Hafgan going to see the thing that Ewolf had become. He would stand and watch his son, sometimes he would try to talk with him. With each visit he lost more hope, the traces of humanity left in Ewolf seeping away, fading slowly from his dark eyes. Still he visited him, standing there for hours as Ewolf shrieked and roared through the bars.

Arnulf rose unsteadily to his feet, the shaggy grey hound coming back to his side. 'Stay boy,' Arnulf commanded. The hound shrank away whenever Ewolf was near, and he would not accompany Arnulf into the room where they kept Ewolf's cage. It was better he stayed here in Arnulf's rooms.

'I want to see him,' Arnulf repeated, then staggered towards the door.

***

Erran sat on his straw stuffed cot and gently wiped the oil from the keen blade of his sword. It was his prize possession, a gift from his father. The old horse merchant was a rich man and had presented it to him when he first swore into Lord Arnulf's service. Erran was all too aware it was a princely gift, far above his position.

It was a blade of bronze, a raised fuller running its length. It was thin near the hilt and flared slightly mid blade before tapering off into a deadly point. It had no crosspiece at the hilt like the newer iron weapons becoming popular with smiths throughout the realm, its hilt short with enough room for a single hand before a pommel of two spiralled bronze coils set next to each other. It was a beautiful sword, even Arnulf and Hafgan had said as much, and he treasured it, making it his daily ritual to clean and oil it after the sun set.

It was not the weapon he would wield this evening, however. He leant over and slid the bronze blade back into its hide covered scabbard and took up the dull iron sparring sword resting against the wall beside him. It was an ugly dented thing by comparison.

There was a knock at the door to his quarters. *It is time.*

Astrid appeared around the doorway, her long dark hair pinned braided back against her head, her expression ever stern. His stomach knotted at the sight of her. *Fierce, yet so very beautiful.*

'Are you coming?' she asked.

He nodded, not letting his gaze linger in case she somehow read his thoughts through his eyes, and rose to her summons. 'Are you well this evening?' he asked as they walked.

'Aye, boy. Are you ready this time?' She glanced at him with a wry sideways grin.

'Always,' he replied. He stood tall and stuck out his chest. 'Are you?'

She snorted a laugh. 'In your dreams, boy.'

You have no idea.

He followed her to the courtyard. The denizens of the Citadel went about their business as they passed. Most would be off to their homes, or to a hall to eat and drink their daily troubles away.

Erran was struck by how different life within the Citadel's walls felt. It was grim and sombre, so much different from the lively mead halls of his homeland in the north. He wondered if it was just the sickness hanging heavy over the capital, or if it was always like this.

He spared a thought for his father and Ravenshold, wondering if it had been re-built or whether it still lay in ruin. He sighed. His home would likely never be the same again.

He laughed and joked with Astrid as far as he was willing to push his luck, noticing she had softened her severe attitude towards him somewhat over these past weeks. He wondered at that. Hafgan had warned him away from her, but there was something enchanting about the shield-maiden. He had learnt much of swordplay and combat from the Death Nymph's daily beatings, a pain he was happy to endure just to spend time in her company.

A small group of cloaked figures slipped from the shadows as they passed under a low arch between some buildings. The sudden appearance startled the young warrior, but Astrid barely flinched, despite the palpable air of menace he sensed from them.

'Astrid!' hissed one of the figures in a woman's voice. 'What are doing with that little rat again?'

'You dare question me?' snapped Astrid, placing her hand on her sword.

The woman whirled around and stood defiantly before them, barring their way. She lowered her hood as the others drew to a halt in a circle. Erran recognised her as one of the Death Nymph's fellow shield-maidens.

'You dishonour us, Astrid,' said the woman, malice in her glare as she looked Erran up and down. 'You spend more and more time with the rat-boy. Will you be drinking with us in the hall tonight, or will you have something better to do with your time?'

'I do what I want with my time. It is not your place to question me, Hild. How dare you?'

'Some of us have wondered if you still honour the oath we all made. Some think you dishonour it.'

Astrid dropped her blunted sparring sword to the ground and it clattered loudly on the cobbles. She whipped her sword from her scabbard. This was no training blade. It was sharp and deadly, the spiller of many a man's blood.

'You challenge me?' Astrid growled, levelling her sword at the woman. She glared at each of the cloaked women in turn. 'I hold your oaths, and unless you stand aside and show me the proper respect, I will strip you of your weapons and cast you from my service. You will be nothing but wretches at the mercy of the wilds once more.'

Hild stood scowling a moment longer, then stood aside with a face like thunder. 'Come on,' the shield-maiden said to her companions. 'You heard what she said. She no longer listens to her sisters. We have no right to question the mighty Astrid.' Hild gave a small mocking bow before storming away.

'I will listen to what counsel I see fit!' Astrid shouted, her voice dripping with threat. 'This is not done, Hild!'

Astrid sheathed her sword and Erran gawped after the shield-maidens in shock. 'Would you fight her?' he asked, unsure if the idea of Astrid fighting her own shield-maidens was terrifying or exhilarating.

She shot him a glare and retrieved the practice sword from the dirt. 'She challenged my leadership. I will not stand for that, she knows it. If she pushes me, I will have no choice.'

'I'm sorry,' said Erran. It seemed a useless remark, but he didn't know what else to say.

'Why?' she snapped. 'What did you do?' Her tone told him she did not want an answer. She walked on and he followed quietly into the courtyard.

She was not a dozen steps into the yard when she rounded on him, drawing her sword and swinging it wildly at his head. He barely avoided the blow, stepping back just in time, ducking and weaving until she ceased her attack.

'Good,' she growled.

'You could have warned me!' Erran puffed, hurrying to catch his breath. He set a stance and raised his blade.

She swung again, a flurry of blows this time, and Erran parried frantically. She was like a wild cat, slashing and swiping, all claws and bared teeth. 'Why should I warn you? Battle can come at any time. Be ready, fool.'

The Death Nymph cut at him again, and Erran felt her anger vibrate up his arm, an anger that was not usually there. She attacked again, battering his sword. She was not normally so savage. He got too close and she kicked him hard in the stomach. He doubled over and she swung at him with a snarl.

The blow never landed.

She stopped short, her blade hovering above his face.

Panting, her face twisted in a scowl, she glared at him. Eventually, her arm dropped, and her blade eased away. 'I am sorry. I should not take my anger out on you.'

Erran blinked. *She could have killed me.*

She threw her sword down and turned away from him. With her hands on her hips, she looked up into the evening sky.

'There was a moment there where I would have caved your skull in and not even cared.'

'I'm sorry,' Erran said again, kneeling to catch his breath.

'Don't be,' she replied. 'Perhaps now is not a good time to practice. I'm too angry.'

'This is my fault,' Erran told her, unwilling to concede his portion of the blame. 'Your warriors hate me, and I insisted on having you teach me.'

'Aye, but their hate is no fault of yours. They… they don't like me training or spending any time with outsiders, whether it was you or another.' Astrid sighed and sat down on a stack of firewood at the edge of the courtyard.

'Why?' asked Erran, sitting beside her.

She cast him a sideways frown, then looked away as if she'd hoped to avoid that very subject. It was a moment before she answered. 'They don't trust men. Some of them even go so far as hating them.'

'But you all serve Lord Fergus,' Erran pointed out.

'Aye, we need to swear to someone. Food and lodging don't pay for themselves. Some of them would still rather we weren't, but we have little choice. We would have been hunted down as outlaws.'

'What happened to turn them against men?' dared Erran, uncertain at how she would react. He had heard the rumours from Hafgan but he wanted to hear it from her.

Astrid gave him a long, dark look. There was a past there, hidden deep behind the bravery and honour, scars that cut deep, shadows his young mind had not yet encountered. 'It was men who stole away their lives. Some of us suffered greatly…' She shrugged and looked out over the yard. Not far from them, a servant walked the grounds lighting torches against the night. As a chill bit the air, folk hurried to shelter in the warmth of halls and chambers. 'But we had our vengeance. Many will never trust a man again.'

'But not you?'

'No, I was just the same. I didn't for many years, but time passes. Some of you aren't so bad,' she said, pushing him with her shoulder.

He smiled but said nothing. She hadn't been this candid with him before, always more standoffish than friendly, but he supposed the fraying relationship with some of her comrades had pushed her towards him. If he was smart, he'd let her talk.

She sighed. 'There *are* men with honour in this world. I know this now, but I fear some of my warriors will never see it that way.'

'What are they like with Fergus?' asked Erran. 'He has a twisted sense of humour, and I hear, an eye for women. How has he not ended up with his balls in a cup?'

She grinned, a mischievous gleam in her eyes. 'Oh, there have been times when I thought one of them would relieve him of his manhood altogether, but they aren't that stupid. For one, I would gut them, and two, Fergus is the son of a high lord. They would not dare, for all their spite. For all his talk he's not so bad. A lord of good humour is better than a man with a spiteful heart.'

Erran laughed and dared another question. 'Why anger them so much to spar with me? What makes me so special?'

'Erran, you are a good boy,' she said with a knowing nod.

'Boy?' he objected, feigning an incredulous gasp. 'I can't be much younger than you.'

She smiled cryptically. He still had no idea exactly how old she was and it didn't look like she was going to tell him, but he suspected she could not be far past her twentieth year.

'Few speak to me as you do,' she said. 'You're a good man, and there's a kindness in your eyes. Few have spoken to me as an equal, or better, regardless of my fame. They just fear me or lust after me. There is no middle ground.'

'You are a warrior of high renown, Astrid. *I* was terrified of you.'

'Was?' She smirked and he raised his hands defensively, shaking his head. 'Fear goes a long way. Most men only understand fear, so that's what we used as our shield against them. But still, many ignore my valour and see only...' She looked down and gestured to her chest and legs. She was a well-built woman; strong, athletic and lean. She was neither scrawny nor voluptuous, as a well-trained fighter should be. Still, she had a pretty face and a shining smile when he had the fortune of seeing it. 'Some men just see this. They find out the hard way that there is much more to me than a good set of tits.'

Erran grimaced. He could just imagine what that realisation had involved.

'You, however, treat me as you would any other. You have made me laugh too. I thank you for that, Erran. Truly.' She held his gaze an instant longer than usual before breaking it.

For a moment, Erran swore he could see the young girl she had once been peering back at him, then her eyes turned back to their familiar stone. 'Come,' she said with another smile. 'I shan't beat you senseless tonight, but I would still talk with you a while yet, *boy*. Let's have an ale. Fuck what the others think—let's get drunk.'

***

Arnulf steeled himself and pushed open the door.

With a throat-ripping roar, the creature threw itself against the iron bars. Filth smeared arms stretched towards him, grasping and clawing uselessly at empty air. Chains rattled and creaked but held firm.

Slowly the futility of thrashing and straining, howling and shrieking seemed to dawn and the creature became subdued. A low threatening growl emanated from its throat like that of a wounded dog.

Arnulf stepped as close as he dared, just out of the creature's reach. It stooped, half crouched, ready to spring forward at any moment and renew its savage struggle against the chains which held it. Arnulf stared into its glowering eyes. There was such hate there, such anger — the bestial fury of the untameable wild.

'Hello, son,' said Arnulf. His voice was low and laced with sadness.

There was no reply. The creature just stared back hatefully. Given the chance, it would rend him limb from limb. *How could this creature once have been my son?*

The clothes he had once worn hung in tatters from his lank frame. The obliterated remnants of rodent carcasses littered the floor of the cage. Across the room, lay a discarded bowl, its contents splattered against the wall. The guards had said he would not eat the food brought to him, hurling it away and screaming ever more. He did, however, seem to have a taste for rats, snatching up any that strayed too close. Was it flesh he craved, still flushed with warm, pumping blood? The dank little cell stank of faeces and piss, a dark, damp nightmare — a fitting prison for such a wretched mockery of man.

Arnulf paced before the cage, his eyes fixed on Ewolf. *My son...*

Without warning, Ewolf launched another futile tirade against the iron containing him. He snapped his teeth at Arnulf, snarling then sinking back to the floor and with a baleful glare .

Arnulf searched and searched, peering through the spite and anger, hoping to see some trace of warmth, some remnant of his son.

Nothing.

A tear rolled down his cheek.

'You must have hope, my lord,' Hafgan murmured from the doorway. 'There is still a hope.'

CHAPTER TWENTY

Forbidden Knowledge

Luthor pored over the leather-bound grimoire on his desk. 'Eldrick's work was quite remarkable. The sketches, the anatomy work — were these drawn from actual specimens?' he asked, leafing through the pages with a look of morbid awe.

'They were, master,' grimaced Duncan, remembering those gruesome dead eyes staring at him as Eldrick worked. He sat on a chair on the end of Luthor's desk checking through the catalogue of findings, a candle burning on the desk beside him casting ruddy light onto the pages.

'That must have made for grim viewing,' commented Luthor. 'I see now the need for such seclusion.'

'They were sights I will not forget,' replied the apprentice, shaking away the macabre visions from his mind. 'I feel I let Master Eldrick down, though. I had no stomach for such things.'

'I imagine few do. Don't let it bother you, lad.' Luthor waved away his worry and turned another page. 'If you'd had the stomach for it you would likely not be here. You'd be in Old Night's cold halls with the others.'

His master's words were meant as a kindness, but they did little to lift his guilt. He managed a weak smile and glanced away, not wanting to meet Luthor's eye. Instead he looked down at the grimoire and frowned. 'I have come to know this book well. I worked from it many times of late. Other than the ghastly dissections, I see nothing in any of Eldrick's earlier study that could possibly have caused this.'

Luthor grunted as he picked up and began reading through a

loose parchment.

The apprentice felt the carved swirl of the wooden charm hung at his neck, a symbol of the old god of air and wisdom, hoping to find some protection in its touch. 'Perhaps the gods were displeased with the butchering of the dead and threw a curse upon all who lingered up there. Perhaps the *gods* did this.'

'That's the explanation you want to give the council?' Luthor looked up with a raised eyebrow.

The apprentice's face flushed with the heat of embarrassment. 'I would not. Still, I don't think any of this was responsible for those ghastly tales we heard at the council. Whatever caused it happened after my departure from the camp. If I remember correctly, he had nothing else planned except further dissections.'

'Hmm,' Luthor mumbled, returning his gaze to the open book.

And the ritual, thought the apprentice. How long would he have to keep up this farce? Perhaps forever? The guilt swirled in his belly like curdled milk. He knew full well what caused this. *They must have tried again.*

The memory flashed through his mind — the dead man clawing across the ground towards him, hungry eyes fixed and unwavering, drawn to his life's warmth.

He had trapped himself with his deceit, though; bound up in his lies and compelled to maintain them. He hated it but it was too late. He could not go back on his testament before the council. His words had damned his master's memory, but there was no other choice. If his deception were discovered, he would be cast out of the College, or worse.

'But what of this ritual?' asked Luthor, rubbing weary eyes. 'The report I have from Rodrik states they found evidence of some strange ritual left unfinished. Could it be Eldrick somehow performed some sorcery?'

Steer him away, he must not discover the truth, murmured a thin reedy voice in Duncan's head, and he started at the sound.

Luthor stared at him curiously.

'Sorry, I thought I saw something behind you,' Duncan said, clumsily covering his tracks.

Luthor shook his head and went back to reading as Duncan's heart pounded.

'Will they really destroy his grimoire, master?' ventured the apprentice, changing the subject.

'Aye, most likely they will burn it, and make a show of it too. It would give the wrong impression if the College were seen to do nothing. The council will be eager to distance themselves from all this. Eldrick will be publicly disgraced.'

'I see,' replied the apprentice softly. 'So much work, wasted.'

'I don't know what they are going to do with this nasty little thing, though.' Luthor produced a twisted dagger, its hilt wrapped in black leather.

The dagger! Duncan started again and scrambled to hide his surprise, raking his hand back through his lank hair. *Eldrick's ritual dagger.*

The sight of it drew forth memories he had tried to forget, images of it piercing, cutting, the trickle of blood on pallid skin. He suppressed a shudder.

'Do you recognise it?' asked Luthor.

You must retrieve the dagger, whispered the voice. *It should be yours.*

'I do!' said Duncan, feigning relief. 'It's my dagger. I thought it lost! Where did you find it?'

Lies.

'Your dagger?' frowned Luthor.

'Yes, it was my father's — a family heirloom, in fact. I thought it was lost forever.'

More lies.

Luthor studied him carefully. 'It was found at the ritual site in the north. Why would it be there?'

'Eldrick had it,' replied Duncan.

Luthor's eyes narrowed slightly. 'And what use would Eldrick have for it?'

'He always liked it,' admitted Duncan with a nonchalant shrug. 'I let him use it for his work.'

'So, it was *this* dagger he used for his experiments?' Luthor's long fingers unfurled towards the grimoire, but he held on to the knife, not laying it on the desk or handing it to Duncan. The apprentice's hands itched to take it.

Duncan waved dismissively, as if it were of little consequence, while his mind spun. He had to get it back, and he had no idea why. He was driven, desperate, drawn to it, holding himself back with each passing second. 'He used many others, but I'm so glad it was found. May I have it back?'

'Uh... No,' said Luthor, shaking his head. 'Perhaps in time, but I do not think it a good idea at present. It is part of the evidence presented for investigation, and should remain with the other items found. If the council were to learn I gave it to you...'

'I see,' said Duncan, letting his face fall in disappointment then painting on a hopeful smile. 'I understand, of course. Please keep it safe, master. It is the only thing I have left of my father.'

Luthor sighed and regarded him sympathetically. 'When this is all over, I am sure arrangements can be made.' His master regarded him thoughtfully a few moments then turned his gaze back to the open book before him, laying the dagger in the far end of the desk. Luthor flicked through more of the pages. 'I believe some of this work could still be of use.'

'It could?'

'It would be unwise to repeat his experiments, but Eldrick was a visionary in his field. It will all need to be scrutinised by the council, of course. I will vouch for it, and you, as much as I can, but I must counsel caution. You are on thin ice.'

Duncan nodded and swallowed his anxiety. The thought of the council scrutinising any of his work filled him with dread. 'What about his work on the ritual — will that be destroyed?'

'Probably. It does make for some dark reading. Trying to raise bones from a cairn, seeking to extend or resurrect a life. It's unnatural. I can't imagine old Eldrick attempting something as mad as *sorcery*,' he laughed, as if the very idea was preposterous. 'Sorcery... I can't believe we are considering such fantasy.'

'Now you have seen it, what are your thoughts on the ritual texts, master?' ventured Duncan cautiously. His brain screamed at him to flee from that ritual, to never look back or even cast it another thought — it was too dangerous — but some dark compulsion drove a malignant desire. The knowledge to command life and death itself, that terrible power he had seen with his own eyes, a power that could be wielded by the wise, it proved too alluring to simply let slip back into the dusts of time.

Luthor turned the pages towards the back of the grimoire and the apprentice caught sight of the strange glyphs inked on the pages beside Eldrick's scrawled annotations. 'He made some interesting assumptions, and he did indeed use my translations in part. Some of his conclusions are... questionable.'

'How so?' asked the apprentice, placing his scroll on the desk and leaning towards the grimoire.

'Well, look here—this glyph,' said Luthor, pointing at the page. 'He has taken the meaning as *eternity* or something to that effect, but I have seen it used elsewhere, and believe it to be nearer to *abyss* or *dark*. And these here,' he said, running his finger under another line of symbols. 'I have never come across these glyphs before. They are very strange. Did he ever mention where he found these?'

'He did not, master. We made many rubbings of the stones and obelisks around the ruins. Perhaps it was one of those...'

Luthor turned the pages, squinting at the various passages of strange glyphs. 'This part of the text appears to be missing...' He leaned closer, as if to see better, and Duncan followed.

'Yes, I remember that one. We found it on a broken stone at the ruins.'

'I have seen this sequence before...' muttered Luthor. He rose from his chair and hurried across the room to his bookcases. He ran a finger across the leather-bound spines. 'Ah-ha! Here it is!'

He cradled a book and came back to the desk, placing the old volume down and stabbing a finger at the open page. Duncan stood, pushing himself up on his good leg and leaning over to examine the text.

There was a sudden flicker of shadow at the edge of his vision and he shuddered as a cold draught brushed his skin.

'He has substituted these symbols,' Luthor continued, unaware of Duncan's distraction, 'but here, I think this is what he was looking for.'

The apprentice compared the pages, trying to ignore the dancing shadows emerging around the room. The pattern of glyphs was indeed identical, but Luthor's was a more complete specimen.

Duncan's stomach knotted with excited realisation. *This could be it. Was this what Eldrick was looking for?*

Behold, apprentice, murmured the voice. *You know in your heart this is the key. These are the answers your master long sought.*

He started again and looked around. They were alone.

'Why do you haunt me so?' Duncan muttered under his breath.

'Are you well, lad?' asked Luthor suddenly. He was staring at him with a touch of concern on his face.

'It's nothing, master,' replied the apprentice hastily.

'You were talking to yourself,' said Luthor sceptically.

'It's nothing, really. My leg is causing me much discomfort, that's all.' Duncan cleared his throat and pointed at the book. 'Where did this come from?' He asked as casually as he could, hiding his interest. He did not want to arouse suspicion in his new master.

Luthor regarded him a moment and turned his eyes back to the book.

'It is a compilation of First Son's writings,' he replied. 'Most is indecipherable. It was compiled by a Master Corinus, I believe. I used it to draw texts for translations.'

'I'm sure Eldrick would have liked to have seen it,' said the apprentice sadly.

'There are likely other copies somewhere in the archives, if he had but asked...'

Seek the book, finish what he started, whispered a watching shadow.

'May I borrow this?' asked Duncan, forgetting himself.

Luthor turned his full regard upon the apprentice. There was a long moment of silence as Luthor studied him with a frown and Duncan regretted his request immediately. 'Duncan, you swear you had no part in your master's pursuits?'

'No, master. I swear. He cast me away for my objections.'

There was another pause.

'I am merely curious,' the apprentice hurried on. 'Maybe I could find where Eldrick went wrong. It might help us undo this wrong. The creature they brought... the council said we were to...' He trailed off, lost for the right words.

Luthor sighed and again rubbed his weary and reddened eyes. 'I hope your intentions are pure, lad, I really do. I don't think it wise for you have this, though. You must understand. For your own good I forbid you to explore your old master's studies. Even if you only mean well, even if you only intend to help that poor creature they brought south, I dare not allow it. If the council were to find out...'

There was a loud knock at the door and Duncan jumped. Luthor looked behind him to a little door leading to another of his rooms.

'Enter!' Luthor called loudly.

Duncan's gaze drifted to the book, his fingers gently lifting the cover up from the desk so he might examine its title. The leather was old and cracked, the hand written title faded.

A Codex
of Ancient Writings;
The First Sons
and Other Lost Peoples

Compiled by
Master Corinus

He burned the title into his memory and let the cover fall back to the desk as someone bustled through the door. A short, fat man hurried in, the entry barely wide enough for his girth, and Luthor turned to greet him. Duncan's gaze fell on the ritual dagger then, and he swiftly snatched it up and tucked it inside his coat, certain Luthor had not seen a thing.

Another man followed the rotund little scholar into the study and a cold hand of fearful awe clutched at Duncan's guts. The man was tall and muscular and had to duck through the small doorway, rising to his full impressive height behind Gideon. His skin was a dark, rich brown, almost ebon black, the like of which the apprentice had never seen before. He had seen the dusky skinned folk of Telis, and had only heard of the people from the far southern continents. He stared at the newcomer, unable to hide his awe.

The man wore breeches and an open white shirt, and his broad chest and arms were hard with corded muscles. The dark man grinned at Luthor, his teeth gleaming white in contrast to his dark complexion.

'Gideon!' Luthor greeted the scholar warmly. 'How is our guest?'

'Ask him yourself,' replied Gideon with a grin.

'Greeting, Master Lutor,' said the big man in a deep, heavily accented voice.

Luthor seemed taken aback, and for a moment he did not reply. 'Hello Jasper,' he said finally.

'Remarkable,' Gideon nodded approvingly to the big man.

'Good see you,' ventured the dark man, struggling with the strange tongue. 'I learn much.'

'Yes, you certainly have.' Luthor marvelled at the man, his pleasure evident in his voice.

Gideon grinned at Luthor. 'Incredible, isn't it? He shows an extreme level of intelligence.'

'How is this possible?' asked Luthor, awe struck.

'My theory is that he has been amongst the people of Arnar for longer than we thought. Gods know how long he was on that ship, learning all the while. And he has been here a turning of the moon already, listening, picking things up,' Gideon explained quickly, unable to hide his excitement. 'I'd wager he was playing us dumb for a while until he was sure of us. We have made remarkable progress these past two days with the proper tutelage.'

Gideon seemed to notice Duncan for the first time and his excited rambling halted.

'Oh, goodness—I did not know you had a guest!' apologised Gideon.

'Ah Gideon, meet my new apprentice, Duncan,' Luthor introduced him to the rotund scholar.

'Pleasure to meet you, lad.' The scholar gave him a tight smile. Although he seemed pleasant, Duncan could not help but notice the wary gaze the man cast from head to foot, taking in the pale hair and his heavily splinted foot.

Jasper stood silently, regarding Duncan in a manner that reminded him of his father looking down on an ailing farm animal that should be put out of its misery. He must have looked sickly and pathetic to such a brawny giant, but he did not care for the dismissive look in the man's eyes.

Ignoring the onlookers, Gideon leaned in closer to Luthor, pressing against the desk with his gut. 'Did you hear?' he asked in a hushed voice.

'Hear what?' replied Luthor.

'About Sareb?'

The mention of the councillor's name drew Duncan's attention and a sour taste into his mouth. He had no love for the spiteful councillor.

'What of him?' asked Luthor curiously.

'He's *dead*,' declared Gideon.

Duncan felt he should be shocked and saddened by that news, but he wasn't. He did not have any love for that vicious, spiteful man, a man who appeared not to have a shred of kindness in him.

Councillor Sareb had been quick to condemn him and Duncan vividly remembered his purpling face as he berated at him. Instead of sadness, Duncan felt a cold indifference at the news, he was almost glad to hear it, but he kept his face passive, pushing away a smirk that tried to curl from the corner of his mouth.

'What?' exclaimed Luthor. 'W — wh — how?'

'Have you been shut away in here all day? It's all over the College.'

Luthor's shock at the news was written all over his face as he stepped back and sat down slowly in his chair.

'How? Was it the sickness?'

'That's the story,' nodded Gideon. 'But there's darker rumours.'

Luthor raised an eyebrow as Gideon shuffled forward, relishing his role in delivering the gossip.

'There's talk of *murder*,' Gideon hissed, leaning closer in almost a conspiratorial whisper. 'I heard they found him mauled and mutilated. There's talk of it being linked with the unrest — a vengeance attack. The council are insisting it was plague, but you know how folk like to talk.'

'Dark times feed dark minds,' Luthor told him, his voice low and his brow knitted in a frown. 'The council won't want panic.'

The apprentice was struck dumb by the news of the councillor's demise. Only yesterday Sareb had shouted him down in the chamber, the embarrassment still a raw wound. Whether taken by the plague or some other fell means, the news was dire. Either way, death stalked the halls of the College, and he should have been sad, or worried, or frightened. Yet a wicked, selfish part of him couldn't help but feel glad, despite the gnawing guilt.

His eyes darted to a flicker of movement in the gloom by a dusty bookcase. The candle on the desk cast strange shadows, looming menacingly and unseen behind the others. He thought for a moment he could hear rasping whispers, not just in his head but with his ears this time, and his head began to swim. His senses overloaded, the unfamiliar guests and their uncomfortable stares, the pain in his leg, the sheer fatigue of knitting new bone in his ankle all weighted heavy and his head spun. Duncan steadied himself on the desk.

Luthor and Gideon continued talking, but their voices seemed distant. Luthor was speaking in fits and starts with the dark man,

Jasper, and the apprentice vaguely heard his new master ask Gideon, 'Does he know of the plague?'

Apprentice, whispered the voice in his mind. Without thinking he stood and put his weight on his ruin of a leg. Crippling pain tore up his leg and into his belly, and cried out as darkness enveloped him.

He blinked hard, and as his vision cleared, he found himself still on his feet but barely. Something was holding tight to his arm.

'Are you alright, lad?' Luthor's voice reached him through the loud buzzing in his ears.

Duncan focused on the sound and searched for his new master. He found him standing beside Gideon, both scholars staring at him with unveiled concern. The grip on his arm shifted and he glanced sideways, realising with a jolt that Jasper had hold of him in his huge, strong hands.

'Duncan, can you hear me boy?' came Luthor's question.

'Is he sick?' The apprentice heard Gideon exclaim fearfully. 'What was he saying just then? Was it some odd language Eldrick had him learning?'

He shook his head to clear his vision and Jasper handed him one of his abandoned crutches before stepping back, examining him as if he'd grown a second head. Luthor waved his colleague into silence.

'I do not feel... well,' managed the apprentice.

Luthor and Gideon exchanged glances.

'I think perhaps I have pushed myself too hard,' Duncan said apologetically. It was an easy excuse, and it wasn't entirely untrue. His ankle might as well have been on fire. His stomach rolled and flipped and his skin beaded with sweat. 'My leg is... unbearable.'

'I think you'd best get some rest, lad,' Luthor told him. 'I can continue this on my own for now. Go, and we'll see how you are on the morrow.'

'Thank you, master,' muttered the apprentice, his cheeks flushing. He had made a fool of himself. He steadied himself with his crutches and shakily limped towards the door.

The book, hissed the voice in his thoughts.

He flicked a glance over his shoulder at Luthor's old book, still open on the desk. Luthor slipped past and opened the door to the entry hall, the young guard waiting idly outside drawing himself to attention as the apprentice emerged. There were College sell-swords there too, and he presumed they were guarding Jasper. Apparently he was not the only one at the College with an armoured shadow.

'Off you go,' said Luthor, glancing at the other guards crowding the hall. 'Get something to eat, then some rest. I'll check on you in the morning. Send for me if you have need.'

Duncan offered his master a weak smile, and a nod, but his eyes were drawn to the desk and the book. He tore his gaze away again and left.

He swung himself in an unsteady jerking motion along the short hallway within Luthor's rooms and stopped before the old door to the courtyard. His guard opened it and he continued into the cold air and bright sunlight.

He began his long painful hobble back to his chambers, when the voice hissed in his mind, *The book.*

The apprentice stopped in the middle of the courtyard. He turned to his guard who watched him with a dismissive mix of disdain and impatience.

'I almost forgot,' said Duncan, feigning frustration. He was getting good at it now, painting a face for others while he thought and felt otherwise inside. 'My master instructed me to fetch him a book from the archives. I should do that before I retire.'

The guard grunted in reply. He didn't seem to care.

The apprentice lowered himself onto a chair in his chambers with a grunt. It was good to take the weight of his feet finally. His shoulders, wrists and elbows ached from leaning on the crutches, and bruises were already forming on his palms. He sighed and rubbed his eyes, then reached inside his robes and drew out the slender ritual dagger. Holding it up, he turned it to the light.

The hilt was bound in black leather, with a small, plain cross guard and a round pommel fashioned into a skull shape. It was a thing of grim beauty and his eyes traced the steel to its point. It had a slender, undulating blade that reminded him of a snake. It was a spitefully pointed thing, a trace of dried blood still crusted along its length. A smile crept onto his face as he gazed at it.

Mine now, he thought.

He opened a drawer in his desk and secreted the dagger inside, then cleared a space for the heavy book. He had made his armoured shadow unwittingly carry the heavy tome for him, he doubted he could have managed it on his crutches.

Duncan's smile broadened further. He had it — he had the answers his master had so long sought. He lifted the heavy cover and flicked through the pages. The ancient glyphs of long dead peoples had been reproduced on each page, along with descriptions and attempted translation scrawled in faded ink beside them.

As he leafed through, the familiar shadow flickered at the edge of his vision, as if trying to peer over his shoulder. The room grew colder with each turn of the page until his gaze fell upon what he was searching for. His skin prickled to gooseflesh. The page detailed ancient markings, first laid down on a stone tablet by a hand long turned to dust.

This is it.

A sense of fear crept over him. What was he doing? If Luthor discovered this book, or found out what Duncan was about to do…

Finish what your master started, whispered the voice from the shadows.

He reached across his desk and lifted up his grimoire, placing it beside the old book. His own tome dwarfed the older book, and he ran his hand over the cover. It had been a gift from Eldrick, a sign that he was coming to the end of his apprenticeship. Anger boiled to the surface of his mood, clearing his uncertainty and bolstering his resolve. It galvanised his decision, justifying the risk.

He had worked so hard for so long. He should be a master in his own right by now. He should be choosing his own apprentice and embarking into his own studies. Eldrick had said as much as he had handed him the grimoire with a rare look of pride on his face.

Damn the council! They had denied him and his long years of study; denied him the position that was rightfully his. And now they insisted he repeat his final apprenticeship! The thought galled him. He felt robbed. He should be a Master. He had done his time. *Damn them.*

'I will show them all,' he muttered and flipped open his grimoire.

Hurrying through the pages, he bypassed the records of his

study, all laboriously copied into his first grimoire, as was the custom. He leafed past hours and hours of work, past his study of the moon, past Eldrick's own studies which Duncan had taken care to copy out in the High Passes. Finally, he came to the last entries; *The Bone Ritual,* and his master's final work from his journals, work Eldrick had entitled, *The Ritual of Flesh.*

There was no mention of this in Eldrick's grimoire — he would not have entered it until it was complete. With his master's journals lost, this was the only remaining copy, a secret knowledge that would remain hidden, for Duncan alone.

He opened a drawer and produced an inkwell, plucked a writing quill from a rack over his desk and leaned forward. With a dip of his quill into the dark ink, he began transcribing from the old book.

You will show them all, apprentice,' whispered the voice.

'Yes, I will show them all,' he repeated.

CHAPTER TWENTY-ONE

His Heart's Home

Bjorn stood watching the landscape slowly drift past, the oars dipping in and out of the river, the peaks of mountains visible over the treetops. *I know this land. I know those mountains.*

The river's course would take them to the foot of those mountains and the forest stretching away to the distance. *The old forest... Home.*

In his hands Bjorn held the stone knife Tung had made. The light shone across the multifaceted surface of the flint blade, a crude, yet beautiful thing. He remembered watching the Wildman as he wrought it from the stones at his feet that fateful night many weeks ago, revealing in stark clarity his intelligence and skill. Bjorn had learned quickly that there was more to the Wildman than met the eye.

He regarded Tung, who sat oblivious at the front of the longship, watching the world pass by in wonder. The Wildman had been at his side ever since that night at his campfire, yet he remained an enigma. Bjorn pushed the flint knife back into his boot and looked out again at the lands through which the river coursed.

'You said you knew these lands?' asked a voice behind him. Archeon's warrior, Daeluf, stepped up beside the hunter and joined him at the ship's rail.

'Aye, I grew up in these parts,' replied Bjorn with a gesture at the approaching trees. 'I walked those woods as a boy and my father paid his silver to the lord in High Stones.'

'He was an oathless man?'

'Aye, a hunter,' nodded Bjorn. 'The lord demanded a tithe of any man who lived on his lands and who was not oath-sworn to him.'

'Your father was proud,' commented Daeluf.

'Yes, but he was free of any oath but his own. He had no obligation to serve any lord's bidding. I live the same.'

'Living for silver — not a life I would choose.' Daeluf shifted his stance to compensate for the gentle rock of the ship. 'It brings me honour to serve my lord, and he rewards me well. A better way to get my silver I think.'

Bjorn said nothing and stared out at the passing scenery.

'This village you spoke of, how far is it?' asked Daeluf.

'A little further upstream, but not far.' Bjorn lifted his chin to indicate the direction of the travel. 'We'll be there before nightfall. There will be horses, alehouses. I know the place.'

Daeluf nodded. 'Better than sleeping on the river another night.' There was a hooting sound from the front of the longship and Daeluf threw a glance at the prow. 'Ten nights since we left Grimm's Crossing, and still he spends all day scrabbling about up there. What is he doing?'

Tung crouched at the very front of the ship, leaning over the prow, peering at the water and poking at it with his spear.

'I don't know,' admitted Bjorn. 'I don't think he's ever been on a boat before, probably never even seen one. What would you do in his place?'

Daeluf grunted in amusement. 'You keep strange company, hunter.'

The Wildman pointed out at the woodlands ahead and stabbed at the water again. Tung turned back to Bjorn and bobbed his head excitedly, seemingly eager to be amongst the trees again, back in the wilds. *He's always more at ease in the woods.*

They had sailed from Grimm's Crossing and taken the river south-east. The river made swifter travel than attempting to cross the rough country which lay east of Oldstones — that overland route could take weeks of struggling through rocky ravines and briar. They left the main river channel before reaching the sea at the harbour of Porth, and rowed upstream to the north-east along a wide tributary which flowed down from the fast mountain streams around High Hall.

A crow cawed at them from the branches of a tree beside the riverbank. The sleek longship had its mast lowered and the benches were full of oarsmen on each side of the deck. It sailed past the tree with its black-feathered herald and with each heave, surged against the sluggish current, the blades of the oars rising and falling rhythmically.

'Still reckon we should have travelled by sea,' Daeluf insisted. 'Taking a ship south from Porth along the coast would have been faster.'

Bjorn cocked a dubious brow at the warrior. 'It's less than a moon til midwinter. I'm no sailor, but even I know it's not a good season to be out on the sea.'

'Rough seas, aye,' he conceded, 'but I know men who have done it.'

'Still, better to stay inland where the weather is fairer. It will be quicker by the river, I promise you,' the hunter assured him. In truth, Bjorn was ill at ease on the open water. He was a man of the wilds, preferring to keep his feet on solid ground. 'We'll stay at the village tonight and ride for High Stones in the morning. There are trade-wharves on the river not far to the south. We can take another ship straight downriver to Arn.'

'The village around the trade-wharves has grown to be a fat little place, more a small town now,' added Daeluf.

'And full of greedy merchants,' sneered the hunter. 'Sometimes we would take pelts there to sell, and the buyers weren't known for their generosity. Passage on a ship might be costly.'

'Do not fear, hunter. I will speak with Lord Hrothgar at High Stones. He is Archeon's most easterly oath-man. He will provide us with another ship. but it may take a day or so to prepare it.'

Bjorn glanced at the woodlands as wild fowl darted amongst the reeds lining the riverbank. The countryside of rolling green dales had begun to give way to forest as the woodland lining the northern bank grew ever closer. Long had he avoided returning here...

'It will be two days ride to High Stones, and the best part of another to prepare the ship down the river?' asked Bjorn.

'Aye, I reckon,' replied Daeluf.

'So, we should be departing for Arn in three days?'

Daeluf nodded.

'Then there is something I must see to. When we make berth at the village up ahead, I must leave you for a time. I'll be back before we sail.'

The warrior's brows rose in surprise. 'Our task is quite pressing, hunter. Is that wise?'

'I swear, I'll meet you at the trade-wharves south of High Stones before we sail, I'll be two days at most.' His assurance did little to convince the warrior, who stood at the rail looking at the hunter with a doubtful frown. 'There's someone I need to see — someone I should have come for a long time ago.'

***

He let his horse pick its way through the trees. They passed amongst wide trunks of old oaks, the ground littered with browning autumn leaves, long since fallen from above. Dappled light spilt down onto the forest floor through the latticework of bare branches overhead, the sky beyond heavy with dark grey clouds.

His horse trotted through a shallow stream. He thought he recognised the bend in the bank away to the left. The trees looked familiar, as did an outcrop of stone nestled at the bottom of a steep bank. It was a map of landmarks, etched in his memory. He was close.

He dismounted and struggled up a muddy rise towards a ridge cloaked in tangled roots. The hunter pulled himself up beside a big old oak that commanded the top of ridge, its branches hanging down over a low craggy cliff. He peered around the tree into the vale below that he knew so well.

The cottage was still there, just as he remembered it; a little building of low, rounded stone-pile walls. It sat squat under a thatched roof that almost touched the ground at the eaves, vegetable gardens nearby cleared and tilled, ready to be sown with next year's crops. He had dug some of those vegetable patches with his own hands, many years ago.

His heart lurched as he spied a wisp of smoke drifting up from the central hole in the thatch. Someone still lived there. He stood a while watching from behind the old oak, suddenly unsure and very nervous.

There was a rustle of leaves on the slope behind him and Tung crouched beside a tree, sniffing the air. Bjorn motioned for him to stay, the Wildman bobbing his head then glancing at the surrounding woodlands. Voices reached him on the wind and Bjorn looked back at the little cottage. When he glanced back at Tung, the Wildman was nowhere to be seen.

Bjorn's heart sank as a man emerged from the cottage. He wore a long cloak and the hunter caught a glimpse of a bearded face before the man pulled his hood up.

Then he saw her.

Khyra...

She emerged from the doorway wearing a long green dress, her raven-black hair just as he remembered. Bjorn fixed his gaze on her face. She was still beautiful, despite the years that had passed. The pair exchanged a few words, then she waved the cloaked man off, watching him disappear down a winding track that led away into the woods. With her hands on her hips, Khyra surveyed the holding, its wicker fence and the vegetable garden.

Her face turned towards the ridge.

Bjorn shrank back into the shadow of the tree. *Did she see me?*

He watched her, frozen as she stared straight at his hiding place for a time. He wanted to step out and reveal himself, but his courage failed him. The moment passed.

'I'm a fool,' he muttered. *She did not wait for me. She married... and can I blame her? It's probably best if I just leave her to live in peace.*

Eventually Khyra turned and stepped back into the darkened doorway, then paused. She turned and stared back up the slope. 'I know someone's there,' she called.

A long moment passed.

'It's rude to spy on a lady,' she said, scanning the ridgeline.

Bjorn took a deep breath and emerged from his hiding place behind the wide trunk of the old oak.

'I mean no harm,' he called as he descended the steep slope towards her, slipping on the loose ground. As he drew closer, recognition crept onto her face in a look of disbelief.

'Bjorn?' she gasped. The colour drained from her cheeks, as if she'd seen a ghost.

'Khyra,' said the hunter. He stopped within arm's reach, desperate to touch her, but stayed his hand. She'd probably break it off.

'Is it really you?'

The hunter nodded, and her shock dissolved into a scowl. 'You never came back.'

'I wanted to—'

She slapped him hard across the face. 'I *waited*, but you never came! I thought you were *dead*... then I heard about you winning some great prize in Barrowford. The famous Bjorn.' Khyra glared at him. 'I waited but you never came.'

'I'm sorry, Khy. You've never been far from my thoughts.'

She slapped him again, her eyes brimming with tears. 'Then why didn't you come?'

Bjorn rubbed at the stubble on his chin. 'I suppose I deserved that.' He gestured down the track. 'Is he a good man?'

She looked confused a moment, then folded her arms, affronted. He hardly had a right to ask, he supposed. 'As good as any.'

'I—I'm happy for you, Khy. If I had known...' He trailed off, not sure what to say.

'You would not have come.'

'I wanted to come. I always knew I would return, but before I knew it years had slipped past—too many years. I should have come, I am sorry. I was passing close by and I had to know. I had to know if you were still here...'

'Oh, so now all of a sudden you care?'

'I always cared,'

Her expression softened a little. 'You look thin, Bjorn.' She reached up to touch the hair at his temple, but her fingers never quite reached him before she pulled back. 'You're going grey. Not the young man I fell in love with.'

Her skin still smelt just like he remembered—lavender and the forest after rain. She smiled. *That smile*... A smile that captured all the beauty in the world and held it behind her eyes.

'Why didn't you come back to me?'

Bjorn chewed the back of his lip, trying to find the right words. 'I knew if I came back, I might never leave. I was young and ambitious then. I didn't see what I had right in front of me. I thought I had to wander the wilds, make a name for myself. But there was always a regret hanging over me... it was not coming back to you, for leaving it so long.'

'Well I'm glad your reputation was more important than me,' she snapped. 'So what happened, had enough of fame and adventure?' She awaited his reply with her hands on her hips, her face twisted with a scowl.

'I made my name, hunted beasts in every corner of the realm,

I've seen things most men never see but with it... I have seen so much death, Khyra. I have seen more blood spilt than any man should ever see. I have seen the darkness that lives within men's hearts, and I do not wish to see any more of it. I needed to come back. I was a fool to leave you here — all this time without word — but I needed to see if there was still someone waiting for me... But I fear I waited too long.' He glanced down the track leading away from the house. 'Your husband is a lucky man.'

'My husband?' Khyra raised her brows and snorted dismissively. 'He's not my husband.'

'Your man then,' he said with a wave in the direction of the track.

'He's not my man, either. My man promised he would come back.' She folded her arms and eyed him. 'I only wish he had come sooner.' It struck home then just how selfish he had been, just how much he had hurt this woman. She hadn't moved on, and he could see in her eyes she was still hurting from being left behind.

'Can you forgive a wandering fool,' he asked, unsure if he really deserved it but thought it worth a try.

With no reply she considered him a moment longer. Finally Khyra snorted a laugh of disbelief at her own foolishness and shook her head at herself. She shot him a withering glare and then gave a sharp jerk of her head to indicate he could follow her to the house.

Inside was much the same as he remembered; bunches of herbs drying from the roof, a raised hearth beneath cooking pots and cauldrons. She still had the chair he had made that rocked back and forth, and her shelves were stacked with books and old scrolls. The back rooms of the cottage were partitioned with an embroidered hanging of a deer and a wolf — Hjort the Hart stag and Varg the wolf — the gods of the hunt, amongst other things. Bjorn smiled; he had missed this place.

There was movement on a chair in the nearest corner, and an ancient black, long-haired cat sat up and yawned.

'Macumba!' he exclaimed. 'You still have her?'

The cat sniffed at his hand warily before allowing him to stroke her, waving her bushy tail and nuzzling his hand. He remembered carrying her through the forest in his pack as a kitten. He had been a young man then, and the kitten had poked her head out, watching the passing woodlands as he brought her as a gift to a beautiful young woman.

'Oh yes, she's still here. Still a pain in the arse too,' replied Khyra.

The cat stretched lazily and sniffed the air at her words. Bjorn could have sworn he saw a barely perceptible look of defiant smugness on its whiskered face. Khyra sat in her chair and motioned for him to sit beside the hearth.

'So, who was he — your visitor?' asked Bjorn.

Her brows rose again. 'Jealous?'

He shrugged, hoping the gloom of the cottage might hide the heat in his cheeks.

Khyra leaned forward and eased a pot onto the fire. 'He came for a remedy.'

'You've become a witch!' he laughed.

'I prefer *wise-woman*,' she corrected with a wry smile. 'Healing, the odd ritual, or assisting a birth. I took over from Old Tanya. She lives back in Garbeck now, with her daughter. She's very frail — shouldn't be living out in the woods on her own. Folk come to see me from the villages and I get by well enough.'

'Have there been others?' Bjorn asked tentatively, morbid curiosity getting the better of him.

'Others?' she sat back in the chair, locking eyes with him. She understood his meaning.

'Other men,' he said.

'I'm not sure that's any of your business, or why you would want to know?' she replied in a cool tone.

He shifted in his chair, uncomfortable under the intensity of her glare. 'No, probably not.'

She sighed. 'I never married. I made a promise — the foolish promise of a naive girl — but a promise nonetheless. In truth, your leaving made it hard to trust that another would not do the same given half a chance. I've been angry with you a long time, Bjorn.'

'I am sorry,' Bjorn told her. He didn't know what else to say. He had left her behind, without word of whether he was alive or dead for too many years. She'd be within her rights to slam the door in his face.

'I can slap you again if it would make you feel better?' She smirked and he thought she might do it just for fun.

He'd arrived on her doorstep with nothing. Tung was out

there wandering around, both of them living off the land as they needed to. He hadn't even thought to bring a gift, or a token of his remorse...

Khyra stood and made her way to a sideboard, 'I suppose you're thirsty?' she said pouring him an ale from a jug and handing it to him without ceremony.

He mumbled his thanks.

'I'm doing a stew too if you're hungry, just vegetables, nothing fancy. I got a rabbit in the snare this morning. I was going to let it hang a few days, but I could put some meat in?'

'No, no meat,' said Bjorn quickly, almost choking on his mouthful of ale.

'No?' she asked with a frown. She would think that odd, but he still couldn't stomach the stuff.

'It's a long, dull story you don't want to hear.' Bjorn waved his tankard, hoping that was enough to deter her questions. He could see them piling up behind her inquisitive eyes. 'Vegetables are just fine. What is that you've added to the ale?'

'Burdock root,' she replied as she busied herself adding herbs to the simmering cauldron.

'It's good,' he said and she smiled a little. It was the weary smile of a woman who lived behind walls and kept her guard up. It was the smile offered to hide the true feelings that hid deep below. It was still as lovely as he remembered but it was dampened by something—something he suspected was entirely his fault. 'I always wondered if you had gone back to the College?'

'No, my place is here,' she replied. 'I love the woods and the open places. I couldn't imagine not living here. Occasionally I'll hear from them—once a scholar, always a scholar they say.' Silence filled the room and for a time, the only sound between them was the crackle of the fire and the bubbling of the pot. 'Bjorn, tell me, who is your skulking friend outside?'

Bjorn glanced up quickly, scanning the door and the small window on the opposite wall. 'Oh, he's a friend. His name is Tung. He's a Wildman. I'm surprised you saw him.'

'A Wildman?' Her eyes grew wide, but she showed no sign of fear. 'And you left him outside like a dog?'

Bjorn licked dry lips, embarrassed by her admonishment. 'He loves the forests, Khy. He never seems at ease indoors. I'll check on him, but I imagine he's quite happy out there in the trees doing, well, whatever he does.'

She smirked again and shook her head.

'I'm sure he'll be fine, though he'd probably appreciate some food, if you have anything to spare.'

Khyra stopped stirring the stew and looked at the hunter. 'So, I'm feeding you and your friend? I suppose you think you're staying the night?'

'I don't want to impose, but I—'

'Oh shut up, you old fool. We'll see—I can hardly turn you out now you're here.'

They sat and talked as the sun sank below the horizon and darkness fell amongst the trees. They ate and drank, and he took a bowl out for Tung. He was tempted to whistle for the Wildman, but he decided against it. The Wildman was no doubt lurking somewhere nearby, but he would not stray far. He tended to his horse before returning to the fire and the company of Khyra. He had not realised just how much he had missed her until she sat before him again.

The years had not been unkind. She was still heart-wrenchingly beautiful, and as quick-witted as ever, her sense of humour razor-sharp. He had forgotten just how sharp until she cut him with it. It was a good sign, though. She was always hardest on the people she liked. Her voice was low and haunting, as it always had been, and his heart stirred every time he looked at her. Seeing her again re-ignited a feeling inside him, a feeling that had slowly dimmed as each year without her had passed. *I have been a fool to stay away so long. Now I am finally home.*

After a while, talking beside the fire, it was as if no time had passed at all. He talked of his wanderings, regaling her with tales of his adventures. He told her everything, from the year he had left right up to recent events; of Archeon, and the terrible Wildmen, and of Tung and his pursuit. He spoke of the manhunt and the rumours of trouble across the realm.

She told him of the local news, of old friends and folk he had once known. Much had changed here, yet much was remained just as he'd left it.

The night grew darker and the conversation eventually slowed until they were both left staring at the crackling fire. Khyra turned to him. 'It's late. I think my bed is calling.'

She rose and considered him a moment. 'You may stay.'

He looked up, a small hope igniting in his heart.

'But you sleep out here, by the fire. There's more timber by the door if you get cold, and furs in the chest under the window.'

Bitter disappointment snuffed out his spark of foolish hope. He nodded and bade her a good night.

She turned to regard him. 'It has been good to see you again, Bjorn.' She offered him a final sad smile before disappearing through the embroidered hanging into her backrooms.

Bjorn longed to follow but he knew he was no longer welcome there. He sighed.

The old cat came and curled up beside him, taking some time to finally settle and purring as he stoked her between her ears.

Regret washed over him as he stared into the dying fire — this was not the welcome he thought he was going to get. How had he been so foolish to expect otherwise? To expect her to welcome him with open arms after all these years. He had wronged her greatly, he had been selfish beyond measure, and that now came with a price he would have to pay to win back her heart. If he wanted her trust again, her love, he knew he would have to earn it the hard way. He drifted asleep haunted by regrets and guilt gnawing at his heart.

***

He awoke to the sunlight streaming in through the window. Khyra was already awake, pottering about as if he were not there.

'You're still here,' said Khyra as she knelt stoking the hearth fire.

The morning light pulled his thoughts back to his impending task. *The ship would be ready soon.* He knew he had to get back, after all, a meeting with a king awaited him. He sighed. *How can I tell her I am leaving so already.*

'Aye, lass, I'm here.'

'I thought I might awaken and you would be gone,' she said.

He smiled, 'I wouldn't go without saying goodbye.'

'But, you are going though aren't you,' she said sadly. 'The audience with your king?'

'Aye, lass.'

'I thought as much. You never could stay in one place for long…'

'I must go, but I will be coming back this time. I promise. This is my last job and then I will return, if you will let me prove my-self.'

'I could make you promise me on the gods, on your precious honour and reputation that kept you away so long. Go ahead, promise me that I will see you again, but I can't help remembering what little good it did last time.'

'You have my word, Khy.'

She shrugged.

In silence, they prepared a simple morning meal of bread and cheese, and Bjorn made ready to leave. Khyra paused as she wrapped the cheese again, and Bjorn grew still as she looked out at the new day beyond the door. 'I had a dream last night. I would consult my cards before you go, if you've time to wait?'

'A dream?' asked the hunter. She had been known to have them when they were together and had been haunted by them through the day many times. They hardly ever bode well.

'A dark dream. We were both there but... I must check the cards,' she said, taking a small wooden box from a shelf.

He placed his gear beside the door and sat across the table from her, watching intently as she opened the box and drew out a wooden seer's deck.

The cards of the god's eyes.

It was known the gods spoke through such cards, sometimes revealing truths or foretelling the path ahead. She shuffled the cards and held them out to him. 'Pick some.'

'How many?'

'As many as you need.'

He plucked four from the deck and handed them back to her. One by one she turned them over, each painted with an image or symbol. There was a wolf, a hooded man, a skull, and a crow.

'What do they say?' he asked when she did not speak.

Ignoring him, Khyra studied her cards then looked up with a frown. 'Portentous,' she replied. She collected a bag from beneath her chair, and from it, drew a handful of stones. She scattered them on the floor, each smooth stone marked with runes and symbols.

'Take another four cards and lay one beside each of the others,' she said, her voice serious. He did as he was told, the four cards showing a crown beneath the wolf, a blind beggar beneath the

248

hooded man, a stag beneath the skull, and fire beneath the crow.

His heart thudded a little harder when again, she said nothing. 'Khyra, what do you see? What does this mean?' asked Bjorn.

She looked up, lines of worry creasing her brow. 'These are not good cards. The runes are the same. There is a darkness in your path. Tread carefully, Bjorn. The crown and the wolf are royal symbols of Arnar. There is a king in your path, or a war. The hooded man can sometimes be Old Night, and the blind beggar with him tell that death is coming, unseen or unexpected perhaps. I'm not sure.'

'My death?'

'I cannot say, perhaps not.' She stood beside the table and her gaze fell back to the cards. 'The skull and the stag, again death but Hjort will guide you, use his cunning. Crows and fire reveal more dark portents. Bjorn, this a warning. None of this is good, and I have a feeling this is bigger than just what lies your path.'

'I will be careful,' he promised, rising from his chair as she scooped the cards back into the box. Some might have dismissed Khyra and her scrying as superstitious nonsense, but he knew better. The shadow of concern in her eyes told him she felt this to her core, and he would be a fool to ignore it. 'I have a ship waiting at High Stones to take me downriver. I must go or they will sail without me.' He smiled and dared to reach and squeeze her hand. She did not pull away, but he let her go.

She followed him outside and stood by as he saddled his horse. The bowl he had left for Tung lay empty outside the door, and Khyra stooped to collect it, hugging her shawl closer about her shoulders. Bjorn looked into the trees and whistled. After a moment a figure emerged from the woodlands.

'Is this your Wildman?' asked Khyra, watching as Tung jogged from the shadows and into the crisp morning. 'Strange company you're keeping.'

'Tung,' Bjorn greeted his companion with a nod. The Wildman hooted and bobbed his head in reply and Bjorn turned to Khyra. 'He's proven a better comrade than most.' It was true — an unspoken bond had grown between them and Bjorn trusted the Wildman more than any other.

Khyra turned a genuine smile towards Tung. 'Keep him safe, Wildman. It would be nice to see him again.' Tung tilted his head, a confused expression crumpling his face, and Bjorn stared at

Khyra. She meant it, but there was a warning in her kindness. She would not pine or wallow, waiting for him and denying all others. He still had a long way to go to earn her trust.

Bjorn mounted his horse and Khyra smiled sadly, stepping back to the doorway. 'Remember Bjorn, tread carefully. There is a darkness in your path. Death stalks these lands.'

He offered her a warm smile. 'I will return.' He urged his horse forwards and Tung broke into a jog, fire hardened spear in hand. At the top of the ridge, by the old oak, Bjorn reined in and turned his horse to take one last look. The cottage, the familiar woods, Khyra watching him go. He burned the image of her face in his mind.

I will return to you. He held her gaze a moment and clicked his tongue at his horse, urging it onward into the trees. *My ship awaits, and a king.*

CHAPTER TWENTY-TWO

The Watching Saviour

'Is Hrothgar still lord of High Stones Hall?' Bjorn asked as he stared up at the wooden buildings perched high on the mountainside.

High Stones Hall was flanked by two colossal standing stones, landmarks in their own right and visible for leagues around. These incredible menhirs lent the holding its name and Bjorn had always found them incredible. They were hundreds of feet high, perhaps once part of the mountain. No one knew how they got there, or what feat of ancient engineering was used to carve them from the mountain side.

'Aye, that he is,' replied Daeluf.

'He must be old now,' said Bjorn. 'I remember him from when I was a lad. He seemed a good man.'

'He's as grey as snow but he's still hearty. Gods know how he's still hanging on,' Daeluf laughed. 'Lord Archeon values him. As you say, he is a good man.'

Bjorn stood at the stern watching the mountains of High Stones and the trade wharves shrink behind them. Somewhere behind those stony cliffs was the old forest, and Khyra. He'd vowed to return this time, and he meant to keep his promise, whether she believed him or not. The ship had been ready as he rode in, and they'd set sail down river to the great city of Arn and the king.

A good westerly wind meant they had no need to row, the sail full as the ship coursed eastwards along the widening river. To the north, the Spine rose along the horizon, the distant peaks slowly sliding past as the morning wore on.

Daeluf took another bite from the strip of chewy salt pork in his hand then offered a strip to Bjorn. Bjorn frowned briefly at the offered pork, then pulled his face into something he hoped resembled a smile and waved it away, giving a shake of his head.

'A hunter that doesn't eat meat?' commented Daeluf with an amused smirk. 'Strange times.'

'The irony is not lost on me,' Bjorn muttered. 'I haven't been able to face the thought of touching it since…'

'Aye, I remember your tale.' The guard captain glanced suspiciously at his salt pork. 'Understandable, I suppose.'

'You said before that you had news you thought might interest me?' asked the hunter.

Daeluf's expression darkened. 'I spoke with Hrothgar. A rider arrived just yesterday, talking of skirmishes in the west, but he had no word of Archeon's forces meeting the enemy in pitched battle. Folk still think it's raiders.'

Bjorn sensed the captain's doubts. 'But you don't?'

'No.' Daeluf frowned.

'You think another rebellion is brewing?' ventured Bjorn, thinking back on the claims of the man he and Tung had tracked and captured.

'I truly hope not, but that is my fear,' the warrior captain admitted. 'Those men we ran down, the man's words before we stuck him in that gibbet… The wind is whistling through his bones, yet his words still haunt me.'

Bjorn shrugged. 'The defiance of a condemned man.'

'Perhaps,' Daeluf sighed. 'Yet there was something about that man. I am almost certain they are the survivors of the old rebellion. That somehow, they survived out there in the Storm Waters, regrouped and formed an army. Now they are returning to take another stab at us.'

'Will you speak your mind to the king?' asked Bjorn.

'Privately, aye.' The captain nodded. 'Archeon has told me as much. He wants the king to know our suspicions but does not want it spoken of it in front of the court. He does not want the whole realm hearing of it and thinking him weak.'

'No, of course,' said Bjorn.

'There is more. Hrothgar has lost contact with many of his holdings to the north. I told him of the savages you spoke of. He was most concerned. He knows how fragile this situation has become and told me he knows of lords who have ridden north, but none have returned. There have been no messages, nothing.'

'The savages?' exclaimed Bjorn. A dark cloud of worry settled over him. If the Stonemen had come over the border, they would be killing Arnar folk in droves, hunting them, eating them. He shuddered at the thought.

The Wildman, Tung, loitered nearby staring up at the flapping sail. He turned at Bjorn's outburst.

'It must be.' Daeluf shrugged.

'I warned them. I warned you,' said Bjorn. 'They're not just mere savages. These Stonemen are killers, beasts. They are feeding on the folk of Arnar.'

'I know, friend,' said Daeluf gravely. 'With most of Archeon's warriors marching west, I fear we find ourselves in a dire situation. We need more men. We must have warriors sent to the frontier, and for that we must convince the king. We cannot fail, or there is a very real chance the Western Mark will fall. We cannot fight invasions on two fronts.'

'We won't fail,' replied Bjorn. 'The king will send his banners. I will tell them all what I saw. I will tell them that the horrors of the Stonemen are real. I will *make* them listen.'

After several days on the river, they passed the town of Barrowford. The ancient ford, where the river ran shallow, lay before an intersection of two large tributaries. A channel through the ford had been deepened so boats could sail freely past, and a bridge now spanned the banks.

The joining of the two rivers had given birth to a town which sprawled the land stretching between them. One of Arnar's largest central settlements, fed by river trade from the east and the rich lands of the south west, Barrowford was a hub for traders and merchants serving the interior.

There had been a great battle here, long ago, spoken of in the Sagas. The huge burial mounds were clearly visible from the river. The bones of thousands were said to rest under those grassy cairns, brave souls lost like grains of sand in the oceans of centuries.

Bjorn and his companions didn't stop at Barrowford, but sailed onward. He watched the houses and people slip past, going about their business ashore until their boat left the sprawl of Barrowford behind, surging eastward along the river. Arn was only a day or two downstream. It would not be long until they reached the capital.

***

Duncan hurried as quickly as he could manage along the narrow corridor, his crutches clacking loudly on the floorboards. He had been summoned by his new master, Luthor's message speaking of travelling to the Citadel to see this cursed son of the northern lord, the one who had become more beast than man. He was curious beyond measure to see the man for himself, and he moved faster than his body liked, all his aches and pains protesting his speed.

How could Eldrick's work have done this? he wondered. He wasn't sure he believed it was connected to the dark meddling in the passes. He had seen dusty bones rise, seen life breathed into dead flesh once more, but the man the king's chancellor had described was not like anything he had seen, nor heard his previous master speak of.

His haste was not only to meet Luthor, but to return the book he had taken from the archives. If Luthor discovered he had found a copy against his express instructions, it would be the end for him at the College. His heart pounded, his pulse thudding in his throat. He had disobeyed his master, he had lied to the council, and to the chancellor.

If they discover what I have done, I am a dead man.

His guard trailed along behind him, emotionless and probably bored out of his skull. Duncan was growing used to their constant presence. It had been nearly a week now, each day a different guard trailing behind him everywhere he went like a grim-faced shadow. Duncan hobbled through the narrow corridors of the Scriptorium, the shortest route to the archives. Scholars sat at easels in little cells lining the passageway, each busily scribbling away with ink and quill. Ahead, loud voices echoed against the walls.

A cluster of young women rounded a corner, their voices growing louder as they approached along the narrow passageway. He stopped to let them pass.

'Urghh,' sneered one of the initiates. 'What happened to this one?'

The other girls giggled cruelly. The one who had spoken looked down her nose at him, her top lip curling. By her clothes, she looked to be noble-born—some lord's daughter, no doubt. Duncan tried to push away his innate disdain for the highborn offspring who filled the College halls. They never stayed long, using the College as a means to learn their letters before returning to their father's household. They had no respect for the institution or its purpose.

'How dare you speak to me like that?' he snapped. 'Who is your master?'

'What's it to you, cripple? You're only an apprentice.' The girl gave a derisive snort. 'You're nobody. Don't you know who my father is?'

'I don't care,' retorted the apprentice. 'He holds no sway in these halls, *initiate*.'

The girls laughed and anger surged in his belly, accompanied by something else.

Shame?

Humiliation?

No. He looked the girl over. Heat rolled through his belly, a wave of vengeful, creeping lust. She was young, barely a woman, but the slight curve of her hips and the hint of her breasts beneath her tunic drew his eye.

He found himself stood, leering at her wordlessly, thinking of all the things he would like to do to her. He felt heat creeping across his face as his thoughts made him blush. He averted his eyes and caught the lingering shadow again, dancing at the edges of his vision.

The girl laughed at him. 'What are you staring at, creep?'

Bitch! I would teach her some respect. He opened his mouth to give her a scathing reply but no words came, instead he found his mouth suddenly dry. He could feel his face burning, which only made it worse. He met her dismissive gaze and immediately looked away at the floor, ashamed. His fight suddenly gone, his old self returning. He had always been nervous in front of girls.

'Out of our way, you creepy little man,' the girl scoffed, pushing her way past. Her entourage hurrying to continue along the passageway to the Scriptorium.

He stood a moment, wrestling with his outrage as he stared

after them. *I'll show you!*

His guard grunted in amusement. 'Not much of a lady's man, eh lad?'

Duncan had no reply. Embarrassed and angry, he hobbled away towards the archives. He would show them all.

***

The rain poured from the cloud-laden sky, and Nym stood out in it with her tattered old cloak wrapped tightly around her shoulders. It was sodden, but it was all she had to ward off the torrents lashing down upon her head. She pulled her scarf in around over her face. It offered little protection from the rain either, but it was a forlorn hope against the encroaching sickness.

There was a body every few strides now, laying in the gutter, the twisted dead frozen in their final agonised throes. Stiffened, bloody death masks, nightmare faces choked with dark blood and flies. Many houses had been daubed in red paint, a sign that all inside had fallen victim to the blood plague. Houses of death, some had yet to be cleared. The carts rumbled along Arn's streets, day and night, wooden wheels churning the rain-soaked mud into a black filth.

The markets had been near empty again. Yesterday, Jor had managed to return with something, but today she made her way back to the house empty handed. *What will we eat? There is little left.*

Many traders had closed up, while other stalls stood ominously empty. The few merchants still open for business had scant wares, and there was hardly any food to be found. Nothing was coming in from the farms to restock the stalls and stores, the farmers had stopped bringing food from their fields in fear of the plague. The fish markets and docks were no better. The boats weren't going out for there were no sailors or fishermen left to crew them. There was just nothing.

She turned onto the now familiar row of dishevelled houses marking the outskirts of the slum district. A grisly monument to the dead adorned the gutter on one side where folk had dumped the fallen at the top of the narrow winding street. The sight stirred a queasiness in the pit of her stomach.

The horror of looking upon the dead wherever she walked

had not lessened, though they had become a common sight. She hurried past an emaciated man clad in rags picking over the pile of dead, searching desperately for anything of value.

It'll do you little good, friend. There's nothing to buy, thought Nym bleakly. He threw her a nervous look, like a wild animal deciding whether or not to bolt. No one seemed to care that he was desecrating the bodies. A few residents watched from their doorways wearing haunted faces, all hope long departed, all honour for the dead long forgotten.

One face stood out to Nym as she passed, and her pace slowed just a little. The witch. *There she is again, always watching.*

Her pronounced, angular nose reminded Nym of a bird — her narrow, painted eyes framed by long black hair, she could have been a crow. Mysterious trinkets adorned her clothes and hair, and she stood watching the street with a cloak wrapped around her. Her hood was down, seemingly unbothered by the rain. Nym had grown used to her now, catching sight of the woman so often that she almost wondered if she stepped out of her hovel just to watch Nym pass. *What could she possibly find so interesting about me?*

Nym thumped into something hard and staggered backwards in the mud. 'Hand over the bag,' a harsh voice demanded.

She glanced up into the sheeting rain to see a man's scarred and scowling face glaring down at her. One hand brandished a knife, the point angled towards her, its blade rough and dull.

'I *said* hand over the bag!' the man repeated, his tone hardening further. He was covered in the black filth off the street, his clothes shabby and his sneer revealed more gaps than teeth.

Nym took a couple of quick steps back, looking around desperately. Doors on both sides of the street creaked shut, faces disappearing into the gloom.

Her heart sank. *Won't anybody help me?*

The man snatched the limp bag from her trembling hands and pulled it open, shoving a hand inside and groping around. His expression morphed from a victorious smirk to a frustrated, angry glower.

'There's nothing in here!' he snarled. 'You've got it hidden. Hand it over now or I'll cut that pretty throat of yours wide open.' He started forwards, jabbing the filthy knife at her.

'Please!' pleaded Nym. 'I have nothing.' She was trembling,

trying not to think of the few coins she had hidden in her bodice. 'There was nothing left at the market... Please—'

'Leave the girl be,' said the accented voice of a woman.

Nym turned towards the sound and gasped. It was the witch from across the street, standing a foot or so distant, unafraid of the man and his knife.

'Stay out of this, bitch,' snapped the cutthroat, brandishing his knife.

'Leave the girl be,' the woman said again, 'or I will cast your soul to the abyss. You will never find peace in death. You will be cursed until the end of days. This I swear.'

'You wouldn't dare,' the man sneered, but uncertainty flashed in his eyes.

'The gods speak through me, fool. I can do as I please,' the witch replied.

The woman cast a handful of bones at the thief's feet and began mumbling, drawing strange symbols in the air.

'No!' shouted the man, shrinking back and dropping the bag. 'I never harmed her!' He stumbled backwards, before fleeing down a nearby alley.

The woman narrowed her eyes. 'Fool.'

Nym trembled where she stood. She wanted to thank the woman, but only tears came in the place of words.

'Be calm, child,' the woman told her. Her accent and her complexion marked her as someone from far beyond the borders of Arnar. 'He will not trouble you again.'

'Did you?' Nym whispered, glancing at the alley where the man had disappeared and at the bones at her feet. 'Did you *curse* him?'

The old woman laughed and Nym backed away, terrified. 'Be calm, child. I will not harm you.' She offered Nym a smile. 'We women must look out for each other, no?'

Stooping to collect the bag the thief had dropped, Nym stepped away. 'T—thank you...' she stuttered. 'Really, thank you, but I must go.'

Nym turned and ran. Seth's house was only two streets away. She left the strange woman standing in the middle of the muddy street and did not look back.

CHAPTER TWENTY-THREE

The Beast in the Cage

The palisades of the Citadel loomed over the water as the boat drew close to the moorings. The apprentice stared up at the figures along the top of the wall, some pacing slowly, others motionless sentinels, the wooden ramparts made even taller by their reflection in the sluggish waters of the Bane River.

Duncan had never been inside those timber walls, but had lived within sight of them nearly all his life. He often looked up here, imagining the ancient towering walls of cyclopean stone that had once stood in place of the cluster of wooden halls perched on the crown of the hill. Legend had it that the wooden halls of Arnar's king were built on the crumbling foundations of ancient stone, he was eager to see if any such stone still lingered within the Citadel. There were few buildings in Arnar that could claim any of the ancient stone as part of their construction, especially since different building techniques had begun to creep over the seas from Telis.

The boat drew closer to the wharf with each pull of the oar, his guard pulling in unison with the boatman. Today his minder was an older man, the leader of those tasked with following in his shadow wherever he went. Master Luthor was also aboard the boat, sitting on a bench in front of Duncan, with Jasper beside him. Gideon sat next to the apprentice, taking up more than his fair share of the bench.

'This creature,' murmured Gideon, breaking the gentle sound of oars dipping in the water. 'They say it howls and shrieks night and day.'

'So I hear,' replied Luthor, his breath misting in the chill air.

'Do you think it's true, master?' asked Duncan nervously.

'It's true, lad,' the warrior put in as he pulled on his oar. 'The screams fill the Citadel, keeping us all from rest.'

'Wilhelm, isn't it?' asked Luthor politely.

'Aye,' replied the old warrior. Duncan's face flushed. He had been so nervous under his guard's watch, it had not occurred to him to ask their names.

'They say the creature was once a man.' Gideon spoke in a low, almost conspiratorial whisper, as if to even mention it would land them in trouble.

'Aye, I saw it the day they brought it before the king in the Throne Hall. It was the son of a lord named Arnulf.'

'Poor devil,' Gideon said, shaking his head.

'What is it now if it's not a man?' Duncan addressed Wilhelm directly for the first time.

'Varg be damned if I know, lad. You'll see for yourself soon enough. But I'll say this — don't get too close it.'

'Our best physicians should be examining it as we speak,' said Luthor.

'And we must too?' asked Duncan, pulling his cloak tighter to ward away the cold. 'What use are we if they are already there?' He was not looking forward to confronting the terrible thing after all the talk he had heard.

'The council commands it,' replied Luthor gravely, looking out over the sluggish river. 'We are to search for any connection between the creature and Eldrick's work. If it bears signs of being experimented upon or of ritual markings, the council must be informed immediately.'

'And him?' The apprentice gestured at Jasper. The big man intimidated him, and he was sure if asked, he could snap Duncan in two. Whether he would was another matter entirely, but the man's obvious strength gave him pause.

Luthor shrugged. 'Jasper is here to assist you actually, Duncan. I thought it best. We will have a bit of a walk and getting about will not be easy as you have already noticed.'

The apprentice had been surprised when Jasper had lifted him into the boat without warning. Jasper had paid his startled objections no heed, strong hands lifting him and placing him on his bench. He had been grateful though, Duncan had been stood eyeing the rocking boat with apprehension, thinking he might fall overboard and drown as he struggled to climb aboard with his crutches. Duncan nodded, understanding now Jasper's actions. Duncan looked across at his new helper, Jasper sat watching the oars rise and fall into the murky water. Duncan had learnt from his master that the man had once been a slave, chained to an oar on the ship they thought had carried the blood plague to Arnar's shores.

The apprentice watched him closely, wondering what Jasper was thinking as the oars rose and fell. What terrible memories did he harbour from his forced labours? And how had he survived the very same sickness that was sweeping through the city and into the countryside, while the others aboard took ill?

'In truth, young Duncan, it was my idea,' admitted Gideon, 'I was also curious to accompany your master to see this creature for myself. I have heard such tales of it. And I do not like to leave our guest alone for long. Jasper has been cooped up at the College for weeks so I thought I would take the opportunity to make him useful and perhaps also show him some of the city.'

Jasper turned to regard them at the repeated mention of his name. He smiled, then returned his gaze to the river. The apprentice wondered how much he understood of their words.

'We have learnt much from him these last few days,' continued Gideon. 'I would repay him, even if it is only with some freedom about our great capital.'

'Some gift,' muttered Wilhelm from in front.

'Why so?' asked Luthor curiously.

Wilhelm grunted. 'The sight of the twisted dead, the stink of corpses? This is no time to go sight-seeing around Arn. This is a city of death.'

The boatman secured his oar through an iron ring and rose from the bench to throw a line over the mooring. Wilhelm sat with his oar in his lap as the boat gently coasted towards the wharf where a group of College sell-swords waited. The council were clearly taking no chances with the safety of their folk.

'The gates aren't far, but we had best put these on — we should have been wearing them before we left.' Luthor sighed and reached into a bag at his feet, lifting out an elongated mask and raising it to his face. It covered the lower half of his face, containing his mouth and nose, his eyes peering over the top. Luthor offered one to Wilhelm, but the warrior shook his head and pulled a scarf up over his mouth and nose. Luthor passed the bag back to Gideon, and Duncan fished a mask out of the bag for himself when it reached him.

The council had advised that all members of the College were to wear protective masks if venturing into the city. Many didn't like them though, Luthor amongst them. Duncan had heard folk call them "plague beaks" or "Caleb masks", and they had become a regular sight within the College compound. The apprentice turned his beak-mask over in his hands. It was made of leather and stuffed with fragrant herbs which Councillor Caleb believed kept the sickness at bay. It was long and tapered, resembling the hooked beak of a rhann, which seemed apt considering the grim circumstances of its purpose.

'Careful, lad; don't let any of it fall out,' cautioned Gideon as he strapped his own mask over his mouth and nose.

'Must wear,' insisted Luthor, trying to persuade Jasper to wear a mask. The big man seemed to find their appearance quite amusing.

'Like bird,' grinned Jasper. '*Jhet ac anarou.*' He motioned the flapping of a bird with his hands.

Luthor turned questioningly to Gideon who shrugged in reply.

'Yes.' Luthor nodded, showing Jasper how the mask worked. 'You must wear this to go inside,' he said, pointing at the Citadel.

Duncan raised his own mask and fumbled with the straps as he fastened it behind his head. It was heavy, the straps pulling on his neck, the scent inside strange and cloying. In truth he agreed with Jasper—he thought they looked ridiculous. It was tempting to refuse and laugh at the idea, but he would rather be safe than sorry, or dead. The others raised their hoods before alighting. Duncan raised his also; he thought to help keep out the cold, and perhaps, he hoped, the sickness too.

As they stepped off the boat and made their way up the dockside street, the apprentice could not help wondering at how they must look like a surreal murder of crows — dark robed, hoods pulled up, grotesque hooked beaks jutting from underneath—the walking embodiment of the rhann and its crow kin. He and his companions were like the birds of death, come to stalk these corpse littered streets as the heralds of Old Night.

The gates were indeed not far, Duncan reluctantly accepting Jasper's assistance as he struggled through the mud with his crutches, but even on such a short walk, the horrors of the terrible blood plague were unavoidable, no matter how quickly he averted his eyes from the dead dumped at the sides of the street.

The heralds of Old Night indeed…

Warriors admitted them through the tall gates of the Citadel's outer palisade and into a packed sprawl of buildings, stables and forges. The apprentice glanced around, and found himself disappointed at the lack of obvious ancient stone. It was a lot less impressive than he had envisioned.

'They're keeping the creature in the outer gaol now, away from the stables. The fucking thing was spooking the horses,' drawled the warrior who escorted them from the gates. 'Been frightening half the Citadel. Aye, few will be sorry to have it gone, that's for sure.' He motioned them inside a thick framed building that looked to have sunk into the ground. More warriors stood guard beside an interior door, eyeing the College group menacingly, then staring wide-eyed at Jasper.

'A few of your lot are already in there,' the warrior continued, unlocking the door.

A blood curdling roar exploded from behind it and to a man they flinched back from the sound. His master exchanged a nervous glance with Gideon, before shifting to rest on Duncan. He said nothing, readjusting his mask and continuing after the warrior leading them.

'Is that…?' asked Gideon apprehensively.

'Aye that's it.' The warrior cleared his throat to cover the waver of his voice. 'They're in here.' He stopped before another door, unhooked a ring of keys from his belt and set about working the lock.

The apprentice stood staring at the monstrosity locked within the cage, unable to tear his eyes away from it. It was bestial and primal. Matted hair hung in its face, it stooped in a crouch, torn remnants of clothes dangling from its body, a low growl emanating from its throat.

The cage had been placed in the centre of a long room sunk into the ground below street level, natural light spilling in from barred windows near the roof. Torches burned in sconces around the room and a pair of the king's warriors stood watch by the door.

A cluster of College scholars and their sell-sword companions stood around examining the beast as it threw itself against the bars, swiping a filthy hand at the nearest observer. Its intended prey flinched back out of reach, and it let out another frustrated roar. One of the beak-masked observers noticed their arrival and broke away from the group to approach them.

'Ah, Luthor!' the muffled voice of a man greeted the master from within the mask. 'They're calling it a Cursed One. A very curious specimen, wouldn't you agree?'

'Master Hobar,' Luthor acknowledged him with a nod.

'I see you have your own curious specimen.' The scholar gestured at Jasper and Duncan saw Luthor grimace, as if referring to the man as a "specimen" made the master uncomfortable.

'His name is Jasper, and he accompanies us to aid my apprentice.'

'Did you confirm that he is indeed a man of Myhar?' asked Hobar, looking Jasper up and down. Jasper ignored the bobbing scholar, no more bothered by him than a horse is by a fly, his attention firmly fixed on the creature in the cage.

'Aye,' replied Luthor.

'Quite interesting,' said Master Hobar. 'I have never seen anyone quite like him. I was one of the first to examine him, you see, on behalf of the council when he first arrived. It was I who guessed Myhar. I imagine few alive have found themselves so far from home has he.'

Hobar's tone dripped of self-congratulating importance, and Duncan noticed that Luthor offered no reply. Instead he watched the creature thrashing at the bars of the cage, howling with a bestial rage.

Seemingly unable to impress Luthor, Hobar turned to Gideon and nodded a greeting. 'Does he speak?'

'Aye, a little,' he replied, his usual excitement on the progress of Jasper blunted by the clamour of the creature. Gideon too had his eyes fixed on the cage.

The creature was attempting in vain to tear away the bars. It howled again, unable to budge the sturdy iron. Even knowing his name, the apprentice did not recognise Master Hobar. He had not come across him at the College. He leaned closer to Gideon.

'Who is he?' the apprentice asked quietly.

'Hobar? He's the College's master physician.'

The apprentice thought it strange he had never heard the name, especially since his previous master had been quite engaged in the study of healing and the body. Duncan nodded as if Gideon had answered his question, and threw a glance of Jasper. The tall man had finally been persuaded to wear one of the beaked masks. It made him look all the more alien, the dark leather of the mask close in hue to his rich ebon skin. His eyes were wide and fixed upon the man-creature held behind the thick iron bars, fear mingling with confusion at the strange and unsettling sight.

'What do you make of it then?' Hobar asked, turning back to Luthor and regarding the cage. 'As I say, it is a curious specimen. He's quite human—I've met his father and others who knew him before he changed. Reports of a monster are quite overstated.'

Luthor nodded. 'What do you think happened to him?'

The scholar clasped his hands behind his back and rocked back on his heels. 'I think he's afflicted with a sickness of the mind, more than of the body. Look,' Hobar said, pointing at the floor of the cage, 'he refuses to eat the food provided. He's eating rats. The poor devil is moon touched.'

The remains of half eaten rat carcasses littered the cage floor, and an upturned bowl of food lay in the corner, its contents splattered against the wall.

He's eating the rats! For the first time Duncan was thankful for the mask to cover his shock. Why was he eating rats and not the food given to him?

'I'm curious...' Hobar's tone was conversational, somehow unperturbed by the thrashing ruin of a man in the cage, but there was sinister curiosity there. 'May I ask why one of our best scholars in language and texts has been summoned to examine a *creature* in a cage?'

'We are here to see if his affliction is the result of experimentation.'

'Experimentation?' exclaimed Master Hobar.

Luthor nodded in reply.

'Well... I suppose it *is* possible. It's not unheard of for a mind to break under torture or extreme circumstances. I once—'

'Is it alive or dead,' asked Luthor suddenly, interrupting the master.

Hobar stared sidelong at Luthor and raised his eyebrows, mouth agape. 'Alive, of course. At least, from my examination at this distance, I would presume so. He *looks* rather animated. I would like to get him sedated so I might perform a proper physical examination.'

One of the scholars with Hobar, an elderly fellow with long grey hair and his face mostly obscured by his beaked mask, stood by the cage waving a set of antlers around in the air. The antlers were secured to the end of a staff and had been draped with trinkets and fine chains. The man-creature lashed out a claw-like hand towards the old scholar as he moved purposefully around the cage, chanting under his breath.

'What are they doing?' Duncan asked to no one in particular.

'Master Edwith is an expert in matters concerning the gods and religious rites.' It was Hobar who answered. 'I believe he is attempting a blessing from Hart, intended to exorcise the evil from this poor wretch. Mind you, I have my doubts.'

'Perhaps we should speak with him, master?' the apprentice suggested, leaning towards Luthor. 'He may be of some help with our ritual.'

'Quiet, lad!' snapped Luthor, perhaps a little too sternly, and Duncan bridled at the sudden rebuke.

'Ritual?' Hobar inquired.

Luthor shot a dark look at Duncan and he recoiled, leaning back on his crutches as his master turned to the curious scholar. 'Our current study is a matter of the utmost secrecy, and I cannot say much. The council deems it sensitive. With all the trouble, you understand...' He nodded towards the cage and left his words hanging.

'I see,' Hobar said, nodding and frowning over his mask. 'Experimentation, secret rituals, this moon-touched devil. I must confess I am quite intrigued.'

'I wish I could say more, but I simply cannot,' Luthor murmured to Hobar as if he were about to let him in on the secret. 'The council values your discretion, Master Hobar.'

'Of course, of course!' Hobar rubbed at his mask, itching to know more. He stood close to Luthor now, almost too close for Duncan to see his face. 'Still, I would be keen to hear about it all when you are at liberty to discuss it.'

Luthor gave his fellow Master a tight smile. 'Hopefully soon. Now, you must excuse us. We have much work to do. Have you finished here?'

'Yes, yes. Be my guest. I can do no more today. I will be requesting he be moved to the College for further study, since the journey through the city has become... perilous. I hope you will support my request? It would save us all precious time if he is closer.'

Luthor nodded.

'Well, I will leave you to your work. Be careful; he is quite savage,' said Hobar, glancing at Jasper. 'Good day Luthor, my learned friends.' He nodded to the rest of them before calling for his sell-sword bodyguards to follow him.

A sudden commotion erupted by the cage, and Duncan spun around on his crutches. Old Edwith was screeching at the man in the cage, who now had hold of the antlers and was yanking them up and down. The staff tore from Edwith's grasp and the creature began smashing the antlers against the bars, violently trying to pull them inside the cage.

One of the hired-swords levelled a spear at the creature and it abandoned the antlers, dropping them and snatching at the spear. He wrenched the weapon from the guard's hands and the man shouted out in alarm, quickly backing away. The spear splintered as the man in the cage tried to get it inside the bars and he whacked the ruined remains of the spear against the bars with a roar of defiance. Other men moved in, threatening him with brandished weapons.

'Hold!' someone shouted.

The sell-swords stopped dead in their tracks and Wilhelm strode forwards from beside the door.

'If any of you fools harm him, the king will have your head nailed over the gates. That there,' he said, pointing at the man-creature, 'is the son of a lord. His name was Ewolf. Now stand down!' The sell-swords retreated, and old Edwith hurried away, shaking his head.

'It's no use!' he muttered as he hurried past. 'The gods have forsaken him. I wish you luck with your studies.' The old man's gaze lingered on the apprentice, then he scurried after Hobar.

Duncan watched the men leave, then limped forward to join Luthor nearer to the cage. The wretched thing inside snarled and growled, leaning out and clutching desperately at the air trying to reach them.

'Don't get too close,' cautioned Wilhelm, lifting a wary arm between them and the cage. Without answering, Luthor began walking round the cage, keeping his distance.

'I see no sign of any markings on his skin,' Luthor said. 'Perhaps it is as Hobar says — the lad is moon-touched.'

A familiar chill brushed against Duncan's awareness, and a shadow flickered in the corner of his eye as he looked into the face of the madman. He was smeared with filth and blood, presumably from the rats, but his hands and arms were cut and covered in blackened scabs from throwing himself at the bars. The room stank too, but hardly any of that registered as Duncan recognised something cold and familiar in the man's darkened eyes.

'Strange,' Luthor murmured. 'He seems to have calmed.'

'Don't let him fool you,' Wilhelm warned the master. The creature stared back at the apprentice, a low growl emanating from his throat. Perhaps he saw something in his own eyes. That same darkness lurking inside him.

You can help him, whispered the sibilant voice.

'How?' muttered Duncan under his breath.

The book... the ritual, it will reverse what has been done.

'Are you sure? I don't know how...' he whispered.

I will guide you.

'I see no signs of experimentation,' Luthor went on, not noticing Duncan's whispering. 'I had feared to see some glyph or symbol etched onto his skin. I am relieved. There appears to be no obvious link between Ewolf here and your last master, Duncan. We will have to await Hobar's examination... Duncan, are you listening?'

'I think we can help him,' he blurted, startling Luthor and Gideon with the volume of his voice.

'And how do you propose to do that?' His master frowned, watching him from the far side of the cage, just to one side of Ewolf and through the hard steel bars.

'Perhaps Eldrick *did* do this, and if so, perhaps we can *undo* it, reverse the ritual somehow.'

'I told you I forbid it!' snapped Luthor, his words echoing off the walls of the cell. 'I will hear nothing more on it, and you will leave this alone. Do not make me regret helping you, Duncan.'

'I am sorry, master — you're right — there is nothing to link him to Eldrick. Forgive me, it was a foolish notion. I feel sorry for him, for what he has become, that's all.'

Luthor's stern regard softened. He shook his head. 'You are a kind fool, lad. But I fear his salvation is out of our hands. If anyone can save him, I think it will be the physicians. You must drop this, this *fixation* with Eldrick's study. You said it yourself it never worked. It was a fool's endeavour. Take my advice and distance yourself from it, do all you can to discredit it or you may be tarred with the same brush, your career over before it has begun. Is that what you want?'

'No master, I will do what you think is best,' replied the apprentice humbly.

'Good,' Luthor said, satisfied. 'Now let us return to the College. There is nothing more to be done here until Hobar has examined him further. We must report to the council in the morning.'

Luthor turned and made for the door, Gideon and Jasper following at his heels. Duncan however did not, instead lingering for a moment and looking into Ewolf's primal eyes. He calmly stared back. *There is something in those eyes... something familiar.*

He shook off the idea and left the cage behind him, limping after the others on his crutches, struggling painfully to keep up.

We can save him, whispered the voice.

CHAPTER TWENTY-FOUR

Making it Right

Finn crouched low, sticking to the shadows.

There he is.

He had spent the previous night lurking outside the tavern and sure enough, the man with the scarred face had been there. The man who blinded Seth. The man who had taken his rage at Finn out on someone who did not deserve it, leaving Finn wracked with guilt over what had happened.

Jor was still furious, and even though Seth was kind about it, he had changed. The burgeoning friendship he had been building with the lute player was ruined. Worse of all, Nym had something in her eye whenever she looked at him; anger, sadness, disappointment. He had to do something to make amends.

The old barkeep had forbidden him to go out, so he waited until he had fallen asleep then snuck out. His courage had failed him last night, and Finn had merely stalked the drunken scarfaced man, following him to a low building.

Finn had watched the big man fumble with the door and slip inside, just as he had done tonight. *This must be where he lives...*

Finn waited a good while before he crept forward. The street was much like any other in the district—low, squat wooden buildings lining a churned up street—not an affluent area.

He approached cautiously, checking there was no one about and that he had not been followed, then he ducked around the back. The alleyway beside the house was filthy, full of refuse and rotting food, and there was a lingering smell of death, the ever-present reminder of the sickness. Finn hoped there wasn't a body nearby. He imagined one of the twisted dead, laying forgotten on the dirt floor of a nearby house, or worse under the heaped rubbish he silently stole past. He pulled his face-covering tight over his mouth and nose, then checked the house. There was no light in any of the windows.

Alright, let's do this.

He crouched below a narrow window and peered through the slatted shutters, moving silently along the wall to check every vantage point. He could see the main room, but it was mostly dark and empty. Glancing down the alley, he scurried back around to the deserted street and tried the front door.

It opened, and he held his breath.

Nothing.

He slipped through and stood inside the door a moment as his eyes adjusted. The faint light of a dying fire illuminated a chair and a table beside the hearth, a cluster of objects littering the floor around the chair. He could make out shelves, but it was too dark to see anything more than shadowy shapes upon them.

What am I doing here? he thought, realisation creeping over him. *If he finds me, I'm dead.* He thought of Seth's eyes and shuddered, his fear losing out to the guilt of the damage he had caused. *I will make this right.*

There was a door leading to the back room. Finn could hear the drunk snoring from behind the door. *He's asleep.*

Finn spied a hopeful object in the corner and moved nearer. It was a chest.

He deftly felt for a latch and smoothly opened the lid, carefully resting it against the wall. He gently ran his hands over the objects hidden in the gloom of the chest. Mostly cloth — clothes probably. Then his fingers brushed against something hard. He carefully lifted it out and turned it toward the weak light.

A dagger.

It was not the one he had seen the man wearing. *A man with more than one dagger is not someone I want to wake...*

He slid it from its sheath and the blade shone as he gently tested the edge with his thumb. It was as sharp as he had ever felt a knife. Finn doubted this was a knife used to cut vegetables. *A killer's blade.* He tucked it into his belt, a wave of vindictive triumph warming his chest.

Finn felt deeper into the chest, his hand grasping at something familiar at the bottom. He heard a slight metallic clink. *Ha!*

He slowly drew out the purse and untied the draw strings, revealing a few coins. Holding them up to the light he could see they glinted silver. *This will help make it right.* He tucked the purse inside his coat and turned to leave.

Something stopped him a few steps from the exit. He slowly turned, his gaze falling on the other door. Was it greed he felt? He touched the dagger at his belt. *No, I will make this right. By the gods, guide me.*

He stepped towards the bedroom door and listened. The sound of snoring was still audible and he edged open the door. The man lay sprawled on a cot, stinking of stale beer and sweat. Finn crept closer, eyes fixed on the shadowed face of the sleeping man.

He unsheathed the dagger. *I will make this right.*

Guilt and shame boiled into anger, into the steel for vengeance. He took two quick steps then staggered to a halt.

What am I doing? I'm going to get myself killed. I already robbed him. The gods have favoured me enough. Yet he could not move. He stood there in the darkened room, hesitating, dagger in hand. *How would I even do it? Could I do it?* He looked down at the dagger. He turned to leave and his foot struck something.

A clatter louder than thunder crashed through in the silent room and the man jerked awake. Finn's heart froze over with terror.

'What's that?' slurred the man, flailing around, still drunk and in the clutches of sleep.

Finn swallowed hard. *I'm dead.*

The man lurched up, struggling to find his feet, eyes focusing on Finn in the dark. 'Who the fuck are you?'

Finn panicked and lashed out with the dagger. The drunk cried out and recoiled from the biting steel. Whether he tripped or was still blind drunk, Finn could not say, but the man with the scarred face tipped over backward, legs and arms wind milling wildly.

I have to make this right! Fuck it, I'm a dead man anyway.

Finn darted towards the man and clutched a handful of greasy hair, pulling the drunk's head back.

He screamed as Finn drew the sharp blade across his face, his hands driven by desperate anger, his arms strengthened by the need to survive. *Vengeance!*

Slowly but forcefully, Finn scored the knife across the man's face, the blade biting into flesh and glancing off bone. A warm gush of blood washed onto his hands .

An eye for an eye.

The man thrashed wildly, clutching his face. He lashed out, but Finn let go, darting back. Excitement mixed with sheer panic rushed through his veins as he dashed for the front door, leaving the man thrashing angrily, unable to see where his attacker had gone.

There was a roar of fury and pain from the house as Finn ran into the street.

Voices rose from the darkness nearby, torches approaching as the street stirred, alerted by the scarred man's cries.

'You there!' someone shouted, but Finn didn't answer. He plunged into an alleyway and ran. He dared to laugh in triumph as he sprinted between the buildings, still clutching the bloodied dagger.

An eye for an eye. I made it right.

***

'Where in the hells have you been?' Nym hissed as her brother slunk through the door.

Finn's face twisted with panic.

Is that blood on his hands? Nym baulked, her anger abating. 'Are you alright? Is that blood?'

She threw a look at the chair where Jor slept, his head back, his mouth gaping open and snoring. The old man had drunk the evening away and finally passed out, and Finn had been nowhere to be seen since. It couldn't have been more than an hour...

Finn whirled around and peered through a crack in the door, watching the dark street outside. He let out a long breath. 'No one saw,' muttered her brother.

'Saw what? Finn, what have you done now? Why is there blood on your hands?' She felt a cold shiver of shock at the sight of blood.

'I did it, sis. I did it...' Finn sank to the floor. His face was pale with shock.

'Finn?' Seth asked from the corner. 'What have you done?'

'I couldn't live with… with the guilt. I felt terrible. I was so sorry for what happened, I had to make it right. I didn't mean for anyone to get hurt.'

'Tell that to Seth,' Nym growled. 'He might never see again.'

'I can hear you, you know,' said Seth.

'I'm sorry, you *know* I am. I hope the gods give you your sight back, really, I do. But I had to make it right. I did it for you, to make it right…' Finn was babbling, shock taking over, shaking his voice and his hands.

'Finn?' Nym stepped towards her bother, her frown deepening. He had something in his lap, something that shone with the light of their fire, a wet sort of gleam along a hard, sharp edge. 'What have you done?'

Finn threw Nym a long searching look, blinking as if he'd forgotten she was there.

'I robbed him — if Seth can't work I thought it was the only way to get the money we need to get out of the city, and why not take it from man who did this to him — but then I had the knife and…' He looked around wild-eyed. 'Then I blinded him as he slept. I wasn't gonna — it just happened.' Finn gulped air, still catching his breath, the tremors in his hands getting progressively worse. 'I got vengeance for what he did to Seth.'

'Oh no,' gasped Nym, raising her hands to her lips.

'I did it for you, Seth.' Finn nodded vigorously. 'I made it right.'

CHAPTER TWENTY-FIVE

The King & the Council

'I, Councillor Merwyl, current elected speaker of this council, hereby convene this meeting of the council open for discussion. We are here to report our latest findings before our lord king, the chancellor and the noble lords of the royal court. We are honoured by your presence, my king.'

Merwyl bowed to the king and his advisors and Duncan stared at them in awe. He had never seen the king so close, sitting only a mere stone's throw away.

King Rhagnal wore a silver circlet over his hair, and a fine green and red tunic with several rings of silver and gold around his upper right arm. The king's warriors stood behind him at attention, their spears held rigid, the wolf of Varg emblazoned on their shields. Beside the king, Duncan recognised the chancellor, the same man who had promised him death for treachery, the same man he had then lied to. He glanced away nervously, unwilling to catch the man's eye or his attention.

There were others, lordly men in fine clothes and armour. Some drank wine, several already looked bored of Councillor Merwyl's drawn out ceremony. The royal delegation once again sat at a table in a position of honour beside the speaking floor, it and the crescent-shaped council table arranged imposingly around any who were summoned to the floor to speak. Duncan noted an empty chair on the Councillors crescent shaped table, Councillor Sareb's chair.

'The wishes of our lord king have been forefront in our minds, I assure you,' continued Merwyl, droning on as the king nodded.

'As promised to the lord-chancellor, we have doubled our efforts on the matter of the plague. We have also investigated at length the matter of the troubling incident reported in the north.'

The king rose to his feet and Merwyl fell silent.

'Very good. I dearly hope you have some good news for us, councillor. I read a recent report estimating that half of the city has already fallen victim to this sickness. Thousands, perhaps tens of thousands, have been sent to Old Night's cold embrace, not just here but in the surrounding towns also.' He grimaced and shook his head. 'I cannot stand by helpless while this evil afflicts my people.'

'We are doing everything that can be done, my king,' said Merwyl with a bow.

'I pray to the gods it will be enough,' said Rhagnal with a sigh. 'I am sure most of you have heard the rumours of my daughter's illness. These rumours are true.' King Rhagnal's voice broke slightly in distress. His face stiffened. 'Now, first and foremost, tell me what progress you have made on a cure? Give me hope that she may be saved?'

The apprentice watched on as various members of the College were called to speak, rising to nervously deliver their reports in front of the councillors and the lords of Arn. It would not be long before his own master was called forward for their report, and he dreaded the thought of being required to speak before the council again. He hoped he would not be needed.

It seemed there were few words of comfort for the king. The physicians spoke with some hope, summoned to the Citadel as soon as Princess Alethea had fallen ill, but none of them would confirm a diagnosis of plague, suggesting other ailments in an effort to avoid the truth. The king listened to them all in turn, his lips pressed in a hard line.

The series of reports seemed to drag, each scholar attempting to impress their lordly guests with their work, and to persuade them of their worth. Duncan suspected some were manoeuvring for future positions at court or upon the council, and he quickly lost interest in what they had to say.

He stifled a yawn and leant down to rub the ache in his ankle. It did nothing to lessen the throbbing in his mending bones. The splint dug into his skin, and he adjusted it slightly, unable to move it far as it was tightly bound into his bandages.

Beside him sat Master Luthor, watching the meeting with a great deal more attention than Duncan could manage to muster. Two guards stood close behind Duncan's chair, Wilhelm and another, both in the king's livery. Gideon was there, as was Jasper. Many others had gathered in the chamber to see the king, scholars of varying rank, and Duncan noted the envoys from Telis quietly watching, likely passing silent judgement on the government of Arnar.

The learned men from Telis seemed to be everywhere these days, observing the affairs of the College. Lofty and shrewd, he suspected the Teliks thought the College inferior to their own older and more famous institutions back home.

Merwyl cleared his throat. 'Master Luthor?'

The apprentice's stomach knotted, breaking his reverie. To his relief it was Jasper they wanted to talk about, and Luthor and Gideon led the big man down onto the speaking floor.

'So, this is the man of Myhar?' asked King Rhagnal, sitting forward, blinking a little as if to clear his thoughts. 'The only survivor of that cursed ship.'

'Yes, my king,' confirmed Luthor.

King Rhagnal rose and moved around the table towards the tall man from Myhar. Two warriors followed at a respectable distance, but they were never so far away that they couldn't defend Rhagnal if the need arose. Jasper's eyes followed the king as he paced in front of him.

The two men made quite a sight. One, tall and ebon skinned, the other, broad shouldered, his bronzed skin pale in comparison. Yet both were heavily muscled and walked with the gait of warriors, both with a certain nobility in the faces.

'I was told he cannot understand our tongue,' said Rhagnal, turning to Luthor. 'Have we learned anything of him, anything of use?'

'You are... king? Chief of these lands?' Jasper's deep voice rolled through the silent room like thunder.

The king turned in surprise. There were gasps from the gallery.

'In my lands, we call king *"dejem"*.' Jhasper bowed slightly and pressed his fist to his chest. '*Jhas p'her deilem.*'

The king stared, lost for words. Duncan supposed even a king could be caught off guard.

'It is part of a ritual greeting, my king,' said Gideon, shuffling forwards. He fumbled with his hands awkwardly as the king regarded the rotund scholar. 'He greets you, and says his name is Jhas p'her.'

'He speaks our tongue?' asked the king.

'Some. His learning of our language has been rapid and quite staggering this past week,' replied Luthor.

'It appears he has a very quick mind. I would say he possesses a quite remarkable intelligence and cunning,' said Gideon, his words tumbling out.

'Was he not an oar-slave?' asked Rhagnal.

'Indeed, sire.' Luthor nodded.

'Princes and kings alike have met such a fate.' The king turned his thoughtful gaze upon Jasper, then nodded at the dark man with a smile. 'Well met, friend.'

'Does he know of the plague?' asked Chancellor Alfric from his seat at the table.

'We have questioned him regarding the plague,' replied Gideon. 'He calls it *Daresh K'hir*, or "Blood Death" as a close translation. It appears it is known in Myhar.'

'Do you have any records on it from Myhar?' asked the king, hope igniting in his eyes. It must have been a tantalising thought, that somewhere out there, someone else might have found the answer to stopping the sickness.

'Unfortunately, we have scant little on the southern continents across the Great Sea.' Gideon glanced at Luthor for reassurance, and the master nodded. 'We scoured our archives but there is no mention in the little we have from Myhar.'

The king's face fell, and his shoulders dropped. He turned, and resumed his seat behind the table.

'Master Luthor?' Chancellor Alfric addressed the master, filling the king's silence. 'You were assigned another task if my memory serves, however it is a private matter between the king and this honourable council.' He looked up at the gallery and the gathered onlookers.

'Yes, yes; of course, my lord,' said Councillor Merwyl. 'There is little more to report about the plague. We shall adjourn, but before we do, there are two other matters I wish to address.' Merwyl looked up and scanned the room, ensuring he had the rapt attention of the gathering before he went on.

'As you may be aware, a young man has been transferred to

the College infirmaries from the Citadel. He was said to be monstrous creature, but this is nothing but rumour. He is merely a man. He is to be treated by our physicians and we will do what we can to cure him.' Merwyl paused and sighed, glancing down at his papers as if he did not wish to put voice to his next announcement. 'Secondly, it has been decreed by this most learned council, for committing crimes against the realm and bringing disgrace on this institution, Master Eldrick is to be cast from the memory of this honourable College. His work disregarded and destroyed.'

There was a gasp in the gallery and Duncan's heart leapt into his throat. Buzzing filled his ears, muffling the rush of chatter in the gallery.

'Eldrick is believed to have perished in the High Passes, as a result of his own misdeeds,' continued Merwyl. 'His actions were that of a madman and unacceptable for a man of this College. There will be a report in time, if any are interested in the specifics.'

The College folk around Duncan talked excitedly amongst themselves, a few even shouted demands for the report to be released immediately and seeking confirmation of Eldrick's demise. Duncan sat dumbstruck as the chamber broke into a commotion around him.

It was rare for a scholar to be cast out in disgrace, the perpetrator of a crime. It was rarer still for that scholar to be an anointed master. And Eldrick had been *his* master, *his* teacher, *his* mentor. Now he would no longer be able to speak the man's name without fear of derision and retribution.

'There will be a report!' Merwyl called holding up his hands to pacify the objectors. 'Now, this session of the council is closed. We have matters to address with the king.' He gestured at the doors, and they swung open. Slowly the College folk began filing out, muttering and talking as they did. Luthor remained where he was, but Gideon ushered Jasper towards the door, and Duncan struggled to his feet, eager to follow them and escape the scrutiny of the council and the king.

'Apprentice Duncan, you will please remain also,' called Merwyl.

His heart sank and he trembled as he made his way down the wooden stairs to Luthor, to face the regard of the Council, and the king. The remaining stragglers finally left the council chamber as a chair was brought forth for Duncan, and the heavy doors closed with an echoing boom, leaving the room quiet.

Exposed before the council table, serious, studious eyes regarded him. The stern glares of the councillors and of the assembled noblemen terrified him. He stole a nervous glance at the king, and almost choked on his own tongue when he saw the man looking straight at him.

'Master Luthor,' the chancellor began, 'have you looked into the work of this renegade master?'

'I have, my lord. And we examined the cursed man yesterday also.'

'Was there any connection? Was this Eldrick responsible?'

'There seems to be no link between the two, m'lord. There is nothing in any of Eldrick's writings, no mention of experimentation on a living man. They are unlikely to be connected, as far as I can see.'

'I see,' replied the chancellor, his fingers steepled thoughtfully. 'Can Ewolf be saved?'

'Not by my work... But I believe Master Hobar is treating him. I hope the gods see fit to help,' said Luthor with a faint, sad smile. Something in his tone told Duncan he had little hope of such a blessing.

'What of Eldrick's work from the High Passes in the Old Lands?' enquired the chancellor as the king poured himself more wine.

Luthor glanced at the apprentice, hesitating a moment. 'Eldrick undertook gruesome and in-depth work with corpses. There are many drawings, anatomy work for medicine as far as I can see. The other work was on this ritual, studies into ancient texts left by the First Sons. A sinister pursuit by all accounts, but there is no record to indicate he was successful.'

Duncan said nothing. The memory of those bones rising like a terrible puppet from that grim altar sent a shudder through him, yet he remained silent. The only record of the successful experiments were in his master's journal, long lost in the mountains, and the copies he had made in his grimoire before he left. He wouldn't speak of it though. He would not reveal what he knew.

Luthor had never laid eyes on his grimoire, nor had he mentioned it, even though he must know Duncan had one. Duncan had spoken of it at the council, and all apprentices kept one at the end of their study, in preparation for becoming a master, but its existence must have slipped Luthor's mind. It was a reminder of how tantalisingly close Duncan had come to finishing his apprenticeship. The thought stung him. He should be a master, yet he remained an apprentice, denied what was his. He ground his teeth at the thought.

'There was no mention of corpses in the ritual, only bones.' Luthor shuffled his feet and shrugged, ignorant to Duncan's bubbling anger. 'For divination I presume, but no talk of corpses, no experimentation on living men — nothing to link Eldrick's work to the claims of the dead walking.'

'The lords from the Old Lands, Arnulf and Fergus, they claim they saw the dead walk with their own eyes. There are warriors of renown with them who swear it also. Eldrick *must* have been responsible!' snapped the frustrated chancellor. 'The site of his expedition is the centre of all this.'

'Something happened up there,' replied Luthor, nodding in agreement. 'But his work gives us no answers. Perhaps he *did* succeed in conducting something dark and terrible, perhaps he found something through his dark pursuits, perhaps the gods cursed them all and brought the dead back for their vengeance. We will likely never know.' He paused, opening his hands towards the council and the king as if appealing for understanding. 'I do think that his anatomy work should be reviewed by the infirmaries. There may be much of use for the physicians. But there is nothing in his work other than dead texts, old rituals and the scrawling of an old man losing his mind up in the dark places of the mountains.'

The council muttered amongst themselves and eventually Merwyl came to his feet.

'Let the physicians have what they will. The rest will be burnt. Cast this man's memory from our minds. The king's justice must be served.' Merwyl bowed towards the king's table. The chancellor nodded in reply.

A courtier quietly entered the room and hurried over to whisper in the king's ear. The king's face instantly changed, a dark cloud falling over him. 'No...' he muttered. 'I must go to her.'

'What is it?' asked Chancellor Alfric, glancing around, eyes wide. 'What has happened?'

'The princess, my lord. Her sickness has worsened. She's at Old Night's gates,' replied the courtier.

'May Hjort save her,' muttered Alfric, the council bursting into concerned chatter. Rhagnal was already on his feet, and Alfric followed, catching the man's arm. 'No, my king. You cannot risk the plague to be with her. The realm needs the king, now more than ever.'

'I must go to her… she's still my little girl,' said the king, his face lined with heavy worry.

'Rhagnal, you must not risk yourself,' the chancellor murmured, his own face a picture of grief. They can't have been easy words to say, but Duncan found himself strangely unmoved. He knew in his head this was dire news — it was well known that the princess was beloved by many in the city — yet in his heart, he wasn't sure he cared. He watched the scene play out as if he were watching a play upon a stage, a mere observer.

'We will send our best physicians to her. Send someone now,' Merwyl snapped at a waiting scribe. 'Go now. Tell them to do what they can immediately.' He turned to the king. 'My king, I assure you we will do everything we can. Our best physicians will be sent to the Citadel.'

'Your best physicians have already attended her these past days.' Rhagnal's top lip curled, and he all but sneered at Merwyl. 'What more could they possibly do?'

Merwyl was at a loss for words. His mouth moved, but nothing came out. *Old fool…*

'Alethea is dying!' The king's voice rose, pitching against the roof, desperation echoing against the beams. 'I can't lose her!'

This is your chance, speak now, whispered the voice.

The apprentice opened his mouth as his conscious mind fought to close it. *What am I doing? This is madness!* 'Most learned council, may I speak?'

'Not now, Apprentice…' Merwyl shushed him with a frown and a wave as Alfric tried to comfort the king and dampen the man's increasing hysteria.

'Let him speak!' demanded the king, a glimmer in his eyes that might have been hope but was more than likely tears.

'After a thorough examination of Master Luthor's extensive works, I believe I have discovered the truth. I believe I know what happened up in the High Passes.' The words came tumbling out, outside his control. All he could do was sit behind his own eyes and watch it happen, listening as his voice spoke words that were not his own.

'What? No!' Luthor spun around and loomed over Duncan's chair. 'I told you, boy!'

'Let him speak!' barked the king.

The apprentice glimpsed the flicker of shadow as the room seemed to darken, seething shadow dancing at the edges of the light. A draft of cold air prickled his skin to gooseflesh. His eyes were drawn to the council table, and a figure stood unseen by the others. It stared at him.

The dark figure stood behind the councillor's table, wrapped in a cloak, its hood raised. He could do nothing but stare into the darkness of the void dwelling beneath that hood. It stared back at him, icy claws clutching at his heart.

'Eldrick got it all terribly wrong. Without the correct texts to conduct the ritual as he intended, he may have succeeded in resurrecting not a living soul, but just an empty shell, a mindless corpse.'

There were gasps. Councillor Caleb slammed down an angry fist on the table. 'Impossible!'

Good, Apprentice. Distance yourself now, so they will hear you, trust you.

'I was glad to have no part in it.' Duncan's heart pounded. He walked a fine line between truth and fiction here. One wrong move and he might hang himself on a tangle of his own lies. 'Since returning, and with the help of Master Luthor, I have uncovered the texts Eldrick needed, and with these texts I believe it may indeed be possible to *prolong* a life, or even return someone from the deathly halls of Old Night. It could even reverse what has been done to that wretched creature we hold in the cage.'

'There is no proof the cursed man is even connected,' exclaimed Luthor.

'I must stress the work he was attempting was wholly unnatural.' The apprentice dismissed Eldrick's work with a wave, ignoring the shouted protests from the council and his master. Luthor had stalked away and was pacing a trench into the speaking floor. Several councillors were on their feet, and the king and the chancellor looked on in open mouthed shock. 'This ritual has rightly been forbidden by this learned council. Such secrets are best left unknown, and this work should be destroyed.'

Yes, nicely done.

'You can save her?' The king's voice was barely more than a whisper.

Duncan shrugged a shoulder. 'Perhaps, if Old Night takes her, there is at least a chance. But the council forbids it, so I must not.' He bowed his head a little and waited, his heart hammering in his chest.

What have I done?

'My king, this man's claims are unproven,' shouted Councillor Caleb. 'He cannot do what he claims. Luthor, what in the gods is going on here?'

'I agree, my king,' the chancellor said, glaring at Duncan. He had to stop himself smiling, the corners of this mouth twitching upwards against his will. He had them nibbling the bait, but would Rhagnal take it? 'I would not let him anywhere near the princess.'

'Apprentice Duncan, you will remain silent!' snapped Councillor Merwyl. 'We will deal with your insubordination later.'

'Master Luthor, what do you say on this?' asked Councillor Uriah.

Luthor spent a long moment looking at Duncan, and the apprentice stared back. He saw the anger, the disappointment, in his master's eyes. He somehow knew he could do it, and he didn't care if he took Luthor down with him. 'I think the boy has the princess's wellbeing at heart but his words are folly. They will only bring hope where there is none. I think he wants to see some merit in his previous master's work, some lingering nostalgia perhaps. I have told him to leave such foolishness in the past. He has disappointed me greatly.'

The courtier slid through the council chamber doors again and hurried to speak with the king. The man's eyes widened, and tears welled afresh. He cast around, his fingers curling into a fist.

'No...' He shook his head, his features crumpling as the courtier's words sank in. 'NO!' he roared, anger blazing with sorrow. Wordless wails of grief ricocheted off the chamber's walls, Alfric dropping hard into the chair behind him, his face in his hands, whispers racing through the gathered councillors as the courtier whispered the news to Merwyl. Duncan glanced at Luthor, their dispute forgotten, hope and opportunity igniting in Duncan's chest. The king sank to his knees in a silent council chamber and wept into his hands.

Princess Alethea was dead.

CHAPTER TWENTY-SIX

Defiance

'What do you mean they have taken him?' demanded Arnulf.

'I've just heard. They moved him this morning,' Hafgan replied.

'Moved him *where*?' Arnulf half shouted his question, his mood darkening.

Hafgan hesitated. 'The College, lord.'

Arnulf's anger boiled over, clenching and unfurling his fists over and over, as he paced the length of his guest chamber. 'How *dare* they?'

Fergus stood behind Hafgan, leaning against the wall. Frowning at Arnulf, he held his hands out in a plea for calm. 'Now, old friend. It might be for the best.'

'For the best? For the *best*?!' Arnulf repeated uselessly, the pitch of his voice rising.

Hafgan and Fergus shared a look, before the warrior turned back to Arnulf. 'I hate to say it, lord, but they could be his only hope.'

Arnulf levelled a foul glare at him in reply.

'Aye, listen to your man, Arnulf. I have heard a great deal about this in the Throne Hall of late,' said Fergus. He strode forward and poured himself a goblet of wine from Arnulf's table. 'Word is, the College have expelled those involved. Most are dead so it matters little, and the apprentice who returned is apparently innocent.'

Arnulf latched onto the word, spinning around. 'The apprentice is *innocent*! Still alive and well, yet he was up there in those passes—impossible! He's as guilty as the rest of them.' Arnulf screwed up his face in anger. 'Fergus, what do you know of him? Tell me what you have heard.'

'Some young lad. He's here in the city, at the College.' Fergus shrugged. 'I heard he defied his master up in the passes and was dismissed for objecting to the rituals. They have decided he is innocent in it all. I heard he's helping unravel that book we brought; they think he might be able to help.'

'What?' Arnulf hissed, incredulous. Arnulf levelled a glare at his old friend, hearing this news had been kept from him was like having a cold knife driven into his back. 'Why did you not mention this?'

Fergus took a sip of wine, staring at Arnulf as though he was being entirely unreasonable. He might well have been, but that wasn't the point. 'I'm telling you now. The boy could be useful—he might even be able to help Ewolf.'

'Anything else you've been keeping from me that you'd like to mention now?' Arnulf snarled.

'I have barely seen you in days, Arnulf. You've been shut away in here, not been at court, not been in the hall.' Arnulf waved his words away but Fergus went on, unperturbed. 'I have been assured that the College leaders want to fix this. Our accusations have severely damaged their reputation.'

'Reputation?' snapped Arnulf. 'They are snakes. They have no *reputation*, no honour.'

'It appears some are not entirely without honour.' Fergus eyed him carefully.

'Do not speak to me of honour. You saw what they did, what happened to my home, to... *Aeslin*...' The memory of it, the grief, it stole his words.

'Lord,' attempted Hafgan. 'I have served you many years now. I have always known you to be a man of honour, a reasonable, fair man. I have never known you condemn anyone on suspicion alone. Perhaps there truly *are* some at the College who might want to help.'

'Haf, has the way of it,' Fergus said quickly. 'Now, I don't like this anymore than you—none of us do—but we can't just let Ewolf rot in a cage.'

Hafgan nodded in agreement and Arnulf slumped in his chair, the fight rushing out of him. Arnulf had been to see Ewolf most days this past week, but today he just couldn't bear to go, and now regret clawed at him. *When will I get to see him? What if I never see him again?*

'I would do anything for Ewolf, you both know that, but *them*? Letting *them* take him, after all that has happened? They just want to experiment on him. For all we know they could be deceiving us, taking him from us to finish what they started. That's *my son* they have.'

Arnulf sat up and levelled his gaze at Fergus, a finger pointed straight at him. 'You say you have heard much in the Throne Hall?'

Fergus nodded and sipped at his wine.

'Then answer me this. What of vengeance? Who will answer for what they did? Who will pay for the lives of my people? The cost was heavy, and I have heard no one speak of aid. Am I to bear this alone? Why is it my people who pay the price while they curse our lands, create vile abominations, and let them walk free?' He slammed his fist onto the arm of his chair. 'I came for *vengeance!*'

Arnulf rose to his feet and took up his axe.

'Arnulf, what are you doing?' asked Fergus, swallowing hard as his eyes narrowed on the axe. Arnulf noticed his old friend's hand subtly move to hover near the hilt of his sword.

'I will go to the College,' replied Arnulf defiantly. 'I will not be denied the right to see my son. Let any man try and stop me.'

'Arnulf,' Fergus cautioned, taking a step to put himself between his friend and the door. 'You cannot. You know well the king has forbidden it.'

'But I *must*,' he hissed, desperate to do something, anything, to soothe the pain.

'Lord, please listen to us,' said Hafgan. 'If you defy the king, what will happen? You would lose everything.'

'Not to mention your head,' quipped Fergus.

'What would you have me do?' said Arnulf. He rounded on them both. Didn't they understand?

'Speak with Rhagnal.' Fergus came towards him, speaking as though Arnulf were a wild, wounded animal. 'Swear him an oath, that on your honour, you will do no harm to any at the College. Swear you will act with honour, and he will probably allow you to go and see your son.'

Arnulf ground his teeth, glaring at Fergus and Hafgan. As much as it galled him, he saw no other way. 'Very well,' he growled.

***

'And you swear this?' asked Chancellor Alfric.

'I do,' replied Arnulf, doing his best to remain humble and calm. 'I swear I will cause no trouble at the College, I merely wish to visit my son.' The Throne Hall had its usual crowd of local lords and courtiers. Most looked upon Arnulf with haughty expressions, whispering amongst themselves as he entered. He wasn't surprised — he could hardly command respect after his ejection from the hall by the king. It was an act he had come to deeply regret.

I have damaged my honour in their eyes, no more than a vagabond lord from the north with no idea of how to act properly at court. Let us show them a lord from the Old Lands.

He bowed respectfully to the chancellor. 'Please let me speak with the king? I will swear to him myself.'

'The king does not wish to be disturbed,' replied the chancellor sadly. 'I am sorry Lord Arnulf. The princess succumbed to the sickness only a few hours ago. King Rhagnal is to be left to mourn.'

Fergus sighed. 'That is grim news. I am sorry to hear it.'

'A terrible omen indeed,' said Hafgan.

'Aye,' said Arnulf. 'I know what it is to lose a daughter. There is no greater pain. It is why I must see my son. He is all I have left.'

'I am sorry, Arnulf.' The chancellor shook his head. 'I know Rhagnal will see you in time, but he must grieve in peace.'

A courtier hurried over and whispered into the chancellor's ear.

'He *what*?!' exclaimed the chancellor, staring at the courtier in disbelief.

'Is everything alright, lord?' Fergus moved towards the chancellor, glancing at Arnulf and Hafgan.

'The king has left the Citadel,' the chancellor replied, rubbing at the bridge of his nose in frustration. 'He is going to the College.'

The crowded Throne Hall rippled with muttered words as

courtiers bridled at the news. The chancellor turned, speaking in urgent, hushed tones to servants and sending folk off with orders.

Why would the king be at the College? Does this have anything to do with Ewolf?

He couldn't leave it to chance. Seeing his opportunity, Arnulf bowed to the chancellor. 'I can see you have much to do, lord chancellor. We will not trouble you further.'

The chancellor nodded distractedly and waved them away.

Turning away, Arnulf glanced up into the rafters at the hundreds of banners hanging there. *The banners of every lord in Arnar, all sworn to the realm, to Arnar.* There amongst the colourful sigils, in a glorious tapestry of honour, Arnulf saw his black axe on a crimson field. Pride filled his chest as he made for the doors. He would bring honour back to that banner.

'Arnulf, where are you going?' Fergus whispered, hurrying after him.

'You say there is an apprentice at the College who was in the High Passes? And the king is there also? Where better to speak with him and this apprentice? I just swore to the king's chancellor that I would cause no trouble at the College, and in all this confusion, I can claim I thought I was permitted under that oath to go and seek Rhagnal there.'

'Is this wise?' asked Hafgan from behind him.

'Perhaps not, but there is only one way to find out. Let us go and speak with Rhagnal.' Hafgan tried to object but Arnulf cut him off. 'Ready an escort, we ride for the College.'

The last light of the day was quickly fading, it was late, nevertheless the streets of Arn were much quieter than Arnulf had expected, and the sight that greeted them beyond the Citadel gates was appalling. He knew there was a sickness in the city, but he had not come close to predicting the scale until he rode out the lower gates and onto the wide thoroughfare.

The city was a festering ruin. Dead littered the gutters, just left on the street, denied the honour of a proper burial or the dignity of a pyre. The smell was unbearable, the mud of the street churned into a black stinking filth. Folk stood aside from the horses, thin emaciated creatures, staring at them as they passed.

Is there no food for the low-folk? By the gods, the poor bastards are starving. Arnulf stared back with unveiled pity.

He rode with a full escort, Hafgan and Erran at his side. The pair always made a strange contrast—the big warrior dwarfing the young lad. Erran was of a much thinner build, his mail coat hanging from his wiry frame and his fine sword buckled at his belt. Hafgan wore plates of steel over various parts of his mail, and Arnulf's remaining warriors rode behind them, similarly attired. They all wore scarves over their faces as shields against the foul air that many thought caused the sickness.

Fergus rode with them, his shield-maidens with him, and more than once Arnulf had seen the glances Erran threw at Astrid. She'd given him a subtle nod in return and ridden on, her face a stoic mask, set hard as stone.

The Death Nymph is softening towards him, I'll give the lad that. Arnulf had heard the talk swirling through the Citadel about the pair of them. Word was they were often together, training according to most of the rumours, but many suggested there was more between them.

The great hound, Fear, loped alongside Arnulf's horse. His tongue lolled from his mouth, seemingly oblivious to the death and suffering around him. Fear seemed excited to be out of the Citadel, running along the streets with the horses, and Arnulf wished he felt the same.

There had been talk of unrest in the streets, and neither he nor Fergus had any desire to encounter it. Arnulf's crimson banner snapped in the air above as they rode, Fergus's blue with a white swooping falcon beside it. They made a fearsome and glorious sight, a show of strength to the folk of Arn, a display of wealth and authority. All would know these were the mighty lords from the north and the townsfolk would not block the path of his small host of warriors.

The sky above the banners was clear, but clouds loomed on the horizon, blotting out the sunset, heavy and dark, likely pregnant with the snows of winter. Silhouetted against those approaching clouds were hundreds of tiny dark shapes. They wheeled over the rooftops and through the hearth smoke, carrion birds spiralling over the city as if it were a battlefield. The birds swooped down to perch atop twisted corpses, unperturbed by folk walking by. *They have come to feast on an entire city...*

'That is a foul omen,' Hafgan muttered.

'Big fuckers, aren't they?' Erran screwed up his face as they passed one of the huge birds ripping at dead flesh.

It cawed angrily at the approaching riders, glaring with defiant black eyes. It was as if these streets were no longer fit for men to walk upon. The bird cawed again, proclaiming the streets of Arn as the domain of Old Night and his carrion birds. The hound, Fear, charged the menacing creature, barking and slavering as he bounded towards it. The bird took to the air with a single massive beat of its huge wings and Fear barked at it as it soared away.

Truly heralds for the God of Death. He is here, walking the streets of Arn, thought Arnulf.

CHAPTER TWENTY-SEVEN

Portents in the sky

Duncan found himself standing again on the vast plain of dead. He stumbled past those familiar dead faces, vacant eyes staring into nothingness. The crows cawed angrily at his presence as they hopped from corpse to corpse.

The stench seemed worse every time he came here — his dreams had wandered here each night this week — and still the putrid reek of decomposing flesh made him heave. There was no escaping it. He breathed through his mouth, hoping to avoid the worst of the thick, cloying smell. The buzzing of flies thrummed around him in great swarms hovering above the ground, the foreboding sky cast with hues of red and purple, the colours of a winter sunset. As he watched, tumultuous dark clouds raced and boiled overhead obscuring the oddly coloured sky.

Duncan moved across the plain, his eyes fixed upon the curious monoliths rising in the distance. Somehow, he knew answers lay there, but thousands upon thousands of corpses littered the ground between him and his destination. He placed his feet carefully to avoid stepping on the rotting dead around him. Some were long gone, covered in moss and mostly skeletal, skin clinging to bone like thin parchment. Others still bore the wounds of battle, great bloody rents cloven through cloth and armour, innards spilled across the ground. Some faces he recognised, old friends and acquaintances. He had seen his father, his brother, even Truda. The worst had been a glimpse of what could have been his mother, looking away as soon as recognition crept over him, not wanting to look too closely upon the desiccated faces of his dead loved ones, hoping it was not really them.

He thought he heard uttered words on the breeze rolling across the plain. Duncan stopped and searched for the source. All at once the dead stirred, slowly and awkwardly rising to their feet, joints popping and cracking like old men awoken from the longest of cold nights.

The dead had awakened.

They shambled forwards, rotting on their feet. He recoiled as one staggered near him. It snapped its head in his direction to regard him with cold, lifeless eyes. Its mouth hung open, exposing the upper jaw, its decomposing face a thing of nightmares. It paid him no heed and stumbled onwards.

The distant monoliths loomed above the horde. He walked onwards. The dead barely seemed to notice as he wove between them, as indifferent as they had been while they lay still in their deathly repose.

Apprentice.

He stopped in his tracks, frozen.

The word seemed to come from a thousand mouths at once, hissing from the lips of the dead stumbling around him; a thousand whispers joining in one great cacophony and rolling through the air like distant thunder.

Apprentice... A single voice this time, weaving through the crowd, the same voice that so often haunted his thoughts.

Through the parting crowds of dead, he saw it. The cloaked figure stood motionless, seeming to watch him from within the shadows of its dark robes. He mastered his fear and with morbid curiosity, he stepped closer.

Apprentice, it repeated, its voice like the gravelly hiss of rasping chains. *There is work to be done.*

***

Duncan awoke in his chair, a candle still flickering on the desk in front of him. It was quiet. He judged it was late evening by the look of the dark sky outside his window. He must have dozed off after his sizeable evening meal. He still was ravenous though, and he rubbed at his eyes. He couldn't have slept long if the candle was still burning. Its smoke drifted lazily towards the ceiling, and he could swear the putrid stench of rot wafted with it, following

294

him from his dreams into waking life.

Just another dream, he thought. The dream of wandering the plain of dead had become all too frequent these past nights, the horror of it diminishing as he struggled through the deceased hordes, trying unsuccessfully to reach those distant monoliths.

The cloaked figure was always there, faceless and watching with unseen eyes beneath that darkened hood.

'Just a dream,' he muttered as his eyes adjusted to the gloom. He pulled himself upright in his chair, the disturbance sending a lance of hot pain shooting up his leg. He winced and sucked air between his teeth. At least when he dreamt, his legs were whole.

He caught a glimpse of something in the corner.

He turned with a start and froze, his heart hammering in his chest. The cloaked figure stood in the gloom by his wardrobe, and the candle guttered, plunging the room into deep shadow. Flaring back to life, light bloomed in the room and the figure was gone. Duncan scrambled, his hands grasping across his desk to find another candle. He fed it on the flame of the first and held it towards the corner casting a ruddy light into the shadows. There was nothing there.

Just a dream.

'Work to be done,' he muttered to himself.

The agony of heaving his broken body had begun to lessen, though it was still a chore to heft himself out of the chair and hobble to the window. A breeze blew in from across the river, the shutters banging gently on the wall outside. There was no cloud as the sun set outside, the clear sky setting a chill in the air. The first stars glimmered in the darkening sky overhead. He could see in the distance, to the west, a thick cloud bank was drawing in. The snows would come any time now — probably within the hour. The night was drawing in fast, but there would be no moonlight to illuminate the eves of the nearby College buildings tonight. It was as he predicted. A dead moon was rising, a moon that gave no light and rose as a black disc into the night.

He searched the sky where he knew the moon should be rising based on his recent observations. There is was, barely visible. Placing his candle down beside the bowl on the table under the window, he picked up his ironwood shard and carefully lay it in the bowl of water. It spun slowly on the surface before coming to a stop pointing north. Leaning his weight onto the crutches, and clamping them under his armpit, he scribbled a note on the moon's position compared to his bearing. He remembered from his work in the passes, Eldrick's ritual had worked best during a dead moon. One crutch slipped and he staggered forward, his broken foot coming down to catch his fall by instinct. There was a flash of pain. Cursing his leg, he shoved the crutch back into place and finished scrawling his notes in a little leather-bound book.

Limping back to his desk, he slumped into his chair and once more elevated the injured joint, relieving the pressure, if not all the pain. With a grunt, he reached for a quill and ink, pulling his grimoire into position with his other hand.

As his quill came down on the parchment, there was a knock at his chamber door, and he arrested the nib with a start before the ink could drip. *A visitor, at this hour?*

He climbed to his feet and hastily slid the grimoire off his desk and into an open trunk. Dropping the lid shut, he turned and quickly arranged the clutter on his desk. There was another knock.

'I'm coming,' he called, clumsily hurrying to the door. He pulled on the handle. 'I'm sorry, master, you caught me sle—' His words faltered as he registered the person standing at his door.

'Apprentice Duncan?' King Rhagnal asked, his voice stern and commanding.

'Y—yes,' the apprentice stammered in shock. 'My king?'

Several men in armour crowded the hallway in escort, their grim, hard faces and oiled steel glaring at him in the light of the hallway torches.

Do they know I lied? Have they come to have me executed?

The king's expression crumpled. 'She is dead. My daughter is dead, and I need to know—is it true? Can you bring her back... back from Old Night?'

Duncan eyed him warily, suspicious of some trap or ruse to make him reveal his lies.

Help him, Apprentice... you must, hissed the voice over his shoulder. *I will guide you... you will succeed.*

'I can,' replied the apprentice.

The king's eyes flashed with hope. 'Truly, it can be done?'

'It can, my king. The council would deny you, but I cannot. I think I can save her. But we must go now, and quietly. I must perform the ritual.' The apprentice bowed, averting his gaze.

'I don't care what it takes. I will try *anything*,' the king said desperately. 'Make haste, Apprentice Duncan, and gather what you need. I have a boat waiting.'

What am I doing? thought the apprentice as he scrambled through his chamber to gather what he needed. Last, he removed his grimoire from its hiding place. *This is madness.*

I will guide you... you will succeed, hissed the voice. *The moon is risen, you know the words, the symbols. You can be greater than Eldrick, greater than them all.*

He looked down at the large leather-bound cover, his eyes tracing the silvered corner pieces and clasp, at the words *Master Duncan* etched in a flowing hand. As he turned, he noticed Master Logan's staff leaning by the door. He picked it up, turning it in his hand, examining the strange carved runes at its head. He grunted, the corner of his mouth twitching to a smile. It was one of his last surviving possessions that he had carried at the last ritual in the passes — it seemed fitting to take it now he was to attempt another. He cast aside his crutches and took up the walking staff once more, hopping as he settled his weight against it, and then he hobbled to the door.

Have no fear. I will guide you, Apprentice. You will not fail.

***

'What is that?' said the warrior beside him.

'I don't know. Smoke?' replied another.

The two warriors from Daeluf's escort had joined Bjorn at the prow, drawn by the strange sight. Bjorn stood silently, watching the sky ahead as Tung knelt beside him peering out from the prow of the longboat. The two warriors kept a cautious distance from the Wildman. Most of them did.

The sky ahead swarmed with a strange shadow, the river guiding them straight towards it.

'That can't be... Is it Arn?' asked one of the warriors.

'It must be,' replied the other.

Bjorn stared. *Could it be?* The hunter was not sure he believed his own eyes.

'It's birds... crows...' muttered Bjorn. 'I've never seen so many.'

Thousands of black wings wheeled against the clouds ahead.

Numbers of such magnitude, they darkened the evening sky like a pall of slowly swirling smoke.

'Daeluf!' shouted one of the warriors. 'Come see this.'

The captain strode forwards, his face a picture of confusion as he peered up into the sky.

'By the gods,' he muttered. 'Is it burning?'

'That's not smoke, friend,' said Bjorn. 'They are carrion birds, flocking as they would over a great battlefield.' *She was right. Death is coming. A darkness in my path.*

'So it is true...' Daeluf shook his head, dismayed. 'I had hoped they were exaggerating.'

Bjorn looked at him questioningly.

'The river traders at High Stones,' explained Daeluf. 'They spoke of the sickness. Hundreds, perhaps thousands, are dead. But I never imagined anything like this.'

There is a darkness in your path, Khyra had said. *Crows and fire.*

She had foreseen this, and now a great calamity loomed on the horizon. He grimaced and threw a glance back west. 'I will tread carefully, my love,' he muttered to himself.

They all stood watching the ominous shadow which smeared the sky; a plume of wheeling shapes, thousands upon thousands darkening the sky over their destination. Enthralled by the eerie sight, they barely noticed as the first flakes of winter's snow began to fall around them.

CHAPTER TWENTY-EIGHT

A Scholar's Honour

The College gates were sealed shut. There were torches casting a ruddy light over the scene, and the first flakes of winter snow drifted down from a cloudy sky as night set in. A small crowd still milled in front of the gates, watched carefully by guardsmen from the town. The movement of torches along the wall marked the guards standing above the gate and on the rooftops of the College, the sell-swords eyeing the crowd as well. The crowd shuffled back from the gates, and Arnulf watched the guardsmen haul away a bound man into a nearby building with a number of guards outside the door. Another man looked up wide eyed at the approaching riders and fled, limping away into an alley.

'What is going on here?' Arnulf demanded, trotting his horse towards the gates. 'Has there been fighting?' Wounded townsfolk lingered amongst the crowd, one man laying against a nearby building nursing a bloodied face.

'This is what I spoke of.' Fergus reigned in beside Arnulf. 'They have been rioting.'

'Seems it's not just us who have a problem with the College,' Erran observed dryly.

A commotion broke out in the crowd as the remainder of Arnulf's warriors arrived behind him. Some folk panicked at the sight of them, scattering into the shadows between buildings, others watching on uncertainly.

'They think we're here to put down the trouble with force,' Fergus muttered, and Arnulf grunted in reply. He wasn't about to order his warriors into a fight that wasn't his.

Fear seemed uneasy at the crowd and hung back close to Arnulf's horse.

'Stand aside!' Hafgan called to the gathered city folk. 'We have business at the College. Stand aside!'

What remained of the crowd parted, hurrying to clear a path for the mailed warriors, their spears scraping the evening sky, banners trailing, axes hung at their belts and broad shields on their backs.

Arnulf rode through the gap, eyeballing the guards, searching for their commander. 'Open the gate,' he ordered, his tone leaving no room for argument.

'Yes, lord. At once,' replied a sergeant, coming forwards and bowing his head respectfully. The gates swung open slowly and Arnulf nudged his horse into the courtyard beyond.

The College's main courtyard was bordered with a circle of straight walled buildings, with a stable beside the gate. From what Arnulf could see in the darkness, the compound was enclosed by an outer wall, shielding an extensive array of buildings that were consumed by shadow. The complex of buildings appeared to continue all the way down to the river bank, but it was impossible to see how far that was at this time of night.

It's larger than inside the Citadel, and they clearly do not like townsfolk wandering around inside.

'They must wield some coin,' Fergus commented, looking around. He brought his horse to a stop and swung down, nodding in appreciation. 'Impressive.'

The buildings were all of a similar construction, though some had a second storey, their roofs sloping down, some even tiled. The ground around them had been paved and set with flagstone in places, providing a much firmer surface than the hard-packed soil of the city streets that turned to sludge at the first sign of rain.

'I want most of the men to wait here,' Arnulf said, looking to Fergus and then Hafgan.

'Aye,' agreed Fergus, 'Astrid, have them to tend to the horses, and remain ready to ride out. I won't be too long.' The shield-maiden answered with a curt nod. Arnulf swung down from his horse and handed the reins to a stable boy loitering nervously nearby.

'You heard him!' said Hafgan loudly as he also dismounted.

'Stay out of trouble. We will not be long.'

Hafgan gestured for Erran and another warrior to follow, Fergus dismounted and joined Arnulf also as Astrid began issuing orders to their waiting warriors. A big woman in dented armour, made some objection to Astrid but was swiftly rebuked. She did not look happy with the command and scowled after Astrid as she stalked off to speak with the other warriors.

A robed man hurried towards them, his shoes slapping the wet paving stones. 'My lords, we were not expecting you.' He had an officious tone to his voice that Arnulf did not like.

'We are here to speak with the king,' said Arnulf, resting his hand casually on his weapon.

'The king?' The man cast around, eyeing the warriors and wringing his hands a little. 'The king left several hours ago. He attended today's council meeting then left.'

'We had word he returned this evening,' said Fergus.

'Not that I am aware of, you must be mistaken,' replied the scholar.

Arnulf cast a frown at Fergus and the red-haired lord shrugged. 'Strange. Maybe Alfric's messenger was mistaken?'

'Or perhaps the king did not want it known he was here,' suggested Hafgan.

'Perhaps you can help us with another matter.' Arnulf addressed the man once more. 'We heard the son of a northern lord was brought here. He is said to be cursed.'

'Aye, that it was. It is in the infirmaries with the physicians. I can find the name of the master who is examining it, if you like?'

It? They dare call my son "it"?

'*It* is a *man*,' snapped Arnulf. He fought to control his anger and forced a smile. 'You will not refer to him as "it".'

The College man baulked and paled. 'I apologise, lord. I will have you taken to him right away, lord.'

'Perhaps it would be best if we find the king first,' Hafgan cut in, 'and find out if he *is* actually here somewhere.'

Arnulf shot the big warrior a look, and after a moment nodded grudgingly in agreement.

'I can send word to the dockmaster and find out if he returned by boat without my knowing,' offered the scholar.

Arnulf nodded.

'In the meantime, tell us this,' Fergus said, stepping towards the man. 'Is there an apprentice here who once studied under Master Eldrick? Do you know of him?'

'Ah yes, he has become the topic of much talk here of late,' the man replied, nodding furiously. He seemed eager to please, or perhaps just eager to get them out of the College and back on the other side of the gate. 'Apprentice Duncan is no longer a student of Eldrick though. Eldrick has been struck from the records in disgrace. We haven't heard the truth of it yet but there are rumours throughout the College.' The man leaned towards Arnulf and Fergus, as if to share a great secret. 'Some say he lays dead in the mountains. The lad is now apprenticed to Master Luthor.'

'Luthor, eh?' replied Fergus. He cast a sly look at Arnulf. 'Well, perhaps while some of your men see whether the king is indeed here, you can take us to this Master Luthor.' Hafgan's brow furrowed, and he opened his mouth to say something, but Fergus waved him to silence before he could and continued without pause. 'We would very much like to speak with his new apprentice.'

***

Luthor leafed through the velum pages of the heavy grimoire. His candle flickered as he turned to a page of First Sons glyphs. He sighed and rubbed his face, pushing his crude spectacles up onto his brow.

'Eldrick, old friend,' he muttered, 'what were you trying to do up there?'

He cast a look around the room, boxes of findings and research, curious old stones, pressed samples of flora, sketches of fauna, maps and charts of the decaying ruins hundreds of miles to the north all cluttering up his study. Apprentice Duncan claimed there was some dark connection between the rituals Eldrick was attempting and the terrible claims of dead men walking, but Luthor could not see how it was possible.

He glanced back at the page. 'Definitely First Sons glyphs... But they make no sense...'

He picked up another tome, the codex by Master Corinus on ancient writings — the very same book his new apprentice had paid so much interest in — and leafed through the pages until his gaze fell upon a similar inscription.

This is the same. He glanced between both pages of script. It was one of the many un-translatable texts discovered throughout the known realms. The only footnotes to accompany the transcription read; "*...discovered amongst the ruins which once lay beneath the town now known as Oldstones*". There was no attempt at translation.

Oldstones... A place built amongst the menhirs of a forgotten time.

There was a loud knock at the door, cutting the thread of his thoughts. Luthor looked up sharply and closed the grimoire. *Strange... a little late for visitors.*

'Enter!' he called to whoever it was outside. A dark robed man bustled into the room.

'Master Luthor, I am sorry. They insisted...' the man spluttered and Luthor watched in nervous confusion as a group of armed warriors pushed their way into his study past the flustered scholar.

'Err,' Luthor ventured, his voice edged in fear as he looked from face to face, each wearing equally grim expressions. 'May I help you?'

A man stepped forward. He had dark long hair past his shoulders and wore armour. Not just any armour — this looked expensive — made of intricately stamped leather and mail. He wore rings of silver around his wrists and carried a fierce looking axe.

This is no common warrior.

'Master Luthor, I presume?' There was something hostile in the man's stare.

Another finely armoured man with bright auburn hair entered and stood at his shoulder. A large formidable looking warrior loomed behind them, accompanied by another, much younger man, who glared at Luthor with as much malice as the rest.

'I am,' Luthor replied, uneasily eyeing the speaker's axe. 'I don't believe we have met. Who are you?'

There was certainly something unsettling about how the man glared at him before he replied. 'I am Lord Arnulf, of Ravenshold and the Motte. This is Lord Fergus of Weirdell,' he said with a gesture at a flame-haired nobleman beside him.

'My lords,' said Luthor with an awkward bow. He gestured to the room and its assorted clutter. 'Forgive the mess. I wasn't expecting visitors.'

'I understand you have a new apprentice, one who once studied with Master Eldrick,' said Lord Arnulf.

Luthor nodded.

'I assume you are aware of this Eldrick's recent *work*, and the rumours of the dead rising in the north?'

Luthor swallowed a lump from his throat. *Should I be speaking of this?*

'I am, my lord, but I must admit I find the rumours quite hard to believe,' replied Luthor.

'Believe me, scholar, the dead walk. I saw it with my own eyes.' Lord Arnulf levelled a stare at him that left him in no doubt.

Luthor's eyes widened. *These are the lords mentioned at the council...* 'You are the northern lords I have heard spoken of?'

Arnulf gave a slow nod, his eyes tracing the desk, stopping at the grimoire. His expression darkened. 'Where did you get that?' Arnulf snapped.

'It is Master Eldrick's grimoire.'

'I know that all too well, scholar,' snapped Arnulf. 'It was me who found it. Why do you have it?'

'The council requested I study it, to find out if there is any truth to be found about the claims against Eldrick.'

'So, the College doubt my word... my honour?' snarled Arnulf, taking a threatening step towards him. 'They do not believe what I have told them?'

Lord Arnulf's hand moved to his axe, and the big warrior placed a restraining hand on his lord's shoulder. Luthor stared at the menacing axe.

'No, no, lord...' spluttered Luthor. 'It's just, it is our way here at the College. Everything is studied and checked, tested for accuracy. There is a lad here, suffering with a strange and terrible malady of the mind...'

Luthor suddenly remembered.

'The lad I speak of, the one from the Citadel, he is your son?' asked Luthor, looking between the two lords before him.

A pained look passed across the face of the one called Arnulf. 'Aye, he is my son.'

'It is why we have come,' said the big warrior behind him, speaking for the first time.

'The physicians are doing their best for him, I assure you. I am studying this grimoire, in part, in the hope of finding some way to help him. If there is a connection between his condition and Eldrick, the answer will be in here.'

'Have you found anything?' asked Lord Fergus.

'Not yet, I am afraid,' replied Luthor.

'I assume you are also in possession of that foul dagger we found in the passes?' asked the big warrior.

'Yes, I have it here somewhere,' replied Luthor. The scholar began lifting sheets of parchment, searching for the blade. He moved books and ink pots, pushed aside candles and yet, the knife was nowhere to be seen. *It's gone.* Luthor felt a shiver of suspicion crawl up his spine. *Duncan...*

'It is gone,' Luthor admitted finally. 'I... I think my apprentice may have taken it. He said it was his father's before he let Eldrick use it in his work.' Luthor frowned. 'There are several things I wish to ask my apprentice in the morning. This I will add to the list. I was hoping he could shed some light on Eldrick's thinking, and he should not have taken the dagger without my say.'

Arnulf and Fergus shared a glance.

'Is it true that he was up there?' asked Arnulf. 'Was he up in the passes with Eldrick?'

'He was, although Eldrick dismissed him for protesting the subject and manner of their work up there.'

'Do you know what part he played?' asked Lord Fergus.

'Aye,' added Arnulf with a dark tone to his voice. 'This I would like to hear. If it turns out he had a hand in any of what happened, I *will* have my vengeance.'

'The lad seems innocent, and he may yet be of help,' said Luthor. Luthor's doubts and suspicions nagged at him even as he spoke. It had been hard not to notice Duncan's strange behaviour these past days, and he seemed far too interested with Eldrick's work. Luthor hoped he was wrong. He had even considered mentioning his fears to the council but if it was revealed Duncan had lied, that might mean his death—he had to be sure before condemning the poor lad.

'Innocent?' snapped Arnulf. '*Innocent?* He was up there with them! I saw what they were doing. How could any of them be innocent? Because of what they did, my son is cursed by gods knows what. My home is in ruins, my hall burnt to the ground.' He slammed his hand onto the grimoire. 'Because of this!'

'I am sorry to hear...'

'My wife,' growled Arnulf, interrupting Luthor, 'burned alive in my hall. She held our daughter in her arms.'

'Mother save them, I am sorry,' muttered Luthor as Arnulf went on.

'They are gone... because of this.' Arnulf's voice dropped, cracking as his grief welled behind the wall he had built to keep it contained. 'Someone will pay for this, in blood.'

Luthor shrunk away from his words and Arnulf breathed heavily through his nose, his face twisting with rage and anguish. The lord took a minute to compose himself before breaking the pregnant silence.

'I must see this apprentice. I would hear his story before I decide whether to take his head,' he said patting the axe hung at his side.

'If he is guilty, he should face trial and justice,' replied Luthor. The lord seemed taken aback at his reply but Luthor pressed on. 'If Duncan has lied — I hope he hasn't, but if he has, and did in fact have a hand in any of it — I would cast him from my service without hesitation. He would deserve the full measure of your justice and vengeance,' shrugged Luthor.

The lord stared at him a long moment and then slowly nodded. 'I am surprised to hear you say that,' admitted Arnulf.

'See, old friend,' said Lord Fergus. 'Not all here are without honour.'

'I swear to you now, Lord Arnulf. I will do everything possible to help your son, as will the others in the infirmaries. If we can return your son to you, we will,' said Luthor. He meant it too. Pity rested heavy on his heart. 'I am truly sorry about your family, Lord Arnulf. To lose them in such a way must be unbearable. I doubt I would be able to endure such a terrible thing. You are made of sterner stuff than I.'

Lord Arnulf's scowl lessened. He gave a slight nod in appreciation of the compliment.

'I am sorry this had anything to do with our College. Please do not judge us all too harshly, though I imagine I would if I were in your place. Eldrick was meddling in some dark and terrible things; things forbidden by the College. Do not let his madness tarnish us all.'

'And what of your apprentice?' asked Fergus. 'It is strange you would speak of him so.'

'He served me once before. He was a good lad. I trusted him then.'

'And now?' pressed Fergus.

'I just don't know anymore,' admitted Luthor finally. Saying it out loud breathed bitter life into the terrible suspicion of treachery. Had he been deceived and betrayed, used like some unwitting pawn in the apprentice's scheme? 'He was convincing — *sincere* — when he returned. He was badly injured, a cripple now, but something in him has changed. He seems strange now, different.'

'How so?' asked Fergus.

'He talks to himself and is preoccupied with Eldrick's work. It is perhaps understandable, but still, something feels... off. There have been moments recently when I have wondered at his honesty in all this. Only today, he defied me and claimed he could use Eldrick's work to help the king to return the dead. It was then I suspected he knew more than he first told us, that I might have been deceived. He has an unhealthy interest in Eldrick's Bone Ritual.'

Fergus flashed a glance at Arnulf and then frowned, stroking his braided beard thoughtfully. 'Where is he now?'

'I can summon him so you may speak with him, hear it for yourselves?' Luthor offered.

There was a knock at the door.

'More of your people?' asked Luthor.

Arnulf threw a glance at the big warrior, obviously his second in command. The man shrugged.

'Come in,' Luthor called.

Another armed man entered but this one Luthor recognised. This was one of the huscarl's men who had been haunting Duncan's steps since he was ordered under guard at that fateful council meeting.

The guard looked surprised to find the study already crowded with warriors.

'Master Luthor, I am Wilhelm, one of the men assigned to guarding your apprentice. We spoke the other day...'

'Yes, yes, I remember,' Luthor said, ushering him in. 'How can I be of service?'

The warrior glanced at the others in the room and a look of recognition spread across his face as his eyes fell upon the two lords.

'My lords,' he said, saluting with a fist on his chest.

'You are one of the king's men?' asked Fergus.

'Aye, lord, sworn to Huscarl Warrick. I remember you from the Throne Hall, I was standing guard the day you brought the creature to court.'

Luthor saw Lord Arnulf stiffen at the word *creature*.

'Sorry it's late, and I can see you have company,' Wilhelm continued, 'but you asked me to inform you if Apprentice Duncan did anything out of the ordinary?'

'Aye, that I did. And…'

'Duncan is gone. I thought he might be here or at the council.'

'What?' exclaimed Luthor.

'He was taken under an armed guard, accompanied by the king himself.'

Luthor frowned. *I don't like the sound of this.*

'The king *is* here!' Arnulf turned to Fergus and the others, as if Wilhelm had confirmed something the man already knew.

'Was,' replied Wilhelm.

'Was? Have you any idea where they have gone?' Fergus asked.

'I am sorry, lord, but no.' The warrior's brow creased with concern. 'King Rhagnal dismissed my men, who then reported straight to me. As I said, I had hoped they would be here. Lord Warrick will have my balls for letting him out of our sight.'

'But surely if the king has taken him, you will not be held to blame?' offered Lord Fergus.

Wilhelm did not look so certain.

'If he was at the council, he would have been summoned there with me. There are no council sessions tonight,' said Luthor with certainty.

'Then where are they?' demanded Arnulf.

'I don't like the sound of this,' muttered the big warrior.

'Let me guess, a bad omen?' finished his young companion with a weak grin, the feeble attempt at humour betraying the young man's uneasiness at the events unfolding. Lord Arnulf flashed them an irritated glare.

'Perhaps King Rhagnal has taken him to the Citadel?' suggested Wilhelm.

'For what purpose?' Fergus said. Rapid fire questions and answers flew across the room, almost too quickly for Luthor to track.

This definitely doesn't feel right. A terrible cold fear crept into Luthor's belly. 'He wouldn't...'

'Wouldn't what?' demanded Arnulf.

'I believe he may attempt the ritual to save the princess.'

'The princess is already dead,' said Fergus, dismissing the suggestion.

'Exactly, but he told the king at council that he believed he could bring her back if the worse happened.'

'By the gods...' The true scale of the horror dawned on Fergus's face. 'But if he attempts Eldrick's ritual *here*...'

'We must find them,' Arnulf insisted. 'We must stop this.'

CHAPTER TWENTY-NINE

Escape

'It's time,' said Jor.

'He's back?' Nym asked apprehensively.

'He is,' replied the old barkeeper. 'It's time to go. Don't forget anything.'

Nym shifted her gaze to Seth, his ruin of a face wrapped in bandages. He fumbled for a grip to pull himself to his feet and she rose to help him up by his arm.

'I'm alright, lass,' he told her with a strained smile. Only his nose and chin could be seen beneath his dressings, the tip of a scabby scar protruding from under the wrappings. He seemed to know it was her although he could not see.

He had looked so young and handsome when they had met him. She was sure other girls thought so too, but now, how many would look upon him with only pity or revulsion? She could not truly gauge his feelings, his eyes gone, a terrible scar warping the skin of his face. His eyes had been so emotive, and now he had only his smile to convey his thoughts. She offered him an unseen smile as she steadied him. If he could smile through all this, she would smile for him too.

Her brother was on his feet, clutching what few possessions he owned in a small dirt covered sack, the dagger strapped to his belt. When questioned by Jor, he claimed he had found it in the street. The old man was suspicious, but he didn't pursue the matter. The tavern keeper seemed oblivious to the news on the street of a knifing nearby.

Probably for the best.

Things were still awkward between her brother and Seth, but something had changed. Seth appeared to have developed a grudging respect for Finn and it seemed there was a chance he might forgive her brother one day.

Finn had hovered by the door since the message had arrived earlier, waiting while the others prepared. Jor had kept a pack ready since they'd met Roark at the tavern, and had urged the rest of them to prepare a bag each so they might be ready to leave at a moment's notice.

'Come, we have to go,' Jor insisted. He picked up his provisions and ushered them outside with the stump of his arm.

Nym grabbed her bag and helped Seth towards the door.

Outside, a hooded bargeman in dark clothing and holding a spluttering torch introduced himself as Whistler and then hurried them away along the narrow street. It was well after sunset, the claws of winter closing tight around the city.

'It's snowing,' Nym gasped as she hastened to keep up.

Delicate flakes of white drifted down from the heavy darkening clouds overhead. An icy crust had already begun to settle on the roofs and eaves of the surrounding buildings. She guided Seth as best she could through the cold and the dark. Blind and stumbling in the mud, he moved as quickly as he was able, his lute case hugged close to his chest with one arm. Finn followed closely behind Jor and the man leading them to their escape.

'You got my coin?' Whistler growled back at Jor.

'Aye,' replied the old man. 'And you'll have it when we get there.'

Whistler glanced at Jor, then down at the dagger at the old man's belt. He'd likely already noticed that Finn was armed too. 'You better,' he said in a low voice.

'It's what we agreed with your employer,' said Jor.

'Keep up,' he snarled back at Nym and Seth, struggling along behind everyone else. 'We won't wait for stragglers.'

Jor started but kept moving. 'We? You're coming with us?'

'Aye, I'm getting me and my own out of here tonight. This is Old Night's town now, only a fool would stay to die.'

Worry rose in Nym's chest. She didn't fancy the idea of being trapped on a barge amongst cut-throats and gutter scum like the man who had accosted her in the street. These were the sort of people who would slit their throats, take what they wanted, and dump their bodies in the river. The terror of having that knife waved in her face still set her heart to racing. As if their plan weren't dangerous enough, they now risked being trapped and murdered as they made their forbidden escape. And, what if they were all caught by the guards? No one was permitted to leave the city. With each step closer to escape, the apprehension grew in her belly.

'How will we get past the guards?' Nym hissed.

'What guards?' Whistler snorted. 'There's hardly any left. They're all either dead or refuse to hold their posts. Would you?' he asked, throwing a glance back at her.

She gave no reply.

'If the king's warriors live, they have all pulled back to the Citadel and are hiding behind their palisades, or they've taken to their longships on the river. We have seen no patrols in the city for days, but the gates are sealed everywhere. They've just fucked off and left us to die, trapped like rats.'

'The king wouldn't do that,' Nym insisted out of instinct, but in truth, how could she know?

'Well, where are they then?' he snarled. 'Fuck the king, and his lords. It's every man for himself now. I'd have tried to sneak out already, but there are still warriors on the walls. If they see anyone trying to get out that way folk say they get a chest full of arrows. I heard a few have made it through, but the boat is still our best bet.'

'How far to the boat?' interrupted Jor.

'West wharves, not far. Come, this way.'

He led them through winding streets. The city was horribly quiet. Although it was getting late, there was usually still the sound of folk about, the flicker of hearth fires through windows, but tonight, there was nothing. The hovels in this particular slum were dark and near empty.

Are they all dead, the whole street? Or have they fled? Nym looked into the sky. Snow swirled down from the inky blackness, flakes catching the light of the few torches dotted here and there along the street. She wondered if the hundreds of crows that circled overhead were still up there, swooping amongst the drifting snow flakes. *Did they even fly at night?* She had no idea.

A scream punctured the air from somewhere nearby.

They ignored it and hurried onwards. The street opened out

into a larger thoroughfare; the intersection marked by the macabre monument still adorning the gutter where the slum street met the main avenue. It was the very place Nym had been attacked, the place where she had been rescued by the witch-seer. Nym shuddered at the creeping memory of her watching eyes.

Holding his torch high to light the way, the bargeman led them through the god's district towards the docks, a place of temples and shrines. A place once revered by the folk of Arn, it seemed to have been abandoned by everyone, including the gods — how else could such a tragedy befall the city or the people of Arnar?

The glow of torches along the wooden walls of the Citadel could be seen, even from this distance. *Some guards remain then.*

The west wharves lay in the shadow of the Citadel, and they would be sneaking out right under the noses of the king's men. The thought made her shiver.

The wharf looked quiet, a lone barge bobbing gently at the closest mooring. Nothing stirred, just the wind laying snow down in a white blanket over the black filth of the street and the wooden planks of the wharfs. A series of oil lamps and torches had been lit at the dock, the scent of burning whale oil wafting in the night air. The flickering light illuminated two carts left by the far wharf, still laden with their grisly cargo of bodies, waiting a barge in the morning to the pyres. The only witnesses to their escape were the dead.

'Here we are,' Whistler said. 'Our way out of this shit hole.' Jor hurried forwards, but the bargeman stopped him with a firm hand on his chest. 'Hold on, old man. There's still coin to be paid.'

'We're not paying until we're out of the city.'

'You'll pay now, or you ain't getting on my barge.' Whistler held out his hand, the other hovering near his hip as if he might have a weapon under that cloak.

'Surely we can settle this on board? Come on, let's go. Before someone sees us.'

'Let me see your coin, or none of you is getting on.'

The old tavern keeper grew still, both men glaring at each other as Nym's heart leapt into her mouth. Jor conceded first, grumbling as he fished in his clothes for his purse. He plucked out the remaining silver for their passage and handed it over, dropping each coin reluctantly into the bargeman's outstretched hand.

The man grinned. 'Pleasure doing business with ya.' He motioned for them to board the waiting barge. Nym guided Seth towards the wharf, Finn following closely as Jor led the way. She had not taken half a dozen steps when a harsh voice rang out across the silent dock.

'Going somewhere?' the voice sneered. A spiteful laugh echoed out onto the water.

'Well look what we got here,' said someone else. 'It's her.'

Nym slowly turned. A gang of murderous looking thugs emerged from the shadows, the man who had assailed her in the street amongst them.

'What is this?' Jor demanded, a touch of fear edging his voice.

'Roark, we had a deal you sack of shit!' Seth snarled, turning towards the sound of the voices.

Whistler slunk away and melted into the darkness behind the cut-throats.

'Ah Seth... You know, someone knifed up Skag, and after what he did to you there's folk who think you had a hand in it,' said Roark. 'Were not people to be messed with boy.'

Nym recognised the speaker as the same man who had taken their silver at the tavern. Finn clutched tightly at Nym's dress, tugging her back from Seth and the thugs but staying behind her as if he were still a bairn.

'And *she* set the witch on me!'

Nym eyed the thief, waving his knife at her again.

'Is that her, is it? Pretty little thing. Maybe we can have a bit of fun with her,' Roark purred, looking her up and down. 'No witches here to save you this time, lass.'

A tremor of terror rippled over her.

'He's already got all our silver,' Jor insisted 'We've nothing else—'

'Oh, I doubt that, old man,' Roark snapped, cutting him off. 'But don't you worry. We'll make sure to check, but none of you will be breathin' when we do.'

Roark laughed and brandished a savage looking blade. Nym heard the crunch of boots on snow as a pair emerged from the shadowy belly of the barge behind them. *They have us surrounded. There's no way out.*

Jor drew his dagger and dropped his bag, readying to face the advancing cut-throats. 'I fought in two wars,' he snarled in defiance. 'I killed more men than I care to remember. Come near us and I promise you, you're dead.' He put himself between the men and Nym, but she couldn't see how the old man stood a chance against them while she held on to Seth, and Finn clutched at her in turn. The old man stood protectively over their little huddle, defiant and brave.

A strangled sob escaped her throat, snow swirling gently around them, settling into an ever-thickening blanket over the ground. Blades glinted in the dim light and the men slowly advanced, each glaring with vicious, cold eyes.

The only witnesses to their murder would be the dead in the carts. They knew what awaited Nym and her family.

Death is coming.

CHAPTER THIRTY

A Ritual of Flesh

An archway of ancient stonework yawned in front of Duncan. Set a few feet inside, where the archway narrowed, were a set of heavy wooden doors of much more recent design, their fixtures hewn into the old stone. He stared up in wonder at the huge blocks of ancient stonework.

So here it is. The great old stones on which Arn's Citadel was first built. It's true then – these are ruins of the First Sons. He thought it did indeed bare a resemblance to the crumbling ruins in those cursed passes, but these had not been left to fall into disrepair. These had been maintained for generations by Arnarian hands. *The hands of our kin.* He hobbled closer and placed his fingertips on the coarse stone. *Cold.*

'Where are we? What is this place?' Duncan asked as he brushed the snow from his robes.

King Rhagnal turned and regarded him. 'The Crypt of Kings. Much of this place is built upon these great stones. It is very old, built by ancient men.' He paused and pushed open the heavy wooden doors, taking a torch from its sconce as he stepped into the darkness beyond. 'They brought her down here. Come.'

Duncan hesitated, watching as the king disappeared down a flight of steps, the torchlight illuminating a stone passageway that descended beneath the earth into the realm of the dead. He glanced behind him, wishing some means of escape, but the archway behind him was crowded. Four mailed men blocked the way, eyeing him closely and waiting for him to follow the king. The only path was downward into the crypts.

The apprentice descended the stone steps, worn by centuries of uncounted footfalls. Each step into the darkness sent a jolt of pain shooting up his leg. He leaned heavily on his staff, praying it wouldn't slip on the uneven steps, his hands and wrists screaming in protest at the strain. He began to regret the sentimental decision to bring his staff instead of his crutches.

The passageway was cold, and it grew colder the further down he went. It smelt damp and musty, the smoke from Rhagnal's torch drifting back up towards him, stinging his eyes. The torch-light threw dancing shadows against the huge stone blocks of the tunnel's walls.

How could men make this so long ago? he pondered in fascinated bewilderment. It was work beyond the skills of most stonemasons living in Arnar today.

Suddenly the steps ended and the passageway levelled out. The corridor opened out into a warren of many interconnected chambers, wide columns of rough-hewn rock supporting the cavernous ceiling. Duncan passed dark alcoves cut into the rock, deep voids yawning beside him, glimpses of skulls illuminated by the torchlight grinning back at him from the shadows of each recess.

'Bones,' he muttered.

'Yes, lad, old bones,' Rhagnal replied without turning.

'Who are they?'

'Great lords of Arn. Some of them were kings, some folk given a place of honour. My fathers and kin lie amongst them. I come here sometimes to think, sometimes hoping to hear the wisdom of my forebears...' He trailed off as a glowing light appeared ahead of them. 'They brought her here...'

The light flickered from a chamber ahead, and as they passed into the room, Duncan realised they were not alone down here.

The princess lay on a stone plinth in the centre of the room. Three women moved about attending the princess, preparing her for her final rest. Her golden hair tumbled over the side of the plinth, one of the women brushing it until it shone. She saw them enter and stopped.

King Rhagnal halted and raised a hand to his mouth. His eyes fixed on his daughter as she lay cold and still. The women bowed their heads and stepped back. One woman quickly finished wiping the Princess's face with a cloth and stepped back to join the other maids.

Rhagnal gasped a ragged sob from behind his hand, as if he had been holding his breath. 'Alethea...' he gasped, tears rolling down his cheeks.

The apprentice limped forward to look closer. Princess Alethea was breathtakingly beautiful, even in death. Intricate braids had been carefully woven into her locks of golden hair. Her lips were full and slightly parted, her eyes closed as if asleep. Her skin was indeed pale, a pallid ivory, and she had been dressed in a fine gown and many spectacular jewels.

The apprentice was surprised. He'd seen the tortured poses of the plague victims, but there was no sign of such rigorous distress here. Her face had been cleaned of blood, though there were still stains of red lingering in the wells of her eyes and crimson glistening in the corner of her mouth. In her haste to make way for the king as he entered, an attendant had left a slight smear of blood trailing from Alethea's lips across her porcelain skin.

'My king,' the apprentice ventured. 'Time is of the essence.'

Rhagnal took a step closer, still staring. 'Can you truly save her?'

'Yes,' he replied.

'Proceed, apprentice.'

'My king...' spluttered one of the king's warriors lingering at the doorway. 'Is this wise, sire?'

'Get out!' Rhagnal snapped, rounding on the warriors and attendants. 'Get out, all of you! You are dismissed. Wait outside the doors.' When they hesitated the king's hand fell to grip his sword. 'Do not fear. There is little this scholar can do to harm me. Besides, he would not harm his king. He is here to save her. Now go. Must I say it twice.'

The warriors backed away hesitantly, but eventually disappeared into the darkness of the crypts. The women hurried away after them.

The king stepped forwards to stand before the plinth, looking at his daughter with teary eyes. The apprentice hurried, his staff clattering on the stone floor, to a nearby flattened stone. He removed his grimoire from a satchel and laid the heavy book down on some kind of altar beside a wall. A recess yawned before him, and on a slab, hidden in deep shadow, were more bones, old shields and spears leaning in the corners. He looked up at a lintel stone set over the recess, squinting at the faint old runes.

Arn.

The apprentice looked back at the bones in awe. A skeletal grin smiled from a dusty skull set with a crown of cobwebs. A sheathed sword lay upon the skeleton's chest, once clutched by bony hands which had long since lost their shape and collapsed onto the stone in a vague order.

The great king himself. The first king of Arnar.

He looked around and saw tattered and faded banners hanging against the shadowed walls, a strange sense of reverence settling in the pit of his stomach. A ripple of cold washed through his bones. He shuddered. Dark shadows encroached at the edge of his vision, dancing with the flickering flames of the torches. The feeling grew, a feeling he knew. He was being watched.

He began flicking through the pages of his grimoire until his gaze fell upon the symbols of the ritual. Memories of the High Passes ran through his thoughts. He remembered the preparations he had once performed with his old master, Eldrick.

He set to his task. Torch in hand, he moved around the chamber lighting all the other torches hanging on the rocky walls. They bathed the chamber in orange flickering light, glinting off steel and old treasures guarded by their skeletal owners in darkened alcoves. The faded details on the old war banners of Arnar became clearer — the wolf, the Hart stag, a tree, and many more sigils of glory now long forgotten.

He collected the grimoire and placed it on the floor, then took a lump of chalk from his satchel. He began marking out a great circle, shuffling around, crawling on his hands and good knee and dragging his ruined leg behind him as he drew the ancient glyphs onto the floor.

If only Eldrick was here to see this — the final culmination of his great work, perfected by my own hand. He chuckled to himself as he scrabbled around, his hand seemingly guided by an unseen force as it swept the chalk in great confident arks. After he was done on the floor, he marked the walls and the plinth. It was a while before he was satisfied. He finally pulled himself to his feet and held up the grimoire, his staff locked under his arm as he carefully checked the circle and the symbols against the pages of his tome.

It is done, whispered the voice. He nodded in agreement.

The apprentice limped towards the plinth where the princess lay, King Rhagnal standing by her side. Duncan's gaze lingered on the princess, almost forgetting she was a corpse. He had never been so close to such a noble beauty.

'I will have to mark her,' the apprentice warned, his words mingling with the sibilant whisper in his head, speaking in unison. Rhagnal looked at him, slight surprise in his eyes, as if he'd almost forgotten Duncan was there. The man was wracked with grief, his hand stroking his daughter's hair.

'I can use charcoal for some of the symbols, but some will need to be cut into her skin,' the apprentice continued, listening as the words spilled from his lips, giving over control of his tongue.

'Cut into her skin?' Rhagnal repeated uncertainly.

'There is no other way. The glyphs will call her spirit back to her body and return her from Old Night's halls. I will chant the words of the First Sons, those that will guide her spirit and grant her the warmth of life once again.'

'She will be saved?'

'She will,' assured the apprentice. He felt himself smile.

'Then do as you must, apprentice.'

'Perhaps it would be best not to witness the preparations, my king,' Duncan suggested. 'It may be distressing for you to watch.'

The king nodded slowly. 'My father's bones rest not far from here. Perhaps I will go and speak with him a short while.'

The apprentice bowed respectfully. 'I will call for you when it is time.'

The king placed a kiss on his daughter's brow and with a last lingering look, retreated into the shadows.

The apprentice sighed as he looked upon Alethea's corpse. It was a true tragedy to see her laid out before him, and the world would be a less beautiful place if he could not bring her back.

You will not fail, said the voice.

Taking a piece of charcoal from his satchel he began marking her skin. Her skin was soft but so very cold under his fingers as he brushed a golden curl from her face then marked her forehead. She was so beautiful, even in death.

He had watched beautiful women all his life, never daring to dream he could ever have one himself. He had wanted Truda, but had never said anything to her, and there were young acolytes at the College, but they were always so pretty, yet so spiteful. They might have been interested in him before, but now they only looked upon him with scorn and revulsion. He stared down at the still princess before him and realised he had never laid his hands on such beauty, and likely never would again.

The grimoire lay open on the plinth beside her. He looked back and forth, transcribing the symbols from page to skin, recalling how he'd carved these same symbols into old bones up in the passes. Now he knew the proper sequences and knew the missing glyphs, all thanks to the unwitting Master Luthor and this strange veracity that seemed to guide his hand. He doubted he even needed the grimoire, so certain was each stroke.

He marked her arms, parted her clothing and drew markings on her shoulders, on her collar bone. He moved lower, turning his back to the direction the king had gone. He exposed a breast, his eyes lingering on the exposed flesh a moment before he began etching black symbols on her chest. His hands brushed the skin and he let them loiter there, groping.

He marked her legs, lifting up her skirt to reveal her stomach. His hands slide over her skin, outside his control, yet he did not fight it. His fingertips brushed the fuzz of hair between her legs as he drew the dark glyphs on her cold skin, horrified, yet enthralled and excited. He thought of Truda as he worked, and how he would have liked to have touched her in such a way. This woman before him bore a beauty far beyond that of his old friend, and here he found himself, with his hands where many a man could only dream of.

The realisation that he was touching a corpse only vaguely repulsed him. *What am I doing? She is dead.*

Not for long, murmured the voice.

Duncan felt his mouth twitch up in a dark smile at that reply.

He pulled her clothing back into place as he worked so the king would not see. Rhagnal would take his head from his shoulders if he even suspected such defilement.

Time for the blade.

The apprentice took the ritual dagger from his belt and held it up to examine its beauty once again. *Eldrick's dagger.* He chuckled. The same blade used by his old master would now see his work come to fruition as he, Duncan, finished what Eldrick started.

Duncan lowered the blade to his hand. He did not wish to cut his palm and so pierced the back of his arm. He winced as the cold steel bit into his skin, blood trickling down his arm to the curves of the steel blade. He spoke strange words, the guttural consonances and smooth vowels of the First Sons. He wiped the dagger's flat edge across his forearm, bathing the blade in the trickle of his blood. It dripped onto the hilt and over his fingers.

He began cutting. He carved a glyph into her cheek. The flesh parted easily. He cut another series over her breastbone. He cut over the charcoal wards and bindings, carving new glyphs and bindings, now in flesh and blood.

She is ready.

'Let the ritual begin,' the apprentice muttered. 'This ritual, of flesh.'

Duncan called into the darkness that he was ready to begin, his voice echoing through the tomb. There was a long moment of silence then King Rhagnal appeared from the gloom and approached him. The king looked down at his daughter, still and cold on the hard stone, her skin pale, the radiance of life extinguished. Rhagnal's eyes traced the arcane symbols adorning her skin, drawn in charcoal and cut into her soft flesh, then he looked at the apprentice.

'Begin,' he commanded. 'Save her.'

The apprentice nodded and began speaking, reciting the text from his grimoire. He spoke words his old master had once translated. He remembered Eldrick's droning voice, his own now taking a similar inflection. His mind wandered to the memory of that last ritual in those passes in the north. The scene around him did not look so different, the chalk circle of glyphs daubed onto stone, the skulls and bones bearing witness. The plinth had become an altar.

The ancient chamber beyond the circle was plunged into such a darkness by the glare of the torches, it was impossible to tell if he were again on that distant hilltop of crumbling ruins or in a tomb of kings beneath the Citadel.

The incantations echoed through the chamber as he chanted in an eldritch tongue, the language long since forgotten, and like Eldrick before him, he repeated the same phrases over and over.

He could almost see them, his old friends Truda, Logan, and Master Eldrick, all cloaked and hooded standing around him, now mere spectres of memory.

As he spoke, darkness seemed to shroud them. A terrible chill descended upon the chamber, stirring the air, kicking up a gust of wind which appeared to blow from the very walls around him.

Smoke from the torches thickened and swirled to form terrible faces, dead things coalescing and dissipating in the dark smoke.

King Rhagnal looked at the apprentice, wild fear in his eyes. 'Apprentice Duncan?'

The apprentice ignored him, his eyes flicking momentarily to his king before returning to the words in the grimoire. The other voice spoke with him, the sibilant voice merging with his own.

The apprentice felt the power and the presence, that same terrible chill he had long remembered in his darkest of dreams. The icy breath of the restless dead turned his skin to goose flesh and their unseen, spiteful eyes bored into him. The skulls of long dead kings stared from amongst their worldly treasures, the resentful shades stealing not only his life's warmth but drawing off and devouring his very will. The malign presence grew, a presence he had come to know from his dreams, that sense of being watched, a presence that haunted his steps. He knew there was no escaping it.

All was pitch black beyond the swirling smoke and torches. They were no longer alone in the cold crypt. He became aware of the spectral figure across the chamber, watching them from beneath its cloak.

His voice rose in a final crescendo, echoed by another, a guttural voice like shifting gravel, their mingled voices repeating the final words again and again before falling silent.

He held his breath and waited.

Moments passed.

Doubt began to set in.

An arm jerked up and grasped the altar's edge.

His skin prickled as his hair stood on end, his heart pounding in his chest. It was happening!

'I did it,' he whispered.

The princess rose from the stone plinth, her movements weak, uncertain. She pulled herself up, moving like a terrible puppet on invisible strings.

The king let out a cry of happiness. He leapt forward to help her. 'Alethea,' he gasped. 'By the gods.'

He pulled her close to his chest and held her. Tears of happiness ran down his cheeks as he embraced her. 'Alethea, you are safe now.' He looked at the apprentice. 'You saved her, lad. You saved her.'

'One last thing,' said the apprentice, picking up his grimoire and returning its weight to the satchel strapped over his shoulder.

Rhagnal looked up gratefully from his embrace and into the apprentice's eyes.

'A sacrifice of blood,' Duncan said with a grim smirk.

Alethea's teeth sank into Rhagnal's neck. His face distorted in pain and shock as he mouthed a soundless scream. The apprentice watched as the king fought to escape his daughter's iron grasp. He reached a desperate hand towards the apprentice, but Duncan merely stood there, watching calmly as the king grew weaker, his eyes dimming as his strength seeped away.

There was a tearing sound and a gush of blood from king's throat.

Blood splattered onto the chalk marked stone floor, and the king slipped from her grasp and crashed down into the puddle of gore. The princess pushed herself to her feet, blood smeared across her face, dripping from her chin. She looked at the apprentice with dead eyes but made no move towards him. In the dim light, a dark pool spread from Rhagnal's limp body. A flash of strange light ran through the chalk markings as the blood touched them. It was as if the blood seeped into those chalk lines. A deep reddish-purple flash rippled through the arcane circle.

A concussive blast of energy suddenly exploded from the circle and engulfed the chamber in oily black smoke and swirling shadow. Another pulse of power tore out from the circle, ripping through adjoining chambers and the very rock itself. Skull faced palls of smoke trailed around the room shooting past him and disappearing into the gloom.

A grin spread across his face as he turned, leaning against his staff. He heaved himself into the swirling shadows and unearthly smoke, hobbling back in the direction of the stone stairway, leaving the risen princess and the dead kings to their crypt.

'I have done it,' the apprentice muttered. 'She lives again.'

You command death itself, hissed the voice.

'I am now truly...'

In his head, their voices again spoke in unison once more.

'Master.'

Part Three

Valour and Steel

CHAPTER THIRTY-ONE

Dead Moon

Clutching the door frame with ageing, work-worn hands, he watched the snow slowly swirl down to settle on the cobbles, illuminated by the shaft of light slicing out into the night from the doorway.

'Wolter, what is it?' she asked from beside the hearth.

'I'm not sure,' he said. 'I felt something strange.'

He took a step outside. The snow was already deep enough to crunch beneath his boot.

'It's really coming down now,' she called after him. 'Put something on before you go wandering around out there.'

'It's fine, Mirim,' he replied and waved her worry away.

He took another step into the snow dusted courtyard and looked up into the sky. Flakes of white drifted out of the darkness in their thousands, kissing his cheeks and melting into icy tears. Flurries danced through the shaft of firelight, settling in drifts by his door.

What was that strange sound, that strange feeling? Something feels odd about this night.

There was no sign of a moon in the clouded sky.

'Dead moon,' he muttered as he peered into the sky. He heard folk in town saying a dead moon was due tonight; when the moon would rise black and spirits would stalk the land. He shuddered at the thought and at the strange feeling that wrapped itself around his guts.

I could have sworn I heard something, he thought. A concussive boom had rolled across the city not more than a few moments ago, strong enough to rouse him from his warm hearth-side and his ale.

He took another step into the courtyard and narrowed his eyes at where he knew other buildings stood in the gloom, searching the sky for some sign of fire or anything that might explain the sound.

Wolter's eyes settled on the dim glow that outlined the Citadel and he froze.

'What in Varg's teeth is that?' he mumbled. *Is that smoke?*

A strange, tumultuous fog seemed to spread from the palisades of the Citadel, obscuring what little light emanated from there. It was somehow darker than the surrounding night sky, a dark cloud. It spread out and up, clawing at the sky, slowly swirling.

A sudden pulse of colour flashed through the fog like lightning deep within a cloud, greens and purples and a deep red all at once. He had never seen lightning like it.

The abnormal cloud and its vacillating light framed a strange shape in the sky.

It looks like a skull!

He recoiled and took an involuntary step backwards, watching with a morbid fascination, a cold sense of dread growing in his stomach.

With a bright flash and a sudden *crack,* a wave of coloured light burst out from above the Citadel, it rolled through the sky and out over the city, like a ripple from a stone thrown into a mill pond. He craned his neck back as the shockwave passed overhead and carried on towards the city limits. Within the roiling colours he could have sworn he saw awful, drawn out faces fixed into silent screams, but they vanished, dissipating into the boiling cloud.

'God's save us,' he whispered.

The cold dread wrenched at his heart, an icy hand clutching at him. He shuddered and turned to flee for the safety of his hearth. He would lock his door tight this night.

A strange sound stayed his hand before he could reach the latch.

He couldn't help himself, and turned slowly towards the noise.

A deep groaning punctuated by a scraping sound echoed

across the courtyard, but this sound was not high above or deep down in the earth. It was right here, in his courtyard, in the shadows by his feet.

***

'Mammy!' she squealed with excitement. 'It's snowing!'

'You should be in bed, dear. What are you doing up?'

'I heard a sound, and then I saw it was snowing.' Elsie jumped up and down, wriggling like a puppy.

Her mother frowned, hiding a smile. 'Come on you, you can see it in the morning. Back to bed — it's late.'

'Please, let me watch it a while first,' pleaded the little girl.

'No, back to bed.'

'Aww,' Elsie groaned, her face falling as if her entire world had been crushed.

Edith couldn't resist that face. 'Go on then, but just for a moment.'

Elsie ran to the window and stared with the amazement at the small square of light spilling from inside the house, the falling snow illuminated by the pale glow. Edith smiled as her eldest daughter bobbed up and down, watching the snow slowly blanket the ground. Her youngest nestled close against her chest, a mere babe of only weeks. This would be her first winter, if they all survived the sickness stalking outside.

The baby was finally asleep. She had been crying all evening, no doubt keeping Elsie awake longer than she should have. Edith rocked the babe slowly and gently lifted her into her crib. She stirred slightly and Edith held her breath, waiting until the baby settled before she let out a sigh of relief. She glanced over at her eldest, and saw Elsie on her knees, clutching at the window sill with both hands, her chin resting upon it as she stared out into the night.

Edith joined her at the window, a chill draught blowing in through the open shutters making a shiver run over her. 'We shouldn't leave this open for long, your sister will catch a cold.' She gently wrapped her arms around her daughter. 'And, so will you if you sit here too long.'

'It's so pretty, Mammy,' Elsie replied.

'It is,' agreed Edith, looking out into the falling snow. 'Do you know about Bheur?'

'What is that?' asked the little girl.

'*Who* is that?' her mother corrected. 'Bheur is the goddess who brings the snows.' She pulled Elsie close to her and continued. 'Some say she is an old woman. Some say she is the Crone herself with another face. But she lives in the mountains where the snow never melts, in a mighty ice palace, waiting to cast her cloak over the lands each year.'

Elsie looked at her mother and smiled. She did love a story.

'This is Bheur's snow, so remember, always whisper a thank you to her when you see the snows fall.'

Elsie turned back to the window. 'Thank you, Bheur.'

'That's my girl,' said Edith, placing a gentle kiss on her head. 'Now you, let's shut this window before the cold spirits get in.'

Elsie drew in her breath sharply.

'Quick, quick, close the shutters,' Edith said with a sing-song voice and a grin. They pulled the shutters closed in a mock panic. 'There, we're safe!' She let out a dramatic sigh of relief and Elsie grinned up at her. 'Now, back to bed.'

The little girl nodded reluctantly, climbing the wooden ladder back to the sleeping platform. 'Good night, Mammy.'

'Good night, sweetheart,' replied Edith with a warm smile. She watched her daughter disappear into her bed and moved to the hearth to warm herself. She checked the baby then settled down in her chair beside the glowing hearth.

***

The cart lurched, the wheel slamming into a protruding rock.

'Dammit,' Barden swore, pulling back on the reins squinting into the shadows of the street ahead.

It was getting hard to see now. Night had arrived and he should have been home long before now, there just seemed to be more than ever to collect. The twisted dead piled outside of plague marked houses seemed endless, but at least now his cart was full.

He caught a whiff of the putrid stench wafting from the back of his cart and wrinkled his nose, turning the cart towards one of the new grave pits. Some of the dead were burnt but people had been saying that the smoke was spreading the illness, so most

were now being interred in the ground. He had heard they would
build a mound over them once this was all over — a great memori-
al for the dead, like the fallen of the battlefield.

He would be glad to get this night over with. The snow was
coming down heavily, and it was bitterly cold. The wheels of the
cart carved black ruts through the snow into the muck beneath.
He longed for a hearth and an ale. Probably a few ales actually —
anything to erase the memory of the bodies he had hauled away.
He was becoming dulled to it, yes, but their faces haunted his
dreams.

A concussive *boom* echoed across the night sky. He spun
around, pulling the horse to a stop, scanning the sky behind him.

Thunder?

Thunder-snow wasn't unheard of, but it was...

A wave of oscillating lightning flashed along the belly of the
clouds, a burst of multi coloured light rippling from the area near
the Citadel.

'By the gods,' he muttered. He couldn't believe what he was
seeing. The surge of pulsating colours raced overhead and disappeared into the distance. The Citadel seemed to glow, illuminating a dark shape in the sky above it.

Witchfire?

He had never in his life seen anything like it.

The air turned frigid, colder than any winter he had lived
through, and he pulled his cloak in tighter, adjusting his face
scarf. In the darkness of the dead moon night, Barden swore he
heard a whispering voice on the air. He shuddered, gripped by a
sudden need to get this cart delivered and to take shelter in his
home as quickly as possible.

'Cursed dead moon,' he muttered, and flicked the reins, urging the horse onwards.

Something grabbed his shoulder with a grip like a vice of iron.
He let out a cry of shock and twisted to see who had hold of him.

Someone is on the cart!

He turned and saw a blooded hand grasping his shoulder,
emaciated and pallid, the hand of a corpse.

He jerked away, wrenching himself back from the clawing
grip but it would not release him. Sensing his panic, the horse
threw its head, braying and screaming, thrashing against the harness and breaking into a blind gallop.

Icy sludge and dark filth sprayed up from the wheels as another pair of hands clamped onto him, wrenching him backwards. He screamed as they pulled him from his seat and into the back of the cart. Dead faces descended upon him, eyes milky and blank, hands raking and grasping at his limbs.

Rotten teeth sank into his arm and he screamed, his flesh giving way to the force of the bite. The cart careened wildly out of control, the wheels slamming into hidden rocks, jolting violently. He shoved at the corpses as bodies were thrown from the cart, thumping down in its wake to lay crumpled in the street. In the dim light of the houses nearby, he watched in horror as they rose unsteadily to their feet.

The dead surged over him, obscuring his view and he let loose another scream, teeth sinking into his shoulder. He tried to fight his way free, but they pinned him, their rooting limbs somehow stronger than steel. He couldn't believe what was happening.

These people are dead!

Warm dampness flooded across his skin and soaked through his clothes. He was vaguely aware that it was his own blood, its warmth quickly sapped by the cold.

With a loud *crack* a wheel broke and the cart flipped. Horse, cart and its grisly cargo careened through the air and smashed into a low round building.

Twisted and mangled, with a pool of blood spreading beneath him, Barden lay amongst the writhing corpses and stared at the sky.

They were biting me... eating me.

Around him the dead began to slowly stagger to their feet, lurching into motion.

He could hear screams. They sounded far away, distant.

The world faded to black.

***

The old man clutched at his arm as he staggered through the door.

'He bit me!' Wolter said.

Mirim spun around in alarm. '*Bit* you?'

'Aye, some drunk stumbled into the courtyard. Took a chunk right out of my arm.'

She stood quickly and rushed to her husband. He was pale,

and his hands trembled from the shock. Dark blood dripped through his fingers as he clutched at his wrist. Glancing out into the courtyard, she saw a trail of crimson emerging from the darkness through the soft white snow. She closed the door and turned her attention back to his arm.

'What happened?' she asked, trying to keep the worry from her voice as she led him to his chair by their hearth.

'Heard someone over by the gate. I asked if he was alright but he just groaned.'

Mirim recoiled. 'Oh gods, was he one of the sick?'

'I don't know, it was dark. Seemed drunk to me.'

'Where is he now?'

'Ha, well I threw him off me, and gave him a good kick in the ribs. Bastard. He took off into the street.'

'Sit down, love. Let me look at it.'

Wolter lifted his hand away from the wound, revealing a deep bite gash, the puncture marks of teeth at its ragged edges. The bastard had torn quite a chunk from Wolter's arm. She looked into her husband's lined face. Gods, he was pale, his lips and cheeks drained of all colour. Had he already lost so much blood?

'This will need stitching, dear,' she said as she examined the arm.

'Can you do it?' he asked.

'Aye, that I can. Push down hard on it though while I get a needle ready.'

He did as he was told. In thirty years, he had learnt that when she used that tone he would do well to comply. She hurried off to find thread and a needle, collecting a dusty bottle from a shelf as she returned.

'The good stuff?' he asked. His words slurred slightly.

'Aye,' she said, dousing the wound and handing what remained to him. 'Take a deep swig, love. This will hurt.'

Mirim set to work sewing the gaping hole in Wolter's arm, doing her best to ignore how he winced and grimaced at the first few needle pricks, but he seemed to calm as she worked. The liquor was doing its job, then.

'There,' she said, examining her handiwork and splashing a little more alcohol across the stitches. 'That should hold. I just hope to the gods it doesn't go bad. I told you not to go wandering around out there, you old fool. It ain't safe.'

'Aye, lass.' He smiled, his skin crinkling with a hundred lines. 'Saw something in the sky, just now.'

'What are you talking about? That drink's gone to your head,' she scoffed. She wouldn't let him grin his way out of this one.

'There were lights in the sky, like a wave. It's a bad omen,' he said.

'You're not making sense...' She frowned at him, his eyes seeming more than a little glassy as he glanced towards the window. He didn't seem quite right; distant, absent, as if his mind was elsewhere. Perhaps it was just the blood loss. She didn't press him further, leaving him slumped in his chair as she cleaned up the blood and her needle.

'I'm hungry,' he muttered.

She made up a plate—cold ham and the last of the bread. She'd have to go looking for more—

He struck without warning, pain exploding in her face as he punched her hard in the mouth. Then again, and again.

She fell to the floor screaming, pleading for him to stop. His eyes were blank, devoid of emotion, filled neither with love nor anger, just cold indifference as his fists hammered down into her face again and again.

Her skull cracked as he muttered to himself. 'Sorry, my love.'

Before the world went black, he bit her, tearing at her flesh, blood running down his chin.

'I was hungry,' he said.

***

Edith awoke with a start. She must have dosed off, but a deep, resonating boom had woken her. Or was it a dream? She leaned over and checked the crib. Her baby still slept quietly.

She rubbed her eyes. She had not meant to fall asleep. She had to finish this sewing by morning or she wouldn't get—

A scream pierced the night, echoing from nearby. She shuddered, trying not to think of what it was. It was not uncommon to hear such sounds of late. Since the sickness came, it was more likely to hear a scream of pain or wail of grief than a peel of laughter or a joyous melody on the night air.

Another scream followed the first, and she put down her work. Something wasn't right. That time it was closer. She walked to the window and peered through the shutters. The street outside seemed quiet.

A figure ran into view, a girl, glancing fearfully back down the street. 'Somebody help me!' she cried, staggering and falling over in the icy sludge of the snowy road.

Edith glanced at the crib and bit her lip, then slipped out the door. Snow crunched under her feet as she hurried towards the distressed girl. 'Hey,' she called. 'Quickly, this way.'

The girl saw her and scrambled to her feet, running awkwardly across the distance between them. 'We must run!' the girl gasped, clutching onto Edith.

Edith cast a look back down the street. A group of people staggered towards them.

'This way, come inside,' Edith urged, eyeing the dark figures. Were they drunk? It was hard to tell at this distance, but none of them seemed steady on their feet. She circled the girl in her arms and guided her towards her door.

Her heart froze.

A man stood between them and her door. He'd appeared as if from nowhere, and he sniffed the air, tilting his head like a curious bird. There was something very wrong with him.

He darted forwards and Edith let go of the girl, staggering away. The girl raised her arms protectively as the man barrelled into her, her screams echoing off the buildings as the pair crashed to the ground. The snow turned to a filthy slush as they struggled in the space before her door, Edith watching on, frozen in horror and unable to move. The man sank his teeth into the girl's neck, and with a sickening tear, ripped her throat out.

The girl's screams turned to strangled gasps and Edith regained control of her legs, slowly backing away, her eyes fixed on the man. He flashed her a glare, teeth bared, bright red in the light spilling from her doorway, before turning back into the ruin of the girl's neck.

He's eating her!

The girl coughed a wad of blood and finally fell still, a crimson stain expanding through the white snow. Edith tore her gaze away from the dead girl's eyes to look at the group the girl had been fleeing, realising with a start that they were nearly upon them. Others had appeared from between the houses, drawn by the girl's screams, swelling the group's numbers. Edith glanced down the other end of the street, hoping for an escape, only to see another group stumbling towards her, the encroaching crowd surrounding her in every direction she looked.

The man snapped his head around to glare at the approaching strangers and let out an animal like snarl before he abandoned his gruesome feast and loped into a dark alley between the houses. As he fled, he ran using both his hands and feet, like some warped beast.

Edith shuffled backwards on numb feet until she thumped back against the wall of her neighbour's house, unable to look away from the crowd. The closest was a woman, her limbs jerking as she staggered towards Edith. The woman reached towards Edith, her hand grasping at the air between them. Dried blood crusted her eyes and nose, her face covered in ragged craters, as if carrion birds had been ripping at her flesh. She had no lips, and a great sheet of skin hung from her jaw, revealing her broken teeth.

She's dead. Edith recoiled in terror. *This must a dream, a terrible nightmare. It can't be real.* Her eyes darted from face to face, each as grisly and gruesome as the last. *They're all dead!*

She turned and scrambled up onto a water barrel, then onto the thatched roof of the house, desperately clawing away from the grisly rotten abominations behind her. Her foot slipped and she slammed down hard on the wet thatch, her skin and clothes tearing. For a terrible moment she thought she would fall back down.

The dead crowded beneath her and she snatched her legs away from their grasping hands. Their nails scraped her skin and she screamed, her heart thudding in her chest. There were more of them, shuffling forwards, drawn by her screams. The rooftop was surrounded, there was no way down now.

I'm trapped!

She stared down in horror at the gruesome victims of the plague, risen again into a mockery of life. Crusted blood had dried around their mouths and eyes, dark, blank stares locked on her face, somehow full of malice. They moved with a jerking motion as if stiff limbs were being forced to move by some terrible malign power, sickening marionettes controlled by an eldritch puppet master.

She dragged her eyes away from the groaning dead and cast her gaze to the streets beyond. Beastly forms darted through the faint pools of light emanating from nearby houses, some bounding along on all fours with a terrifying speed. They appeared to be human, but nothing about their movement seemed human. She watched as a fleeing figure was run down by one such creature, and everywhere the staggering dead could be seen, slow and inexorable. Townsfolk began screaming, their shrill voices rising into the night.

What are these monsters? There's so many, they're everywhere.

The orange glow of a fire grew brighter as several buildings across the city were consumed by the flames, illuminating the snow laden clouds as flakes continued to cover everything in an ethereal white.

Bheur, what are these horrors that you have brought with your snow? Hjort, save us, she prayed.

The Citadel caught her eye as she climbed to the apex of the roof. A huge dark shape loomed above it in an unnatural black cloud. She gasped. It looked just like a skull, the eye sockets staring into her soul, hungry for her warmth, stealing away her hope. *Is it Old Night himself? Save us.*

'Mammy?'

Edith's heart skipped and her eyes slid closed, a tear tracking down her cheek. *No.*

'Mammy?' Elsie called again.

Edith turned and looked back across the street to her front door, and Elsie standing on the step. The door to their house was still open, the body of the dead girl cooling in the churned snow, but Elsie ignored it, looking up at her mother and clutching a bundle to her little chest.

The dead turned towards the voice, lurching around to consider the source of the new sound.

'No!' shrieked Edith, reaching out in vain. 'Elsie, *run!*'

She started the scramble back down the roof, ignorant of the danger, desperate to get between her children and the walking corpses. The dead staggered towards the little girl, but Elsie didn't move. She looked from them to her mother, frozen in place, the little bundle clutched to her little heaving chest.

Elsie held the bundle up towards her mother. 'But Mammy… the baby is crying.'

CHAPTER THIRTY-TWO

The Bite of Steel

A rumbling boom shook the air, stealing Nym's breath as the concussion wave struck her. The dark waters of the river rippled and shivered, the surrounding buildings, the piers, even the very ground trembling and creaking as the force rolled through them. Every person at the dock flinched and ducked instinctively, turning to search for the source. They looked up at the nearby palisades of the Citadel and the eerie mass of dark fog billowing out from within the Citadel's doors and windows. Nym swore she heard whispering as the wind swirled the snow, a pulse of light flashing away across the clouds.

'What the fuck was that?' said one of thugs, looking around in confusion as his companions muttered to each other and shrugged. The murderous cut-throats hesitated only a moment, but when they did not perceive a further threat, their attention once more settled on Nym and her companions.

Jor stood protectively in front of them his knife drawn and Nym had no doubt he would use it. He had to, or they were all dead. She glanced back at Finn and gasped as he took out his own knife. Stepping forwards, he brandished it bravely beside old Jor. Finn wore a facade of brash courage, but the knife trembled in his hand. Seth clung to her, turning his head to catch any sound from the menace that bore down upon them.

Had it always been a trap? Did they ever have a chance of escape from the city, or had Roark just seen a chance at for vengeance for what had happened to one of their own? It was as good a chance as any to prise what silver they had from their dead hands, leaving another few bodies to greet the dawn in a city wracked by plague. There would be no justice for them. No one would mark them gone.

What did you do little brother? she thought, looking at Finn. *You have killed us all.*

Two of the thugs charged the old tavern keeper and he lunged, batting a knife aside with the stump of his arm. The blade bit into his skin, but Jor surged forwards with only a grunt of pain, plunging his knife into the thug's throat. The man's face twisted in shock as Jor yanked the knife free and blood gurgled from his neck.

The other man was on Jor before the old man even turned, chopping with a hatchet. Jor twisted and narrowly avoided the descending axe head, and with a horizontal slash, he opened the man's throat then plunged his knife into his chest.

Finn still stood protectively in front of Nym and Seth, watching in awe and trembling with fear. Seth clutched tightly to his lute case, looking sightlessly around as the three of them backed away, leaving Jor to stand over the two dying men at his feet. The whole thing had been so quick, the cut-throat's surprise evident on their faces. They must have assumed these folk would be an easy target.

For a moment Nym saw a glimmer of the warrior Jor had once been. She imagined him standing side by side with her father under a banner on distant battlefields. He would go down fighting, no matter what.

'What's going on?' Seth demanded. 'Da, are you alright?'

'Aye, lad,' Jor replied without taking his eyes from the would-be attackers hesitating at the edge of the light. The old man was breathing heavily, and a trickle of blood dripped from his arm stump.

Nym looked around desperately for an escape route, but the thugs had her family pinned at the end of the wharf, uninviting river water stretching out behind them. *There's too many*, thought Nym hopelessly. They wouldn't underestimate the old man a second time.

'Take him down, lads. Make it quick,' barked Roark.

They came on as one, all at once as to overpower the old tavern keeper. Jor managed to stab one but another seized him from behind. A man with a big scar down his face used a wide-bladed knife to chop at the tavern keeper's good hand, and Jor cried out in pain, his knife falling to the ground, splattering the snow with crimson blood. A solid punch to the side of the head dropped the old tavern keeper to his knees.

'Bring him to me,' commanded Roark. They dragged Jor away as some of the others rounded on Nym's little huddle. The man nearest to her grinned menacingly.

It was then Nym saw them—a dozen or so figures wandering out of the shadows around the warehouses. She looked over as more figures climbed from the back of the cart at the far end of the dock.

'Boss, it's an ambush,' cautioned one of the cut-throats.

Roark laughed. 'Can't be, there's no way the little singer boy knew we'd be here.' He turned to the approaching figures and shouted, 'Not healthy hiding amongst the dead, I assure you. Well, you're too late anyway. We found 'em first.'

With those last words he dragged a knife slowly across Jor's throat.

Nym screamed, her hands gripping Seth's coat tighter than ever as tears streamed from her eyes.

The tavern keeper choked and spluttered as blood poured from his neck, his wide eyes darting to Nym and then to his son. Life faded from his gaze, taking with it the expression of sadness and he flopped down to the ground.

'Da?' Seth called. '*Da*?'

There was no answer.

'Nym, is my Da, okay?' Seth pleaded.

Nym chocked on a sob. She couldn't answer.

'What have you done to him?' Seth shouted, his voice racked with sorrow.

'Boss…' one of the men said carefully.

Roark rounded on the approaching figures. 'Don't know how you managed this, Seth, but they will die, same as your pa.'

'No!' Seth moaned. 'Nym…'

'*Boss!*' the man shouted again. 'Look! There's something not right here.'

The men circling them threw uncertain glances at their leader and Nym watched the unknown saviours staggering and lurching forwards. She had no idea who they were, and she was certain they had nothing to do with Seth—he would have said something by now.

The dockside had become bitterly cold, snow coming down heavily.

'Lads, take care of these fools first. The girl and the blind fiddler can wait.'

Several of the cut-throats charged the figures, brandishing their weapons, a young lad striking with his hatchet, scything into the lead figure. The axe head sank into the stranger's shoulder and Nym stared.

The figure barely flinched.

Instead of falling to the ground and writhing in pain, it seized the young man by the throat. The lad kicked and screamed as he was lifted off his feet, and his comrade recoiled. He tried to retreat but a figure launched at him, driving him to the ground, biting and tearing.

'Demons!' shouted a cut-throat.

'No, they're *dead*!' screamed one of the thugs. 'They're fucking *dead*!'

'What in Old Night's hell is this?' someone shouted as another man was attacked, the stumbling figures descending on him as the others tried to flee. Finn started shuffling backwards, pushing Nym and Seth towards the empty barge.

'What fucking sorcery is this?' Roark bellowed as the dockside descended into chaos. Nym could hardly breathe as corpses walked into the faint light of the torches and tore into the street gang.

One of the dead lurched close enough for her to see it clearly. It was a man, his jaw hanging loose where one of the thugs had tried to kill it before being pulled to the ground screaming. The dead man's skin was pale and thin, his face and hands gaunt and shrivelled. His eyes turned towards her, a cold, black hate dwelling within them.

She screamed.

Roark ran desperately towards the barge, his footsteps thumping loudly on the wooden planks, but the dead cut him off, dragging him to the floor screaming. His screams suddenly intensifying into a stomach curdling gurgle before being cut short. Her mind reeled as the corpses descended on the traitor. *This can't be real.*

Finn pulled urgently on Nym's arm and she tore pulled her

eyes from the dreadful scene unfolding before her.

'Nym, look,' Finn said, pointing in the direction of the city.

She saw it too. The way was clear. The dead had eyes only for the street-gang, drawn to them by their screams and cries for help.

'Seth, we need to run,' she said, dragging the blind man towards the dark streets. Finn was already running, and she hurried after him to the entrance of the dock. Seth stumbled and slipped on the snowy ground but by some miracle remained on his feet, the polished lute case never leaving his hand. She clung tightly on to his coat, fearing if she let go she would lose him too. He said nothing as they ran, and she was certain that if he had eyes, he would have been weeping.

Poor Jor. I will remember you, old man.

She threw a look back into the chaos of the docks. To her horror, she saw their escape had not gone unnoticed by malign dead eyes. The dead man with the horrific hanging jaw had been joined by several others who now slowly staggered after her. Men ran out onto the piers, jumping into the river to escape, but the dead followed relentlessly, pitching into the dark water after them. Others were trapped, desperately fighting against the grasping hands, their weapons seemingly useless. The dead barely noticed the wounds being inflicted upon them. They seemed unstoppable. More dead clambered down from the carts. There were dozens of them now, swarming the street gang.

They didn't stand a chance.

CHAPTER THIRTY-THREE

The Examination

'He's sedated?'

'Aye, he's out cold,' replied the assistant.

Master Hobar nodded. 'Excellent, let's make this quick.'

The hinges screamed as the cage door opened, his apprentice, Enid, wrinkling her nose at the smell. The floor of the cage was soiled in urine, weeks of human filth and rotting rat carcasses — no one had dared get close enough to clean it.

The chains rattled as they lifted the limp form onto the examination table.

'Shall we unchain him?'

'No, leave them as a precaution.'

Enid gave a sigh of relief. 'Very wise, master.'

'Quickly now,' urged Hobar. The master leaned over the gaunt form of Ewolf and felt for breath with the back of his hand. 'He's breathing steadily.'

Hobar peeled back Ewolf's eyelids and recoiled.

'What is it, master?'

'His eyes… look.' Hobar leaned back, allowing Enid to see for herself. The blood vessels had turned a blackish-purple, marbling the whites of his eyes. His pupil looked distorted, pulled into an unnatural shape, and blackness within had the depth of a void, like something eldritch and terrible dwelt within.

Enid gasped. 'What could do that?'

Master Hobar let the eye close and shook his head. 'In all my years, I have never seen anything like it.' The pair shared an uncertain glance and continued.

'How long will the mixture last?' Enid asked with an anxious look at the unconscious form of Ewolf.

'Should be a few hours at least. I've seen it knock men out for a day, so we should have plenty of time.' Master Hobar pushed aside the ragged remains of Ewolf's filthy shirt. He was emaciated, his ribs protruding, his skeleton clearly visible beneath stretched skin.

'You can see how they thought he was dead. He looks like a corpse,' Enid said.

Hobar nodded. 'He's in a terrible state. We should try and get some food and fluids in him while he's out.' Hobar touched Ewolf's pallid skin. The same dark veins that could be seen in his eyes ran beneath his clammy skin, and the master traced one with his finger. The younger man's chest rose and fell rapidly, his breathing more like an animal panting.

'Very concerning,' commented Hobar.

'Master?'

Hobar pressed against the young man's abdomen with his fingers, his ear on his chest, listening to his breathing and heartbeat.

'Master, look!' Enid exclaimed. 'His eyes.'

Hobar raised his head to see Ewolf's eyes stirring beneath the closed lids. 'Can't be...'

Suddenly his eyes snapped open, the dilated and distorted pupils focused on the shocked master hovering above him. The chains rattled as the limp man stiffened, his muscles spasming.

The master started and tried to pull away, but hand shot up and seized him by his hair. Master Hobar yelped and Ewolf snarled, thrashing against his chains and yanking Hobar's face down towards the table. A burning sensation exploded in his cheek, teeth slicing through his skin and pinching together. He screamed and tried to pull back, but Ewolf held on, tearing at Hobar's face until a chunk of flesh came free.

Hobar screamed all the more, and his apprentice bolted for door, her cries for help echoing throughout the infirmaries.

***

The old man lay limp, his breathing heavy. He was still awake, but too terrified to move.

Ewolf had not felt such things as terror since the darkness took him. He felt rage and hunger, but not fear. He looked at the chains and the cage, and rage filled him again. He grasped a nearby chair and hurled it across the room to crash into the cage which had held him for so long, splintering with the impact. He let out a roar. He saw a key on a nearby table and snatched it up, quickly unlocking his chains. *I am free!*

He once again looked at the old man trembling on the floor. His prey's scent was already beginning to change. Its wounds already smelled different, more familiar, like himself. It would become like him if he left it alone.

He had a choice. He could feed now, gorging himself on the sweet flesh before it was consumed by the darkness, or he could leave the prey and allow it to change, to become an ally, another for the pack.

He had seen the other one flee in terror. He heard it fumbling with the lock on the other side of the door. He would not be locked in a cage again.

***

Enid heard a terrible bestial shriek echo within the examination room and hurried to secure the door's lock with trembling hands. A sudden pang of guilt struck her at the sound.

I'm sorry, master!

A mighty impact shook the door and the wood panels cracked. Enid took a step back, eyes wide with terror. Her back came up against the wall and another shriek pierced the silent corridor. *It's trying to get out...*

The creature hurled itself against the door again. The hinges creaked and a panel broke. A wild, primal eye glared through the hole. That door wouldn't last long, yet she was petrified, unable to do any more than watch as the horror unfolded.

With an explosion of splinters, the door tore off its hinges the cursed man barrelled into her, knocking the wind from her and sending them both crashing against the wall.

***

A swipe of his claw-like hand opened the prey's throat. With a surge of spiteful malice, the one once known as Ewolf unleashed a

344

flurry of savage swipes, tearing at its torso, life pumping away onto the floor, but the release felt good. His prey lay gurgling blood, fighting vainly until it fell still.

Ewolf's body was wracked with pain. From his fingernails to the bones in his limbs, he was changing. His hands were already more like talons, and while he could still taste the blood in his mouth, and feel the slivers of flesh between his teeth, a dull ache throbbed through his jaw as his teeth shifted. The change was so painful he unleashed a bestial roar, agony fuelling his rage.

It's the flesh, the feeding — it's bringing the darkness closer, it's changing me. I can hear it whisper. This change is a gift.

Behind him a familiar scent grew stronger and he looked back at the wounded prey he'd left in the examination room. He had resisted the urge to feed, despite waiting so long to taste it. The prey's wounds were not fatal, it would live. Even now it stirred, the darkness taking hold. Soon it would join him, and they would hunt as one.

He looked down at the prey at his feet. A fresh kill. He would feed on this one. He tore into its neck, ripping away the sweet flesh. Blood ran down his chin as chewed, his eyes rolling back in ecstasy — he had waited so long. Madness had taken him while caged, unable to hunt, unable to feed. Now he was free and he gorged himself on the human flesh before him.

As he ate the memory of who he had been began to fade, the last threads of humanity still lingering somewhere within him growing ever distant. Something of his old life had remained during his time locked away in that cage, but it disappeared, replaced by the need to feed as instinct took over. A figure joined him beside the corpse.

So, it turned. We are pack.

He stepped back and let the new one feed, taking a moment to survey the corridor. Splintered wood that had once been the door littered the dim hallway. His ears pricked at the sound of a commotion nearby, and he sniffed the air. More prey — he could smell their fear on the air.

Then he caught the scent of something else, something he knew. It was faint but he was certain of it. The one who had locked him away to rot for weeks was nearby. Rage seethed inside him and he growled.

Father...

CHAPTER THIRTY-FOUR

A Night for the Dead

'Jasper?' Gideon asked as he waddled into the room. 'Did you hear that, it sounded like thunder?' Gideon found Jasper stood staring out of the window. 'What are you up to?'

'What this that comes from sky?' Their guest stood at the window of his room, staring out at the night sky.

He must never have seen snow, thought the scholar as he joined Jasper at the open slatted window. *I don't suppose they have snow in the desert lands of Myhar.*

'That is snow, my friend,' Gideon told him. 'It comes in the cold parts of winter instead of rain.'

'It cold,' said Jasper.

'Aye, that it is, Jasper,' Gideon agreed.

The dark man turned an amused glance to the rotund scholar who now stood beside him. 'Jhas p'her,' he corrected.

'Oh yes, I know, I am sorry. Does it bother you that I cannot pronounce it? I shall endeavour to —'

Jasper dismissed Gideon's scramble for an apology with a chuckle and a wave. 'No matter. Call me what is best in your barbarian words.'

Barbarian words... Ha, he calls us barbarian, and we him...

'Is there no snow in Myhar? Not even in the mountains,' Gideon asked curiously.

'I have seen mountains from far away. I have never been to mountains. I have seen white stone on high mountain, but never this... snow in sky.'

'It is probably snow you have seen from a distance. It often crowns the high peaks here in the north, and I imagine it is the same in Myhar despite the vast arid lands we hear word of.'

Jasper grunted and gazed back into the falling snow.

Gideon retreated to the table with a shiver. 'It's cold with that window open,' he grumbled. He lowered his bulk onto a chair, opened a ledger on the table and read through the last entries. The scholar had brought a bowl of sweet breads, and he plucked one and took a bite.

Gideon looked up. 'I am curious, Jasper,' he said with his mouth full. 'Tell me, how long have you been able to understand us. You have made incredible progress these last days. You cannot have learnt the language so quickly. You must have been listening and learning for weeks.'

Jasper turned his regard on the scholar. 'Yes, I listen. I speak small. I learn quick, I learn before you know I learn.'

'Indeed.' Gideon nodded. 'Did you understand the sailors aboard the ship?'

'I listen on ship. I listen here. I speak your words.' He shrugged. 'My teach-men tell me I learn quick.'

'Your teach-men? You had tutors? Teachers?'

'Teach-men,' Jasper repeated with a nod.

'Incredible,' Gideon muttered to himself as he scratched away in the ledger. 'You were not born a slave, were you, my friend? Who are you? How did you come to be a slave?'

Jasper took a moment, looking out the window as if gathering his thoughts. 'We fight Kayobash. I lead many spears. It was trap. We lose many men. I become prisoner, a slave.'

'Who are the Kayobash?'

'Enemy,' Jasper replied with a grimace.

Gideon scribbled in the ledger. 'What else can you tell me about your homeland? We know so little of it. What is Myhar like?' He awaited with a quill poised, ready to note down everything the man said.

'Hot,' Jasper said with a smirk.

Gideon smiled and shook his head. 'What else?

The big man shrugged and sighed. 'Will I see my lands again? I am far from home.'

Gideon lowered his spectacles and looked over their wire rims. He put down his quill and sighed. 'I truly hope so, my friend. Jasper, you said before you saw the sickness in your homeland?'

Jasper nodded, 'We call it *Daresh K'hir*, the blood sickness, yes I have seen it. Same as you have here. Blood sickness is death. I am sorry for your people.'

'Is there a cure?'

'Daresh K'hir is death, death for many,' replied Jasper with a shake of his head. 'I not heard of cure.'

Gideon looked disappointed.

Well at least we know now.

'What that sound?' Jasper turned sharply towards the door, frowning.

Gideon listened also. He could not hear anything until a distant scream bled through the door. 'Probably from outside the compound. The poor townsfolk have been suffering terribly — well, you saw it yourself. I have often heard screams from the streets beyond the College walls in the dark hours of the night.'

Another scream pierced the dark night, closer this time. Jasper and Gideon shared a look.

'That was *inside* the walls,' Gideon whispered.

'Something happening,' said Jasper, purposefully moving towards the door.

'No, Jasper, wait,' Gideon warned, but his words fell away. He could think of no real reason not to go, but that scream had stolen his courage. Gideon was not a superstitious man but still he had no desire to wander outside in the darkness of a dead moon.

'Come,' Jasper said, turning to Gideon. 'We go help.'

Gideon flinched as another screech echoed through the College hallways, and followed him into the night.

***

Duncan's staff skidded across the stone paved ground hidden beneath the deepening snow. Muffled screams emerged from the crypt behind him — shouts of alarm, cries of terror, all echoing along the ancient stone passageways, distorting into unearthly sounds that made the hairs on his neck prickle. The thick ethereal fog billowed out from the Crypt of Kings, swirling around the courtyard he now hobbled through. It was hard to see more than a few feet in any direction.

He had no idea how to get out of the Citadel, unable to retrace the steps he had taken to reach the crypts. Unfamiliar buildings reared up through the fog as he limped onward, lost and uncertain.

I do not recognise this place. He looked desperately for something familiar to guide him. *I must get out of the Citadel before they find me.* A terrible panic clutched his heart. From the screams behind him he knew his deeds had been discovered. Attendants and guards had rushed down into the subterranean depths.

'Help!' he had cried when they arrived. 'The king needs help!' The guards had rushed into the foggy passageway to aid their king, the attendants following, neither with any idea what awaited them, no idea what he had done. He had lied and demanded the remaining guards let him pass, telling them the king himself had ordered him to see the chancellor immediately, leaving them uncertain and nervous as he disappeared into the swirling fog before they had a chance to object. How far could a cripple get anyway? They could soon chase him down if need be. It was mere moments later when the first screams had followed him into the night.

A dark shape flashed past him through the fog, sending the grasping tendrils of mist into swirling eddies. He started in fright, nearly toppling over as he struggled to maintain his balance. Clutching his staff tightly, his head whipped around to where the dark shadow had flashed by.

The guards. They are searching for me. He swallowed a lump from his throat. *They cannot find me in this mist.*

A dark shape came into focus, moving close and pausing nearby. He could feel its eyes boring into him.

They've found me!

He couldn't see the figure clearly. It was a dark silhouette in the fog, but its head lolled to one side and a strange growl emanated from its throat, like that of a cornered hound. He imagined bared teeth and raised hackles, but it was a human shape, not a dog.

It sniffed loudly, scenting the air.

It can smell me.

He heard whispers in the fog, and was overcome with the same familiar sense of being watched from behind, his skin turning to gooseflesh.

With the sudden snatch of a growl, almost a yelp, the figure darted off into the gloom.

What was that? Something of its movement, its sounds, reminded him of the caged man from the north, the man they called the Cursed One. He dismissed the thought. He knew that cursed man had been taken to the College infirmaries, so it could not be him. Still, something about the animal-like sounds and the strange pose made him shudder.

Duncan let out a held breath. He raised a hand to his throat and touched the trinket that hung there — a fetish to the old gods, the gods of the foolish common folk. He knew better than to put much faith in such unproven beliefs. Yet, it was an old habit and the old superstitions die hard.

Confusion and fear seemed to be spreading through the Citadel like the floodwater from a burst riverbank, people calling and shouting, unseen through the fog. He came up upon an old stone stair that seemed twist down into the gloom between two round-walled buildings. He ducked into the stairwell and took a moment of respite. His leg throbbed and his arms ached from clinging to his walking staff, the ache of his hands and his arms screaming at him to rest. His heart beat frantically, his pulse thudding in his ears.

He looked back the way he had come as he caught his breath. He could see figures running, others walking slowly out of the mists, staggering and limping. They seemed to be grasping at anything that came near. Other things moved low and fast, darting in and out of the shadows. He watched one leap onto a fleeing figure, followed by blood curdling screams. There was fighting, warriors barking commands in the dark.

Duncan knew he should not linger. He turned and followed the stairs down, hoping they would bring him out somewhere near the lower gates. Each step was agony, jarring his ruined leg, taking his breath away. Progress was slow but the way was narrow and hidden in darkness. It was safer than back there at least.

He stopped and stood still.

Suddenly, he laughed. 'I did it! The ritual worked! I am a master. I did what Eldrick could not. They will all call me master now.'

The self-proclaimed Master Duncan continued down the stone steps, laughing into the night.

'The dead, they are rising, and those beasts... they are... they are Cursed Ones,' he muttered between laboured breaths and throbs of pain. He didn't understand it, but he knew he had made them, that somehow the ritual had done this.

I have power over death itself, he thought. *I will bend even Old Night to my command. And, if I can command one god, why not the others.* He laughed again. *Men will kneel before my power.*

He smiled darkly.

Afterall, I have already killed a king.

***

Nym hurried, her heart in her mouth. She cast a look back over her shoulder.

Nothing.

They had escaped the dead.

She still clutched Seth's arm, helping him stumble along beside her while clutching at his lute case, the two of them hurrying in a stunned silence. His father was dead. The man who had been a father to her these past few years was dead. What could she possibly say to comfort him? She could not find the words. Jor had been good to her and Finn, so kind when no one else had cared. Tears pooled in her eyes. He was gone.

Finn jogged along close beside her, constantly throwing anxious looks back towards the docks. He put on a brave face, but she could see he was terrified.

Bile surged from her belly and she fought to stop herself doubling over and heaving into the snow. Her mind reeled. How was it possible? Those people were dead, yet they rose up and descended on the living with a savage malice.

She shuddered at the memory and tried to push it away, but the images were too horrifyingly vivid. Eyes on the dark street ahead, she blinked hard. They had to keep going.

But where would they go? How would they escape the city now? That barge was their only way out. The gates were sealed and they were trapped behind those forbidding city walls, trapped inside with the sickness, and worse, as the halls of the dead emptied into the streets.

There was so much snow now. Every street a stretching expanse of desolate white, illuminated in patches by struggling torches and faint light from the few hearth fires still burning. Flakes whirled through the air, some small and delicate, others a complex crystalline feather, all settling as one on the ground, on the eaves and roofs, growing thicker and deeper.

Snow had always reminded her of the winter festival—a time she had always looked forward to. There was feasting and drinking, children laughing and fighting epic battles with arm loads of snowballs. This winter would not be one of merrymaking. Instead, the streets were empty. This snow did not bring winter's joy, but bleak hopelessness.

No one stirred as they hastened along another empty street. Somewhere in the distance, people were screaming. There was sign of people passing however, tracks left in the powder, the footfalls of those who had come before her, their paths criss-crossing the road. The footprints were slowly being covered as the snow fell, soon there would be no sign at all. She traced a set of tracks leading to an alleyway, and for a moment Nym felt like a hunter tracking her quarry, but she could not escape the feeling that it was she who was being hunted.

The piles of dead that had become a common sight were ominously missing. Had they risen too? It was incomprehensible. Impossible. Yet, where were the bodies?

She had seen the dead walking—she knew it was true. The docks were behind her now, but what if there were *more* of them? Had the halls of Old Night emptied into the lands of the living. Victims of the plague, risen to wreak the terrible vengeance of the envious, restless dead.

Fear ate at her as they rushed along. It came creeping, grasping, like the dead things she had just witnessed. The memory pulled her mind into a dark reverie, a waking nightmare so vivid she could not pull herself free. Her skin crawled and she shivered, the icy wind piercing the holes in her tattered dress, her legs were so cold her skin grew numb. A crippling weariness descended upon her, but she was too scared to stop and rest.

She longed for warmth, for the warm dreams of blissful sleep. Instead there was just the snow, and the fear that clutched at her heart, creeping through that biting cold. There was an ominous menace in the empty streets stretching off in front of her. Those empty streets became a void, and from that frigid void drifted the fear. Icy fingers of iron slowly tightened around her chest. She couldn't breathe. She was drowning in that void and she couldn't find the edges. She was sinking.

With a deep, gasping breath, Nym steeled herself. It was all she could do. She threw a look at Seth and at her brother. She would be brave in the face of this nightmare and show the gods her quality. Fear would not chip away at her resolve, or erode her valour.

It was a small mercy that Seth had no eyes to witness such horror, but he surely heard it, his head shifted, turning in the direction of the distant screams as they ran on. Her brother visibly shook, and she was sure it wasn't just from the cold. He still clutched at his stolen knife, and she wondered if he could let it go, even if he wanted to.

She fought away a shudder. Was it fear or the cold? Her stomach cramped and she tasted vomit in her mouth. Nausea washed over her in waves, slowly rising from her gut. She swallowed it down. It took every fibre of her being to stop herself from retching.

A scream sliced the night air and brought them to a halt. It was close.

They stood a moment, watching, waiting and listening. In the distance, the sound of steel clashing accompanied the shouting and screaming. The city seemed to be slowly awakening to the horror stalking through its streets. Finn threw a fearful look at Nym and she reached over to squeeze his arm, her hand shaking, her fingers numb.

They hurried on towards the end of the street but did she dare glance around the corner? What would they see? Death awoken; grasping, clutching, desperate to draw her into Old Night's cold embrace? If they lingered too long it would surely come for them. They had to get away, had to keep moving — but where, back to the house, the gates, or try and find a boat?

The corner revealed another seemingly empty street. At its end, illuminated by an odd glow, the Citadel loomed up through the flurries of snow. There would be warriors there. It would be safe there.

She motioned her brother onward.

A dark shape darted across the street and disappeared down an alley between two buildings. The sudden movement startled her, and all three of them shrank back into the shadows. They watched and they waited.

Nothing.

'Come on,' she said quietly. 'Let's go.'

***

Arnulf heard shouts and screams from beyond the College walls.

'There's a fell feeling to this darkness,' Hafgan muttered as a woman's screams echoed ominously through the streets. Arnulf threw him a glance and strode back towards his waiting warriors. Hafgan followed at his shoulder beside Fergus, Master Luthor trailing behind them, looking nervously around. Erran brought up the rear, keeping a watchful eye on the scholar. Luthor had insisted on accompanying them and carried the old grimoire that they had discovered in the passes. He clutched it tightly and wore a cloak wrapped tightly around his College robes.

They walked with an anxious sense of urgency. They had to get back to the Citadel and find this apprentice, and they had to stop him attempting another ritual. Arnulf dared not think what terrible evil might be unleashed in the capital if the young man were to succeed.

Snow fell heavily now and crunched loudly beneath their boots as they emerged into the main College forecourt. His warriors looked uneasy, muttering amongst themselves at the screams outside the gate.

'Lord!' Hafgan exclaimed, grasping at Arnulf's shoulder. He pointed into the night towards the Citadel. A strange ethereal mist welled up over the darkened palisades, lit from below by a weird glow, and slowly rolled out over the city.

'That is a bad fucking omen,' Hafgan said, as if it weren't already obvious.

Erran ran up the steps to the platform over the gate, College mercenaries standing motionless and staring out at the pulsing light rippling through the clouds and the city streets below. The young warrior was a picture of fear when he turned back to look at his lord.

'What is it, lad?' Hafgan shouted.

'It's the dead,' he managed.

'Fuck! We're too late.' Arnulf raked his hand back through his hair, casting around.

'No!' Fergus declared in disbelief. 'It can't be.' The red-haired lord ran up the wooden stairs to see for himself. 'No,' he repeated, his voice laced with hopelessness. He turned to look back at them from the platform. 'There's fucking dozens of them. Arnulf...'

Close by, another scream was cut short to an eerie silence.

Suddenly a bestial roar tore the night. Hafgan whipped his sword from its scabbard, the sound making the hairs on the back of Arnulf's neck stand on end.

'That was *inside* the College,' Hafgan growled, easing into a crouch and preparing for attack. Arnulf unslung his axe and as one, the warriors and shield-maidens drew their weapons, stealing singing free of scabbards in the night.

'The infirmaries are that way,' said Luthor. 'It's —'

'It's my son,' Arnulf cut in.

There was a flash of movement.

'Watch out!' Hafgan shouted. A figure bounded from a nearby building, a College scholar by his attire, screaming hysterically. Hafgan braced to defend against the sudden threat, but instead the man fell to his knees before the warriors. He clutched at a wound on his arm, blood welling up between his fingers.

'Please, help me!' he pleaded.

'What happened?' Hafgan barked, his sword levelled at the man. The big warrior must have been a terrifying sight in the half dark, his face shadowed beneath his helmet, his armour glinting in the flickering light of nearby torches.

'The Beast, it's loose. There are others,' he spluttered. 'Help us.'

'Kill him,' commanded Arnulf.

'What?' exclaimed Luthor.

'Do it.'

'No,' Luthor pleaded. 'Please.'

Hafgan looked to his lord as the wounded man knelt shivering in terror, pleading pathetically for his life. Why was Hafgan hesitating?

'He has been bitten!' Arnulf levelled the head of his axe at the man and addressed Luthor. 'The curse will take him, it is certain. He is too dangerous to leave alive.'

'But Arnulf,' Fergus ventured. 'He will rise again. We saw it before, in the passes...'

'Aye,' said Arnulf turning away. 'We're too late. The dead will rise here soon regardless. The curse will take hold of the wounded. This place will become a slaughterhouse.'

'Impossible,' Luthor gasped.

The wounded man hurled himself at Hafgan, shrieking. With practised ease the big warrior side-stepped the man's desperate lunge and brought his sword down, crunching into his neck.

'No!' Luthor cried, almost dropping the grimoire. The man lay twitching as a bloom of dark blood appeared in the snow around his half-severed head.

Hafgan looked urgently to Arnulf and Fergus. 'He changed fast.'

'That was *much* faster than when it took Olad,' agreed Fergus, a worried look on his face. 'Olad took hours. This happened in moments.'

'Aye,' replied Arnulf with a grim nod.

Not again, this can't be happening again.

'It could be different for different people,' Astrid suggested.

'Convenient, I say,' Hafgan said darkly as he watched for danger in the shadows. 'It's as if this evil knows it must spread its curse quickly.'

They stood silent, weapons ready, watching the shadows for the next emerging threat. A fire had broken out in one of the College buildings, shouts of alarm, mixed with the screams of terror rising with the smoke as the fire spread.

'Come, we must move,' Arnulf ordered, breaking the silence. 'We cannot be certain he won't rise quickly also. Whatever is in *there*,' he said with a nod towards the fire, 'will soon be here. We must get behind solid defences. We should make for the Citadel.'

'But how?' Fergus asked from the top of the gate. 'The dead are in the streets. Come up there and look.'

'Could we go by boat?' suggested the warrior named Wilhelm. 'To avoid the sickness on the streets, me and my men have often used the river to travel between the Citadel and the College.'

'Possibly,' said Luthor. 'There will be some boats, but enough for all these warriors? I doubt any of the bigger barges will be docked. I heard talk that the barge captains have been staying up-river because of the sickness in the city. Worth a try though.'

'And if there's no boats?' Astrid asked.

'We fight,' growled Hafgan.

CHAPTER THIRTY-FIVE

Journey's End

The water beneath the hull was dark and foreboding, but Bjorn paid it little mind. His attention was on their destination, and he stood at the rail of the ship, staring up at it. That thunderous boom and the unsettling lights in the sky, the witchfire, it seemed to come from the Citadel. A thick fog rolled over the water. Visibility was poor. Ahead the fortress rose up out of the fog and towered over their ship. The Citadel of Arn was eerily illuminated by an unearthly glow, a lingering remnant of that strange flash of colour that had rolled overhead as they approached the city.

The snow fell heavily, consumed by the dark river as it touched its surface and settling on the ship. The prow's figurehead was frosted, its features buried, a thick layer accumulating on the yard arm. The sail itself had been furled and tied, and snow clung to the windward side of the mast. It gave the ship a ghostly appearance in the light of the rail torches, a vessel of white slowly gliding over the water to make port.

The river was low. Patches of weed and reeds marked the shallows. Partially submerged river weeds lingered on the surface, their positions marked by a covering of snow, like luminous sandbars in the night. Oars dipped in and out of the dark waters as the rowers fought the undercurrent to bring the ship's heading on course to the wharves of Arn.

'Finally,' Daeluf grumbled as the ship approached the jetties. There were a few torches along the dock, but not many, and those that remained were guttering in the wind.

Bjorn nodded in agreement — he would be glad to be out of this cold. Tung squatted beside him, watching the water with the same awe he had shown for the entire trip downriver. The tillerman steered the ship directly towards the huge rocky outcrop of the Citadel, aiming for the Citadel's own private landings. Other ghostly looking ships were already moored at the foot of the outcrop, the snow-covered masts of docked longboats gently bobbing up and down as small waves lapped against their hulls.

The king's ships, thought Bjorn. *Arnar's ships of war.*

The shouts of sailors betrayed other ships out on the river somewhere nearby, though in the dead of night none were visible through the shroud of mist and snow. Only the Citadel could be seen. Even in the darkness Bjorn was awed by the ancient hilltop fortification where Arnar's king made his seat.

'Quite the fortress,' commented the hunter as his eyes scanned the wooden palisade.

'Aye,' Daeluf replied. 'Is it the first time you have seen the Citadel?'

'Aye,' said Bjorn. 'At least up close.'

There was a foul stench in the air, death and decay wafting over the water. It was the same smell that lingered over battlefields when the weapons had been laid down and only the dead remained. He wrinkled his nose. The sickness was reaping its toll on the city.

Khyra's words echoed in his mind; *The hooded man... Old Night, death is coming perhaps unseen.*

'It comes unseen,' he muttered. 'Was it the sickness she spoke of?'

'What's that, hunter?' Daeluf asked, not quite hearing his mumbled words. 'The sickness? If it's the sickness you fear, I imagine we will be safer in the king's hold than anywhere else.'

'Let's hope so,' Bjorn replied, once again looking up to the battlements.

'What was that strange light I saw, have you seen anything like it before?'

Bjorn frowned at the captain. 'Lightning perhaps?' he shrugged. 'I heard thunder, but I have never seen lightning like that in all my years. A dark omen on a night like this.'

Daeluf grunted and turned his gaze back to the Citadel.

The ship's hull bumped against the wharves and men jumped across as mooring lines were cast ashore. Bjorn followed them, his boots crunching onto the snow-covered planks of the jetty. He looked up to the Citadel along a narrow winding track leading upward, passing through a low palisade which formed an outer redoubt, before threading up between the rocks to the gate above. It appeared easily defensible. The king's wolf banner hung either side of the path, a greeting to those disembarking.

Bjorn thought it odd there were no guards or delegation to greet them.

It is late, he supposed. *They must not guard the wharves at night.* Perhaps they relied on sentries along the high palisades, but he couldn't see them from this distance.

Tung joined him and sniffed the air. He was swathed in furs and carried his fire hardened spear, seemingly unbothered by the cold, wearing only thin shoes made of soft leather.

A glow emanated from beyond the palisade, and Bjorn swore he could smell smoke. 'Looks like a fire,' he commented warily.

Something here felt off. The whole situation had an ill feeling to it. He wasn't sure why, but he strung his bow, feeling more at ease with it in hand.

'Would explain the lack of guards,' Daeluf grunted as he stepped off the ship.

'I would have expected someone would greet us, or at least sentries to challenge us,' said Bjorn.

The Captain of Oldstones shrugged. 'They must be fighting the blaze,' he said and waved his honour guard of four men ashore. 'Someone will come. Our ship flies a high lord's banner. They will know us to be Archeon's men. Come, we must find the king. I have a letter for him from Archeon, and he will want to hear your tale. Then we can be gone. There is a foul air here, and I would rather not linger once our task is done.'

Daeluf trudged away, followed dutifully by his warriors, leaving Bjorn and Tung on the dock. His men wore their split black and yellow shields slung over the shoulders and each carried a spear. Bjorn glanced at Tung who nodded in reply and they followed the captain up the trail. They had passed through the abandoned redoubt and wound up a stone stair towards the lower gate. At the top it levelled out and the path ran along the foot of the high palisade.

A blood curdling shriek echoed from above and a figure plunged from the ramparts. The person fell screaming and Bjorn flinched as they cracked off a rock mid-fall, the limp body tumbling the rest of the way in silence to slam into the ground ahead of them.

'What in Mother's mercy happened?' exclaimed Daeluf. The warriors edged forwards to investigate and recoiled from the horribly twisted corpse that greeted them. 'Poor bastard.'

They stood a moment, shocked at the sudden grisly fate of the poor man.

'Perhaps he fell?' offered one of the warriors.

'Well obviously he fell,' Daeluf scoffed. 'Come, we best tell someone.'

Bjorn knelt by the man. He was definitely dead. No one could survive such a fall. His limbs were twisted into sickeningly wrong angles, and there was a lot of blood—the man's body had burst open on impact. Thankfully he lay face down, sparing them the sight of his ruined face.

Daeluf stepped carefully around the body and continued toward the gate. Bjorn made to follow, but Tung grabbed his arm fiercely, making a low hooting sound and franticly bobbing his head, pointing up towards the palisade. Bjorn followed the gesture and strained to see through the blizzard in the dark. For a moment, he thought he saw a shape slink down from the palisade and dart amongst the rocks, but the longer he stared the less sure he became. A trick of the shadows, nothing more.

The Wildman hooted and growled, agitated by something other than the grisly corpse before them. Tung levelled his spear towards the shadows and bared his teeth.

Something is out here with us...

Daeluf turned at Tung's sounds. 'Your friend seems —'

A figure leapt from the shadows. There was a glint of iron in the darkness as an axe swung down, the cleaving blow catching Daeluf in the back of the head. His helmet was sent flying, coming to rest spinning on the flagstones.

Ten hells broke loose.

The warriors of Oldstones bellowed and the attacker lunged at the nearest man, barrelling into him and driving him to the ground before anyone knew what had happened. It was a man, a warrior perhaps, his clothes torn and bloody. He knelt over the stricken warrior in a battle frenzy, foaming at the mouth, abandoning the axe and biting into the fallen warrior's face like a wild beast.

Another warrior thrust his spear into the man's side and he roared with pain, turning to hurl himself towards the man who had impaled him. The other warriors stood wide-eyed in shock at the madman's ferocity. He roared again, trying to reach the terrified warrior, but only pushed the spear deeper. The warrior held on desperately, keeping the madman at bay with the length of his spear. The frenzied attacker hurled his dripping axe instead and it clattered uselessly off a shield.

An arrow thudded into the man's chest. Bjorn lowered his bow, seeing his arrow make its mark. The man's movements became sluggish, a slobbery string of blood oozing from his mouth. He roared in defiance a final time, silenced by another warrior's spear thrust. He went limp.

'Lord Daeluf!' exclaimed one of the warriors, kneeling beside his captain. After a moment, he shook his head. 'He's dead.'

The bitten warrior began shaking and convulsing violently on the ground, his head snapping around. Bjorn saw a madness in his eyes, the same frenzied lunacy that had afflicted the man who lay twitching as his life's blood trickled away, staining the snowy ground red.

The wounded warrior hurled himself at one of his comrades and was rebuffed by his shield. Bjorn fumbled with another arrow. His hands were slow, numbed from the cold. He drew and loosed, the arrow catching the madman in the leg. The wounded warrior stumbled and fell down the steps.

Tung tugged at Bjorn's arm, pulling him behind the cover of a rock at the foot of the palisade. Bjorn and the Wildman watched as the man rose and hurled himself once more at the raised shields of his comrades as they pleaded reason with their friend. It was no use—he was in a blind fury, mindlessly smashing his fists into their painted shields until his hands bled, leaving dark smears on the yellow and black paint. In the end they thrust spears and swung axes, hacking him down until he finally lay still. The men backed away from their dead friend, one of them tripping over the corpse of the man who had fallen from the palisade.

Bjorn let out a breath he hadn't realised he was holding.

Then it happened.

The man who had fallen, that horribly twisted ruin of a corpse, moved. A hand jerked up and Bjorn gasped. Broken bones snapped as the fallen man somehow staggered to his feet and took a shaky step towards the dumbstruck warriors. They edged backwards down the path, back in the direction of the river. From the look of sheer terror on their faces, Bjorn was glad he could not see the wreckage of the man's face.

Impossible! He was dead, I saw it!

The madman who had killed Daeluf twitched, then began to rise like a puppet pulled to his feet by invisible strings.

They were both dead...

Finally, as the once dead men staggered after the retreating warriors, the bitten warrior, the insane man who had been hacked to the ground by his own comrades, rose to his feet also.

Bjorn and Tung shrank into the shadows, Tung whimpering at the impossible sight before them. Bjorn clamped his hand over the Wildman's mouth, praying to Hjort the dead men would not see them.

The dead seemed focused on the terrified warriors in their clattering armour. Three dead men stumbling down the path, arms outstretched, grasping and snarling at the warriors of Oldstones.

Bjorn did not think any less of them when they turned and fled back towards the ship. Had he been able to get past, he would have too. The dead disappeared after them, snarling and moaning as he warily emerged from his hiding place. Keeping as low as he could, he approached Daeluf's body.

He was indeed dead, his skin cooling rapidly in the snow. Without taking his eyes off the motionless corpse, he reached inside the man's cloak and removed Archeon's letter. It seemed foolish, his mind screaming at him to run, but his honour forced him onwards. He had every intention of getting as far away from this place as possible, but he would not have men say he breached his contract and defiled his honour. He would see the king, tell him what he knew, and he would earn his silver.

He hurried towards the gates, throwing a nervous glance back at the lifeless form of Daeluf. He offered thanks to the gods that the corpse remained motionless. He would not hang around to find out if he too would rise from Old Night's embrace. From the high vantage, he saw the ship push off, heard the panicked shouts of sailors. He had no choice but to go forwards now and find another way out of this nightmare.

There is a darkness in your path. He grunted. 'You weren't kidding.'

The gate itself was more like a heavy door cut into the palisade, and it gave in at a push from Bjorn. To his surprise it had been left unbarred and apparently unmanned, and he opened it just wide enough for he and Tung to slip through.

Inside, the Citadel was choked with smoke and a thick fog. Men shouted and he could hear the sound of fighting. They kept to the shadows and kept moving, crouching behind some barrels. Peering over the rims, he surveyed the way ahead. There were buildings clustered around gate that looked to be storehouses, and a track led up a slope, presumably to the king's hall which he assumed would crown the ancient mound.

A man darted out of the smoke, franticly looking for somewhere to hide amongst the quiet storehouses.

'Over here, friend,' called Bjorn. On seeing the pair hiding behind the barrels, he hurried over to join them. 'What in Varg's name is happening here?' Bjorn asked as the man settled beside them.

'The dead...' he stammered. 'The dead are walking. There's a madness in the Citadel, men are fighting each other. Gods save us.'

'I saw them,' replied Bjorn. 'But I can still barely believe it.'

'Stay hidden, and hope they don't find you,' the man told them, giving Tung a strange look. 'We must get to the boats. The Citadel is lost.'

'Good luck with that. The dead are out there too,' said Bjorn.

The man looked at the gate and let out a whimper of panic.

'We can't stay here,' said Bjorn. 'Where is the king? Tell me, friend, where can we find him?'

'I don't know. The hall, probably.' He gestured up the hill with a shrug and pushed himself deeper into the shadows.

Bjorn nodded his head at Tung, indicating that they should move. There was no use hiding here. He led the Wildman up the slope, staying low to the ground, heading towards where he hoped the king's hall might be found through the fog and smoke. The sounds of fighting grew louder but he could not see far through the mist.

A grand looking hall which rose up from the tumultuous fog. There were torches ensconced around the walls, braziers on the halls stone steps, all casting just enough light for Bjorn to make out some detail. The flames cast the sprawling halls in ruddy light, through the fog it gave the whole scene a sinister feeling of doom. Bjorn could make out the eaves of the hall were exquisitely carved with images of horses and ships. The great doors at the top of the stone steps were carved also. Such extravagant craftsmanship to decorate the buildings exteriors, surely this had to be the halls of a king, thought Bjorn.

The sound of battle intensified as they approached. From the mist and smoke emerged a level plaza full of men in pitched battle before the halls steps. Some had formed a ragged shield wall, and half a dozen men slowly edged further into the plaza, trying to break through to the others at the stone steps of the hall. A man in mail and a burnished helmet reflecting the flickering flames of the torch he held stood shouting orders, all the while dozens of animated corpses clawed at the locked shields of the king's men.

Bjorn watched as a frenzied man charged screaming into the warriors on the steps and impaled himself on a lowered spear, thrashing violently like a landed fish. The dead nearby turned on him, biting, clawing, and chewing his body.

Bjorn suppressed the urge to vomit. The dead were eating the fallen. Some lone warriors fought on, and Bjorn watched as one was surrounded, overwhelmed, and driven to the ground, his screams adding to the cacophony of the desperate fighting.

Tung watched, unsettled by what he saw. Bjorn waved him onward and they approached the side of the hall cautiously. The warriors ahead were trying to break through to reinforce the others at the hall's steps. One of them saw him and warned their leader.

The man in the helmet turned to look at them. 'Who goes there?'

'We are friends,' Bjorn called. 'We bring news from Lord Archeon in the west for the king. We must speak with him urgently.'

A dead woman appeared beside the man. With a snarl she dragged her animated corpse from the gloom. She lunged at the warrior and he held her off with his shield. His men were busy edging forward with the dead pressed against their shields, and the Wildman readied himself, thrusting his spear into the dead woman. It had no effect. He pulled it back and thrust again.

Bjorn unhooked his axe and brought it down into the woman's skull. She fell.

'You have my thanks,' nodded the man.

The woman writhed on the ground, the blow failing to still her. She started to pull herself up and the warrior brought his own axe down, hacking until her body was riven into a bloody mess.

The man grimaced. 'Some are saying the king is dead. No one knows what's going on; it's chaos.'

'Shit,' cursed Bjorn. 'Who commands here?'

'I am Huscarl Aellar,' the man shouted above the clashing of iron and wood, and the snarling of the dead. 'If rumour of the king is true, the lord prince rules now I suppose. He's not here. He is aboard his ship. We are trying to get the chancellor to safety aboard a ship too. The Citadel has fallen.'

'We just came from the docks,' Bjorn shouted back.

'Are there dead down there?' The huscarl turned and chopped over another man's shield, severing a dead arm in a spray of blood.

'Some, but nothing like this,' Bjorn replied. 'I would hurry, Lord Aellar.'

'I am no lord,' said Aellar with a grim smile, evidently amused at the title. 'Help us get to the others in the hall. We need every man. The chancellor is in there.'

Before Bjorn could answer, a slavering madman dove headlong from a rooftop above and crashed into Aellar. He wrestled the creature with both hands, desperately pushing the thing away and holding the madman's snapping teeth from his face.

What's wrong with them? It was a creature of nightmare, a thing of savagery and malice wreathed in human skin. Bjorn knew at a glance these things were no longer human. He wanted to help the huscarl, but instead he hesitated.

Another insane creature crashed into the shield wall from above, knocking men off-balance and sending warriors sprawling. The wall of shields crumbled before Bjorn's eyes, the dead assailing them. There were screams of agony as men were torn apart by tooth and nail. A piercing screech marked one of the insane creature's end.

Tung jabbed his spear into the creature savagely clawing at the huscarl from its perch upon his chest, the dead swarming the huscarl before the first creature ceased its thrashing assault.

They were forced to retreat from the advancing corpses, Huscarl Aellar stretching his hand towards them in a desperate plea.

He had the eyes of man who knew his fate had come.

'Run!' His shout turned into a scream as teeth tore open his flesh.

Tung looked like he was about to bolt, the fear evident in his companion's eyes. Tung tugged on his arm and motioned the hunter away back down the hill.

He's right. There is no way through. Bjorn let himself be pulled away. *I am no warrior. Brave, perhaps, but not a man of war.* Bjorn longed to see the wilds again, and he had no desire to die here against these impossible horrors from the grave.

He cast a final look at the slaughter of the plaza. More dead were pouring from the fog. Men taken by a terrible madness turned on their comrades and fought like crazed beasts, hurling themselves at the stricken warriors with wild abandon.

This is a hopeless fight. There are too many.

He ran.

He allowed Tung to lead the way as they fled the plaza, hurrying downhill and away from the fighting. They wove between darkened buildings and old stonework.

'The Citadel is lost, my friend,' said Bjorn, in a forlorn voice. Tung looked back at him as he spoke. 'We should have got back to the boat with the others,' said Bjorn shaking his head. He spoke more for his own benefit than the Wildman, who likely understood little or nothing of his words.

Bjorn did not recognise where he was. He looked for something familiar, one of the buildings they had passed, anything.

This is not the way we came. He cursed again. *We need to get out, out of the Citadel, out of the city.*

Bjorn looked downhill, looking for some way out of the stricken fortress, fog and smoke obscuring his vision. There was no moon to illuminate the darkness and he strained his eyes to see, but it was no use. The track levelled out, but now seemed to be doubling back.

The hunter cursed once more. He had no idea how to find his way to the lower level. There must be a city gate in the lower palisade through which they could escape. They tried a dark stone stairway that seemed like it headed downward, Tung padding beside him, clutching his spear in both hands.

Suddenly the Wildman stopped and growled at the darkness,

levelling the bloodied spear.

One of the primal creatures hurtled from the gloom and Bjorn's axe buried itself into the man's face with a wet crunch. The man-creature collapsed in a daze and Tung raised his spear, plunging it into the man's chest. The man arched his back as Bjorn stepped forward and brought his axe down, chopping into his face. The man spasmed and died.

'What is happening to them all?' Bjorn looked down at the dying madman.

'They are called the Cursed Ones,' said a voice. 'A curse brought from the north by some lord, or so I hear.'

Bjorn wheeled around to the voice and found a crippled man in a dark robe limping from the shadows. His leg was bandaged to a splint and he leaned heavily on a wooden staff that equalled his height. His hair was long and white, yet his face was not that of an old man. He looked like he could be in his early twenties, but his face was tired and drawn. The man wore a satchel at his side, the spine of a large leather-bound book peaking from the top.

Tung pulled his spear free and levelled it at the newcomer.

'Who are you?' demanded the hunter, eyeing the man warily as he hobbled forward.

'My name is Duncan. I am a scholar with the College. And you?'

'Bjorn,' he replied, waving at the Wildman to lower his spear. 'There are dead men walking. They are killing people, eating them.'

'I saw,' replied the man. His voice seemed flat, cold, somewhat indifferent, as if he were merely making observations of a test subject.

'We are trying to find the lower gate—do you know where it is, friend?'

'I had the same thought myself,' said Duncan. 'It is not safe here. I have only been here a few times and do not know the way well. Perhaps we can help each other. I do know the city.'

'Perhaps, but I am sorry friend, if you slow us down...' The hunter gestured to the scholar's ruined leg.

The dead madman snarled suddenly, still face down, sprawled across the snowy steps. An arm shot up mechanically and grasped the stone.

'He is rising!' Duncan said with a gasp.

The dead man heaved himself up, and the three of them backed away down the steps. Bjorn readied his axe. The corpse watching them with cold eyes, moaning but oddly made no attempt to attack. Tung jabbed his spear at it, but it just stood there, staring blankly.

'What is it doing?' Bjorn whispered.

'I don't know,' Duncan murmured.

They backed away further, slowly taking one step at a time, the scholar grunting in pain each time.

The dead man lurched forwards, then stopped again, as if slamming up against some invisible barrier. It just stood there, glancing around.

'Why isn't it attacking us?' Bjorn hissed.

Duncan did not reply at first. He seemed distant, as if listening to something Bjorn couldn't hear. 'It must be the gods,' he said eventually.

Bjorn didn't know what to think. Ever since he had set foot on shore the entire night had become an atrocity of horrors that would forever haunt his dreams.

He shrugged his bow from his shoulder, nocked an arrow, drew and loosed. The shaft disappeared into the corpse's chest, the fletching protruding from his clothes yet he hardly flinched, unaware of the feathered shaft in his cold flesh. Bjorn loosed another, this time thudding into his open mouth, tearing its lower jaw away. Bjorn winced.

Tung crept forward and with a sweep of his spear, struck the man in the knees and sent the corpse tumbling to the ground. He thrust the spear down again and again. Still the dead man struggled to rise to his feet, but yet would not take a step closer or retaliate.

Bjorn strode forward determined to finish the foul creature. With a ferocious swing of his axe, he took the dead thing's head clean from its shoulders. The decapitated body tumbled to the ground, twitching, the head rolling away between two buildings. Bjorn could still hear it snarling and moaning from the shadows. The sound made the hunter shudder.

'Let's move,' Bjorn said. 'Before it decides to come back again.'

The scholar stood a moment, staring at the headless corpse. Then he turned and limped after the hunter.

CHAPTER THIRTY-SIX

The Hunt

The shutters of the window banged loudly against the wall. The wind blew them back and forth, each impact painfully loud, making Gideon flinch. Snow drifted inside on an icy breeze that blew down the corridor. Gideon quietly toed along the dark hallway creeping closer to investigate the shout and a thud that drew their attention.

The doors adjoining the hall led to various private chambers and study rooms of the College's members. In the gloom he could make out several examples of taxidermy lining shelves along the walls, creatures from Arnar and further afield, as well as exotic objects and curiosities from the known world. The reptilian snout of a strange lizard-like creature caught his attention, he had never seen such a thing before. He examined it briefly in the dim light, the shuddering light of the torches making it seem alive.

The sound they had heard had come from a room a little way ahead, through an open door. Tearing and crunching sounds echoed towards him, and he had begun to regret his decision to take a look. He crept to the open door and peered inside.

The room was in complete disarray—furniture smashed to pieces, splinters of wood that had once been a chair littering the floor. Amongst the chaos crouched a fellow scholar with her back to Gideon, bent over something behind an upturned desk.

The door creaked in the breeze. The scholar's head snapped around at the sound and Gideon gasped. He recognised this woman. Yet, she was not the woman he knew. Her chin was smeared with blood, her teeth bright red and chewing, and in her hand, she clutched a dripping hunk of bloody meat.

But it wasn't any of that fixing Gideon to the spot. It was her eyes. Something familiar and terrible burned behind those darkened eyes.

'Master Ardben?' Gideon whispered. 'What—'

The master launched herself across the room and hurtled towards him. The scholar yelped and reeled backwards into the hallway, the madwoman surging forward over broken furniture like a snarling banshee.

Gideon raised his hands to his face in a vain defence.

A hand shot past his face and seized the insane creature by the throat. She squealed in shock as Jasper caught her mid-air, holding her at arm's length, her feet kicking several inches off the floor. The creature that had been Master Ardben twisted and squirmed. She beat at uselessly Jasper's arm, his muscles tightening as he held her firm. Jasper looked into her eyes, indifferent to her snapping jaws and futile snarled defiance.

Jasper hurled the frenzied creature, tossing her back into the room. Gideon watched on, shivering and breathless, as Jasper stepped into the room after the creature. He snatched up a broken chair leg as the creature shook off her daze and sprung back to her feet to renew her onslaught. Ardben attacked again, the headlong charge checked by the swinging chair leg.

Jasper smashed the splintered wood into Ardben's nose, and without pause clubbed it down into the madwoman's skull as she collapsed to the floor. A sickening *crunch* and Ardben fitted and convulsed, writhing pitifully while Jasper stared down, waiting until she became still.

'You killed her!' exclaimed Gideon in horror.

'She try to kill Gideon,' Jasper replied, pointing the bloodied length of timber at the corpse as if Gideon had not seen it happen.

'Well, yes… Thank you. You saved me.'

'Gideon is friend.' Jasper shrugged.

Gideon crept closer, though keeping his distance. 'She must have been insane,' he muttered. 'What happened to her?'

'She like man in cage,' said Jasper.

The realisation dawned on the scholar. That look in Ardben's eye, it had seemed familiar and now he knew where he had seen it.

'You're right. She was cursed, but by Hjorts's horns, how?'

Gideon crept closer still, nervously peering around Jasper's large frame to examine the dead woman at his feet. 'Her arm!'

The dead master's arm bore a blackened wound that Jasper had not inflicted. Dark veins coursed up the limb, creeping into her pale flesh.

'She was Cursed One,' Jasper agreed. 'A she-beast. Like man in cage.'

Gideon nodded slowly. He did not like the thought of that savage beast stalking the College's halls. He must have escaped the infirmary and somehow spread his taint to Ardben. Gideon swallowed a lump from his throat.

His gaze tracked to the space behind the upturned desk. Another body lay there, unseen at first, but it looked like one of the College mercenaries, his abdomen torn open and his entrails spilled across the floor. Gideon heaved as the bile rose quickly, averting his gaze, unable to look directly at the horrific, gruesome remains. Jasper knelt beside the dead man, careful not to step in the pooling blood.

'Weapon not drawn,' he muttered then carefully unhooked the axe and hefted it. He seemed satisfied at its weight. The sight of the muscular foreigner, axe in hand, reassured the scholar.

Gideon imagined the strength and sudden savagery needed to slay the sell-sword, and found it hard to comprehend Master Ardben, with her small build, being able to overpower and kill him before he was even able to draw his weapon. It was then he realised what she had been doing.

She was eating him.

Unable to contain his stomach any longer, he wretched and vomited.

'Gideon, you no see blood and death up close?' Jasper asked. He placed a hand on the scholar's back as he heaved. 'Have no worry. I have.'

The words did little to settle Gideon's stomach, but he appreciated the attempt, nonetheless. Together they left the room and Gideon leaned against the wall in the hallway, fighting another surge of bile from his belly.

'There might be more,' Jasper warned, glancing both ways down the hall.

Forcing the final wave of queasiness away, Gideon composed himself as best he could. 'I hope not.'

A scream echoed along the hall from elsewhere in the College.

Gideon's heart sank and his stomach knotted with fear. 'I think that answers our question, my friend.' He could feel his heart pounding like a drum in his chest at the thought of more Cursed Ones loose in the College.

Jasper stalked off into the gloom and approached a display of artefacts attached to the wall. Feeling suddenly vulnerable and alone in the dark hallway, Gideon hurried after him, catching sight of what had drawn Jasper's attention.

An antique shield hung on the wall. It was a strange oval shape, not of Arnarian design. The warriors of Arnar fought with round shields made of wooden boards and sometimes covered in animal hide. A central iron boss was not uncommon, and they were usually painted over. This shield, however, was made of burnished bronze. It was dented and battered with age but still a thing of beauty. It had two swirling motifs and a decorative border that looked like it had been hammered in by hand. Gideon read a nearby placard, noting that the shield had come from the far shores of Telis and was at least two hundred years old. It looked heavy but Jasper lifted it from its mounting with ease.

Even in the gloom the man made a formidable sight. He held the bronze shield on his left arm and the axe in his right hand, his eyes shining with something that had not been there before. In that moment Gideon glimpsed something of Jasper's former glory, and it was not hard to imagine the man striding across the arid lands of his homeland, leading warriors into war. The scholar looked him over with a pang of jealous awe. He was not a man made to fight, but a man of quills, ink and books.

An ominous groaning caught their attention. Gideon slowly swung his head around, his worst fears materialising. The sound came from the same open door to the room they had just vacated. Jasper turned to the sound and approached, walking in a half crouch with his shield raised and axe held ready. There was a menacing intensity to his gait, as if ready to pounce with a ferocity akin to that of a mountain cat.

As Jasper reached the door the dead mercenary lurched out.

Gideon staggered back, unable to believe the man was somehow still alive and standing. His bowels hung from the gash in his abdomen, swinging freely like a macabre tangle of grisly ropes. His leg was twisted and snapped, yet somehow held his weight.

But… he was dead! Gideon could not comprehend it. *That man is dead! This can't be.*

The dead sell-sword grappled with Jasper, who kept the grasping hands at bay with the old shield. The sudden weight pinned the shield against Jasper, and he couldn't swing his axe, trapped between the shield and his shirt. The dead man's mouth opened wide, bringing his teeth slowly towards Jasper's face.

Gideon had to do something. He snatched up the nearest thing to hand, and stepping up behind Jasper, whacked the stuffed lizard creature across the dead man's snarling maw. The corpse recoiled, glaring at Gideon with a malign glare for a mere second before Jasper's axe crunched into the dead man's skull. The body spasmed, still grasping, unrelenting in its spite. The axe descended again, and again, blood splattering both he and the scholar, until he had chopped the man's head into a red ruin of brains and gore. Finally the dead thing collapsed to the floor, twitching.

Gideon reeled. *That thing was* dead, *an embodiment of some cold malice returned from Old Night's embrace.*

'We should not linger here,' Gideon murmured, his voice coarse as he stared at the twitching body.

Jasper turned a haunted face to Gideon and nodded slowly.

They ran, reaching the end of the hall when a sudden snarl halted them.

They turned back, sharing a knowing, dreadful look before their gaze fell on the corpse of the headless dead man rising to its feet, advancing on them, blindly clutching the air. Master Ardben staggered from the room behind the creature, her eyes dark, blood trickling from her nose. She lurched forward with the same dreadful animation as the headless dead man.

'Run,' Gideon gasped.

***

There were smells everywhere, a world painted in scents. He could smell the detritus of city life congealing in street gutters, the ice in the air, the muddy water of the river, all wafting in from outside. He caught the scent of dusty shelves and mildewed paper, the old books and scrolls that seemed to fill this place. Somewhere nearby he could smell the scent of a dead rodent. He had lived off the flesh of rats for weeks, and he wasn't sure if the smell

373

repulsed him or made his mouth water. He could smell blood, offal and spilt excrement, as well as fear. The stench of prey was everywhere. A long strand of drool spilled from his lips, slivers of flesh still stuck in his teeth, the iron tang of blood lingering on his tongue. Hunger gnawed at him, stronger than ever.

There were others now, their whispering thoughts reaching out to him as each was birthed into the dark — born anew into an eldritch, bestial form. More whispers joined the darkness, their muffled voices coalescing as one, snatches of thoughts revealing they were near. They came to him one by one, subservient wretches grovelling under his dominant glare. He was strongest, the leader. Together they were pack.

Sounds echoed around him. His hearing had sharpened. He could hear footsteps running, the shrill voices of men in panic, of terrified women scrambling for their lives. It was him they fled from, and from the others, from the pack. The others were feasting, bones breaking, flesh tearing. His pack was feeding. Every mouthful of cooling flesh heightened his awareness, a gift from the whispering dark.

There was prey approaching. He could hear its footsteps on the wooden boards, could smell its sweat, could sense its fear, its uncertainty. The others sensed it also, and he watched them shift in anticipation, primal hunger burning within them. The grasp of darkness still tightening its grip. The change still fresh. In their eyes, the memories of their former lives, the revulsion of the feed, faded to a hate-filled insanity.

They awaited his signal to begin the hunt. A look, a gesture, an unspoken whisper in their minds. He was the leader of the pack, the strongest, the first one amongst them.

With only a thought he released them. They darted off, bounding away on all fours.

Then he was alone.

He heard the prey scream, then it was silenced. A fresh kill. The scent of blood found his nostrils, filling him with the urge to claim his fill.

He resisted. He had all he needed here. His previous kill lay splayed open before him, a macabre feast made from cold flesh. On a whim he plucked an eye from its socket. The soft jelly burst, filling his mouth with viscous liquid. He chewed. It was a curious sensation.

He grinned as he squatted on his haunches. He had escaped his chains. He was free, and now there were others.

For so long there had only been him in the darkness. The lone whisper in the spiralling void of insanity had grown louder each passing day. He had waited; alone, trapped in that cursed cage. The darkness whispered to him, calling him. Oh, how he had fought against those restraints, his body withering in that prison, the change slow and agonising, his only friend the whispering dark and his rage. An impalpable anger, all consuming, made him stronger. Those weeks of wind and rain, the smell of horses and dirt, replaced by the salt scent of the sea and the ever-shifting floor, swaying back and forth. And all the while, there was the scent of man-flesh and another — *his* scent. This one he would find, this one he would kill.

He felt its presence before he saw it move, as if the darkness consumed even the dead. His kill twitched. Its arm began moving, groping the floor, its hand feeling out as if searching for something lost.

He backed away — yet another kill disturbed. The dead thing looked at him with its single eye. It had no legs — they had eaten them — so it clawed its way towards him with those groping hands, malice and hunger, perhaps greater than his own, glinting in its eye. It was as if it meant to reclaim its lost flesh. It snarled up at him.

The dead things terrified him. It was a terror born in the deepest primordial depths of his instinct.

He fled, leaving the dead thing to claw impotently. He had eaten his fill, and there was fresher prey.

He moved quickly, skulking in the shadowed corridors, the clawing dead thing left far behind him. He passed the kill his pack had been so eager to chase down. Two wretched creatures stooped over the dead woman's corpse. They flashed fearful snarls in his direction as he emerged into view but he moved onward, uninterested. The kill would likely soon rise, and they would scatter.

He padded through hallways absorbing the beautiful anarchy. People were running, screaming — blissful chaos. His pack tore them down, and the wounded would soon swell the pack's numbers. There must be a dozen or more already. He saw shambling corpses, already risen, scare away the others of his kind and claim a half-eaten kill for their own. The dead rose everywhere, and he knew this hunting ground would soon be too dangerous. He saw the dead clawing at a door, a woman's screams coming from the other side as she fought to keep them out. She would fail.

Then he caught the scent again, *his* scent, the one he knew. His senses sharpened and focused on that faint aroma. *He is close.*

Hate seethed inside him. He crouched on his haunches and sniffed the air, pinpointing the scent's direction. His body shuddered in anticipation. Using his hands to bound low and swift, he surged forward. He would let the pack rampage through this place, and in the chaos his mind blinkered to a singular thought. *Hunt.*

The scent grew stronger.

He turned a corner and flames blocked his way, searing heat radiating out as the flames licked the ceiling and fire consumed all in his path. The smell of smoke was overpowering, the cloying soot smothering his breath. Worse, it masked the scent of his prey.

He scrambled through a window and gasped in a lungful of cold night air. He needed get up higher. He scaled the wall opposite and pulled himself onto the roof.

A great plume of smoke billowed into the night and filled the sky, the oily cloud illuminated by the roaring inferno below. Skulking low, he moved onwards. The rooftop soon ended, and he found himself perched on the eaves. A wide courtyard yawned before him, the snowy vista marred by churned mud and chaos around the compound's gates. The dead clamoured to enter from the city beyond, and those gates would not hold them long.

He hissed at the glint of steel and iron. Men gathered there, formidable prey. He could smell their horses, those same scents he recognised from his imprisonment. He had to suppress a howl of rage, lest he be discovered. His quarry was amongst them, but he waited.

In that courtyard below, stood the only one thing that remained, his one need—to kill that prey. It was his revenge, his vengeance on he who bound him, on the one who had put him in those chains and locked him away in that cage.

Something was growing in him, consuming all. He became stronger, faster with every feed, slowly transforming into something monstrously powerful. He would surpass man and beast and reign over all his eyes surveyed.

His old life was a mere shadow of memory, replaced with the burning hunger. His name had faded from his mind, replaced by endless hate. There was one word which burned in his thoughts, the one remaining spectre of his old life...

Father.

CHAPTER THIRTY-SEVEN

Prey and Flames

'You said there were boats?' Arnulf turned, exasperated.

'Aye,' Wilhelm replied. 'Me and my lads come in by boat to stay off the streets.'

Arnulf cast a glance at the surging gates, the dead massed on the other side, straining and fighting against the heavy wooden bar which sealed them shut.

'We can't get back to the Citadel that way,' Arnulf told them. 'We should take the boats.'

'What about the horses?' Erran asked. 'We can't just leave them here.'

The horses were unsettled, terrified of the dead. They were unridable, thrashing and fighting at the hitches with an unwavering need to bolt free. The hound, Fear, barked at the shadows of the College and at the gates, his hackles raised. He knew what lay on the other side of those gates and this time he had nowhere to run.

'What choice have we,' said Arnulf, looping a leash around the dog's neck. 'We'll set them loose and let them find their own fate. Fergus, can you hold them here?'

'Aye, we'll hold,' replied Fergus, and Astrid gave a grim nod, hefting her weapon and leaving to issue orders to her warriors.

'Hold the gates. If there are boats enough, we will get out that way.'

'Should more of us not come with you, lord?' Erran asked, panicked questions in his eyes.

'The docks aren't far,' Wilhelm told him.

Hafgan gave the young man a slap on the back. 'I'll keep Lord

Arnulf safe, lad. Don't you worry.'

Arnulf looked at his warriors, and then to young Erran. 'You are needed to hold here, to keep the dead out, and watch our backs. We will not be long.' With a nod to Wilhelm and glance at Hafgan, Arnulf said, 'Show us.'

Wilhelm led them through a maze of stout wooden buildings. The College appeared to be built in a uniform fashion, a far cry from the usual ramshackle sprawl of Arnar's towns, where every building differed. The trio moved towards a part of the College complex that looked to be ablaze. Even in the heavy snow, the buildings caught like dry tinder, the fire spreading quickly.

They saw no sign of the dead here, or of the cursed that would surely follow. There must be dead loose in the College — what else could explain the man they had slain in the courtyard and the un- settling screams nearby. The sound of slaughter and panic echoed through the night from deep within the complex.

'We should move quickly. They will be upon us soon enough,' Hafgan growled.

The docks were indeed close by and other than those dreadful sounds, the acts that caused them remained out of sight. Arnulf didn't see another soul as they hurried along.

He did however come over with the creeping sensation of un- seen eyes watching him. As he followed closely behind the warri- or named Wilhelm, he scanned the darkness and the snow clogged alleys they passed.

Nothing.

Checking behind him, he expected to see some horror bearing down on him. He scanned the rooftops and the snow laden sky. Still nothing, but the feeling remained, growing stronger and more sinister with each passing step.

The thoroughfare Wilhelm guided them down brought them closer to the fire. They passed beneath a walkway spanning be- tween two buildings. The inferno engulfed the buildings on one side, and would soon spread to the walkway overhead. They shielded their faces with their sleeves, running past the conflagra- tion and into the only marginally clearer air beyond. The rippling surface of the river appeared ahead, shimmering with the reflect- ed flames.

Hafgan squinted through the smoke. 'There's not enough boats for all of us.'

There were scant few boats, and nothing of any decent size. The two rowing boats, one tiny and the other a longer launch, would not be enough.

'We could get eight or nine of us in those,' guessed Hafgan.

'Perhaps we could signal a ship off the river?' Wilhelm suggested, gesturing to the distant masts of larger ships at the edge of the gloom.

'They will not come,' said Arnulf, shaking his head. 'Would you? The city is cursed, they will watch it burn. Look!' He pointed up at the Citadel. 'Fires are burning even there. There is sickness and death everywhere, monsters prowl the streets.' He looked back out at the silent watching ships. 'They know Old Night walks here, and he is reaping his toll. They will not come. Let's get back to the gates.'

'Aye,' agreed Hafgan.

'We must hurry,' Wilhelm urged, indicating the fire that burnt behind them. The flames had caught in the buildings opposite now, and the enclosed walkway between the first storey of both buildings which was now engulfed. 'That's going to come down if we don't go now.'

He was right. When that collapsed, the thoroughfare they had come down would be impassable.

Hafgan frowned at the flames. 'Is there another way?'

'Yes, but it's much longer, and it sounds like that way is where the dead are. Come on, move!'

Wilhelm hurried ahead, waving for them to follow.

'Let's go, m'lord.' Hafgan clutched Arnulf's shoulder, then jogged after Wilhelm, holding his arms above his head and around his face to ward off the fire and smoke.

Arnulf cast one last glance back at the icy wharfs. He sighed and turned to follow Hafgan and Wilhelm and his skin prickled, an unsettling feeling creeping over him.

I am being watched.

He stopped, searching the shadows, the flicker of the fire making them dance, illuminating objects then plunging them back into darkness. Nothing lurked there, yet eyes bored into his soul. He felt its malign stare with a cold shiver.

'Lord!' Hafgan shouted. 'Hurry!'

Arnulf swore under his breath and lurched into motion. Hafgan and Wilhelm had cleared the flaming walkway overhead and awaited him. The flames roared now on both sides. He sprinted.

Crunch.

The blackened timbers of the walkway collapsed. A great plume of cinders exploded into the air, a wave of heat searing his skin. He raised his arm to cover his face.

'Lord!' Hafgan called again.

Arnulf staggered back from the flames.

He was trapped.

All around him orange fire raged. The buildings beside him were being consumed. Walls had already begun to crumble, burnt away to reveal the skeletal framework beneath wreathed in licking flames.

He held his hand up to shield his eyes, Hafgan only barely visible through the burning debris. It was impassable, the heat too great.

'Arnulf, we're coming!' shouted Hafgan over the roar of the flames.

'There's another way around. Hold on.' Wilhelm pulled at Hafgan, urging him to follow, and Arnulf watched them disappear around a corner. He backed away from the inferno, edging towards the wharf and the cold, dark waters of the river.

He knew he was there before he even turned. He felt those eyes.

A dark figure barred the path, glowering eyes staring from beneath a mop of wild hair, crouched on its haunches with a single hand resting in the dirt. It began stalking towards him, a gloating hunter approaching a snared buck. It exuded the confidence of cold inevitability, its predatory pose coiled, ready to pounce with the vicious ferocity of a hill cat.

Arnulf narrowed his eyes and waited, like an old wolf of the forest. His shoulder draped in a fur cloak, his armour of mail and grey plate. His hide was tough for an old wolf, and he had sharp claws. He rested his hand on the head of his axe, his fingers feeling the intricate knot work wrought into the metal.

The wolf stood his ground, defiant and formidable as the cat stalked, deadly and feral, a grotesque sleekness to its primal gait.

The figure stepped from the shadow into the flickering firelight.

His heart lurched.

He knew that face.

He remembered that face.

In his memory, he played with the young boy it had once been. He remembered how he had loved the winter feasts, how they had played in the snow. He remembered that face as they rode over a heather strewn moor, through forests, that same young man at his side. He remembered hunting together, remembered his smile, the boy who became a man.

Ewolf.

That boyish smile no longer existed. The face was the same, yet it had changed. What lay behind it was different, something terrible and vile. He choked back a sob as he looked upon what his son had become.

Around them the fire blazed, curtains of flame hemming them in. The heat had melted all the snow, the ground had returned to a slushy wet mud. Rivulets of melt-water ran across the ground towards the shallow bank of the river. Behind the ghoulish creature that stood in his path, snow fell on the dark waters of the river. He stood in a world of fire and but yet behind that creature he saw a world of ice and snow.

'Son...' Arnulf held out his hand. An appeal, the desperate plea of a father, an outstretched hand. 'Son, hear me. It's me.'

Ewolf surged forward. His snarl rising to a deathly shriek. His eyes were alight.

Arnulf's axe was in his hand before he knew it was there, a testament to his long years as a warrior. He punched out the haft of his axe. The ancient polished wood crunched into Ewolf's snarling maw and the cursed man crashed to the ground. He recovered and lunged again, not seeming to feel the blow which would have felled any other man. There was such fury in his eyes, the primal look of a wild thing, boiling with hatred.

Arnulf's heart lurched. His stomach coiled tightly. His vision blurred.

My son.

...The little boy laughed. He slashed the air and grinned. Arnulf remembered himself laughing. The sky was iron grey and there was a mist on the far hills. Ravenshold sprawled below them. The boy came on again, darting over the grassy slopes of the Motte toward him. Arnulf parried, and then proceeded to prod and poke the small berserker-mad child, keeping him at arm's length.

382

With each thrust and tickling poke to the ribs, the boy burst out laughing without ceasing his onslaught. Then came the point where the father must let the boy into his guard. Arnulf remembered raising his arms in submission as the young lad hacked away at him.

'You've got me. You've got me. I yield,' Arnulf had said. He had scooped the giggling lad from his feet and held him in a tight embrace as Arnulf's own banners fluttered overhead...

Ewolf lunged, snarling. Again, he was sent sprawling towards the flames that surrounded them. Ewolf hissed as the heat seared his skin and leapt clear.

Time almost stilled as he looked down on the thing that had once been his boy.

'Stop, Ewolf, please...' Arnulf pleaded. 'It's me, your da.'

He remembered holding the tiny squalling pink baby, still smeared in blood and gods knows what. Aeslin had collapsed back on the bed with relief, the women rushed to fuss over her and do whatever women did after a birth. His eyes were fixed on the child in his arms. He remembered staring into that baby's eyes.

'I'm a father,' he'd muttered. 'It's a boy!' He remembered that feeling so clearly, every detail of his boy's face. He had never been so proud, so happy.

His first child. He was a father.

He remembered Aeslin's smile as he handed him to her.

'Ewolf,' he had said. 'Can we call him Ewolf?'

She had nodded. 'Ewolf — my warrior-wolf.'

He remembered that feeling so clearly. He had never been so proud.

My son...

There was nothing left of that child in the thing he saw before him. It skulked in the mud, readying to attack again, no love in its eyes, only hate. He saw only evil through his tears.

He remembered Ewolf as he had once been — his smiling, happy boy who grew into a strong young man. He had always been so proud. He remembered Aeslin, her beautiful face. He remembered Idony, his little girl's mischievous grin. All the images of an old life flashed through his mind. All gone now.

The creature snarled. Behind all the hate and the fury, he saw a son's plea for mercy, a plea for death, a release from the terrible curse from which there could be no escape. His son was gone, and only a beast in a familiar shell remained.

He knew what he had to do.

'I'm sorry, son,' Arnulf murmured.

Ewolf snarled and lunged.

Time slowed. Arnulf ground his teeth as he raised his axe high. He closed his eyes as the axe fell. He let out a roar of pure anguish as the axe came down, his eyes streaming with tears.

He felt a sickening *crunch* as his axe bit through flesh and bone.

All was still.

The fire continued to roar, timbers crackling and popping. Heat washed over him, tears drying almost as soon as they fell, only to be replaced by another. He breathed slowly, completely numb. It seemed like an age before he opened his eyes and looked down.

He choked out a sob.

There in the wet mud, lay his son—cold, still and lifeless— blood pooling in the churned mud. His gaze flicked to the ancient axe-head of his fathers, a single drop of crimson blood falling from the blade. It was his blood on that axe, the blood of his fathers, the blood of his son.

He had killed his own son.

He knelt and cradled the boy's head in his lap and unleashed a howl of anguish as he knelt in the blood and mud. He held the body close, rocking it back and forth. He kissed Ewolf's forehead.

Footsteps ran towards him from behind.

'Arnulf?' It was Hafgan. 'Oh no. Lord, I am so sorry.'

Arnulf didn't turn.

'He is free now,' Arnulf sobbed. 'It was the only way. I had no choice. The curse stole my son from me.' He turned a tear streaked face to the warriors behind him. 'This way he is free.'

Arnulf knew it would not be long until he turned and rose again in un-death, but he would deny the curse its prize. Arnulf lifted his son's body and walked towards the fire.

'You shall not have him,' Arnulf declared defiantly, tossing

Ewolf's body into the flames.

Hafgan joined his lord and stood at his side. He said nothing —
what could he say?

Arnulf watched as the fire consumed his boy. The flames had
taken Aeslin, taken Idony, and now they took Ewolf as well. He
softly sang the refrain of that old song, memories of Aeslin singing it as if it were a lullaby, gently rocking their infant boy in her
arms. Tears streamed down his cheeks.

He was alone now, the last of his line. Everything he had loved
had been consumed by flames. All had turned to ashes in the end.

'We should go, Arnulf,' Hafgan said finally.

Arnulf nodded and the world seemed to blur as his warrior led
him away. He didn't even see where he was being led. He didn't
remember walking, his thoughts completely consumed by a single
thought.

I killed my son.

CHAPTER THIRTY-EIGHT

Reunion of the Broken

'There are the gates,' Duncan said, pointing.

The hunter and the Wildman crouched in the shadows as he stooped above them, his splinted leg preventing him from crouching. The sounds of carnage, fighting and death drifted down the slopes from the Citadel behind them.

'The dead haven't reached here yet,' the hunter noted as he surveyed the courtyard in front of them.

The Citadel's lower palisade rose up from the snowy ground before them. A fighting platform ringed its upper ramparts. Duncan had expected to see warriors patrolling its length, sentries standing guard, but there was not a soul in sight. Snow drifted down from the darkened skies, the ground now thick with it. The few footprints tracked across it were quickly being filled in.

Someone has been here recently, he thought.

'Indeed, we appear to be ahead of them,' Duncan agreed.

Beside him, the Wildman shifted restlessly. Duncan had never seen such a man before, or smelt one. He stank, and Duncan wrinkled his nose at the musty, earthy smell that was mingled with stale sweat. It was quite overpowering and made him gag. He tried to breathe through his mouth, shuffling as far from the Wildman as he could.

The Wildman, who the hunter called Tung, wore only a piecemeal collection of cured pelts, and his hair was a tangled mess of knotted clumps which hung in locks around his face, littered with leaves and twigs. *What a foul, wretched little man.*

The hunter was much different. He had black hair streaked

with grey, and an unkempt beard which looked as if it was usually cropped short. He had an angular face with a strong chin and
said his name was Bjorn. His travel worn leathers seemed to attest
to his claim, and he looked like a man who was at ease in the wild
places of the world, and in the company of a stinking Wildman.

The Wildman made Duncan nervous. *What manner of man is
this? Can he speak? I doubt it.* There was certainly something animal-like about him, something feral.

'There should be guards,' Bjorn muttered. 'Where are the
guards?'

'They must be up the hill, rallying to the fight,' Duncan suggested. He had no idea and he found he didn't much care either.

The hunter grunted. 'You say there are docks close by that the
common folk use?'

'There are berths all along the riverbank, and two of the city's
biggest docks are close.'

'Good,' said Bjorn. 'I need to get to the prince's ship on the river, then I can be gone from this gods forsaken city.'

'Aye, there will be boats. The closest only a short walk from
the gates. I think that is where I will be headed also,' Duncan told
him. *These poor fools will not help me escape the city if they suspect I
had a hand in this, I best play along.* 'I will not be lingering in a place
where the dead walk.'

'Wise,' he commented. 'There must be some dark sorcery at
work in this place, to stir the dead from their graves.'

Duncan was amused by this countryman's superstitions. He
laughed. 'There is no such thing as sorcery, friend.'

'Then how do you explain *that*?' Bjorn pointed back up the hill,
then made a warding gesture and touched an amulet hung at his
neck.

Duncan merely shrugged in reply.

'Come on then,' Bjorn sighed. 'While the way is clear. If anyone challenges us, let me do the talking.' He moved from their
cover toward the tall gates, his boots crunching through the fresh
snowfall. The Wildman padded along, not even seeming to feel
the bitter cold.

They reached the towering wooden gates without challenge
and found them barred, but there was a small door built into one
of the gates. Bjorn got it open and he and the Wildman slipped
through.

Duncan paused. He cast one last look up into the Citadel, peering up to where the Throne Hall would be. A small smile crept over his face. *I did this.*

A faint laugh echoed in his mind. It was that same whispered voice that had haunted him for weeks. *Yes, such power. You did what no living man could. Now you are master of life and death. The harbinger of the dead.* The voice laughed again.

I killed a king, he thought. *The great Citadel fell by my hand and I brought life from death. I am master now.* Duncan smiled, and then he too ducked through the small door and followed after the hunter and his repulsive companion. He left the Citadel behind him, leaving it to the cold clutches of the dead.

The streets outside the gates were eerily empty. A flurry of snow cartwheeled over the white covered ground. The eaves of the nearby buildings were dusted in snow, the thatched roofs no different.

'Which way to the boats?' Bjorn asked, looking down the gloomy streets that converged on the Citadel's lower gates.

'Not far,' Duncan told him. 'Let's head for the west wharves. This way.'

The biting chill made his leg throb as he limped off. Tung made a sound, a strange guttural word perhaps? Duncan turned, and he saw her.

The woman was shrivelled and gaunt. The snow had settled on her hair and clothes. Her skin was pallid, without the rosy tint that came to pale skin in such weather, streaked with old blood, and she staggered out of the mist. *She's dead,* Duncan realised with surprise.

He had imagined the dead were confined to the Citadel, a direct result of his ritual, but here on the cold dark streets of the city, a corpse walked. At first, he was confused, but it slowly dawned on him that his ritual had reached further than he had imagined.

Yes, whispered the voice. *The ritual was powerful. It is at its most powerful during the darkness of the dead moon, and the markings were correct, the words spoken. Such power...*

The dead woman staggered closer. The plague riven husk that had once been a woman had been delivered back from Old Night to walk the city's streets again. Duncan felt a swell of excitement. He wondered exactly how far the ritual's effect had spread. How many had risen? There had been hundreds upon hundreds of dead in the streets courtesy of the blood plague. And what of the dusty bones in the old crypts? Had they risen too? Somehow he knew they hadn't, but now he had so many questions. There was so much work, so much research, suddenly stretching ahead of him, and he would find his answers.

'I thought the dead were behind us,' Bjorn growled, breaking Duncan's reverie.

'Obviously not,' he retorted. He was intrigued by the dead woman. As he stepped forward to examine her — much as Eldrick had once examined those corpses in those bleak passes — the woman stopped moving.

'Watch out, lad,' the hunter warned. Duncan waved his words away.

It will not harm you, said the voice.

'It will not harm me,' Duncan repeated, replying to Bjorn.

'How?'

He suddenly didn't know how to answer.

Tell him anything but the truth, the voice instructed.

Duncan searched for an excuse. His eyes settled upon Logan's staff, upon the runes carved into it. The runes simply spelt the master's name, *Logan,* but written in the old markings of runic script used across ancient Cydor. 'It must be the staff.'

'The staff?' Bjorn frowned. 'Is it magical?'

'It has a blessing from the gods. Perhaps it is indeed *magic.*'

'But you said there was no such thing as sorcery,' scoffed the hunter.

We shouldn't trust this one, the voice warned.

'Yes, I did.' The apprentice shrugged. 'But who's to know the ways of the gods?'

Bjorn raised a sceptical brow, but seemed to accept his words.

They moved off, leaving the dead woman stood oblivious to their presence.

They had barely turned onto the next street before Tung began hooting in alarm. It was a warning. More figures approached through the snow.

'There's more!' warned Bjorn.

'No,' Duncan muttered, straining to make out the vague shapes in the gloom. They were moving differently. *They are not dead... They are survivors.*

There were three of them, and they stopped as the group spotted them. One was a young woman, and beside her were two young men, one slightly older than the other with something wrapped around his head.

'Hello?' the young woman called. 'Please, can you help us? There are *things* in the city...'

'Come forward, lass,' Bjorn replied. 'We have seen the dead and we are quite alive. You shouldn't fear us.'

She led her companions forward hesitantly. She was blonde, her hair pale in the darkness and strikingly beautiful. She seemed familiar, but he could not place her in his memory. A young lad followed her closely, a scrawny thing who even in the dark looked filthy. Recognition dawned as he eyed the older man. *The blinded man, the lute player.* The name came to him. 'Seth?' Duncan ventured.

'You know them?' asked the hunter.

'Aye, well, this one at least.' Duncan hobbled slowly toward them. The girl he recognised too — she had come to visit Seth in the infirmaries. She stood protectively in front of the others and stared nervously at him, her eyes flicking to Tung where they lingered. Understandable, for the Wildman was indeed a strange looking wretch. Duncan was close enough now to see her eyes were red rimmed, as if she had been crying. Nonetheless, she stood there bravely protective.

'Who's that?' Seth asked.

'It's me, Duncan, from the College infirmaries. We shared a room when I broke my leg.'

Seth's head moved as he searched for the source of the sound. 'I remember! It is good to hear your voice, friend. Nym, do you remember Duncan?'

The girl regarded him with the same look of revulsion as she had that day back at the College. She considered the Wildman with a more favourable expression, though for the life of him, Duncan couldn't think why.

'Thank the gods for a friendly voice,' Seth continued. 'I hope your leg is healing.'

'It could be better,' Duncan replied. 'I hope your eyes are healing.'

'Could be better,' Seth said with a weak smile. He still wore bandages wrapped around his head covering over most of his face, revealing only his mouth and nose. All three of the companions looked exhausted, cold, and forlorn.

'We are heading to the Citadel,' blurted the young boy.

'I wouldn't be going there, lad,' Bjorn warned.

'Why?' asked the girl, who Seth had called Nym.

'There's a terrible evil there, lass. We just escaped it.'

'The dead are there too?'

The hunter nodded with a grimace.

'Where will we go?' she said, her voice edged with panic. 'Please, they're behind us. They're after us.'

The hunter did not look impressed at the prospect of more deadwood to slow their progress. For a moment Duncan thought he might send them away, sending them to find their own doom in the city. Instead the hunter sighed. 'Come with us. The city is not safe. We are heading for the boats.'

'The west wharves,' Duncan confirmed.

'No.' Nym went deathly pale. 'No, you can't go there. That's where we saw them. There were dozens of them.'

Bjorn cursed. 'Then where in all the hells *are* we going?'

'We could try the east wharves,' suggested the young lad. 'It's the fishing dock. There are always boats there.'

'Where?' Bjorn demanded.

'That way.' Nym pointed and the hunter looked to Duncan, who nodded his agreement.

'Fine, we go that way. But first I'd have your names. You are Seth and you are Nym?'

'That's right,' said Nym.

'I am Bjorn, this is Tung, and you know Duncan. What is your name, lad?' the hunter turned to the youngest one.

'Finn,' he replied in a shaky voice.

'You stay close, you hear. I won't be coming to find you if you wander off.'

The young lad nodded shakily.

'If any of you see anything, you say. You got it.'

'There are things in the fog, monsters…' Finn murmured.

'Aye, lad; I know, we've seen them too. Now come on, let's move.'

They had only gone a short way back toward the Citadel when the Wildman began making a low hooting noise. Bjorn hissed at them to halt, Tung indicating the rooftops ahead with his spear. Up in the gloom, a creature slunk across the snow-covered thatch.

A Cursed One.

They waited in the shadows, huddled against the side of a building until it was gone, then a little longer after it had gone, before continuing on.

'Who is he,' Nym asked eventually, nodding to the Wildman.

'I told you, lass,' said Bjorn gruffly. 'His name is Tung. He's a Wildman from the north, and he doesn't speak our language, but he is a friend. You have nothing to fear from him.'

The Wildman bobbed his head and sniffed at her. She recoiled away.

'Are you a warrior?' asked the boy, Finn.

'No, lad. I am Bjorn, the hunter.'

'*The* Bjorn?' Seth asked as Nym guided his steps.

The hunter smirked. 'The only one I know of.'

'I've heard songs of you.'

'You have songs?' Finn's eyes were suddenly alight.

The hunter smiled. 'I wouldn't believe everything you hear in those songs, but aye, that's me.'

Finn's reaction amused Duncan, who hobbled slowly along behind them. The boy walked beside the hunter awestruck, quietly whispering questions at him. "Have you killed a bear?" "Could you kill a hill cat?" Duncan sneered at the hunter's immodesty. He strutted through the snow, lapping up the boy's adulation. *Pathetic.*

The girl kept looking at Duncan, and he had hardly taken his eyes off her. She looked nervous, uncomfortable, but that did not stop Duncan drinking in her beauty with his roving eyes.

I would have her, thought Duncan.

Then take her, spoke the voice. *She can be your prize. Get rid of the hunter and the wild thing and keep her as your own. Her companions you can bend to your will.*

'Yes,' Duncan muttered.

Nym cast him another glance and quickly turned away, concentrating on guiding the blinded Seth through the snowy darkness.

One moment the streets were empty avenues of snow; quiet, almost serene, with nothing but the occasional set of tracks to show that they were not alone in the city. The dead woman who had been wandering by the Citadel gates was nowhere to be seen.

Then suddenly, the dead were everywhere.

The shrunken and bloodied corpses that had been stacked in the gutters of every street in the city, corpses that had laid in the filth awaiting the grisly carts, staggered out of alleyways and side streets. To Duncan's bemusement they grew still when he drew near, and he deployed the same flimsy excuse to explain the phenomena. They were superstitious fools and he chuckled to himself.

The gods indeed. He didn't understand it himself but assumed it had something to do with the ritual. In any case, the dead ignored him and those who stayed close to him, barely even registering the group as they passed by. They simply stood still and vacant as he approached, only to lurch into motion as he moved away. It was as if his presence stunned them.

'Don't touch them,' he warned them. 'They will not see us as long as you do not stray from my side, but I cannot promise anything if you touch them.'

'This isn't right,' Nym muttered.

'None of this is right,' replied the hunter. 'None of it, and it's fucking terrifying.'

The dead stood frozen as they each threaded between them. Nym carefully guided his blind friend Seth, whispering instructions while the Wildman nearly prodded one of the dead out of foolish curiosity, before Bjorn managed to stop him.

Should have let the stinking fool do it, Duncan mused. He would not have been sad to see the feral man-beast torn limb from limb.

'How much further?' Bjorn whispered.

'Not far.'

'It's like walking through Old Night's halls.' the hunter commented. 'Like a nightmare. I'll never sleep again.'

'Don't look at them, Finn,' said Nym. By the way she ordered him about, the boy seemed to be her brother, yet for all the authority in her voice, her words wavered as she spoke. Seth, of course, saw nothing, only hearing the terrifying groaning and snarling of the dead. Perhaps in some twisted way it was a kindness that the gods had seen fit to take his eyes. At least one of them did not have those vacant dead faces burned into their memories. Duncan shuddered. He had truly hated Eldrick's experiments, but now, if given the chance, he would gladly trade the sight of these dead things for a hundred of Eldrick's cadavers.

These things were a mockery of life and they made his skin crawl. Yet, there was also a tingle of pride. *I did this*, he thought.

Yes, whispered the voice, *you did*.

Around them it seemed the whole city was crying out in terror as the living fought their futile battle against the risen victims of the plague. The tables had turned, and now it was the plague's survivors who were suffering at the hands of those who had not been so lucky. It was a final revenge for the plague's dead. The gods were cruel. Duncan wondered if those who had died of sickness had the luckier fate. At least they escaped this horror.

A loud scream brought the group to a halt. They stopped, aghast as they watched a small group of the living try to fight off the swarming dead. It looked like a family; a man, a woman, and a child cradled in the woman's arms. The man swung an axe savagely but there were just too many.

'Don't look,' whispered Nym as she covered her brother's eyes with her hands. The girl however was unable to tear her eyes from the scene. The family died horribly, the dead swarming over them like ants on fallen fruit, tearing into their bodies, gorging on their flesh.

There was a shriek and a blur of movement. Something hurtled from the shadows and was suddenly amongst them. The hunter's reflexes were lightning fast. He just managed to dodge the thing, a Cursed One, missing its target and barrelling into the dead. The dead lurched into motion and those corpses not close enough to Duncan staggered after it with hungry eyes. It obviously feared the dead, deftly darting amongst them and avoiding their grasping hands.

It didn't get far though. The dead closed in on the creature in overwhelming numbers. With another shriek of rage, the creature was torn down, the dead hands seizing it as it fled, teeth piercing its flesh.

In Bjorn's sudden motion to avoid the Cursed One, he knocked Finn sprawling into a dead man and outside the radius of Duncan's protective circle. The dead man snarled at the startled boy, as if just noticing him for the first time. It turned its baleful glare on Finn and reached down for him. The boy scrambled backwards, terror stealing all rational thought. In his panic he bolted down a nearby alleyway.

'Finn!' Nym screamed. She dashed after him.

'No!' Duncan called, but it was too late. She had stepped too far and the dead swung their heads toward her. Her scream drew their attention and the corpses between her and the alley closed in on her. She had nowhere to run, and she was too far away for Duncan to reach her in time before the dead got her first, no way to reach the safety he offered. *Damn this leg.*

In desperation she plunged into a gap in the crowd left by those drawn off in the pursuit of the Cursed One. Bjorn took a step forwards to help her, axe in hand, but Duncan grasped his shoulder and shook his head.

'They are as good as dead already,' he said sadly. Duncan saw it in the hunter's eyes; he knew it too. Duncan had probably just saved his life, and he still might need the hunter yet. He could still prove useful.

Duncan watched as Nym fled. *Shame. Such beauty, wasted. I would have made her mine, despite her disgust at my broken body. She would have been mine.*

There will be others, whispered the voice.

Duncan sighed.

The Wildman watched beside Bjorn, all eyes were fixed on Nym as she ran franticly through the horde of the dead, leaving Seth lost without his guide at his side.

'Nym?' he called. 'Are you alright, lass? Nym?'

Seth flinched as Duncan placed a consoling hand on his shoulder. He sighed heavily. 'They are gone, my friend. They are lost to the dead.'

Seth shook his head, his chin trembling. 'No. No, not Nym.'

Bjorn clamped a hand over the blind man's mouth and scanned the crowd of corpses. 'Quiet, you fool,' he warned Seth.

The dead did not appear to see them. Those nearest stood in a frozen reverie while the others staggered after Nym as she fled into the night.

'We can't help them,' Bjorn said. 'I'm sorry, friend. There's nothing we can do. There's too many.'

Seth slumped. He could not even weep for his lost friends. Those parts of his face that were not bound in bandages showed his mouth twisting with emotion.

'How far to the damned boats?' Bjorn hissed.

'Not far,' replied Duncan. 'This way.'

CHAPTER THIRTY-NINE

The Gates

Hafgan let Wilhelm lead them back to the gates and the waiting warriors to share the tragic news of Ewolf's death and the disappointment that there were not enough boats to get them out.

Arnulf seemed lost. He had a distant look in his eyes and he hadn't said a thing on the journey back. His lord had stumbled along beside him through the muddy slush, seemingly unaware of his surroundings. Hafgan could not begin to imagine Arnulf's pain. He had known Ewolf since he was a child, had watched the lad grow into a man, but the loss he felt was nothing in comparison. Ewolf's death had come suddenly, so unexpectedly amid a night of unfolding horror, especially when there had been some small hope that the young man might recover from his affliction.

Hafgan was not a man easily shaken. He had not faltered a step whilst fighting those first dead men in the passes, but the scenes he witnessed now would have halted any man. The gates, and the courtyard before them, had plunged into chaos. The first stumbling corpses had emerged from the College and were attacking anything that lived. There were not many, but the sight of something so unnatural as a walking corpse was enough to freeze any man's blood. There were Cursed Ones just like Ewolf, freshly turned, tearing through the snow to hurl themselves upon raised shields only to be hacked down by grim armoured warriors. The dead staggered forward here and there, having to be savagely dismembered before they finally stilled.

His fellow warriors still held the gates, Lord Fergus amongst them, barking orders. They fought and held their ground, but with the dead straining at the gates to get in, and now more inside the College compound, it seemed to be only a matter of time before the living would be overwhelmed.

One of the wretched cursed creatures who looked to have been a member of the College came loping through the snow toward Hafgan. Its eyes, glinting with malice, were locked upon the stricken form of Arnulf, as if selecting the weaker of the three of them. It carried a knife in one hand and used the other to bound across the ground with three limbs like a small withered bear.

Hafgan's shield was still slung over his horse's saddle, but Wilhelm had his, the king's sigil of Varg emblazoned upon its face. The warrior lowered his spear and tracked the creature with his spear's point. At his left hip, Hafgan carried his sword, and beside it his axe, and he drew both weapons in a flash. He reached across to grasp his sword's hilt with his right hand, and with his left, he seized his axe below its head. As he levelled his sword, he pulled his axe free and slammed its haft onto his leg, sliding his hand into position.

He struck immediately, not allowing the cursed creature to strike first. The creature's knife skittered uselessly across his mailed sleeve and he caught the thing with savage back swing of his axe. His sword followed, skewering the creature down its gullet. He watched the light fade from its eyes, and it collapsed with a shudder, red froth bubbling from its mouth.

Wilhelm gave him a grim nod. 'Let's move.'

The surviving warriors had made a protective ring around the gates and stables, shields raised. Fergus's warriors and their blue painted shields mingled with the reds of Arnulf's men, falcon and axe standing as one. One of Astrid's shield-maidens wrestled with a dead scholar that was grasping at her shield, the Death Nymph herself cleaving the thing's arms from its body with a ferocious swing of her glinting sword, and then rammed its tip into the dead scholar's eye. The thing went down, but still twitched.

Hafgan and Wilhelm dragged Arnulf between them and ran for the protection of those raised shields before some other fell thing took note of them.

'We can't stay here!' shouted Fergus as he saw them return. 'Tell me there's a boat.'

Hafgan shook his head in reply with a bleak expression.

'There's a pair of tiny things,' Wilhelm offered. 'Nothing we can all use.'

'Shit,' Fergus said, shaking his head.

Several warriors heaved against the gates with their shoulders, struggling against the press beyond. Despite their efforts, the gates bulged inward. The heavy timber barring the gate splintered and cracked, straining against its iron wrought fittings.

'This gate is not going to hold. They are coming at us from both sides,' Fergus warned. It was then Fergus saw his oldest friend slumped beside Hafgan. 'What happened, Haf? Is Arnulf wounded? Tell me he hasn't been bitten.'

'It's Ewolf. He's dead,' Hafgan replied with a grave voice.

'No!' Fergus exclaimed. 'Arnulf...' His words failed him and he looked back to the big warrior. 'How?'

'He had to put the lad to peace with his own hand,' Hafgan replied, shaking his head, his throat tightening around the words. 'There was no other way.'

Arnulf stared down at his hands and wept.

Fergus's face dropped with sadness. 'No...'

Arnulf sank to his knees in the filth and churned slush as the timbers barring the gates cracked and splintered.

'We need to go!' Fergus shouted, his face a mask of fearful desperation.

'We will need to fight through them,' Hafgan told him as he retrieved his shield from his panicked horse.

'Don't be a fool,' argued Fergus. 'There's too many out there.'

'You have a better idea, Lord Fergus?' Hafgan challenged.

Fergus opened his mouth and closed it again, shaking his head as he struggled to think of something, *anything*, rather than fighting through those corpse-swamped gates.

'They will tear us to pieces,' Fergus muttered. The fear showed in his eyes.

'There is no other way,' said Hafgan.

Fergus looked to Arnulf in mute appeal, as if his old friend would suddenly reveal some perfect solution. Instead he knelt broken in the dirt.

Hafgan didn't think his lord even heard the words spoken around him, hopelessly lost in a reverie of grief, lost in silence as a cacophony of butchery and death raged around him. Without a better suggestion Hafgan took charge. He spoke for his lord and

Arnulf's warriors listened.

'Listen, lads,' he shouted. 'We're going to fight through them. It's the only way out.'

Warriors looked to each other uncertainly. They knew Hafgan, they trusted he could get them out, yet the fear was written plain on their faces. Beyond those splintering gates stood a horde of undead corpses. Hafgan looked from warrior to warrior, something in his resolute face bolstered their resolve. With that look he would compel them to clutch at those tatters of courage and stand firm at his side.

'Cut the horses loose. Take all that you need, now. Ready yourselves.'

'What about Arnulf's hound?' Erran asked from the stable.

Hafgan looked to his lord, who made no reaction to the question. 'Aye, Fear too. Cut them all loose, let them find their own fate.'

The hound ran to his lord as soon as he was cut loose. He nuzzled the lord's hands, but Arnulf barely seemed to notice. At the sound of a terrible shriek nearby, the hound yelped and bolted into the shadows. The great grey hound bounded away, fleeing the madness that raged around them.

Wise beast, thought Hafgan.

The big warrior turned to Wilhelm. 'Will you stand with us?' Hafgan asked and Wilhelm nodded. 'Might need you to show us the way back.'

Nearby, the scholar, Luthor, stood shivering, completely out of place amongst these warriors. He clutched the grimoire to his chest and tried to keep out of the warrior's way.

He will be little use in the fight.

'You,' he said, pointing at Luthor. 'Stay close. Watch our backs. Try not to get yourself killed.' The scholar swallowed a lump from his throat and nodded.

'I will keep an eye on him,' Wilhelm offered with a thin smile at the scholar, then hefted the weight of his shield on his arm.

'And you up there,' Hafgan called to the College sell-swords still up on the gate's guard platform. 'Will you fight with us? Staying here means death.'

'Aye, we will be right behind you, don't you worry,' one of the mercenaries shouted in reply.

Hafgan took one final glance. *It's now or never.*

'Shield wall!' bellowed Hafgan.

The ash boards of their shields clattered together as warriors formed rank before the heaving gates. Some of Fergus's shield-maidens stood amongst them. Hafgan caught Astrid's eye. She gave him a nod, a gesture of respect between warriors. Fergus, with no better idea, was swept along, helpless to object. Astrid motioned for his warriors to stand with the others.

Hafgan checked the courtyard behind them. It was empty, nothing stirred. However, he was doubtless that the dead stumbled through the darkened hallways of the College beyond, and the wretched Cursed Ones lurked somewhere, perhaps hunting easier prey. But eventually, he knew, they would come.

'Lord Fergus,' called Astrid. 'I think I can draw some of them away from the gates.' She dangled a horn from her hand in explanation.

'Worth a try,' nodded Fergus.

They looked at Hafgan.

'Do it,' he agreed.

'Not too far, and get back here quickly,' Fergus ordered as she climbed up to the guard platform. She scrambled over onto the rooftops that were built up against the compound's walls and moved to position herself further along.

'My lord.' Hafgan pulled Arnulf to his feet. 'We have to move.'

'He's dead,' Arnulf said weakly. 'It's all gone.'

'Keep him close,' Hafgan commanded one of his nearby men. 'Ready, lads?'

There was a sudden silence. They all knew what was about to burst through those gates. Fear was thick in the air and the moment of awful quiet seemed to stretch. The snarls and moans of the dead on the other side were the only sound.

Astrid's horn brayed and echoed through the snowy air. He saw her leaning over the wall banging her sword's pommel on its wooden sides. She blew it again. The horn carried a nasal note, a mournful sound that reminded him of some mountain goat's bleat.

'Steady, not yet,' Hafgan ordered as the shield wall rippled.

'Some are moving away,' came a shout from above.

'Ready lads. Let's show these dead bastards Arnar steel,' said Hafgan. Then he bellowed, 'Open it.'

Someone pulled the timber bar free. The gates swung open. A

horde of bodies surged forward.

'Hold!' shouted Hafgan.

Shields braced. Spears bristled from the second rank. They had brought less than a score of warriors, but more than enough to plug the gateway with shields. It took six men with shields raised to span that gap. More waited to the sides, ready to add their shields to the wall as they pushed out.

Spears thrust and axes came chopping down. Men were shouting, and Hafgan felt the thud of the impact in his belly more than he heard it. The push of the horde reverberated through the entire shield wall as warriors strained against their shields. The smell of rotting flesh assailed him, mingled with the reek of vomit as a few of the warriors emptied their stomachs.

Dead faces pressed in onto their shields, dead hands clutching over rims. The corpses of Arn filled the street beyond, many with signs of plague who had already begun to rot, eyes pecked away. Maggots festered in open wounds and bloodied mouths. Smiths, fishermen, traders, farmers – all reduced to snarling husks of their former lives. Women, children, fathers, mothers; the sickness had not discriminated. Street urchins and whores stood beside rich merchants and ladies; none were spared, all now arisen to bear a seemingly rapacious hate for all things living.

Astrid's sounded her horn once more. Some of the dead in the street turned and stumbled toward the sound. The press lessened slightly, and he heard someone shout, 'Heave!'

The shield wall moved a pace forwards.

Again, and again they heaved, and slowly the stalwart shields of Arnar pushed the dead back.

***

The dead were not distracted for long, the clamour of the fighting drawing the attention of many that were stumbling towards the sound of the horn back toward the gate.

Fergus glanced around to see Wilhelm thrusting his spear over the front rank of shields. Arnulf's young warrior Erran fought on the outer flanks of the wall, bellowing defiance at the dead, the lad's sword smeared in dark blood as it hacked down again and again.

The shield wall had pushed out from the gate in a wide arc.

Twitching bodies fouled their feet, the warriors stepping over the fallen with each surging push. Yet still the dead came on, unrelenting and unyielding like the tides of the sea.

One of the horses, seeing no other escape, bolted through the gates, trampling one of the shield-maidens from behind. She never even saw it coming. The woman collapsed; her skull crushed in her helmet under the beast's iron-shod hooves.

Fergus watched in horror as the shield of the man beside him was torn away, leaving him open to the grasping dead hands. The warrior was torn from the ranks screaming and dragged off into the crowd. One of the man's arms was wrenched away from his torso in a spray of blood and a piercing scream. The blood splattered Fergus's face, his view in every direction nothing but ghastly dead faces.

There are too many.

On the rooftops dark figures prowled on all fours, stooped low, watching, waiting. They were not dead, but they were no longer human.

Even if we fight clear, those cursed things will be waiting for us. He backed away from the front rank, letting his gap be filled by the men either side. Astrid drew back beside him and gave him a questioning frown. He looked for where the dead seemed to be thinnest. *There must be fifty, a hundred of the dead in our path. Who knows how many more between here and the Citadel – hundreds, perhaps thousands?*

The cold grip of panic wrapped itself around his heart.

We are going to die here.

Images of his limbs being torn from his body, torn bloody from their sockets, filled his thoughts. He could almost feel his bowels uncoiling as the dead things pulled them from his belly by their teeth.

'No,' he whispered. 'Not like this.'

He backed away further from the wall of shields, then turned and fled to the safety of the gates. The scholar, Luthor, stood there looking helpless, clutching that cursed book they had brought south.

Somewhere in the press of bodies he heard someone screaming. It petered off into a sickening gurgle before falling silent. Arnulf seemed to have lost his mind, despite Hafgan's efforts to move him, he just sank down again weeping. Fergus knew his old friend was going to die there. They all would.

The boats… That warrior had said there were some small boats. The idea crept into his mind — why should he not save himself? He would be High Lord one day; he was too valuable to die here. *Better these men die, so a few can live.*

'Shut the gates,' he called to the men still waiting there.

Those warriors looked confused, but like him, they were terrified. They didn't need much persuading.

'No!' shouted Hafgan, retreating back to join them as he heard the command. 'What are you doing, fool?'

'Watch your tongue!' snapped Fergus. 'You forget your place, Haf. Would you defy a lord's command?'

'No, lord,' he said sullenly, though the anger was written plain on his face.

Astrid had fallen back with her lord, never far from his side. 'We can't,' she argued siding with Hafgan. 'There are warriors out there. They will die.'

'They're dead anyway,' snapped Fergus. 'Close the gates.'

***

The gates began to laboriously swing shut. Hafgan stood by, unable to do anything, his honour preventing him from disobeying a lord's command. Warriors, seeing what was happening, broke from the wall and fled toward the gates. Some were torn down from behind and dragged away into the mass of corpses. The shield wall fractured into small groups, men and women frantically fighting as the dead surged through the gaps. Some found themselves surrounded, and desperately tried to fight their way clear.

'Fergus, you coward!' Astrid snarled with a look of disgust.

'How dare you, bitch,' Fergus retorted. 'I am your sworn lord. You stand at my side; your sword is mine. Now leave them, help me get to a boat.'

'I will not run. I will not leave them to die so you can live.'

It was then Astrid's eyes found Erran. He was separated, trapped in a small group fighting back to back as the dead swarmed around them.

'You would break your oath, girl?' Fergus sneered. 'You will be nothing.'

'Fuck your oath,' she snapped and ran out through the gates.

It was in those moments, as the gates slowly swung shut, that Hafgan witnessed why they called her the Death Nymph. She was death incarnate.

She plunged into the mass of snarling corpses, sword flicking out, chopping and hacking. She buffeted away their outstretched hands with her shield, ramming its iron rim into gaunt faces. Bones cracked and skulls buckled as they were crushed into a gory pulp. She was agile, her whirling movements sleek like a hill cat, but instead of the grace he had witnessed when she was sparring, there was a ferocious savagery that stole his breath away.

He had witnessed acts of bravery, but the charge of the Death Nymph was something Hafgan would never forget.

'Erran!' she screamed, her voice heavy with emotion.

The young warrior turned as the shield wall disintegrated around him. He and Astrid looked longingly at each other; their eyes locked. The lad smiled sadly, realising his fate.

They will never make it.

He caught one last glimpse of them fighting and then the gates banged shut. He closed his eyes and grimaced. He too knew their fate. Fists hammered desperately on the gates, the pleas of warriors trapped on the other side rising up, voices begging to be let in. Those pleas became screams as the dead reached them.

Fergus watched with indifference as the splintered drop-bar was lowered back into place.

'Arnulf,' Hafgan said, 'please do something.'

'He's dead,' Arnulf repeated again and again.

As soon as the bar was lowered and the gates secured, Fergus fled toward the College docks. The shield-maiden Hild accompanied him, usurping Astrid's place at his side. She had chosen silver over honour and Hafgan spat as he watched them make their hasty retreat.

He raced up to the fighting platform over the gate, hoping somehow to be able to help any survivors to scale the walls. The last brave warrior fell, overwhelmed and dragged under the crowd and out of sight. There was no sign of Erran, no sign of Astrid. All those trapped outside were gone. His heart grew heavy, knowing how they must have died, torn to pieces by the horde of snarling corpses.

They are all dead.

The realisation stung him. Erran was gone. They had been

close in a way. Hafgan had trained him, drank with him — he had grown fond of the lad. He shook his head sadly. He punched the edge of the College walls with a surge of anger and grief then ran back down to Arnulf.

'Lord, we have to move. Too many died out there.'

He caught a flash of movement in the snow behind him. A shout of warning called out from the survivors gathered near the gate. He whirled to meet the attacker, cutting the creature down with a single stroke of his axe before it managed to reach Arnulf. The Cursed One spasmed in the snow as its blood stained the ground. One final swing stilled the wretched monster.

Arnulf barely seemed to notice.

'My lord,' exclaimed Hafgan, 'You must fight with us.'

'He's dead. My son is dead,' Arnulf muttered.

'Then avenge him,' Hafgan urged, thrusting his lord's ancient axe into his hands.

Arnulf looked up and met his gaze, his eyes bloodshot and welling with tears.

'Avenge him,' snarled Hafgan.

Something hardened in his lord's eyes. 'Vengeance,' muttered Arnulf. He looked down at his axe, running his hands over the intricate knot work on its aged head.

The axe of his fathers, thought Hafgan. *It will bring him their strength.* The corner of his mouth twitched in a grim smile as his lord rose to his feet.

The gates heaved again as the dead renewed their assault.

'Behind us!' someone shouted in alarm.

Half a dozen corpses stumbled through the snow, drawn by the sounds of battle from the College's blood stained halls.

'Vengeance!' Arnulf snarled again, and with a bellow of hate, he charged.

He swung his axe with both hands as he reached the first one, cleaving the corpse in two with one ferocious swing. He charged the next one, hacking savagely. He was taken by the blood-frenzy, a battle lust fuelled by hatred and grief. The other men stood by in awe as Arnulf swung his axe in wild abandon, chopping limps and severing heads. He buried his axe into the final corpse's chest with a *crunch* of cracking ribs. It snarled and clutched at him in reply, but he sent it tumbling to the ground with vicious kick.

'Vengeance!' he screamed, as he brought his axe down to split the thing's head in two. He stood there panting, staring down into the blood and brains that had spilt from its cloven skull.

'My lord...' Hafgan didn't know what to say next. Arnulf had unleashed a primal savagery on those dead things, pouring his anguish into a furious rage. Now it seemed spent, released. The fury of it all stealing his words.

The courtyard was deathly quiet, only the moaning of the dead could be heard as the dead strained against the gates. The snow fell silently adding an eerie feel to the scene.

'We need another way out,' shouted Hafgan.

For a moment no one spoke.

'The rooftops,' suggested Luthor. 'There are storehouses built up against the walls on both sides there,' said the scholar, pointing. 'We could use the rooftops to get away and perhaps into the temple district to get back to the Citadel, if that is still where you wish to go.'

'Will it be the quietest way?' asked Hafgan.

'Aye,' confirmed Wilhelm. 'I reckon that's our best chance.'

The gates bulged inward, the timbers cracking loudly.

'Then let's go,' shouted Hafgan. 'If we stay here, we're dead.'

They ran over to the storehouses and Hafgan scrambled up onto the thatched roof, using a barrel to reach up into the eaves. The gates burst open as the others reached them, warriors turning fearfully at the sound. The dead tumbled through, spilling into the College's courtyard. Men franticly pulled themselves up as the dead closed in, Hafgan kneeling at the edge, hauling them up. He counted as he helped each man up onto the roof, bringing Wilhelm up last, the warrior waiting until everyone else was safe, covering their retreat with his spear and shield.

He's a good man, this one.

They had gained three College mercenaries, four of Fergus's shield-maidens, the king's guard Wilhelm and the scholar named Luthor. He sat back and slumped at the count. Less than half of Ravenshold's men remained.

Just six.

Arnulf knelt beside him and looked back at the College. The night was oppressively dark. *A dead moon.* Hafgan grunted at the thought. The lack of moon was portentous; a terrible omen. Some of the College buildings still blazed fiercely, the flames that had become Ewolf's pyre. His body stolen from the fell evil of the risen dead. He noticed his lord's gaze lingered on those flickering orange flames for a long time. He wanted to say something, but no words came.

It's probably for the best, thought Hafgan. He did not want to send his lord back to another dazed stupor of grief.

'Where is Erran, and the others?' asked Arnulf suddenly. 'Where is Fear?

'Erran is dead, lord,' Hafgan replied. 'We lost too many good men.'

'Erran?' asked Arnulf in disbelief.

'He's gone lord,' replied Hafgan gravely. 'He was a good lad. He fought well.'

'And Fear?'

'We cut the hound free when we released the horses. He bolted. I don't know what happened to him. I'm sorry, lord. I hope he found somewhere to hide.'

His lord's face fell at the news, another blow he didn't deserve.

'I don't remember any of it,' Arnulf said, rubbing his face. 'What happened at the gates? Where is Fergus?' Arnulf listened as Hafgan retold the events after Ewolf's death, his face darkening.

'He did what? No,' Arnulf said shaking his head. 'Fergus is better than that. He is no coward.'

'He saved his own skin, and abandoned the rest of us, Arnulf. We all saw it.'

Warriors nodded their heads in agreement, the look of betrayal plain on their faces.

'I can't believe it.' His denial was fading even as he spoke. 'He would not have cost so many good men to save himself.'

'It's my fault. It was my call,' Hafgan told him. 'We had to fight through. It seemed the only way. I got men killed. I got Erran killed.'

'You did what you thought was best at the time,' assured Arnulf. 'I would have done the same. You had to do something.' He paused and frowned. 'If what you say is true, it was *Fergus's* cowardice that got Erran killed, not you, my friend. I still can't believe he abandoned us. He was my oldest friend. I thought he had honour.'

'As did I,' agreed Hafgan.

Wilhelm was already guiding their warriors onto the roofs adjacent which belonged to buildings outside of the College complex. The rooftops of warehouses had been built right up against the College's outer walls, and Hafgan could see some way along into streets of Arn by the light of the blazing fire behind him. He rose to his feet and stepped over the top of the wall and onto a sloping roof, leaving the College compound behind. The buildings were built close together here, and they should be able to stay above ground for much of this particular street and head deeper into the city. He hoped it was not far to the temple district, and he prayed to the gods that the way was not clogged by another rotting horde of dead things.

The street led them closer to the waterfront, the river a wide band of glistening, reflected fire light against the dim country that lay beyond. Hafgan negotiated the rooftop of a large building that looked like a storehouse, and the man beside him stopped.

'Lord, look. On the river.'

Arnulf saw it, and began scrambling to the building's riverside edge before Hafgan could reach him. 'Fergus!' Arnulf bellowed.

There on the dark waters of the great river was a small boat. Its two oars dipped in unison, disturbing the surface and leaving a wake of shimmering ripples.

'Fer—' Arnulf shouted again, cut short by Hafgan's hand clamping over his lord's mouth.

'No, lord. Those things will hear us,' Hafgan warned in a hoarse whisper.

It was dark, the dead moon offering no light, yet there they were, barely visible, waiting, watching with malicious eyes. Across the street Hafgan pointed out the skulking shapes that lurked there. The Cursed Ones—cursed monsters just like Ewolf.

'We could draw more of them,' warned Hafgan. 'We could draw the dead. We must move quietly.'

'Arnulf,' Fergus called across the water.

Hafgan swore.

'Is that you, Arnulf?' called Fergus. Hafgan could clearly see the lord's fiery auburn hair, even in the dim light. It seemed to draw the reflection of the flickering fires, and he thought he saw Fergus's grin. Another figure pulled at an oar beside him, probably the shield-maiden, Hild. 'You're alive?' Fergus laughed.

Arnulf opened his mouth to call out a reply but Hafgan hissed at him to keep his voice down. Arnulf looked at the faces of the men on the rooftop with him. His lord desperately wanted to call out, but knew it could cost them their lives. He remained silent.

Fergus did not. 'I had no choice, old friend. I thought you had lost your mind. I had to retreat.'

'Run like a coward, more like,' Hafgan muttered bitterly.

'I would come back for you, but my father would not be happy if I was not alive to take his place,' Fergus shouted, still laughing as if it were a great joke. 'I am too important to die here. I hope you understand. If that is you up there, Arnulf. I wish you luck and a good death. I will see you in Old Night's hall. We can drink again once more.'

'He thinks we're all doomed,' said Arnulf.

'He could send a boat back to pick us up,' Luthor suggested hopefully.

'He won't,' Arnulf growled. Did he hear something in his old friend's voice, in that familiar laugh, which confirmed his fears? Hafgan thought Fergus's words had an ominous finality to them. It was a farewell wreathed in guilt.

'He won't want us to live now,' Hafgan whispered to the scholar. 'He won't risk it. He knows we would tell folk of his cowardice, and it'll ruin him. I bet he's shitting himself now he knows we're alive. He'll be praying for our deaths. There won't be a boat.'

Fergus was still looking back at them, obviously unsure if anyone was even there. They watched his boat move further away.

'Let's move,' Hafgan ordered.

'Aye, this way, Lord Arnulf,' Wilhelm said from behind them. 'The temple district is not far. We should be able to find somewhere to slip across up ahead.'

'If I ever see him again...' Arnulf spat, his eyes not leaving the little boat as he tracked its slow progress across the river. 'He'll pay for this. The fucking coward.'

CHAPTER FORTY

Alone

She ran on, the dead everywhere she turned. Hjort, the great Hart, god of the hunted, must have smiled on her in those cold dark hours of that fell night.

Dead hands reached for her, gaunt faces looming out of the darkness, closing in, but Hjort was with her. She dodged around them, running through gaps in the crowd before their dead eyes had a chance to register her. Most were slow, and by the time they had lurched towards her, she had already gone. Some however, sprang forward with a terrifying speed; it was as if her life's warmth sent them into a frenzy. They chased her, snapping their jaws at her heels. Some of the dead shrieked and screamed with blood curdling cries as their eyes fell upon her, making her blood freeze in her veins as the horrible sounds pierced the night. She had to get away.

She saw an alley and took her chance, trying to circle back to where she guessed Finn might have gone.

'Finn?' she called in a sharp whisper. She winced as she spoke, not wanting to rouse the attention of some horror in the dark, yet desperate to call out to her brother. 'Finn?'

She cuffed the tears from her face with her sleeves. A horrible feeling boiled in her stomach. She thought she would be sick again. *He's gone. Finn. Finn. No, please. Please don't leave me. Please come back.*

She wove between buildings, clambering over fishing nets and past midden heaps. It was so dark. She felt her way with her fingertips and prayed for sunrise. Rounding a corner she saw something and froze, straining her eyes in the gloom.

It was one of them, one of the dead. A dead woman. She stood there, slowly swaying but unmoving. She had her back to Nym. The woman's hair looked matted with blood and mud, trailed down her bare back. Nym crept silently and passed the alley entrance, desperate not to make a sound. She took another path.

She came to an opening of another street and looked out. Her heart sank as she saw dead milling there. Some knelt eating some poor soul, others slowly staggered toward the macabre feast. She crouched a moment and watched, spying another gap across the street, a shadowy dark void between two buildings. She weighed her chances. *It's dark. They might not see me if I run.*

She took her chance and dashed across.

A snarl, a sound that was part wheeze and part screech, echoed behind her. The dead had seen her. Her stomach twisted and lurched like it was trying to jump into her mouth. She ran headlong for the safety of the shadows. Her heart skipping as something stumbled from the darkness. A corpse blocked her path, its eyes pecked out by crows. With a roar, it dived at her. In a panic she turned and fled up the street, her pulse pounding in her ears.

A huge pair of stones loomed from the dark, illuminated by a pair of burning braziers at their base. She ran toward them. In the flickering light she saw the stones had been worked. They were covered in beautiful patterns. It was a portal, Nym realised – a portal to the realm of the dead.

Beyond the stones the night seemed still, a promise of quiet sanctuary. As far as she could tell there was no sign of the risen dead in that quiet place. As the dead had already spilt into this world, she would take her chances with the ghosts.

She darted between the huge stones. Behind her the dead were still coming, the more agile dead were closing in fast, eyes hungry with malice, and behind them the others continued their slow and terrible advance. The dead were inexorable.

Her eyes had adjusted to the night's gloom, the firelight highlighting the ancient standing stones and the branches of the trees that grew there. There were no houses here, instead there were oaks and elms, bare branches twisting up to claw at the dark sky like spindly fingers. Nym thought it strange that such a place existed amongst the sprawl of the city. It must be a sacred grove, a part of the city dedicated to the ancestors, a place of temples and gods.

She followed an avenue marked by low placed stones and lit with more braziers, leading her deeper into that hallowed realm of spirits. The way was flanked by rock pile cairns and old burial mounds. She prayed to any god listening that nothing stirred within the old mounds, but if those dusty bones had risen too, surely the groves would be teeming with ancient withered corpses? Yet the place was deserted, the air still, just the ghosts watching her with ancient ethereal eyes. She was an intruder in their domain.

She reached into her pocket, her fingers brushing against her comb. It had been her mother's — the last physical link she had to her parents. She hoped by touching it that link would strengthen, that her mother would know she was there. She thought back to the ritual at Anchorage's God's Circle. That was the last time she had walked in the realm of ghosts. She'd felt her parents watching her then, as she felt the ancestor's spirits watching her now. She prayed her parents were amongst them, that they were close. Again, her eyes searched the gloom, longing to see the apparitions of her parents, smiling kindly from the other world.

She thought of Finn, hoping he was hiding somewhere and that he was safe. He had once told her that he didn't remember what their parents looked like. He was so young when they died, just a tiny child. A tear slipped down her cheek. *Now I've lost him too.*

A shriek behind her announced the dead had reached the standing stones of the portal. She whirled around to look, daring to hope that the magic of the gateway would prevent them from following her inside, that the ghosts of the ancestors would bar their path. Her heart sank as she watched them stagger into the grove. It was as if they had her scent, relentless blood hounds of death. They reached for her and stumbled forwards. Fear gripped her heart and she ran.

Nym came to a ring of the burning braziers and at their centre towered another large stone. It was carved, like the portal stones had been, but this one was adorned in bones. Human skulls, set row upon row, grinning in the flickering shadows from recesses cut into the rock. There were animal skulls too; a stag's skull with huge flaring antlers stared down at her, hung above all others.

'Hjort,' she whispered. She glanced into the darkened sockets, but quickly lowered her eyes, unable to meet its gaze any longer. Clustered around the totem stone were more mounds. Inside she imagined the resting bones of lords, kings and heroes. She could picture those ancient bones laid out on a slab within the mound, still wearing their wargear, swords and axes resting on their chests. Noble and magnificent, even in death. The great warriors of the ancestors that would rise as terrible wights and strike down the enemies of Arnar when the realm was as its greatest peril. She prayed they would rise now and save her.

The dead were getting closer. She heard a creaking sound and turned to see a wooden door set into one of the burial mounds moving between two large pieces of rock and the heavy lintel stone resting above. There were runes carved into the lintel, but she couldn't read modern script, let alone ancient markings. The door creaked open fully revealing a yawning darkness within. Then she caught sight of a faint flicker of light.

She heard a voice whisper, 'Come, child. In here, quickly.' Was it the voice of a mighty ancestor offering her sanctuary in its dusty tomb? A robed figure appeared at the doorway, beckoning with a hand that did not seem rotted or decayed. It was human—a living human. She looked up to the stag, with its magnificent antlers, and whispered her thanks. The gods had heard her prayer.

The dead were still coming, snarling and moaning, one lurching step after another, and she ran for the shelter of the burial mound. She pulled the door closed behind her. To her surprise it had a latch made of rope and old wood on the inside.

A latch on the inside?

She slipped the latch over the hook on the wall. *A latch so the ghosts could seal themselves in, so none could disturb their rest.* She peered back through a crack in the door. The dead staggered up to the stone totem outside, their quarry seemingly gone. She ducked back into the darkness and prayed none had seen her enter.

She closed her eyes and let out a deep breath. Summoning her courage, she turned to peer into the gloom. A dim light flickered at the crypt's far end, illuminating the robed figure.

'You're safe now, child.' It was the whispered, accented voice of a woman, her face obscured by shadow. 'Come back here, away from the door.'

'They are out there, the dead...' Nym whimpered.

'We will be safe in here. They will not find us.'

413

The woman held out her hand and Nym stepped hesitantly forward, allowing herself to be led deeper inside. The flickering light came from a small tallow candle set on a flat stone. The roof was low and Nym had to duck down into a crouch. As the candle-light chased away the darkness, niches materialised along the walls like shelves. Dozens of skulls stared out at her. Bones were arranged on others, all matching. There were no complete skeletons as she had imagined, instead there were the bones of many souls, all separated and grouped together. Here many had become one, a macabre collection of bone.

The central chamber was narrow, a small sarcophagus of flat uneven stones leant together. It was there the tallow candle sat, flickering its meagre light onto the chamber of bones.

The figure turned and lowered her hood. Nym gasped. *It's her!*

It was the witch-seer, the woman who had watched her in Anchorage and again on the streets of Arn. She was the same woman who had saved her from the thug in the street.

A surge of bile burned in her throat. She wanted to be sick, her hands trembling.

'Don't be afraid,' said the woman. 'I will not hurt you.'

'Who are you?'

She smiled. 'I am Ramona.'

'Why have you been following me?'

'Have I?'

'I've seen you watching me,'

'I watch. I have seen you, true. I saw you in Anchorage. I saw you here in the city. I have seen many things though, not just you. Perhaps it is *you* who has followed *me*.'

Nym didn't know what to say to that.

'And now you know my name, child. What is yours?'

'Nym,' she replied. 'You're a seer, a witch?'

The woman laughed softly. 'I can read the cards, yes. I know how to hear the gods. I can see their omens and portents. I know herbs and healing. Here in Arnar, that is what they call us, but I thought I was just an old woman from across the sea living in a strange land.'

'Where are you from?'

'Telis, my dear. I came here a long time ago. You are from Anchorage?'

'Yes, I came here with my brother, Finn.' The thought of him brought tears to her eyes. 'But he's gone. I lost him out there.'

'I am sorry. You will see him again, if not in this life, then in the next.'

'He's not dead!' Nym hissed.

The woman closed her eyes and for a moment she said nothing. 'I do not see his ghost,' she said. 'There is hope yet.'

Nym let out another sob in relief. 'Oh, thank you,' she said. 'I hope he's alright.'

'Are you here alone?' asked the witch. 'Your parents?'

'They're gone,' Nym sniffed. 'They died a long time ago.' Her hand absently clutched at her mother's comb.

'Ah that explains it. I have seen spirits watching you, child. They are watching over you.' She smiled. 'And who is the old man I have seen?'

'Jor? You have been watching all of us?' Nym accused.

'I see many things,' she replied cryptically.

'Jor is dead too, the dead...' She started crying.

'Hush, hush now. Come to Ramona.' The witch pulled Nym into an embrace, and she let herself fold against the woman. 'I will keep you safe.' She rocked her gently and began humming a strange tune.

Nym felt the surge of bile suddenly rise into her throat. She pulled herself away and dashed into a dark corner, retching as quietly as she could manage. It was bad enough that the noise might alert the dead, but it was a grave insult to do such a thing in a tomb.

'Are you alright, child?' Ramona asked, hovering uncertainly.

'I am sorry,' Nym said, rising and wiping her mouth. She noticed the woman watching her warily. 'I don't have the sickness, I promise. My stomach hasn't been right for weeks.'

The witch looked her over then approached. 'Let me look at you.'. She touched Nym's stomach, her fingers probing the skin. Suddenly the witch gasped. 'Do you know?' she asked.

'Know what?' replied Nym.

'I sense something inside you.' She looked deep into Nym's eyes, searching. 'When did you last bleed?'

'Erm...' Nym was lost for words. She'd lost count if she was honest—there had been so much going on that it hadn't occurred to her that something was out of place. It wasn't unusual for her to go without a cycle or two, especially when food was scarce, so she hadn't worried too much. The look on Ramona's face told her she might have been wrong not to. 'A moon cycle, maybe two? It happens sometimes...'

The witch nodded. 'Well you will not bleed again for some time.'

'*What?* Why?'

Ramona laughed. 'Because you are with child, my dear.'

Nym gasped. A pang of numbness struck her and spread through her body at the witch's words. She shook her head. 'No, I can't be.'

'But you are,' said the woman.

Uncomfortable memories flooded back, things she had tried hard to forget. The image of his drunk leering face, the smell of his stale breath, the stink of sweat on his skin, the sound of his grunts as he pumped away on top of her. She remembered the sticky mess he left dripping from between her legs as he climbed off her, and laying there trying not to cry.

All for a chunk of hack-silver. She shuddered and fresh tears welled up.

'No,' she protested. 'I can't be.'

A thump suddenly shook the wooden door to the tomb.

'What was that?!' Nym whimpered.

A snarl from outside answered her question. Something hammered on the door again, scraping across the wooden boards.

'They've found us!' The sound of groaning grew louder. The door shook violently, straining against its old hinges. 'They are going to come through.'

The witch's face paled as she looked at the door. 'Come, child. Find something heavy to put against the door.' Nym looked around desperately but there was nothing but old bones which she dared not touch. 'This,' said Ramona, moving towards the stone sarcophagus. She tried to move the heavy flat stone which served as a lid. Nym moved to help her. Despite their best efforts, it would not budge.

'Why have they found us?' Nym asked, trying to keep her fear from her voice. 'I thought we were safe here.'

'It is fate,' shrugged the woman.

'It's because I was sick, isn't it? I have offended the spirits,' said Nym. She let go of the lid. 'We're making it worse.' She retreated from the cold stone.

'Don't be foolish! This thing is too heavy anyway.' Ramona levelled a look at Nym. 'The dead don't care about this place, and the ancestors would see us live on. We should use whatever we can.'

Another booming thud echoed as some dead monstrosity hammered on the door again. The impact sent a cloud of dust swirling into the gloom. The wood was splintering, their hands and nails scraping against boards.

'It's not going to hold,' Nym told her.

'Old wood,' shrugged the witch. She moved to the door and braced it with her shoulder. Nym did not think her tiny frame would be much use. 'Come on then, girl. Help me.'

Nym reluctantly joined her pushing against the door with both hands. The snarling outside intensified, as if the dead could sense their warmth from beyond the door. It lurched inwards, the hinges starting to give, and the two women forced it back with all their strength.

Nym ground her teeth and dared a glance through one of the cracks in the door. She wished she hadn't. Dead eyes stared at her hungrily, mere inches away, separated only by the splintering boards of ancient wood. The old wood creaked and groaned under the weight of the dead, desperate to claw their way inside.

Suddenly, with an eruption of splinters, a hand burst through and seized a handful of her hair. She screamed as the dead hand wrenched her head into the door, trying to pull her head out through the ruptured wood. Another hand burst through the door lower down, clutching at emptiness.

The witch muttered to herself, a spell or a prayer in a foreign tongue. Nym could do nothing but desperately heave her weight against the door.

A strange clattering sound, and a clanging like a cow bell, or a smith's hammer striking at the forge, rang outside and she heard a wet thud. A splatter of something damp hit her head and for a dreadful moment she thought her scalp had been torn from her skull, but there was no pain. The hand clutching her hair went limp, and something fell onto her, tangling in her hair. She pulled her head away from the splintered hole and something dropped to the floor. It was moving.

She stared down in horror at a severed hand. It was still clenching and twitching. Long strands of her blonde hair still trapped between its fingers. It had been severed clean off at the wrist.

Beyond the door, voices were shouting. Through the splintered hole left by the dead hand, Nym watched an axe head chop down, followed by another wet thud.

There's someone out there!

'Help us!' she screamed. 'Please! Help us. We're in here.' She caught a glimpse of a man in a helmet, of armour glinting in the firelight outside.

'You can open the door. It's safe,' spoke a man's voice.

'Wait,' hissed the witch as Nym's hand moved to open the latch. 'Can you see? Are the dead gone?'

'The dead are slain,' assured the voice. 'But they will be back, we must move quickly.'

Nym peered through the hole. There were corpses littering the ground, hacked into a bloody mess. Warriors stood near the tomb in mail armour, some of their shields painted red with a black axe, others with a blue falcon. One man wore the snarling wolf of the king, their spears and axes blood splattered. She nodded to the witch that he spoke the truth.

'It's safe,' she whispered, her voice drenched in relief.

As the door opened Nym hurled her arms around the nearest warrior. There were tears in her eyes. 'Thank you,' she gasped as she embraced her saviour then stepped back. 'Thank the gods you came.'

'See,' said the witch. 'Ramona knows. The ancestors were watching over us. They kept us safe.' She nodded her thanks to the warriors as she emerged. 'The gods sent you to save us. I never doubted them.'

'It's you?' the warrior said, he sounded surprised. 'I know you, lass.'

Nym narrowed her eyes against the gloom. It was hard to see him in the dark, underneath all the blood and muck. His voice was familiar, but she couldn't put her finger on where she knew it from.

'It is you, isn't it? From Anchorage?' he asked, leaning forward to study her face. 'It's me — Wilhelm. Where's Jor?'

CHAPTER FORTY-ONE

The Death of Knowledge

The College had plunged into absolute chaos. Gideon found himself running with Jasper, the old shield strapped to his arm, the tall man shepherding the scholar into a courtyard ahead, Jasper's thick corded arms and the cold bronze of the old shield pushing him along.

In his panic, Gideon had barely registered his surroundings as they fled. All he could think of was those seemingly impossible corpses which had returned from the dead. They came at him over and over, the memory vivid before his waking eyes. *It is impossible. The dead are walking.*

All around him people were screaming, and realisation slowly dawned that they were his fellow scholars, all fleeing in terror. People were running everywhere he looked and he ran with them. Jasper seemed like a solid, calm sentinel in the tide of horror, his dark eyes darting around, searching for an avenue of escape. Behind them, driving his terror-stricken colleagues onward, came the dead.

Dead scholars lumbering after the living. Gideon flinched as one man leapt screaming onto another, dragging him down into the snow, tearing at his skin with his teeth. *These things are Cursed Ones. Oh gods, what is happening?*

A man lurched from a doorway. Gideon recognised him, but his face had lost all familiar expression. His innards had been pulled out through a gaping hole in his torso, blood dripping onto the snow with every step, entrails swinging back and forth like a gruesome pendulum of bloody chains. Gideon trembled at the sight of him, but Jasper brought his axe down, sending the corpse staggering back into the shadows.

A woman opened a door, bleary eyed and still half asleep. 'What's going on?' she asked.

Her face paled as she saw the approaching dead. Another scholar grasped her shoulders and shouted at her to run. Fire burned everywhere, the acrid smoke thick in the air. There were flames visible over the roofs of nearby College buildings, reaching up to the dark night. To Gideon's horror, he realised the blaze was likely *inside* the College buildings. The place was going up in flames.

They ran on, nearing a woman struggling on the ground, screaming piteously as one of the monsters dragged her down. It began furiously tearing at her with its inhuman claws, tearing her clothes, exposing her skin to begin feasting on her alive. She screamed, whimpering pleas for help.

Why is no one helping her?

No one tried to stop it; they all just ran. Another cursed scholar leapt upon her attacker, attempting to supplant the other and take his turn feeding on the poor woman, like a pair of wolves fighting over a wounded animal. The usurper was knocked away by a swipe of a bloodied hand. The first one roared its dominance and then turned its attention back to the woman, who was trying to crawl away. It pulled her back and tore a chunk of quivering flesh from the wound on her back and began chewing lazily.

Her screams intensified and Gideon averted his eyes, unable to look as they drew close. *She will become like them. She will be cursed,* he told himself as the guilt tore at his conscience. It was a poor excuse, and he knew it.

Jasper however changed direction and ran towards the screaming woman, and with a swing of his axe, dispatched the vile creature in a spray of misted blood. There was another wet thud and her screams fell ominously silent.

He killed her. What else could he do, it was mercy.

Jasper pushed him onwards and they followed the crowd of still living scholars. Former colleagues ripped into each other as the curse took hold, making fellow scholars turn on each other with a primal savagery. There were College guards amongst the crowd, sell-swords who took their silver from the College coffers. Some fought, cutting down the cursed and futilely grappling with

420

corpses. Most just ran like the rest. These creatures brought a terror which few had the courage to face.

The fallen dead rose all around. Corpses slowly clambered to their feet before lurching into motion. Their heads lolled to one side, mouths snarling and biting. Their arms outstretched, desperate to seize at the warmth of the living, desperate to sink their teeth into warm flesh. The slain cursed rose, as did the College folk who were killed before the curse took hold. Soon there would be more dead than living within the College walls.

Jasper cut down another Cursed One with a scything swing of his axe, and then smashed it away with the old bronze shield. The creature reeled backwards, gushing out an arc of blood as it fell. Jasper had already stepped over it and was pushing Gideon onward before the thing had stopped twitching.

Jasper drove him forward. Gideon was a large man—he had always been so, since he was a child—and he was slow. His short legs burned with every step, panting as he struggled to carry his paunch. It was sheer terror that kept him moving—that and Jasper. Without the foreigner, he would have no doubt been caught by one of the fell creatures as he stood watching them in dumbstruck horror. Indeed, if it were not for Jasper, Gideon was certain he would have perished long ago.

They finally found themselves before the large building that housed the council chambers. It seemed the crowd had swept them there, many fleeing there in the hope that this place would prove some kind of sanctuary. It was the centre of their scholarly existence. He saw Councillor Merwyl standing with a handful of others on the building's steps. The College elders were surrounded by guards. Everyone was shouting, councillors watching in disbelief as the growing horde bore down on them. Merwyl was shouting, trying to direct the fleeing College folk.

'The Histories!' he cried out. 'The Great Histories must be preserved!'

'You! Yes, you! Fetch water,' someone else shouted. 'We must put out that fire.'

'Preserve the archives!'

'Save what you can!'

The huge fire blazed behind the approaching dead, corpses silhouetted against flame as they came inexorably onward.

So much work… so much knowledge… all lost.

A man Gideon recognised as Master Hoartwyn stepped in front of them. 'You heard the councillor!' he bellowed. 'Get to the archive. We must—'

The master's words turned to a gurgling shriek as a Cursed One grabbed his hair and wrenched his head back. It flung the master against the wooden walls of the council building with a *crack*. The master went limp and collapsed to the ground, the creature turning a sickening grin on them, its mouth dripping with blood.

Jasper's axe crunched down. 'Go!' he shouted.

'Where?' Gideon spluttered. His mouth was dry. It felt like he hadn't spoken for some time, stunned to silence. He turned to Jasper, gripped by urgency. 'We need to get to my room. We need to save my work.'

Jasper looked down at him with dark eyes. The reflection of the flames gave him a baleful gaze. 'You are wise-man, Gideon. But even wise-man stand behind warrior in battle. Let warrior lead. We need to run.'

Gideon tried to object, but in his heart, he knew the College was doomed. Any who lingered here would die, eaten by those *things*. His spirit deflated at the realisation. All that he knew and loved, all that they had worked for would either burn or be lost to the dead. So many great minds were already gone, so much knowledge, destroyed. He felt sick.

'Show me way out,' Jasper commanded.

Gideon pointed back toward the glow of flames where folk were screaming and dying. 'The gates are that way.'

'No. Too far. This way.' Jasper urged the rotund scholar away from the fire and towards precious archives.

'Where are we going?' Gideon panted.

'Boatman,' Jasper replied.

'There will be no boatman,' Gideon told him. 'And the wharves are near the gates.'

'We swim then.'

'Wait! Councillor Uriah…' Gideon said as an idea crept into his head. 'He has been surveying the river. He believed the dead were fouling the water…'

'We not go back,' snapped Jasper. 'We not save your archive. If you want to live, we run.'

'No, you don't understand,' said Gideon, 'He had a boat, a canoe of sorts.'

'Where?'

'He usually pulled it up on the banks. I know where it is.'

'We go. You show us canoe.'

There were no dead in their path — the carnage had not yet reached this corner of the College grounds. Scholars came wandering out from their quarters to stand in the snow and watch the flames, muttering to each other about the fuss. Gideon tried to warn them, telling them to run, but most just stood in awe, looks of concern and confusion on their faces as they watched the spreading flames.

The fools, they don't know what is coming for them.

He screamed at them to run, told them the dead were coming, but they merely looked at him like he was a madman. It didn't take long for the screams to begin behind the scholar and the warrior as they ran on. The cursed had found fresh meat.

They must be right behind us.

He dared not look back.

Gideon's chamber was in a dormitory complex beside the river. Jasper kicked the door open and hurled Gideon inside, slamming the door shut just before something crashed into the other side. A roar of frustration reached them from outside, then it was hammering and scratching at the wooden boards, trying to get in.

'This way,' he managed, indicating down the corridor with a trembling hand.

The hallway was dark and the dormitory complex was quiet. Doors lined the corridor, all closed. Gideon assumed folk were asleep, blissfully ignorant of the slaughter unfolding behind nearby.

We should warn them, he thought, *but would they believe me? The others didn't. Would trying to explain slow us down, get us killed?* Despite his guilt, he knew it would be pointless. They would not listen and then it would be too late. *I must escape. Their fate is their own.*

The creature outside continued its assault on the door. Surely that would wake some of them.

'Here is my chamber,' Gideon said, peering inside.

'No time,' Jasper commanded with a scowl. 'Where is boat?'

'It's out there,' Gideon waved. 'I will only be a moment, I promise. Some personal effects is all.' He hurried into his room.

'That thing get in soon. We must go!' growled Jasper.

Gideon ignored the man's objections and scooped a handful of books into a bag. He ran to his shelf and crammed in as many of his scrolls as he could. There was a stack of books on his desk, and he paused a moment, looking at them thoughtfully. Some were Luthor's. He snatched them up and waddled back into the corridor.

He heard a crash as the door they had entered had finally given in.

It's inside!

They ran from the sound, Jasper following the scholar down to the door that opened to the river. He used to sit beside it and read as the boats passed by.

The creature loosed a heart stopping howl that echoed along the narrow passage toward them and Jasper pushed Gideon to move faster. They reached the door and burst through, icy cold air biting the skin of his face as they emerged back into the snow.

'There,' Gideon said, pointing with his elbow, his hands too overburdened with possessions to be useful. Pulled up high onto the riverbank was a slender canoe with barely enough room for the both of them. Gideon dumped his books and the bag in the narrow boat and helped Jasper haul it into the water. A horrible scream peeled out from the dormitories behind them and they both rushed to clamber into the boat. Water sloshed into the bottom of the vessel as they managed to climb in and float out onto the river. He was not a small man, and neither was Jasper, and with the two of them and all his books, the canoe rode low in the dark water. Jasper frowned at the books he had tucked into satchels in the hull.

'I had to save my work,' Gideon said defensively.

'If we sink, you lose your work, and you probably die.' Jasper shrugged, dipping an oar into the water. 'I swim good.'

The man from Myhar paddled carefully and the canoe moved out into the safety of the river. Gideon prayed the water would not pour over the sides and plunge the tiny boat beneath the surface. He selected a particularly large tome from his bag and regarded it a moment. With a shrug, he threw it over the side. The canoe somehow seemed less precariously low and Jasper grunted with amusement.

'Better,' he said. 'Not worth saving?'

'Probably not. It was a dull read,' he said with a smile. He felt giddy with relief at reaching the safety of the river. He didn't know if he wanted to laugh or cry, but his body took over and he chuckled involuntarily. The weird elation was short lived and a sombre sense of gravity descended upon him.

'Jasper... I would be dead if it wasn't for you,' Gideon admitted, turning to glance carefully over his shoulder. 'You saved me back there.'

'You are friend. I do not want friend Gideon to die.'

Gideon smiled at that. 'Thank you, friend.'

Jasper nodded in return and paddled the boat forwards as Gideon watched the College slip by. Screams reached them even out here, framed by orange flames leaping high into the night. It looked like whole buildings at the eastern end of the complex had been consumed by fire. How much of the Great Histories would be lost this night? Would the fire spread and consume the entire College? Would the archives burn? He hoped not, and shuddered at the thought of centuries of knowledge and records vanishing in one fell swoop. It would be a great loss to Arnar.

Greater than the loss of learning was the loss of life. What if the dead escaped the College? Thousands would die in the city, and he found himself hoping the creatures would be trapped inside the compound, burning with it. He put his head in his hands, his eyes gritted with soot and ash, his eyes itching from the tears he had shed for his colleagues and his home.

CHAPTER FORTY-TWO

The East Wharfs

'Here we are, hunter. The east wharves,' Duncan said, indicating ahead with his chin, his hands occupied by his staff.

'Finally,' Bjorn muttered. 'There are the boats.'

'What about Nym, and Finn?' Seth asked. He had been reliant on Bjorn to help him walk since the young woman had run off after her brother, but he hadn't accepted they were truly gone.

'There was nothing we could do,' Duncan told him again. 'They know where we were headed. If they survive, they may yet meet us here.'

'Perhaps,' Bjorn agreed, but Duncan could see the doubt plain on his face.

He felt bad for Seth, especially since the man had told them his tale as they walked through the city. Seth had spoken of how his father had died fighting to save them, a one-armed tavern keeper against the cut-throats of the city's gutters. Now he had lost his other companions, the beautiful girl the greatest shame in Duncan's estimation. Seth had lost everybody he held dear, and all he had left was a lute in a case. No wonder he clung to it so fiercely.

Duncan liked Seth. Few had paid him much heed since his return, though Duncan wondered if Seth would have treated him so kindly if he had been able to see his crippled body. He knew he'd lost most of the youth from his face, and his peculiar hair that had been leeched of its colour seemed to put people off. He had become an outcast amongst his own, but not with Seth. Had he made a friend that day in the infirmaries? He felt he wanted to comfort Seth if he could, and if giving him some hope of finding the girl and her brother was what he needed, then so be it.

The hunter crouched behind a barrel, peering onto the waterfront. Duncan thought it unnecessary, as the strange invisible aura of protection around him meant the dead could not see them anyway. He'd been pondering the phenomenon since he first noticed it, and his lie about his staff seemed to be working. The ignorant fools actually believed it!

They were so fabulously uneducated, he doubted any of them could read a single letter. They believed their quaint superstitions; the idea of magic and spirits haunting their everyday lives. He chuckled to himself and hid a smile. Though he wore an amulet too, but it was no more than a relic of his upbringing, a habit borne of the stories his parents had drummed into him as a boy. He knew better of course. Still, the protective phenomenon puzzled him.

Was it an effect of the ritual? If so, it had evidently not worked for Eldrick. Or was it some boon from the whispering presence that haunted his consciousness? At least the aura was some evidence that the voice wasn't just his mind slipping into insanity.

You have doubts? whispered the voice.

'No,' Duncan muttered. 'Show me the way. Guide me.'

'What?' Bjorn asked, whipping around to look at him.

'Nothing,' Duncan smiled. 'Just a prayer to the gods.'

The hunter grunted and turned back to his study of the wharves ahead.

We must discard this one now he has served his purpose, said the voice. *He is too dangerous. Let the dead take him, and his foul companion.*

'When?' Duncan whispered.

As soon as possible. Their purpose is at an end. They should not leave the city alive lest he interfere with our purpose.

Duncan's eyes flicked questioningly to Seth. The blinded man waited patiently.

That one could prove useful, as a companion or a thrall perhaps. He will surely be honoured to stand by your side and join our purpose.

What purpose is that? Duncan thought.

Great things await. All will become clear.

Duncan's looked back to the hunter and the Wildman crouched beside him.

Get rid of them, hissed the voice. *Let them join the ranks of the dead. They are not worthy.*

'Do you think they are alive, Duncan?' Seth asked, breaking the scholar's reverie.

'I do hope so,' Duncan answered truthfully, if only so he might regain his chance to claim Nym as his own. 'I hope they both get out.' He offered Seth a weak smile, which of course, went unseen.

'I hope so too,' Seth replied, his voice bleak.

The first light of dawn edged into the sky to the east, a smear of crimson on the horizon marking the sunrise. *An omen of blood*, thought Duncan.

The coming dawn brought a frail promise of salvation from the horrors of the dead moon, a vague hope that the sunlight would chase the risen dead back into their graves. The snow had stopped, for now, but the sky was still heavy with broken leaden clouds. The dawn light crept out from the horizon, slowly casting a dim wash of colour over Arn.

On the river, Duncan could see longships coated in snow. They were rafted together in the deeper water to create a moored pontoon, and there were no large boats docked at the wharves. These docks were usually for fishermen and barges. On the far side of the wharves, a shingle spit jutted out from the shore to create a little harbour, and beached beside a lone longship were several small rowing boats. Duncan presumed they were used by sailors to row back and forth between the longships moored offshore.

There were half a dozen dead milling aimlessly around the waterfront, all of them seemingly oblivious to their presence as they crouched and watched from the shadows of a dockside warehouse.

'One of those should get us out of this accursed city,' Bjorn said, gesturing to the row boats by the spit. He eyed the lumbering corpses warily. 'If we head over to the far side and down onto that beach, we can push one of them out and be away from this gods forsaken place.' He turned back to Duncan and Seth. 'Agreed?'

Duncan nodded.

'But what about Nym and Finn?' asked Seth again. Bjorn threw a piteous look at him, then shrugged at Duncan helplessly.

'There are other boats. If they make it, they can follow us,' was all the hunter could say to comfort him.

Seth hung his head and Duncan patted his shoulder with his

free hand, the other clutched tightly at his staff for balance. What else could he do? It would do the man no good to tell him they were likely dead already.

They set off cautiously across the waterfront, Bjorn in the lead. The hunter kept looking back at him, keeping Duncan close, not wanting to stray too far ahead. The Wildman stalked at the hunter's heels, clutching his crude spear, and Duncan wondered if that savage understood Bjorn's caution, or whether his primitive mind was just imitating him. In any case, he had no desire to travel anywhere with the filthy man, and he needed a way to get rid of him. He followed the hunter so closely, it would be impossible to...

An idea dawned in his mind as the sun lightened the sky, the voice nudging him towards it.

Yes, that could work, Duncan thought.

They descended down a steep muddy bank onto the shingle beach. Duncan again regretted leaving his crutches behind as he laboriously hauled himself across the loose stones. Bjorn, still guiding Seth by the arm, reached the boats first and selected the larger of the two. He placed his shoulder against its hull and began heaving it to the water. At first it didn't seem to move, and then slowly it began to slide, the stones screeching in protest as they scraped its bottom. Tung joined him and strained against its weight beside the hunter. The bow of the boat began to float.

'One last push will do it,' declared Bjorn. 'Ready —'

'Wait! Let me climb in first, I'll never get in on my own,' Duncan insisted.

The hunter frowned at him and then nodded, lifting him from his feet and placing him in the boat. 'Right, you next,' he said grasping Seth's arm once more to help him aboard.

'Nym!' Duncan shouted.

The hunter spun around to glare at him.

'Nym!' he called again. 'There, I see them!'

Seth paused, moving his head as he tried to see, or catch a sound that might confirm Duncan's assertions. 'Nym? Are you sure?' He pulled back on Bjorn's grip, nearly losing his balance.

'Where?' Bjorn demanded narrowing his eyes back towards the warehouses and the streets beyond.

'There!' Duncan said, pointing towards an empty street. 'I swear it was them. They must be too frightened to come out.'

The hunter frowned at the Wildman, and Tung just stared blankly at him, as if wondering what was going on. He had obviously seen nothing and the hunter's brow furrowed.

'Please,' Seth pleaded. 'We must get to them.'

'I don't see them,' the hunter insisted.

'They must be hiding from the dead,' Duncan suggested, putting all his effort into sounding convincingly hopeful. 'They were right there. Perhaps they didn't see we are here.'

'Maybe they did but are too afraid to move because of the dead?' Seth suggested, a spark of hope in his voice.

Bjorn sighed. 'Come, show me where you saw them.'

Duncan looked back up the shingle beach and the muddy path leading down to it with a pained expression. 'I don't think I can get back up this, and Seth can't see where he's going.'

'Well what do you want me to do?' Bjorn hissed at him, glancing around, eying the dead loitering nearby.

'There aren't many of them.' Duncan nodded at the milling corpses. 'They would be easy to avoid. You're both quick and you can fight the odd one if it comes to it, can't you?'

Bjorn began to shake his head.

'We'll stay here with the boat, one last shove and it will be away,' Duncan suggested. 'You go fetch them and we'll be ready and waiting.'

'No,' said Bjorn.

'Please,' Seth begged. 'You are Bjorn, hero of many songs. The great huntsman. I have heard tales of your bravery and skill. I know you can do it, and if you do, I will make you a song that will be sung for a hundred years. Please, save them. They are all I have.'

Bjorn regarded the dead, weighing his chances. Eventually he nodded. 'Fine,' he snarled. 'I'll get them but be ready to heave those oars. We'll be running, and those things will be after us.'

'We'll be ready,' Duncan nodded, making a show of determination with his face.

The hunter turned, stones clattering as he ran back up the beach trailed by his Wildman shadow.

Duncan smirked. *Fools.*

***

A Ritual of Flesh

Dead faces turned, eyes trained on Bjorn before he had even reached the top of the muddy bank, the nearest dead snarling viciously as they lurched into motion. There were three nearby, and two further along the wharf, all of them now aware of his presence. They were spread out, they were slow, and he was Bjorn. The lad was right—these few would be no match for him and Tung.

Tung followed close behind, and he glanced back to see the Wildman's look of fearful bewilderment. Tung likely had no idea what was going on, and he was looking nervously back at the waiting boat.

I'm sorry you followed me into this mess, my friend, but following me was your choice.

Bjorn gave the dead a wide berth, threading between and easily out-pacing them. He quickly reached the entrance onto the street where the scholar had indicated and found it littered with nets and wicker crab cages. It was narrow and crammed with empty sailor's taverns, sail makers and fish traders. For all the debris on the road, there was no sign of Nym or her brother.

Niggling doubt set in.

Something didn't feel right, and it hadn't since the scholar first claimed to have seen them. He threw a quick look back down to the beach to where the blind man and the cripple waited with the boat.

'Nym?' Bjorn hissed. 'Come on, lass; come out. We have a boat. We have to get going.'

Nothing.

His words brought no reply, but the dead heard him though. All around, from alleys, darkened doorways, and around the walls of the houses, corpses stumbled into view, the street filling with the snarls of the dead.

'Nym!' he shouted, giving up all pretence at stealth. 'If you're there, it's your last chance, or I'm going back without you.'

Still there was no reply. *She's not here. Either that scholar was badly mistaken, seeing things, or he lied.*

'Shit,' snarled Bjorn.

Suddenly Tung began squealing and hooting, gesturing franticly. Bjorn cursed again. His anger flared and he ran for the beach.

The blind musician had already pushed the boat out and

431

clambered aboard, he now sat beside the scholar, but they had not waited.

'Fucking cowards!' he shouted as he and Tung hurtled back down to the waterfront. He couldn't believe he'd fallen for such a ruse. Why leave them? He had done nothing but help the both of them.

The scholar hauled on the oars, and the little boat surged away from the beach and out onto the river. He knew they had no intention of returning to shore.

'Bastards!' the hunter bellowed.

The dead swarmed down from the street, slowly surrounding them. Every moment that passed closed off another avenue of escape as they became choked with corpses. One lurched into their path from the direction of the waterfront and Tung stabbed with his spear, skewering it to the spot. Bjorn chopped his axe into its face as he ran past. The impact made the thing reel back and they ran on.

They reached the muddy bank and began scrambling down, as behind them, a snarling horde burst onto the waterfront. The mud and snow were slippery and treacherous, his boots sending stones spraying as he sprinted towards one of the remaining boats.

'You fucking cowards!' he bellowed again.

Bjorn slammed his shoulder against the hull of one of the remaining row boats, the stones shifting with a harsh hiss as the boat edged into the water. Behind them the dead were tumbling down the bank onto the stony beach. Some had already regained their feet and were slowly lurching toward them. The hull of the boat began to float and he called for Tung to jump. With one last heave they were afloat and Bjorn splashed into the shallows and scrambled over the side.

'Shit,' he spat. 'There's no fucking oars.' He spotted them laying on the beach, no more than a few dozen feet away, but they were too close to the approaching dead now.

Why did they do this? Why have they tried to leave us for dead? The little rowing boat drifted impotently out onto the river, at the mercy of the current.

Ahead Bjorn watched the other boat's oars dipping and rising rhythmically. They were already several hundred yards away, heading to downstream to the south east and away into the delta.

The first of the dead splashed into the tenebrous water, flailing around, as if unsure what to do. Still, they were relentless, piling into the cold waters in pursuit.

'I hope they can't swim,' Bjorn muttered. 'And I hope they don't float either.' His heart rate slowed as he watched the dead floundering in the shallows.

The boat drifted away from shore, carried out by the tidal currents and by the waning impetus of his final heave. Tung bobbed his head up and down as he watched the dead intently, the boat rocking gently from side to side. Bjorn reached over and tried to paddle with his hand, but progress was pitiful.

'I hate boats,' he said with a sigh. Tung glanced at him a moment before turning his attention back to the dead at the shoreline. 'And I hate this city. And, I hate those bastards.' He watched the boat ahead pull further and further away. He cupped his hands over his mouth and shouted, 'Duncan, Seth — I swear to the gods I *will* find you. You *will* die for that, you bastards!'

CHAPTER FORTY-THREE

Battle Song

'Lord, they're coming.'

Arnulf glanced around. 'How many?'

The man's face was pale. There was little hope in his heart. 'A lot. Maybe hundreds.'

'We need to keep moving,' he bellowed. 'So much for the temple district being clear.'

The rest of Arnulf's survivors were taking a moment to catch their breath. They had moved quickly through the darkness, not stopping until now. The men and women he led were weary.

'It is what it is,' Hafgan said from beside him. 'We got this far. There could have been a lot more in our path. This was still a wise route, lord.' As the big warrior spoke, he watched the skulking cursed creatures. They had stalked them from the rooftops since they first set foot amongst the old mounds of the temple district.

'Why don't they attack us?' asked Arnulf.

'Perhaps they fear us,' Hafgan suggested. 'They will come, have no doubt. They are cunning. They are waiting for their chance.'

'Let's not give them one,' Arnulf replied.

Shields clattered, weapons clinked against armour, and the brave few he led made ready to continue their flight through the sacred places of Arn. Arnulf watched his warriors hurry two women away from a burial mound to join them.

A totem stone of Hjort, crowned with the mighty skull of some great stag, dominated the grove. He kissed his amulet and whispered a quick prayer to that god of luck and speed.

'The gods watch us,' Hafgan said, seeing his lord looking at the totem.

'A good omen?' asked Arnulf.

'Perhaps,' replied Hafgan. 'Let's give them a good show.' He gave Arnulf a weary smile.

The undead horde that the other warrior had spoken of could be heard not far off, approaching at a steady rate from the far side of the grove. If they had arrived any later, he would have found the area choked with corpses and the mound breached, the women surely torn to pieces. It seemed the gods had brought them by just in time.

'This way to the Citadel,' he shouted, pointing with his bloodied axe down a wide avenue which led away from the sound of the dead and appeared to lead straight to the foot of the Citadel's palisades. The high wooden ramparts were silhouetted against the gash of red dawn that broke the eastern horizon.

'Blood in the sky,' commented Hafgan. 'Now that *is* a dark omen, lord.'

Wilhelm ran over, and Arnulf looked at the terrified young woman he led with him. Behind her walked an older woman, a mystic by the look of her. She nodded at Arnulf, her face was set with a grim look, her lips pressed together in a hard line.

His warriors had heard their screams and had seen the dead trying to force their way into the old burial mound. It had indeed seemed the gods had fated his arrival. He feared their displeasure at allowing the wretched dead to desecrate that ancient resting place. He ordered his men to cut down the dead, to rescue those innocents from a terrible fate, and maybe the gods would smile on him again.

Wilhelm was talking to the girl, and there seemed to be a familiarity between them.

'Wilhelm,' Arnulf called. 'You know this young woman?'

'Aye, lord, I do. She is the charge of an old friend. I know her from Anchorage. She says she was with others who had come from the Citadel, but they told her the Citadel had fallen.'

Arnulf's heart sank at those words. 'Is it true? You were at the Citadel?'

Her hands trembled but she straightened her shoulders. 'Yes, lord... I mean no, lord.' She glanced at Wilhelm, as if wondering what to say next.

'You are safe now,' he said, trying to reassure her. 'Please, tell me your name?'

'Nym,' she whispered.

'And you?'

'I am Ramona,' said the mystic.

'We are headed to the Citadel. We need to know what's there. Can you tell me what you saw?'

Nym shook her head. 'I wasn't there, lord. We were down by the docks when the dead came. Jor died and we fled into the city. A hunter found us. He said he was Bjorn and he had come from the Citadel with some others. He said the dead were there. I didn't see it, lord, but they did. He said the king was dead.'

Arnulf cursed. 'The king is dead? Are you sure?'

'I don't know, lord. It's what the hunter said.'

'Where are they now, this hunter and the others?'

'I don't know,' she said, shrinking back a little from the barrage of questions. 'We got separated. I can't find Finn. I need to find my brother.'

'Where were they headed?' Wilhelm asked gently.

'The fishing wharves.'

'The east wharves?' asked Wilhelm.

The girl nodded. 'The dead couldn't see us, but then they attacked us. Finn ran away. I need to find him.'

Luthor stood nearby, listening intently to the girl's words.

'The horde behind us is coming from that way, lord,' Wilhelm said to Arnulf over the blonde woman's head.

'Did this hunter say if any warriors remained alive at the Citadel?' Arnulf asked, looking ahead to the palisades.

'I don't know.' Her voice began to crack. 'That's just what they said.' She broke down in tears and the mystic took the girl into her arms, scowling at Arnulf as he stepped away, leaving Wilhelm beside them. Luthor drifted closer. Something about the girl's story seemed to intrigue him.

'Bring them with us and keep them safe,' Arnulf said to Wilhelm as gestured to his warriors to continue moving. Their reprieve was at an end. Wilhelm nodded in reply, hefting his shield and spear.

'Do we still make for the Citadel?' Hafgan asked.

'What choice do we have?' grimaced Arnulf.

The Citadel loomed up in front of them, perched on its high hill, an ancient hillfort of old people. The sky was lightening behind it, the dawn chasing away the shadows. Snow lay thick on the ground but had stopped falling. It told a tale of the night, imprints revealing the chaos that gripped the city. The black filth of Arn's streets showed through where it had been disturbed.

Arnulf and his companions left their own black footprints behind them as they hurried onwards. There were other footprints, evidence of violent disruptions and ominous smears of crimson blood staining the perfect white. In the haunting stillness of dawn lay a foreboding and silent tale of the night's passing, a terrible chronicle of slaughter and death. Arnulf saw the doom of a city written in that snow.

They emerged from the stone marked causeways and mound dotted groves, a place strangely detached from the surrounding city, and spilled onto streets lined with thatched roofed round houses and the small halls belonging to Arn's wealthier folk. The dead stalked those streets. At first there were just one or two, easily dispatched and hacked down by the mail clad warriors who charged from the fleeing gloom bringing swift retribution, axes scything, spears thrusting. Arnulf followed the wide thoroughfare towards the Citadel's gates, now clearly visible in front of them.

His warriors were weary. He had pushed them hard through the temple district. Luthor and the two women rescued from the mound were struggling to keep up, helped along by Wilhelm and some of the others.

'Arnulf!' Hafgan exclaimed between laboured breaths. He was looking ahead.

Arnulf could see it for himself. There were warriors there, and his heart dared to hope for an end to all this. There were perhaps twenty of them, some holding blazing torches, their shields locked into a thin shield wall around the gates. The warriors seemed to be protecting a small group emerging from the gates, and a few surviving townsfolk. The folk of Arn had no doubt fled to the protection of the Citadel. The group left the gates and the protective arc of shields began to retreat north toward the river.

There must be boats, Arnulf thought.

Arnulf also saw what lay between him and those shields, what those shields were defending against. Between his ragged band of weary warriors and those raised shields were the dead. They only barely outnumbered the living, but more were closing in.

Again, Arnulf touched his amulet and thanked Hjort for guiding them. It seemed that his arrival was fated. The warriors must have only just emerged. They couldn't have been there long, otherwise the place would have been swarming with the dead by now. He felt a glimmer of hope. Just maybe, the gods were watching.

'I see them. Keep moving,' he called to his weary warriors. 'We hit them hard, smash through before those things know we're here. We add our shields to that wall and fight out way to the boats. You got that?'

He heard mumbled acknowledgements. Those too tired to speak just nodded.

'One last push, lads,' Hafgan urged.

There was a cheer from the beleaguered shield wall as Arnulf's warriors charged. They struck hard and fast. The dead had not noticed their arrival, so focused was their malice on the warm flesh behind those shields. Shields smashed dead flesh, corpses sprawling to the ground under the impact. Axes chopped down, the dead caught and crushed between two walls of wood and steel. Arnulf brought the hammer and the Citadel's shields were the anvil upon which the dead were smote, sent back to the halls of Old Night.

It was pure savagery. Arnulf lost himself in vengeance, the details blurred. He remembered glimpses of grey pallid flesh, suddenly riven apart and mangled into a gory ruin. He remembered grasping fingers, distorted dead faces. At some point he threw down his shield, using both hands to swing his axe around him in a wild slaughter. His arms burned by the end but still he kept swinging. He remembered the splatter of dead clotting blood. He heard the snarling of the dead, but he roared louder, screaming defiance as he swung his axe home.

Then came the cheering. He looked around him at the ruined bodies; arms, heads and legs riven from their twitching torsos. The mouth of a severed head snapped open and shut and he kicked it away. The snowy ground before the gates had become a churned mire of black slush, but it was clear of the dead for now.

The peace would not last, for already corpses came stumbling towards them along the avenues that converged on the Citadel's gates. The dead emerged from every direction, drawn by the sound of battle, and soon the mud before the gates would again be filled with the walking dead.

'Fall back!' came a shout. It was Hafgan. The shield wall edged backward.

'Join their wall,' bellowed Arnulf. He heard the staccato sound of shields clattering together. Arnulf found his shield in the snow and snatched it up, running to join his comrades.

Warriors stood shoulder to shoulder; their shields raised to protect the man beside him. The red shields of Arnulf, mingled with the blue shields of Fergus's remaining shield-maidens, all beside the snarling wolf of Varg emblazoned on the shields of the king's men.

'Steady,' Hafgan called. 'We fall back to the river but stay tight, stay ready.'

The man under guard was shepherded towards the water by the same group of guards that had emerged from the gates. But now Arnulf could see the man they guarded.

'Thank the gods you came,' he called when he saw Arnulf commanding the new arrivals. 'I don't know how much longer we could hold them.'

Arnulf let another take his place in the shield wall and approached. 'Chancellor Alfric, where is the king? We need to get out of the city.'

'Aye, that we do. Men are saying the king is dead. We have not been able to find him, it is possible. These things...'

'I tried to warn you!' Arnulf snapped, letting his anger and fatigue get the better of him. 'Gods, I tried. I told you what we saw and now it's here.'

Something in the tone of Arnulf's voice made a guard lower his spear, ready to defend the chancellor, but Alfric waved the guard away. 'You spoke true, Lord Arnulf. You were right that day. I can barely believe what my eyes have seen.'

'Where are the ships?' Arnulf asked looking to the river.

'We managed to signal one of the boats that came in close. It wouldn't dock. They've seen the dead, they're not fools. But they said one of the prince's warships is on its way. It's coming to the shore, it should be able to beach and get people out.'

Men stood at the riverside, waving torches as a ship surged towards the banks. A small crowd of terrified townsfolk huddled by the water waiting for rescue to end their nightmare, the warriors of the shield wall were all that stood between those piteous folk and a grisly end at the hands of the dead. More dead were coming, slowly and not many, but they were coming.

The first of the dead reached the shields as the ship ground to a halt in the shallows. The dead came slowly, sparse and spread out, spears did little but knock them back or skewer them in place. It was the axes that hacked and chopped, dismembering the monstrosities piece by piece until finally they could no longer animate their wretched bodies.

People began splashing into the river, wading out to try and reach the waiting ship. Panic gripped them as danger pushed from behind and salvation lay so close at hand. Some just stood waiting to be told what to do, too tired to think, while the Citadel's warriors shouted at them to make way and let the chancellor through.

It was then they struck.

While the shield wall slowly edged backward, occupied by a handful of corpses, and the townsfolk stood defenceless by the river with only a few warriors to guard them, the Cursed Ones took their chance.

They leapt from rooftop perches, several of the creatures tearing through the snow, howling and screeching with their bestial fury. Some hurled themselves into the shields and died alongside the corpses, while others tried to run and leap over the shields. Most were caught and impaled but a few somehow made it over.

Rather than turning, it ran on, hurtling toward the folk of Arn beside the river, and the chancellor, protected by three of the Citadel's warriors. Wilhelm was there too, watching over Nym, Ramona and Luthor.

'Hold the wall!' Arnulf bellowed as he broke off and sprinted to aid them. Four of the creatures had broken through, but only one was enough to wreak terrible havoc amongst townsfolk.

The creatures approached like a pack of wolves, attempting to split the crowd and separate the weak. *Foul, cunning wretches!*

The first was taken in the throat by a good spear thrust from an exhausted looking man amongst the survivors. It seemed they weren't as defenceless as Arnulf had assumed. These people had survived the night, not through blind luck, but by taking their fate into their own hands. They were fighters.

The other creatures shrieked as one of their pack was slain, then leapt vengefully at the man. He had no chance, screaming as one of the cursed tore bloody furrows with inhuman claws. Another tore his throat out with its teeth.

Arnulf reached the man too late to save him, but he disembowelled one of the things with a wide rising cleave of his savage axe. The cursed wretch fell, mewling pathetically as its entrails splattered onto its feet.

Wilhelm speared another, forcing it down into the snow and pinned it there. A woman set upon another creature, hacking it with a hatchet until it was still. The last one tore away through the crowd, like a hound let loose amongst fowl. People scattered from its path, screaming and pushing, shoving each other in sheer panic. An arrow struck the beast in the shoulder, the feathered shaft flying in from nowhere. Arnulf spun around to find a grizzled College mercenary lowering his bow. The creature roared in pain but still bounded onwards.

All Arnulf could do was watch in horror as the thing lashed out at any who were too slow to get out of its path. It charged towards a screaming girl, only a child, but it was checked by a warrior's axe. The chancellor's guard had barely left his side during the chaos, and did nothing to help as Arnulf and the townsfolk fought the creatures off. He gave them a glowering look and spat into the snow.

Cowards.

Only one man amongst them had the courage to wade into the fight. He was a huscarl, and it was he who saved the girl. Her sobbing mother snatched the girl up in her arms and hurried her away as Arnulf stalked towards the chancellor's warriors, his bloodied axe hanging from one hand, his blood boiling.

'Why didn't you fight?' Arnulf roared.

The warriors shrank away from his words, glancing at each other as if they had no answers or excuses.

'The chancellor boards first. We need to get him to safety,' one of them insisted.

Arnulf lashed out and struck him with the back of his fist. 'No! You fight!' he snarled and turned on the chancellor, gesturing at the stranded townsfolk. 'What about them? We need to save these people. What good are warriors if we let innocent folk die? You tell your men to fight. We need to hold here until everyone is on board. We save as many as we can.'

'That's madness,' gasped the warrior he'd hit.

Arnulf laughed manically. 'Yes, it is!'

'Lord Arnulf is right,' the chancellor said suddenly. 'We must stand here and get these people on that ship. Another will come for us.' He looked at the growing press of dead battling the shields of the warriors before him, then turned to Arnulf. 'Can we hold them?'

'We are here to defend Arnar. We have fought these things all night, and for *my* warriors, this is not for the first time. We will hold, lord chancellor.'

With a nod of acknowledgement from the chancellor, Arnulf stalked away into the crowd of refugees. Some amongst them had only survived the night by fighting desperately with improvised weapons, others had armed themselves with axes and old spears. The women, as stoic and well-armed as the men, stood protectively over crying children. Arnulf thought it a miracle any child had survived the night. They must truly be blessed by the gods to have lived through the horrors of the dead, but looking at those fierce protectors, he suspected having such strong parents certainly helped. He nodded at a woman cradling a baby in one arm and holding an old spear in her other hand, struck by a wave of sadness that he had not had not arrived in time to save his own family. He cuffed a tear from his eye and looked away.

'Arnulf!' Hafgan called from the edge of the fighting. 'This one is wounded.'

Haf led a man by the arm, tired looking and dressed in filthy clothes. He had been unlucky enough to get too close to that last cursed wretch and had a slash across his arm. Arnulf stared at the man a long moment, regarding him with pity—they all knew what fate lay ahead of him.

'I am sorry,' said Arnulf with a grave voice. He turned away from the man and back to the chancellor. 'You need to kill him, quickly. He will turn soon.'

'We can't just *kill* him,' Alfric objected, wide eyed.

'That man must die before he turns on us. He will become one of *them*,' insisted Arnulf. The chancellor shook his head, his mouth opening and closing.

He hasn't the will to do what must be done.

Arnulf turned back to the wounded man who looked up at

him with resignation in his eyes. 'Listen, you have two choices. I can kill you now and I'll make it quick and painless, or you run back into the city and take your chances with the dead, but you cannot stay here. I am sorry. You *will* turn and you are too dangerous to remain amongst us.'

The man trembled, tears streaming down his face. 'Do it,' he whimpered. 'Kill me — don't let me become like them.'

No one spoke for a moment, the only sound coming from the approaching dead and the warriors in the shield wall.

'Kneel, friend,' Arnulf said. The man did as he was told, trembling despite himself. As the man closed his eyes, Arnulf thought he faced his fate with bravery.

The axe swung down and the man's head thumped on the ground and rolled away. Blood erupted from his neck and his body fell limp into the mud and snow.

'There must have been another way,' Alfric cried out, a sickened look on his face.

'I wish there was,' said Arnulf.

'You are a hard man, Arnulf.'

He grunted and walked away from the body. There was nothing he could say. He vowed then not to let any man or woman meet the same fate as his son.

'He killed his own son to save him from joining the dead,' he heard Hafgan say. 'Arnulf will do what needs to be done.'

He kept walking, ignoring the wave of sadness as he thought of Ewolf. There had been no choice. His son was at peace, amongst his fathers in the halls of the dead. He had saved him from the fate of rising again as an undead corpse. There was no dignity in that terrible fate.

I saved him, he told himself.

He left the townsfolk to dismember the dead, destroying the bodies of the fallen before they could rise again behind his warrior's ranks.

Those warriors holding the shield wall still struggled against the advancing corpses. He looked out toward the gates of the Citadel and onto the surrounding streets of Arn. The dead were everywhere, emerging by the dozen onto the streets that converged on the Citadel. The horde that had followed them through the temple district stumbled into view, hundreds bearing down on the frail line of warriors.

'Keep moving the line back, lads!' called Hafgan. 'We protect the riverbank.'

Arnulf turned to see people scrambling over the sides of the ship. Men passed crying children up to the waiting hands of the ship's crew, then pulling women and the elderly on board. Any who could fight remained. There were emotionally charged exchanges as husbands bade their wives farewell—promises made to see each other again, but they were promises none could be certain of. They were the words of desperate comfort as families which had survived the terrors of the night were wrenched apart.

The ship's oars began to move leaving so many on the riverbank, safety and escape slowly floating out of reach. The townsfolk left behind shouted their final farewells, terror evident on their faces at being left on that muddy riverbank.

Other ships were rowing in towards them, and one sounded a horn to herald their approach.

'Quiet you, fools!' Arnulf cursed. *They will bring every corpse in the city down on us.*

The horn sounded again, its low braying sound echoing over the water with promise of salvation, but their approach was painfully slow. The horde would be upon them long before those ships could reach them. Arnulf knew they would have to fight.

'Any man who can fight,' Arnulf bellowed. 'Shield wall!'

He locked his shield with the men beside him.

'Men of Arnar,' he shouted, holding his axe above his head. 'I am Arnulf, and I have fought the dead and lived. We *will* hold them here. The boats are coming and the sun has risen. The gods are with us, but I need you to stand firm one more time. Just *once* more against the dead. Only valour and steel can stand against the rising dead.'

The warriors cheered, clanging weapons against shields. They knew they had no choice, but Arnulf's words hardened their resolve. They would stand and fight.

The shield wall was a terrifying place to fight, hidden behind a raised shield, stabbing and thrusting at any gap that opened. The enemy were usually so close you could smell their ale-reeking breath, but this foe was unlike any Arnulf had ever fought. Instead of ale, these things stank of rotting flesh and bone.

A foreboding silence settled over those brave few who remained in the shadow of the Citadel's wooden palisades.

There are too many, Arnulf thought.

The sound of them approaching echoed up the streets and out to the waterfront, the snarling and groaning of hundreds of dead mouths drawing ever closer. Behind him desperate townsfolk splashed into the shallows, wading out waist-deep into the water to meet the approaching ships.

The warriors beside him trembled as death incarnate staggered forwards to assail their shields. The dead would break against those shields like a crashing wave and they would be overwhelmed like the beach in a rising tide. His words had given them courage, but the effect was waning as the warriors stared into a wall of rotting dead.

It was then he heard a voice, rising clear and strong beside him. The melody was mournful yet the words were full of defiance. Arnulf looked to the man beside him. Hafgan watched the approaching dead, his face grim, but his lips were moving. Hafgan was singing. Arnulf felt a pang of emotion. Other voices took up the song.

It was *that* song. Her song. Aeslin's song.

He had heard her sing it a thousand times, and the melody haunted him. He added his own voice to the chorus, his eyes brimming with tears. Aeslin sang along in his head, accompanying them from the otherworld, and the warriors began slowly hammering their shields. The steady rhythm drove the song onward, the glorious *Battle Lament of Thoragallyn*.

Arnulf felt the hearts of men stir as they sang at the tops of the voices in brave defiance.

The dead were a mere twenty paces away, an easy spear throw. Arnulf counted down the steps until they crunched into the shield wall.

The chorus drowned out the hateful snarls of the dead, the words lighting a fire inside him. His soul alight, he saw that same fire burn in the eyes of the warriors around him. Still they sang the famous battle song of Arnar. The gods themselves would hear them.

Fifteen paces.

The spirits of the ancestors would set down their horns of ale, there would be a silence in the halls of the ancestors as they turned to watch this fight against overwhelming odds. The ancestors would cheer as men bled and died. This would be a glorious end.

Ten paces.

Arnulf held Aeslin's face in his mind, Idony beside her. His beautiful daughter smiled from the grave. It was a smile that shone proud in her eyes. He saw Ewolf. Not the creature he became, but the son he remembered. Tears rolled down his cheeks as that glorious song rang in his ears.

Five.

The shields braced. Spears tensed.

Three.

He roared in fury and raised his axe high ready to strike.

Two.

His soul burned for the slaughter.

One.

The shield wall heaved as the dead struck. His axe crashed down and bit into flesh and bone, dead fingers curling around the rim of his shield. Beside him Hafgan roared as he chopped with his axe also. An impossible strength pulled on his shield, trying to wrench it away into the horde of dead, trying to wrench *him* from the shield wall. He set his feet and held.

Further along, a man was not so lucky. He screamed as he was torn from the formation and into the horde. The dead devoured him alive, just paces from his comrades. Arnulf was glad he did not see that poor man's demise. He put his shoulder into his shield and heaved back at the growing crush of the dead.

He saw a dead face appear over his shield. It was a bloody ruin, its eyes writhing with maggots, forcing its way between his shield and the man to his left. It lunged and it bit down on to Arnulf's arm. He cried out in alarm, the teeth splintering on his mail sleeve, unable to penetrate. A spear thrust over his shoulder, plunging into the eye socket of the withered face, but the dead thing just snarled in return until an axe split its skull.

The battle song dwindled to cries and shouts, the glorious song fracturing. He heard the battle cries of Arnar, and he heard men die.

He chopped with his axe again and again, his muscles burning as the heavy weapon sapped his strength, but still it rose and fell, crunching through bone and pallid flesh. The stench of death became overpowering, the stink of rank blood, rotting flesh and excrement assailed him. He fought his heaving stomach as he shoved with his heavy shield. The dead were pushing their line back. He felt his boots squelch into the mud, the snow long trampled into a mire of black muddy slush.

A hand reached beneath his shield and seized his leg. He roared and rammed the rim down with a wet *crunch*. A snarling face appeared, its skull half caved in. It was a horrifying sight. Still it wrenched his leg towards its snapping maw. He rammed the shield down again. There was no room to swing an axe. Suddenly the thing lost its grip and he snatched his leg away, staggering back a little before he shoved his shield forwards once more.

A horn brayed behind them. He dared a quick glance over his shoulder to see two ships waiting in the shallows.

Salvation.

Other men saw them too. Some broke and splashed into the water.

'Hold!' Arnulf bellowed.

'Hold!' Hafgan repeated beside him. 'Hold the wall. Fall back slowly.'

It was useless, like screaming into the wind. Warriors, seeing a chance of escape, broke and ran. Against this nightmare foe even the bravest crumbled. The shield wall began to disintegrate as warriors ran for the safety of the ships.

'No!' Arnulf cried.

A hand grabbed his shoulder and pulled him back.

'Run, lord,' Hafgan shouted.

Shields were abandoned to the clutching dead hands. The corpses pulled the shields into their midst but were enraged to discover that nothing living stood behind them. The warriors fled into the water and the dead were slow. Suddenly there was nothing there, where a moment before there had been living men and women in a wall of shields and steel.

Some unlucky few were seized from behind and wrenched backward as they turned to run, their terrified screams peeling out across the water, but Arnulf did not dare to turn and look. He just ran. Those unlucky few became a macabre feast for the hungry dead, giving the fleeing warriors a few precious moments to escape. The dead swarmed the fallen, tearing with teeth and hands, biting chewing on their warm flesh.

Those who had been in the water had already been hauled

aboard the waiting ships, shouting now for the warriors to run with looks of horror written on their faces. They held out their hands and reached down to help others clamber aboard.

Arnulf sprinted into the cold water. At waist deep he had to wade with maddening slowness, expecting at any moment to be wrenched backwards and set upon by tearing hands and dead faces.

He felt a hand reach down and grasp his mail, and someone hauled him up and over a ship's rail. He lay there a moment, blinking. All he could hear was shouting, and the sounds of the dead. Around him men sat on benches, one standing over him jabbing a spear at something clinging to the sides of the ship.

I'm on a ship. It took a moment for the situation to register. *Did we really make it out?* Arnulf struggled to his feet.

'Pull!' screamed a bosun. Oarsmen heaved on their oars again, the dead clinging to the sides of the ship as it surged away from the riverbank. He swung his axe one final time to send a snarling corpse splashing back into the dark waters.

He leaned heavily on the rail.

Every muscle in his body ached, his heart pounding in his chest. His head spun. Looking back at the shore, all he could see were dead things. Everywhere he looked, a corpse was stumbling with an unsettling jerking motion, flailing in the water, swarming across the banks and clogging the street beyond.

The ship was clear. The bosun shouted and the oarsmen heaved. All around him warriors stood dazed, water dripping from their armour, a distant look haunting their eyes. In his head he still heard that song.

The dawn had broken and brought the golden light of a winter morning creeping over the city. Colour ebbed back into the world and the dead became distant figures on Arn's streets. To the west, from the College, oily smears of smoke stained the lightening sky. To the south, other plumes rose ominously as fires burned across the city. The Citadel stood dark and silent against the dawn sky. A banner flapped on a high rampart, the snarling wolf of a dead king. A doom had settled over this once proud city, and on its streets the dead walked.

CHAPTER FORTY-FOUR

A Court of Ships

'*Fuck*,' Bjorn shouted in frustration. He punched the water. 'This is useless.'

For all Tung's evident bushcraft, he was useless out on the water. He had no idea how to paddle, and instead just splashed around excitedly. With no oars, Bjorn had tried everything, even tying his cloak around his axe to make a makeshift paddle. It was not very effective. All it did was get his cloak soaking wet, and now he was cold as well as adrift.

'I hate boats,' the hunter groaned, rubbing his shoulders. His hands were bitterly cold and his arms ached from the hour or so of futile paddling, struggling against the merciless current. That current had their little boat in its grip, and hand-paddling alone was not enough.

He had seen a longship row past, coursing down the far side of the wide river, heading out to sea. He had franticly waved to it, but the sailors either didn't see him in the dim light of dawn or were purposefully ignoring them.

Too risky, he thought. *They probably think we're infected, or even dead.*

The current pulled their little boat out into the estuary. Eventually it would wash them out to sea and to the mercy of the waves and tides. His only hope was that they would be somehow washed up on a sandbank or on one of the marshy islets. Ending up out to sea would surely spell their doom.

On the south shore he saw a port town. Probably Anchorage, but he had never been there, so knew little of it. The place looked dead, only a few lifeless figures visible milling around its water-front. *So the dead roam here too.*

Khyra had warned him that a terrible darkness lay in his path. She had warned of smoke and crows, and the carrion birds wheeled across the sky wherever he looked. She had warned of death, and death stalked here like he had never seen before. She had warned of a blind beggar, a hooded man, and it was them who had left him to die on that beach.

'Those fucking bastards,' Bjorn muttered. The little row boat had long since passed from view, disappearing around a bend in the river as he and Tung had floundered uselessly without an oar.

He cursed himself. He should never have come here. He should have stayed with Khyra and helped her with her cottage, rebuilding something of a life.

Tung hooted and cooed, saying incomprehensible words, then jabbed him with the butt of his spear. The Wildman was pointing off over the water to the east. The sun was still low, struggling to shine through the grey clouds in the morning sky. Bjorn shielded his eyes with his hand to see. Out of that glare came a dark shape.

Another ship!

The longship surged up the river towards them, its white sail bellied in the morning wind.

Is it the same ship? Could be. Bjorn stood in the boat, making it rock from side to side, and waved his arms, hoping someone aboard would see their little boat.

'Ho!' called a voice.

'Greetings, friend,' Bjorn called in reply. 'We're drifting. We have no oars.'

The longship angled to pull alongside them, sailors spilling the wind from the sails.

'Are you wounded?' the sailor asked.

'No,' replied Bjorn. 'We escaped the city. It's been overrun with dead creatures.'

'Aye, we have heard the tales.'

'I brought urgent news for the king from High Lord Archeon in the west, but we were unable to deliver it. May we come aboard?'

A rope flew through the air and splashed across the little boat's hull. Bjorn grabbed it and heaved the rowboat against the ship's hull. A helmeted face appeared above him. 'If you're wounded, you will be thrown back overboard, you understand?'

'I promise you we are not,' Bjorn said as he grasped an out-stretched hand. He was pulled up and over the side, followed by Tung.

'Then you are lucky, friend,' said the man. His brown hair was stuffed beneath an iron cap, and instead of mail he wore a stout leather jerkin. Few men wore mail at sea for it was a quick death if they fell overboard. His face was weather worn, creased by the spray of the sea and the wind. 'You bring word from the west?'

'Aye, I came with an escort to deliver a message to the king. We were set upon by foul creatures when we landed ashore at the Citadel — dead things, if you can believe it. Only me and my wild friend here escaped.'

'We have heard much the same. Come, speak with our captain. This ship is *Glarkillen*, and Prince Harald commands here. He will hear you.' The man led him between rowing benches towards the prow of the ship. There beside a high figurehead of a carved wolf, stood a man wrapped in a fur trimmed cloak. The prince was a lean man, his dark blonde hair hung long about his shoulders and blew in the sea breeze.

'Lord prince, these are the men we brought aboard. They are messengers from Archeon in the west, and they escaped the city.'

The prince turned to regard them. He was young but had a serious, careworn face, as if struggling with pain and burden in the face of duty. 'Your name?'

'I am Bjorn the hunter.' The hunter offered the prince a curt nod.

'And your companion?'

'He is Tung, a Wildman from the Barrens.'

The prince looked at the Wildman curiously. 'Strange company you keep, hunter. I am Harald, my father is King Rhagnal. You bring him news from Lord Archeon?'

'Aye, I came with a captain of Oldstones, a man named Daeluf, but he fell at the Citadel. His escort fled back to their ship and we were stranded in the city.'

'Aye, we encountered them on the river. I must admit, I found their tale hard to believe, but every one of the survivors tells the same tale — the dead walk?'

Bjorn nodded and glanced at Tung, hoping he wouldn't touch some integral part of the ship. 'We were attacked by the creatures, some were alive—insane and possibly cursed—but the others were...'

Harald shook his head. 'I have seen them myself, but from a distance, for we dared not dock. They would not answer our hails, and as we got closer, we saw... They were all staggering and limping. How is this possible?'

'I don't know,' Bjorn admitted. 'I saw them up close. I even fought them. Those things were not living men. There is a great evil in the city.' He paused. 'My lord prince... I have grave news. I heard rumour from the men in the Citadel, rumour that your father had fallen in the chaos.'

A look of sadness swept over the prince's face. 'I have heard the same rumour. I pray to the gods it is just that; a rumour.'

'I... I did not see it with my own eyes,' Bjorn admitted. 'I hope it is as you say.'

Harald grunted and turned and looked out onto the river. 'What of this message from Lord Archeon?'

'We were to deliver this to your father.' Bjorn rummaged inside his cloak and produced a sealed parchment which he handed to the prince. 'Lord Archeon sent me as a witness, to tell my tale to the king. There is great trouble in the west.'

'Greater than the walking dead?' the prince asked with a rueful smile, breaking the seal and scanning the page.

'We had word of the sickness on our way here, but nothing of the evil we found when we arrived,' replied Bjorn.

'Archeon writes of raiders on the coast, possibly remnants of the old rebellion. He is sending his warriors to make battle and asks for reinforcements,' said the prince. 'It must be dire for Archeon to ask for aid.'

'Daeluf was better informed on that than I, lord prince. I am no soldier.'

'Please, call me Harald. What is this news of Stonemen coming from the Barrens, of villages attacked and strange beasts? He mentions you... ' Prince Harald raised his eyebrows. 'I have heard of you, but I never expected to be pulling the famed Hunter of the West from these cold waters. You are the same Bjorn from the songs? The man who won the tourney at Barrowford without missing a single arrow? The man who is said to be able to hunt any beast. Who slew Geffin the Outlaw?'

'I'm not nearly as glorious as the songs make out,' Bjorn said.

There would have been a time when he would have puffed out his chest and put a swagger to his stride when his name was recognised, but of late that renown and fame seemed a foolish burden. Instead, he felt old and tired.

'Archeon writes that you have a dark tale to tell. Well go on, tell me what you saw.'

Bjorn looked at Tung.

'I have seen the folk of Arnar hunted like animals. Whole families — men, women and children — hunted and slaughtered with indifference. I have seen the Stonemen of old, those same savages spoken of in the Sagas. They have returned to the lands of Arnar and are attacking and raiding all along the northern frontier, taking people, killing whole villages. And worse, they are feasting on human flesh. They are eating people...'

***

Nym wretched over the side of the ship, her stomach lurching and churning with the roll of the river. The ships that had rescued them from the riverbank had been lashed together, three in all, forming a floating refuge anchored upon the river. The three ships were already crammed with the survivors rescued from Arn, folk huddling on the abandoned rowing benches cradling their only earthly possessions. Parents held their children close, while others looked out over the water to the city that had been their home. They all had that same forlorn look about them. A few tried to sleep, but most just sat there, wide eyed and unable to close their eyes, unable to force the horrors of the night from their thoughts.

Nym heaved again.

'Is she sick?' asked a man nearby. 'She's sick isn't she?' He pulled his family away from her. His face a vision of revulsion and fear. 'She has the sickness! She has brought it among us!'

'Shut your mouth, fool,' Ramona snapped. The mystic placed a hand on Nym's back and pulled her hair up behind her head. 'She is with child, you stupid little worm. Don't spread the fear, there's enough of that here without you sowing more.'

'But if she *is* sick, she will doom us all,' continued the man. Everyone was looking at her.

'Say another word and I will turn your bowels to water. I will make your seed barren and your member as limp as a sand eel.

You will never be able to spawn another idiot whelp upon the world.'

The man shrank back at her threats and Nym eyed Ramona with amazement. *Can she really do such things?* Folk certainly thought so. These people all looked at her with respect and fearful reverence of her magic.

'Leave the girl be,' Wilhelm warned, walking over upon hearing the commotion.

The man backed away from the warrior and cast a scowl at the mystic. The woman beside him scowled and he remained silent, cowed by his wife. Only a man with little honour would attack a woman with child, and his wife did not look happy to share such dishonour.

'It's okay, my dear. The feeling will pass,' Ramona murmured, stroking her hair.

Nym pulled herself upright and wiped her chin with her sleeve. 'I am sorry,' she managed. 'There's nothing in me, I'm just gagging now.'

'Poor thing.' She gave her a sympathetic smile.

Nym was still stunned by Ramona's revelation. *How can I be with child? I can't be. I don't want to have a baby.* Her eyes welled with tears and she felt a different kind of sickness, brought on by the memory of that horrible drunk in Anchorage.

The scholar Luthor sat on the bench beside them and offered her a look of pity. 'She's right, lass; it will pass.'

'Oh, and what do you know?' Ramona sneered. 'What does a man know a woman's burdens?'

Luthor looked indignant. 'I will have you know I've studied with the College since I was a mere boy. I'm not wholly ignorant of the world.'

The mystic waved his words away with a dismissive gesture. Wilhelm sat down opposite Luthor and offered the scholar a nod in greeting. 'You're with child? Not to Jor, I hope?'

'No!' Nym snapped, revolted by the very idea. 'I don't want to talk about it.'

'Ah, like that is it?' Wilhelm nodded as if he understood entirely without her breathing a word. He turned and watched a large ship sail towards them.

'Why don't you all find somewhere else better to be,' Ramona said. 'Leave the girl be.'

Wilhelm made a hasty retreat from the fierce mystic, and Nym watched him clamber between the lashed boats, making his way to the outermost edge where it looked like the large longship would dock with their makeshift sanctuary.

Nym couldn't help but notice that Luthor remained. He had hovered around since they came aboard, as if he wanted to say something, but was wary of Ramona's wrath. Eventually, as she sat watching the water lap up against the hull of the ship, he finally spoke his mind.

'Nym, may I ask you something?' He threw a cautious glance at the mystic who eyed him menacingly. It amused Nym how all these men feared the woman. In truth Nym had been terrified of her too, but she had become her protector these last few hours.

'You said,' he continued, 'that you were invisible to the dead? Those words have had me curious since you said it. What do you mean? Could you tell me more?'

'It was in the city, before I lost Finn,' said Nym sadly. 'Our friend was killed as we were trying to get away. The dead came out of nowhere, then they were everywhere, and there were those other things.'

'The Cursed Ones.' Luthor nodded. 'What happened then?'

'We met some others near the Citadel. There was a man named Bjorn and he said the dead were in the Citadel. He had a crazy man with him, like a wild man or something, and there was a cripple too, a scholar like you.'

Luthor sat up at those last words, his attention sharpened to a serious focus.

'He had a magic staff that he claimed was blessed by the gods. Whenever the dead came near him, they just stopped moving and stood still when we walked past. We walked through whole crowds of dead bodies. It was horrible.'

Ramona had stopped scowling and was listening intently to her story.

'I imagine so,' the scholar said with a deep frown. There was an odd look in his eye and an edge to his voice as he spoke, as if she was confirming something he already suspected. 'What was the scholar's name?'

'His name was Duncan, I think. He knew my friend, Seth. I met him once before when I visited Seth at the College infirmary. I didn't like him much; he stared at me all the time.'

'Duncan!' Luthor exclaimed.

Nym started, leaning back, unsure what to make of his outburst. 'You know him?'

'Aye, I know him. Now please, this is very important. Tell me everything, from the beginning. Every detail could be important. Tell me everything you can.'

***

Prince Harald regarded them as they clambered onto the waiting longship. The longship was huge, larger than any Arnulf had set foot on; a proper royal warship. He reckoned it could carry a hundred warriors at least, with thirty oars per side and a mighty wolf's head carved onto its prow. Prince Harald sat on a simple chair in front of the ship's raised steering platform, the chancellor beside him. He had hurried off to meet the new ship as soon as it had arrived. Then the summons had come.

'Is this him?' murmured the prince and Alfric leaned down to speak into Harald's ear. 'Lord Arnulf, I am glad to meet you.'

'Lord prince,' Arnulf replied with a bow.

'Chancellor Alfric tells me you saved many lives in the night.'

'Not enough,' Arnulf said with a grimace.

'But still, you have my thanks, and that of my father... if he lives. Word is he did not survive,' Harald said, his voice slightly ragged at the edges, as if he held tears back that he dared not shed.

'Then you will be king?'

'Perhaps, if no one challenges and the Witan decides as much, but I still hold the hope that my father lives. More survivors are trickling in. We need to find out what is happening. I am crewing as many ships as possible.'

'How did you escape?' asked Arnulf.

'I didn't. I was commanding the fleet last night. I was already out on a patrol when we saw something strange over the Citadel. A fell wind and a mist, then witchfire in the sky. I sent ships to the Citadel as soon as we saw it, but few warriors returned. Men speak of the dead walking. Is it true? Has our city been overrun by corpses?'

Arnulf gave a grim nod. 'They are everywhere. We fought them from the College to the Citadel. The dead fill the streets.'

'I have heard much the same from every man I have spoken with.'

The prince glanced at a weather worn man standing nearby, absently toying with what appeared to be a stone knife. He had a strange man with him, with wild hair and wearing nothing but filthy pelts.

The prince sighed, the weight of a realm recently thrust upon his shoulders. 'That is not all. There is word of dead on the north banks, in the villages, and in Anchorage.'

'So, they are not just in the city?'

'I wish it were so, but it seems wherever there is dry land, there are now corpses walking. Was the plague not enough?' The prince sighed and regarded Arnulf for a moment. 'It was you who first saw this in the north?'

Arnulf nodded.

'I remember you in the Throne Hall that day. I remember the court laughed at your tale, and I am sorry for that, truly. I wish we had listened.' He nodded and looked at the chancellor. 'You helped get Alfric out, and these folk owe you their lives. Your bravery will not be forgotten, Arnulf.'

'I was just doing what needed to be done,' Arnulf replied.

'Dead men walking...' Harald shook his head in disbelief. 'Where did they come from?' He asked to nobody in particular. 'Have the gods forsaken us?'

'I wish I knew for sure,' Arnulf replied, throwing a glance at Hafgan. 'But I believe there is a man who does know.'

The prince looked at him sharply.

'I believe this was the work of a single man, an apprentice at the College who returned from the north not long before we arrived.'

'I know of him,' said Chancellor Alfric. 'I saw him myself at the College council. We had the council watching him, and our own men too.'

'Aye, Wilhelm there was one of them,' said Arnulf with a nod towards the ships that had been lashed together. The warrior had approached the rail of the prince's ship, and stood listening. 'He helped us get out of the College, a brave man. He was with us when the dead rose.'

Wilhelm nodded in acknowledgement.

'It is strange that you were at the College, Arnulf,' Chancellor

Alfric said with a knowing look. 'Especially when you were forbidden from going there.'

Arnulf met his eye a brief moment but looked away, knowing well he had defied the king's orders. 'We went looking for the king, but we did not find him.' The excuse sounded flimsy. 'We did meet a scholar... what was him name?'

'Luthor,' Hafgan murmured.

Arnulf nodded. 'Master Luthor will tell you, as will Wilhelm. Word has it that this very same apprentice I speak of left the College with our lord king.'

'What?!' exclaimed the chancellor. 'This is news to me.'

'It is true,' Wilhelm confirmed. 'We think the king took him back to the Citadel.'

'Why?' gasped Alfric.

'Alethea,' said the prince sadly. 'If he thought someone could help bring her back, he would have done anything to save her.'

Arnulf looked at the chancellor questioningly.

'She was the king's daughter. She succumbed to the plague yesterday. At the council the apprentice told the king he could save her.'

'No,' Arnulf hissed.

It all makes sense.

'I *knew* the apprentice had a hand in this,' Arnulf growled. 'I knew it in my gut. This is the same evil that befell our lands in the north.'

'Luthor!' called a shrill voice from behind them.

Arnulf noticed Luthor clambering aboard, trailed by the two women from the burial mound. A fat little man in College robes was hurrying towards Luthor, and the pair embraced. It was hard not to notice the other man with the fat little scholar, tall and dark, towering over the others. Arnulf had never seen such a man. He looked again at the weather-beaten man and his wild companion, and then back to the round little scholar and the foreigner. *There are strange folk aboard this ship.*

Luthor and the other scholar approached them. The two women they had rescued followed uncertainly, lingering back a little way as the two scholars approached the prince. The elder of the two, the mystic, considered those assembled with a cool regard, but the younger one stared about in wide-eyed awe at being on the royal warship, her eyes flicking between the strange dark skinned warrior beside her, who she seemed uncertain of, and Prince Harald.

'My lords,' said Luthor in greeting.

'Ah, is this the scholar you brought from the College, Arnulf?' asked the prince.

'Aye,' Arnulf replied.

'Greetings, friend,' Harald said, lifting a hand. 'I hope we find more of your folk. The loss of so many College scholars is a sad thing.'

Luthor nodded sadly. 'Are there any others? Surely we cannot be the only ones.'

The younger girl, Nym, suddenly gasped and tried to speak, but the mystic pulled her back and motioned for her to be quiet as the prince spoke.

'So far,' replied the prince. 'I see you have already found Gideon and his companion?'

Luthor smiled. 'I am glad to see them both—they are good friends.'

'My warriors are wary of our dark friend. Men say he is a demon.'

'Jasper is his name,' said Luthor. 'He is a remarkable man, and extremely intelligent.'

'He saved me,' added Gideon, waddling to join them. 'It was Jasper who saved me. He fought those *things*. I would be dead without him.'

Arnulf regarded the dark man. He indeed looked formidable, holding an ancient looking bronze shield and with an axe at his belt. He noticed Hafgan offered the man a nod of respect as their eyes met.

'Tell me, Luthor,' Prince Harald went on. 'Lord Arnulf has told me of this apprentice he seeks. Chancellor Alfric saw him at the council meeting also. What do you know of him?'

'I know the young man, lord prince. In fact, it is news of him that brought me to speak with Arnulf. Nym saw him in the city,' Luthor explained, indicating the young girl at his side. 'I knew him well some years ago. He was once my apprentice before he went to study with Master Eldrick. His last master died in disgrace, in the High Passes, where Lord Arnulf found all manner of fell things, including the first instance of the risen dead. Eldrick was cast out from the College for his foul work, and I was tasked to investigate the evidence that was brought back and to keep an eye on his apprentice, Duncan.'

Nym still seemed agitated, desperate to speak; Arnulf noticed she was staring at the weather beaten hunter and his peculiar wild man.

'He professed his innocence in the events in the north,' continued Luthor, 'and I believed he was. But more recently I couldn't help but notice there was something odd about him. Before I knew what was happening, all this occurred,' he said with a wave at the city. 'I believe he convinced the king that he could raise the princess from the dead using Eldrick's rituals, and in doing so, unleashed unimaginable horror on Arnar.'

'He deceived many,' Chancellor Alfric put in. 'The council, myself... even the king.'

'We must find him,' Luthor pressed. 'Perhaps if we do, we can reverse this evil.'

'Are there no records of this in the College? Some copy of the rituals?' asked Harald. 'Surely there is something in your archives?'

Luthor turned to Gideon, who shrugged.

'Perhaps, lord prince,' Luthor replied, 'but whatever might have been has likely burned in the night. We do have Eldrick's grimoire, the fell book from which the northern rituals were performed. The apprentice's knowledge is based upon it, and with that combined with my study of the book, perhaps we can discover how this was done and undo this evil and lay the walking dead to rest.'

'Haf?' Arnulf turned to the big warrior. 'Do you still have the journal?'

Hafgan felt inside his cloak. 'Aye, lord,' he replied, pulling out the tattered little book.

'We believe this is Eldrick's journal, from the ritual site,' Arnulf said.

'By the gods,' gasped Luthor. 'Please let me see it.'

'There may be something of use in there,' Arnulf continued. 'You have earned my trust, scholar, so I will allow you to study it, but it will not leave Hafgan's possession. Do you understand?'

The scholar nodded his agreement.

Nym finally called out. 'It's him!' She ran forwards and tugged urgently on Luthor's sleeve. 'Luthor! It's him! It's Bjorn.'

'Where? Which one, lass?' asked Luthor.

She pointed to the old weather-beaten man with greying dark hair.

Luthor's eyes narrowed at the girl's words. 'Lass? You are sure that is the same man who was with Duncan when you last saw them?'

She nodded. 'It's him. He was helping Duncan and the rest of us to get out of the city.'

Arnulf's attention focused on the man, the matter of the journal forgotten.

'But where is Seth?' Nym asked softly.

Nobody replied and Arnulf immediately strode over to confront the man, his anger building with each step. 'You were helping Duncan? Where is he?'

'The little shit and his blind friend took a boat and left us to the dead. I don't know where they are,' Bjorn replied as he slid the strange stone knife back into his boot. He turned to Nym. 'We thought you were dead,' he said spreading his hands.

'You lie!' snarled Arnulf.

'Arnulf, what is the meaning of this,' Harald demanded.

Arnulf sneered at Bjorn, 'If he was helping the apprentice, then I'd wager he is in league with him. This Apprentice Duncan raised the dead and brought doom upon the city. If he did go with the king to the Citadel, then he could have been the last man to see him alive. He may well have killed him. Did you help him do it, hunter?'

'This is madness!' snapped Bjorn. He turned to Harald. 'Who is this man to accuse me?'

'This is Lord Arnulf,' replied Harald.

'Well lord or not, tell this fool to silence himself. He does not know to whom he speaks.' Bjorn glared at Arnulf, his hand resting on his axe. 'If I see that little worm again, I promise you, I will kill him.'

'Lord,' said Hafgan. 'He may know nothing of Rhagnal's fate. We don't know anything for sure.'

'I heard of the king's death before I met the scholar,' said Bjorn defensively. 'If he had a hand in it, I knew nothing of it.'

'You still helped that bastard traitor escape. You aided him in his treason.'

'I took pity on a crippled man who promised to find me a

boat—nothing more. He did not even look capable of wiping his own arse, let alone slaying a king.'

'It was he who raised the *dead*, fool, and you helped him escape!'

'I didn't know, I swear,' said Bjorn shaking his head.

Arnulf unsheathed his dagger. 'I think you lie.'

The Wildman levelled his spear at Arnulf, growling with bared teeth like a mad dog.

'Guards!' called Prince Harald. 'Stay your hand, Lord Arnulf. Calm yourself. I will have no bloodshed on my ship. Save it for the dead.'

'Secondly,' said Chancellor Alfric, 'Bjorn is an emissary from High Lord Archeon in the west. He has just arrived in the city. I doubt he was in league with the traitor.'

Arnulf and Bjorn exchanged icy stares as warriors drew them apart. Arnulf slammed his dagger back into its scabbard.

'I promise you, Lord Arnulf,' said Bjorn, 'if I see that scholar, or his blind friend, I will slit their throats. I will not be used.'

'No!' exclaimed Nym. 'Seth is a good man. He would not betray anyone.'

'They left me to *die*,' snapped Bjorn. 'They are dead men when I find them.'

She shrank away, glaring at the hunter, and the witch took her in her arms, holding her protectively.

The prince raised his hands and walked between the two men, trying to diffuse the tension. 'Perhaps I have a solution. Bjorn, you can hunt any man or beast, true?'

'I can,' replied the hunter.

'And, you have a grievance with this apprentice?'

Bjorn nodded with a frown.

'Perhaps,' continued Harald, 'you could track this apprentice, this Duncan?'

Bjorn began to shake his head. 'I am done with killing men for silver. I plan to leave this place and disappear into the forests of the west to grow old in peace.'

'Hear me out. I will not command you, but he betrayed you, and I will pay you well for his capture. Consider this—that man has brought evil upon us all and doom upon our lands, *your* lands. Arnar cannot let this man live for such crimes. Do this one last thing.'

'The vengeance should be *mine*,' demanded Arnulf.

'And so it will be, Arnulf. You will have your vengeance. I promise you will be the one who finally kills him.' He looked at them both. 'What say you? Bring me the apprentice in chains, or bring me his head — it matters not. Will you find him together and bring him the justice of Arnar?'

'I do not know if this hunter can be trusted,' Arnulf said with a scowl.

'I have done you no wrong,' snapped Bjorn.

'Lord,' Hafgan warned and Bjorn cast him an icy stare. 'We will have trouble tracking the apprentice for we do not know these lands. We need this man, and his skills. We cannot let the apprentice escape a second time.'

Arnulf frowned for a long moment. 'You are right, as always.' he reluctantly agreed looking at Hafgan. 'Fine,' said Arnulf finally. 'You may join us in our hunt, but do not think I will trust you.'

'Trust is earned,' Bjorn shrugged.

Arnulf looked at Hafgan as he regarded the hunter for a second and nodded in approval. Hafgan obviously suspected this man could prove to be an ally, despite his own distrust.

'Good,' nodded the prince. 'Make your preparations. I wish you Varg's cunning in running the bastard down.'

'Mark my words, we will find him,' Arnulf assured the prince. 'I will have my vengeance. Too many lie dead in the north because of that bastard and his friends, and now this curse has been unleashed on the city. I will make this apprentice suffer.'

'So be it,' said the prince. 'I wish you luck, but I can spare none of my warriors. Take only the warriors which ride with you. We need every man and woman able to fight. There are too many dead, and not enough living.'

'The Great Histories must be recovered too,' said Gideon suddenly. 'It is our memory, our way of life, our stories. We must save what we can,'

'It will take warriors to clear the College, men I cannot spare right now,' replied Harald. 'My first priority is the people, and we must rescue those who we can. There must be more out there, but we need food, supplies. We have ships enough and I have already sent men to bring back any longship moored offshore around the Citadel. We cannot abandon the capital. We must re-take the city.'

'Aye,' Chancellor Alfric agreed with a grim face. 'There must be an islet out in the delta where no dead roam, or even a village?'

'I have ships searching for such a place,' Harald told him. 'We need supplies and food. There is so much to do. The College will have to wait I'm afraid, but you are right. The ways of our people must be saved.'

'We can study the grimoire for answers until then, my prince,' replied Gideon. He offered a weak smile, but the disappointment was plain on his face. 'When you do return to the College, we will guide your men and retrieve what we can. I am no warrior, but I will help where I can.'

'Gideon, my old friend,' said Luthor. 'I do not think I will be joining you in returning to the College.'

'What?'

'I think that task may be yours alone. I think I must go after Duncan with Lord Arnulf. If you will have me, lord?'

'As long as you don't slow us down,' agreed Arnulf.

'But, why?' demanded Gideon.

'He must have taken his books, and if we can recover them then we have a greater chance of ending this... We need to stop him. I know the lad. It should be me.' Gideon's face fell and Luthor patted him on the shoulder.

'We should leave as soon as possible,' said Bjorn. 'Every moment our quarry gets further out of reach.'

'Hafgan, get the warriors ready to leave,' said Arnulf.

'Aye, lord,' Hafgan replied.

'Wait,' a woman's voice called. 'We will fight with you.'

The two shield-maidens stood nearby, bloodied and exhausted. The rest of their comrades had all fallen, or been abandoned to die by their sworn lord. They had already scraped their shields clean, the blue of Fergus's sigil scrubbed away. The dishonour of that sigil scraped clean, free and no longer bound to their oaths.

'I said we need every warrior,' repeated Harald. 'Take only your sworn warriors. The folk of Arn will stay and fight.'

'We came south with Arnulf,' protested the lead shield-maiden. 'We were sworn to Lord Fergus and he abandoned and betrayed us. Rather than return to the north, we would fight beside you again Lord Arnulf.'

He looked at the shield-maiden who had spoken and then at the woman beside her, both had a steely resolve in their eyes, faces grim and determined. *These women will fight, and fight hard.* He would be honoured to fight alongside them.

'They are not folk of Arn,' added the chancellor. 'They served the north.'

'So be it,' said Harald with a dismissive gesture, 'but the College mercenaries stay with us.'

'Thank you, lord prince,' replied the shield-maiden with a bow. 'Lord Arnulf, may we ask that one day, should we find Fergus again, will you allow us to take our vengeance?'

Arnulf's face hardened, the pain was still raw. He had been betrayed by his oldest friend, left for dead. It would be a hard to permit vengeance, but Arnulf knew he would not forgive him.

'Fergus will pay for his dishonour,' was his only reply, then Arnulf looked out over the river.

The women knelt and gave Arnulf their oaths there and then. They would now paint those bare shields red and place a black axe on those crimson boards. They would serve amongst his remaining warriors, and they would be most welcome. There were few fiercer warriors than the shield-maidens of the Death Nymph. Arnulf was only sorry that Astrid herself was not with them — she had been a formidable ally.

Erran's absence yawned like a great void. He knew Hafgan felt Erran's absence most of all. The big warrior had loved the young lad in his own way, the closest thing he had to a son. Now Erran was dead. He felt a wave of grief. Hafgan too would have his vengeance. *For Erran,* he vowed.

Now, including the two newest oath-sworn warriors, Arnulf counted seven. He regarded each in turn. They were good fighters. With himself, Hafgan, the hunter and his Wildman, and the scholar, they would be twelve. Twelve brave souls to hunt an apprentice through dead, haunted lands.

The prince offered up one of his crews to land them ashore wherever they wished. Arnulf supposed it would be somewhere of the hunter's choosing. It was he who had last seen where the apprentice was heading. *He better not betray us or I will kill him myself.*

Their small warband clambered aboard the longship. Arnulf stood at its prow and looked out south over the river. Hafgan walked up and stood beside him. Neither spoke for a moment, standing in companionable silence. Arnulf ran his fingers absently over the knotted patterns wrought onto his battle-axe by the smiths of his fathers.

'Where are you, apprentice?' Arnulf murmured eventually as he scanned the southern shores. Whether he spoke to Hafgan or merely to himself, he was uncertain. Hafgan made no reply. 'Wherever you are hiding, know this—I am coming for you.'

EPILOGUE

Flight of the Broken

The oars slowly dipped in and out of the still water, the little boat coursing through the labyrinth of creeks and reed-beds. Ducks and waterfowl paddled between the rushes which grew tall all around them. The marshes south of Arn were an expanse of reed choked mud-banks and narrow waterways which emptied into the estuary of the great river.

Duncan had slowed his frantic rowing now and rested his tired arms. They were deep within the safety of the fragrant marshland, the sun climbing higher into the morning sky. All around the sounds of insects and water-birds whirred and squawked, the lingering smell of fetid water filling his nostrils. Stagnant pools and bogs dotted the landscape, cut off from the waterways, and they rowed past islets of spongy yet somewhat solid looking ground. On these refuges grew stunted trees, spindly twisted little things, their clawed roots hanging onto the piti-ful swathes of dry ground, marooned amongst the stinking marsh. Scrubby bushes and other plants vied for wherever space that was left.

The reeds fared much better. They enclosed long stretches of the narrow creeks, leading them into still pools where the reeds and rushes towered menacingly over their little boat. At times, Duncan was unsure that any given narrow passage would in fact lead anywhere at all. He constantly feared to come up against an-other dead end. More than once, he found himself unable to row any further and had to turn back and try another way.

He had no idea where they were or how he had even found his

way there, hopelessly lost amongst the mires. He picked his way through water, choosing which way to take by gut instinct alone. Some ways grew perilously shallow, and he cringed every time their keel scraped the mud. It was gut wrenching.

What if they run aground and got stuck? It would probably be their doom. Yet, by some mad luck, they crept deeper and deeper into the expansive marshlands.

Duncan couldn't help but nervously watch their wake, fearful of a glimpse of the hunter. He'd lost sight of Bjorn as he guided their little boat around a bend back on the river and had immediately made for the marshes. There was no way the hunter could possibly know which way they had gone.

He cannot track us on water. He cannot know where we are.

Still, his nerves would not settle. He meant to put a few leagues between them and the doomed city and the marshes seemed like the perfect sanctuary.

'I think we should be safe now,' said Duncan eventually.

'I can't believe we got out,' Seth said as he lounged against the prow of the boat. 'Do you think the hunter is following us?'

'I can't be sure,' replied Duncan. 'How could he? But still, the thought of it makes me nervous.'

'Even so,' said Seth. 'Surely he will understand. You said it yourself, you saw the dead swarm them. What else could we do? We had to leave.'

'I felt certain they would be killed,' shrugged Duncan. *Lies, such lies.*

'He would have done the same in our place,' Seth assured him. 'Anyone would have.'

'He was most certainly wounded, though.' *Lies.*

'As you said, the madness will take them. Like the others you told me about.'

'The Cursed Ones. Yes, he and his wild friend have likely already succumbed and turned into one of those foul creatures. That is why it makes me nervous. If he does somehow follow us, and he is cursed, there will be no reasoning with them—they will kill us both.' Duncan paused. 'I shouldn't worry too much though. When we examined one of the creatures, it was clear it had the mind of an animal. They couldn't use a boat, so they can't follow us. I should put my mind at ease. I should know better.'

'We're safe,' said Seth. He smiled beneath his dirty bandages.

'You're probably just shaken, friend. It happens to the best of us. Do think we are safe enough out here to play a little? It has never failed to calm me when times seem bad, and this is a bad a time as any, wouldn't you say?'

'Go ahead,' Duncan replied.

Seth reached sightlessly for his case, his fingers probing for the latch. The thing had not left his hands the entire night. Duncan had heard him play once before, that day at the College infirmaries. Seth unlatched the case and carefully lifted out the lute. Truly a thing of beauty. Duncan could see why he had clung to it so dearly during their flight from the city. Seth relaxed, as if simply holding it leeched away his troubles. His fingers explored the dual necks with a familiarity, and he adjusted a tuning peg before he began to play.

'I still can't believe we made it out — a blind man and a cripple — when all those others didn't. The gods must be smiling on us, Duncan.'

Duncan smiled. 'Yes, I suppose so.'

'I do hope Nym and Finn made it though, found somewhere to hide or something,' said Seth.

'It is possible,' replied Duncan.

'She is a sweet thing, young Nym,' continued Seth.

'Aye she was indeed,' agreed Duncan. *Such a shame,* he thought. *I would have used my knowledge to lead them, to keep them safe. She would have realised my qualities eventually, she might have warmed to me – she could have even loved me.* He cursed his crippled ankle, if he could have just moved faster, he might have been able to get to her, might have saved her. Instead she was gone, lost to the city of dead.

Seth smiled sadly, oblivious to Duncan's regrets. 'You know, my father watched over them for years after their parents died — they were friends of my pa. Her father and my mine fought in the war together.'

'Which war?'

'The rebellion — Aeginhall and all that. It's how he lost his arm. He was a brave man, my da. I think her da got him out, saved him in the fighting. He never forgot that debt. Now he is gone.'

'I am sorry,' said Duncan. He wasn't really, but it seemed the right thing to say. He remembered a time when he would have cared, when he would have genuinely felt bad for a friend to lose someone so close, but that part of him was slipping away, lost between his fingers like a handful of sand.

'I still can't believe he's gone,' Seth murmured. 'At least he isn't one of those things now.'

His song took a mournful turn as he slowly picked out a sad melody. He said nothing for a moment, just playing his lute. Duncan let the mournful tune wash over him.

'Everything is gone now, everything I ever knew,' said Seth suddenly.

'Well perhaps the gods spared us for reason. Perhaps they have a plan for us yet.'

Seth sat quietly playing for a while as Duncan resumed rowing.

'Have you ever lost anyone?' asked Seth quietly.

Duncan thought a while. 'I lost everyone before this all even happened. I lost my master. He died back up north with Master Logan. Everyone on that last expedition died but me. After last night, there is no one left. I've barely spoken to my family in years. All my colleagues, everyone I ever knew was in the city. They're probably all gone now too.' Duncan sighed as the realisation hit him.

'Was there not a lady?' asked Seth. His mouth twitched into a smile.

'Aye, there was.' He paused. 'Truda was her name. She died with my master and the others on our expedition...' He trailed off and out into the marshes.

'Pity,' said Seth.

Silence descended on them both once more, Seth idly plucking at the strings of his lute while Duncan's thoughts lingered on Truda. He tried to recall her face, but the memory seemed distant, her image fading. He tried to remember his last words to her, but he couldn't. Regret gnawed at him. *Why did I never tell her?*

'Well at least we got out, friend,' said Seth, his voice taking a conciliatory tone. 'And thank you, Duncan. If not for you, and that staff of yours, I don't think I would be sitting here now.'

Duncan grunted. 'Blind luck.'

Seth snorted a laugh. 'If being blind brings me luck, then I am glad of it.'

'I think we will need your luck in the coming days,' replied Duncan.

Seth nodded thoughtfully. 'What happened back there... It was like a terrible nightmare. I don't know any man who could have seen what you all saw and not be shaking. In some ways I feel it was a kindness the gods robbed me of my sight. I am glad I did not have to see those things. The sound of it though... I think that will haunt my dreams for the rest of my days.'

'Aye,' agreed Duncan absently.

But it was my doing. It was all me. Duncan shuddered as the enormity of his actions began to dawn on him. Hundreds, maybe thousands were dead by his hand. He had unleashed the dead on an entire city. There would be hordes of them roaming the land by now. *What have I done?*

He caught a flicker at the edge of his vision and a shiver ran down his spine, prickling his skin. That now familiar malign sense of watchfulness wrapped itself around him once more. He tried to look, jerking his head to catch a glimpse of the shadow dancing at the edge of his vision. As he turned, his stomach knotted. There amongst the mires and bogs of the marsh, the dark figure stood alone, cloaked in black.

His heart froze.

There was no face below the hood, just a yawning abyss of darkness. It stood motionless watching him.

You doubt yourself, spoke the rasping voice in his mind. He knew that cold voice was that of the watching apparition in the marsh. *You should not. Expel your doubts. You have commanded death. You have wielded such ancient knowledge, such power. A power not seen in long ages of men. You have taken your place as master – your dream accomplished without doubt or peer. You are the apostle of the grave, Master Duncan. Beloved of the darkness.*

But so many died, thought Duncan.

True, there was sacrifice, replied the voice, *but for great knowledge there must be great sacrifice. Dwell not on what was lost, but what has been achieved. Dwell on what more can be achieved. There are secrets still yet hidden, awaiting such a disciple of knowledge as you.*

What secrets? asked Duncan.

The ritual breathes life into death, brings life again to dead things, perhaps into... broken things. It is just a matter of experimentation to uncover these secrets. We will guide you, as we have always done, breathed the voice.

'Is it possible?' muttered Duncan.

'Did you say something?' Seth asked from the prow of the little rowboat.

The rasping voice fell silent. The marshes stood empty. It was as if the shroud of shadow had suddenly been lifted from his eyes. Duncan blinked in the vivid light of the morning.

'Just a thought. I was thinking out loud,' Duncan told him, rubbing his face.

Seth laughed. 'Talking to yourself? They say it is the path to madness.'

'You have no idea,' muttered Duncan.

Seth shrugged. 'What now then, Duncan?'

'Oh, there is much to do. I have just had an idea! How did I not think of it before? There is a ritual we can try, a healing ritual. A powerful old magic... but maybe, just maybe...'

'What is it?' asked Seth curiously.

'First, we must get further from the city, well away from the dead and the curse that has fallen there. We must get out of these marshes and find ourselves somewhere safe, but if I am right, there is something that could fix us both. Fix my leg, and perhaps even return your sight... How would you like to see once more, friend?

Here ends
A Ritual of Flesh

Volume II
of
The Dead Sagas

A NOTE ON
THE DEAD SAGAS

A Ritual of Flesh will soon be followed by
Volume III of *The Dead Sagas,* and will continue this epic saga of
the struggle between the living and the cursed dead.

*Only valour and steel can stand
against the rising dead*

I would like to thank you for reading.
If you have enjoyed this book, please could I ask if you would be
so kind as to leave a review somewhere,
in particular on Goodreads, or Amazon.
Every review and rating is hugely appreciated.

For more information, and for Lee's mailing list please visit

www.leeconleyauthor.com

ABOUT THE AUTHOR

Lee is a musician and writer in Lincolnshire, UK. He lives with his wife Laura and daughters Luna and Anya in the historic cathedral city of Lincoln. Alongside a lifetime of playing guitar and immersing himself in the study of music and history, Lee is also a practitioner and instructor of historic martial arts and swordsmanship. After writing his advanced guitar theory textbook *The Guitar Teachers Grimoire*, Lee turns his hand to writing fiction. Lee is one of the founders of *Bard of the Isles* literary magazine and is now also studying a degree in creative writing while working on his debut fantasy series *The Dead Sagas*, which includes the novels *A Ritual of Bone* and *A Ritual of Flesh*, as well as also generally writing speculative fiction and horror.

CPSIA information can be obtained
at www.ICGtesting.com
Printed in the USA
LVHW040059131120
671604LV00012B/435/J